WHEN DARKNESS COMES

JOHN ANTHONY MILLER

— All the best —

John A. Miller

WHEN DARKNESS COMES

John anthony Miller
ISBN: 978-1-943789-60-3
Copyright 2016

Cover layout by WhiteRabbitGraphix.com

Printed in the United States of America

This book may be purchased through

Amazon and Amazon Kindle
Taylor and Seale Publishing
Barnes and Noble
Books a Million
and in other fine book stores

This novel is a work of fiction. Names, characters, places and incidents are the product of the author's imagination and are used fictitiously. Any resemblance to actual persons, living or dead, events, or locales is entirely coincidental.

Taylor and Seale Publishing, LLC
Daytona Beach Shores, Florida 32118

Phone: 1-386-760-8987
www.taylorandseale.com

A note from the author...

When I started *When Darkness Comes*, I wanted to write about a man who gave up everything to save others – his wealth, his reputation, his family, his future – and I created Julian Junot. But often when a novel is conceived, and other characters developed, their stories become just as intriguing.

While researching the book, I created Paul, Claire, and Rachel from fragments of sentences I found in historical records. Each described tragedies endured by those in the French Resistance – a man who lost his wife and daughter, a young woman killed by the Germans, a teenage Jew who defied the Nazis. I thought they deserved more than a few words in a forgotten WWII journal and felt compelled to tell the stories, even if fueled by my imagination.

I also read about a French homeowner forced to board a German officer, a very polite man who replaced a wine glass broken accidentally. From this brief paragraph, General Berg emerged. A devout churchgoer who doted on his granddaughters, he loses his life not because of who he was, but because of what he represented – like many millions of others in the Second World War.

Lastly, the book contains horrific tragedies. Although not based on anything specific, each can be traced to thousands of similar events that actually occurred, spawned by a global catastrophe that should never be forgotten.

DEDICATION

For my mother—Mary Lucy Josephine DeMarco Miller

ACKNOWLEDGEMENTS

Special thanks to Cindy, Chris, Danielle, Steffany and Mark, my agent Donna Eastman at Parkeast Literary Agency, my publisher Dr. Mary Custureri and editor Dr. Linda Straubel at Taylor and Seale, and all the advanced readers who helped make the book the best that it could be.

Chapter 1

Paris, France
July 17, 1942

It was the French police who came for the Jews. Over thirteen thousand were selected, their names chosen by raffle. But they were foreign Jews, mostly from Eastern Europe. It should have been acceptable to a city crushed by the Nazi occupation. But it wasn't.

The Abzac family avoided capture. A customer in their shoe repair shop was friendly with a French policeman. He told Rachel, the sixteen-year-old daughter, what was going to happen. "Don't go home for the next two nights," he warned. "After that it'll be safe. I know you understand, but your parents might not. They're too trusting of a world that no longer exists."

Rachel convinced her parents they were in danger. Even though it made no sense to them, for they had no enemies, they huddled in the tiny shoe shop for the next two nights: father and mother, Rachel, and little brother Stanislaw. It wasn't until the third day that they returned home, assuming it was safe, arriving at their apartment after dark. Many in the building had been taken; some doors hung on broken hinges. Others, like the Abzacs, had notices posted at their residence, ordering them to police headquarters. Some apartments were spared completely.

Rachel glanced up and down the corridor, dimly lit, the paint fading. When convinced no one was looking, she tore down the notice and led her family into their flat. Just as they entered, she saw the landlady exit the stairwell. A middle-aged woman more interested in her tenants' lives than her own, she stood at the far end of the hallway, watching.

Their apartment was undisturbed. After ensuring their belongings were safe, mother and father prepared Stanislaw for bed, and they followed soon after. Rachel went to her room but remained awake. She kept thinking of the landlady's face.

The footsteps were sharp and distinct, the strides long and measured as boots pounded the hardwood floors. They came to a sudden halt and Rachel bolted upright, hearing gruff voices in the corridor. She jumped from the bed and leaned against the wall, placing her ear against the cracked plaster where the wallpaper had peeled away. She heard the landlady talking, providing locations of different apartments, the Abzacs' flat among them. Then they went across the hall and knocked loudly on a neighboring door.

Rachel knew she had to act quickly. She went to the adjacent bed and shook Stanislaw. He opened his eyes, sleepy and confused. "Stanislaw, hurry!" she said. "You have to get dressed." She ran to the next bedroom and awakened her parents. Her father sat up, placing wire-rimmed spectacles on his nose.

"What's wrong?" he asked, speaking in Polish.

"The police are outside," Rachel said, breathless. "Get dressed. We have to hide. They're coming for us and any other Jews that escaped." She ran to her room and dressed hastily. Then she helped her brother.

"Rachel, can't we try to reason with them?" her mother asked as she buttoned her dress.

Her parents clung to the old ways, searching for Poland in Paris. A new world was hard for them to comprehend. A world controlled by a hostile enemy was even harder.

"It might be a misunderstanding," her father said, hoping to avoid a confrontation. He pulled his black suspenders over his shoulders.

There was a knock at the front door, insistent, loud and rhythmic.

They froze and glanced at each anxiously, fear masking their faces. "What should we do?" the mother hissed.

The knock came again, louder.

"Wake up!" a voice commanded.

Rachel tried to stay calm. She knew their lives depended on it. She looked at the trunk beside her parent's bed and to the wardrobe against a far wall.

"Open the door!" the policeman yelled.

"We have to hide," Rachel whispered, her eyes wide. She frantically surveyed the tiny apartment – closets, walls, and then the windows.

"We can't," her father whispered. "It's too late."

"We're breaking down the door!" a voice warned harshly.

Rachel took Stanislaw by the hand. She ran to the window in her parent's bedroom and opened it, her hands shaking, and motioned to her father. "You go first," she said softly.

"Rachel, we're on the sixth floor! Are you mad?"

"On the ledge," she said firmly. "Hurry."

Her father looked at her with amazement, surprised by her courage. But he obeyed, and climbed out the window.

"Mother, you're next," she whispered. "And then Stanislaw."

The butt of a rifle crashed against the door, the wood cracking under the onslaught. The policemen continued pounding, shouting warnings, demanding surrender, until the door crashed open, the jamb splintered and broken, and they burst into the apartment.

Rachel was scrambling through the window when she heard them barge in. A policeman searched the parlor, a second went to her bedroom. She eased the window down, trying to make no noise.

The wall faced a narrow alley, an adjacent building two meters away. The ledge was twenty centimeters wide, barely enough to stand on, and Rachel looked down, dizzy, her stomach lurching. A German soldier, dwarf-like from such a height, patrolled the alley, ensuring none of the Jews in the building escaped. If he looked up, he would see them. Rachel consoled her brother as he wept quietly; her father comforted her mother. The seconds passed with agonizing slowness, the policemen searching the apartment, the sounds coming closer. Rachel looked down again. The German was directly below, pacing, a machine gun slung over his shoulder. She squinted in the darkness, leaning forward, and lost her balance. She shrieked, not loudly, but the night was so still it echoed, and she struggled and almost fell, balanced on the edge, her shoe slipping from her foot and plunging into a pile of rubbish.

The soldier turned, startled by the noise, but not sure where it came from. He moved the gun from his shoulder, poking the barrel into the trash.

Rachel grabbed the window molding, her knuckles white, clinging to life and teetering on the ledge, her upper body swaying to and fro. Her mother extended her arm as

Stanislaw pulled her towards him, and she regained her balance and pressed against the wall, frightened and breathing heavily.

In the alley below the soldier left the rubbish pile and walked towards the road where a bus was parked on the street. Jews were being led to it – those like the Abzacs who thought they had escaped: young and innocent, old and wise, parents and children, forming a long, single line that wound its way down the road. They carried small suitcases and parcels filled with their prized possessions, forced to take only what they valued the most.

Rachel could hear the policemen in the apartment enter the main bedroom. They flung the wardrobe doors open and threw the trunk lid to the floor. She saw a reflection by the window, blocking the light, a policeman centimeters away, the brim of his hat pressed against the glass as he peered out. She tensed, inching from the window.

Chapter 2

In the small Normandy village of Giverny, Paul Moreau cautiously approached a parachute caught in the lower branches of a chestnut tree. He couldn't tell how long it had been there, or if it was British or German. He moved tentatively towards it and saw a British airman lying at the base of the tree, a leather cap and broken oxygen mask covering his face. His leg was caught in a shrub, twisted, his leather jacket torn.

"Papa, who is that man?"

Paul turned to find his five-year old daughter. "Sophie, get back," he said anxiously.

His wife Catherine was a few steps behind her. "Is that a parachute?" she asked.

"Don't come any closer," he requested.

Catherine didn't listen. She moved beside him and saw the airman. "We have to help him," she said with no hesitation.

"It's too dangerous," Paul hissed. He glanced around warily.

"Why is he sleeping?" Sophie asked innocently.

Paul knew she would never understand. She lived in a fairy tale filled with imaginary playmates. She couldn't comprehend war. But then, neither could he.

Catherine bent over the airman, a straw hat covering her sandy hair. "He's breathing," she said, "but I can't tell how badly he's injured."

"Should I let him play with my doll?" Sophie asked.

"Catherine, please," Paul pleaded. "Take her inside."

He looked at Sophie, her cherubic face framed by blond curly hair. He didn't want her exposed; he wanted to protect her. Northern France had been occupied by the Germans for over two years. If they were caught aiding the enemy, the punishment would be severe.

"What are we going to do?" Catherine asked. "We can't leave him here."

Paul looked at the River Seine behind them. There were no boats, no people on the far bank. He surrendered and said, "I suppose we should get him to the barn."

They then heard the sound of a motor, distant but growing louder. Vehicles occasionally passed on the quiet country road, normally not even noticed. But now it was different; their lives were in danger. The parachute flapped in the breeze, clinging to the tree, visible from the road.

"Quick," Paul said. "Hide behind these bushes." He grabbed Sophie, wrapping his arms around her. Catherine crouched beside him.

The vehicle rounded a bend and they could see it through the trees as it approached. It was large, the pitch of the engine deep, maybe a German troop truck looking for the airman. The driver shifted gears, the motor whining as the vehicle slowed.

"Why are we hiding?" Catherine asked.

"If anything attracts their attention, and they look from the road, they'll see the parachute," Paul replied.

They saw the front bumper through the trees and then the rest of the faded green truck, loaded with freshly cut logs. The driver, alone in the cab, guided the vehicle past them, his eyes on the road.

Paul sighed with relief and led them from the shrubs. "Go wait in the barn," he told them. "I'll bring the pilot there and then come back for the parachute."

The airman's eyes were closed, his lips bruised and bleeding, his right eye swollen. Paul freed his foot from the shrub, cringing as he realized how awkwardly it had been bent. He studied the parachute dangling from the tree. It could be seen from the river, or the air if a plane flew low overhead. And the Germans could arrive any minute. Paul unbuckled the parachute straps from the flyer's chest and scooped the airman up in his arms. He was heavy, and Paul struggled not to drop him. He carried him into the barn, a stone building with a thatched roof, and gently laid him on the ground.

"Be careful with him," Catherine said. "We don't know how badly he's hurt."

Paul removed the airman's cap and the remains of his oxygen mask. He was young, barely a man, with red hair and freckles.

Catherine got some water from a rain barrel and splashed it on his face. After a few seconds he woke and gazed about the barn, confused and disoriented. When he regained his senses, he bolted upright.

"Easy," Paul said in English. He gently pushed him back down. "You're safe."

"What happened?" he asked groggily.

"Your plane was shot down."

"Now I remember," he said. "There were two German fighters. I didn't have a chance."

"You must have ejected," Paul informed him, "and your parachute got caught in a tree."

"Where's my plane?" he asked.

"I don't know," Paul said. "I didn't hear a crash, and I saw no sign of wreckage."

"It can't be too far away. I'm sure the Germans have found it by now."

"Are you all right?" Catherine asked as she knelt beside him.

He flexed his foot, trying to move it in the leather boot. "I think my ankle is broken," he said, moving his torso and arms, stretching his back. "Other than that. I'm all right. A bit bruised, I'm afraid. Who are you?"

"Catherine Moreau," she said. "This is my husband Paul and my daughter Sophie."

"Did he fall out of the sky?" Sophie asked.

Catherine smiled. "Yes, Sophie," she replied. "He dropped from the clouds."

"Tommy Dover," he greeted them warmly, adding a broad smile accented by the freckles on his face. "Thanks for helping me." He extended his hand.

Paul shook it, conscious that his palm was wet and clammy, his heart racing, his stomach queasy. He didn't take risks. And helping a British airman was a huge risk. Paul touched Dover's ankle and manipulated it gently. "Does that hurt?" he asked.

Dover gasped and his body tensed. "A bit," he replied, wincing. "But I suppose it could have been worse. Are there Germans in the area?"

"A few," Paul said, "although they normally leave us alone. But I'm sure they're looking for you now."

Dover frowned. "Can you hide me?" he asked. "At least until my ankle is better."

"I suppose so. But first I have to dispose of the parachute. Before someone sees it."

"I'll stay with him," Catherine offered.

"I don't think you and Sophie should be here," Paul said firmly. He knew what the Germans did to those who opposed them.

"Get the parachute," Catherine said. "I'll stay until you return."

Paul grabbed a shovel and hurried towards the woods. He noticed a small boat had arrived, an older man in the back, holding a fishing rod. He was tall and slender with wire-rimmed spectacles, a floppy hat upon his head. He seemed preoccupied, enjoying a peaceful morning, presenting no danger. Then, just as Paul reached the chestnut tree, he saw movement on the far bank, behind the boat. The bushes were parted, but not naturally as the breeze would blow the branches.

Paul watched a German soldier emerge from the brush and stand on the river bank, hands on hips, his gray helmet glistening in the sunlight. A machine gun was slung over his soldier. He gazed in both directions, up and down the waterway.

Paul ducked behind the tree, his eyes wide, his heart racing. He looked at the parachute, dangling from the tree, then to the German. He was staring down the river. Maybe that's where the plane had crashed. If Paul climbed the tree to untangle the parachute, both the German and the fisherman could see him. The fisherman seemed harmless; the German was not.

The German called to the fisherman, but Paul couldn't hear what he said. The fisherman turned, muttering a reply. The German looked across the river, towards Paul. He then poked around the brush before leaving.

Paul climbed up the tree, pulled and tugged at the parachute until he freed it, and let it fall to the ground. He scampered back down and rolled it into a ball. It was bulky; it took almost thirty minutes to bury it. Then he covered it with leaves and branches. With sweat dripping from his forehead, he returned to the barn.

Sophie was by the doorway, talking to her doll and drawing in the dirt with a stick. She had lost interest in their guest. Paul bent over and kissed the top of her head. "Is everything all right?" he asked Catherine as he entered the barn.

"Not really," she said. "He needs a doctor right away. His ankle is badly broken."

Paul considered his options. Giverny was a small town, just downriver from Paris. Although the cottage had been in his family for decades, he lived in Paris – and he always had. The cottage was for weekends and summers; he didn't know the people in the village that well. But there was one man he assumed he could trust – a life-long friend. He was suddenly overwhelmed with the full realization of what he was doing. Why would he ever risk his life and family for a stranger? He wanted to help the flyer, but was it worth it?

"I think I can manage on my own," Dover said, seeing the apprehension on Paul's face. "Just let me stay until dark. Then I'll be off."

"No," Catherine said. "We'll help you."

Paul looked at the young face, the freckles, pale blue eyes, thick red hair. He couldn't desert him. "There's a doctor in town," he said. "I've known him all my life. He was a close friend of my father's."

"Dr. Durant," Catherine confirmed.

"Yes," Paul said. "I'll go and get him."

"I haven't eaten in over a day," Tommy mentioned hastily. "Any chance of a bite before you go?"

"Of course," Paul said, feeling like a poor host. "I'll get you some food."

Paul passed Sophie, who was now dancing across the lawn, doing pirouettes like a ballerina. He looked at the fisherman casting his line, absorbed in the fish he couldn't seem to catch. Nothing seemed amiss; he noticed nothing unusual. Paul got some bread and cheese and a bottle of wine, found some fresh fruit, apples picked that morning, and started back to the barn. As he left the house and crossed the yard, he suddenly froze as a German staff car turned into the lane in front of the cottage.

Chapter 3

On the *Boulevard Saint-Germain*, near *Rue de Cardinal Lemoine,* sat a book store owned by Claire Daladier. Passed through her family for generations, it had lasted over a hundred years and survived two wars. Cluttered with wooden shelves crammed with leather volumes, and comfortable chairs in which to sit and read them, the store was a favorite among Parisians. It now thrived during the German occupation, the rare books that filled the shelves desirable to the enemy as were all things French.

Adjacent to the store was an arched doorway with fluted moldings, small cherub statues adorning each side. It opened to a black and white tiled vestibule, and a staircase made with decorative iron spindles that led to the apartments above. Just after seven a.m., a frightened Rachel Abzac stood at the building entrance. She gazed up and down the street, studied the passing pedestrians to ensure no one was watching and entered, quickly closing the door behind her. Then she went to Claire Daladier's apartment on the third floor.

Rachel worked at the book store on Mondays and Thursdays, earning money to help support her family. She had met Claire months before, after a man in her father's shop saw an old, leather-bound Talmud behind the counter. It was rubbed and cracked, having spent many years in the Abzac family. The man told her father it could be valuable, and he knew a woman who might buy it. Although her father doubted the worth of such a book, he wrote down the woman's name and address.

The next day, Rachel took the Talmud to Claire Daladier. She liked the bookstore owner instantly; her smile and twinkling brown eyes were warm and inviting. Claire not only bought the Talmud but also gave her a job after learning of Rachel's love of books.

Rachel knocked on the door, timidly at first and then more forcefully, terrified of waking other tenants. The hallway was deserted, the ornate doorways closed and quiet. Rachel stood there patiently, short and slight, her brown hair brushed back from her forehead, her simple green dress buttoned to the neck.

The door opened a crack and Claire Daladier peeked from behind it, a gray robe pulled tightly around her slender frame. She had short brown hair, cut just below the ear, and bright brown eyes, searching and sensitive. A childhood scar, shaped like a hook, left an inch-long indentation at the top of her cheek, just under her left eye. Her expression was curious, but upon seeing Rachel, she smiled.

"Claire, please help me," Rachel whispered urgently. A tear dripped from her eye. And then another.

Claire showed no hesitation, instantly flinging the door open and leading Rachel into the parlor.

"What's wrong?" she asked anxiously.

"The police came in the middle of the night," Rachel said, choking on the words. "They were arresting people and putting them in buses."

"Is your family safe?"

"Yes, we climbed out the window and waited on the ledge until they left."

Claire could envision the carnage: doors broken down, occupants screaming, innocent people led from their homes. Others waited anxiously, hoping they weren't next, while the Abzacs stood on a window ledge, terrified.

"Where is your family? They didn't go back to the apartment, did they?"

"No, they are hiding in my parents' shoe shop," Rachel replied.

Claire realized how precarious the situation was. Eventually the police would go to the shop. Maybe not that day, but soon. "They can't stay there," she said. "It isn't safe."

"Am I safe here?"

"I'm not sure," Claire mused aloud. "But it's the best place for you right now." She considered her own safety. She had to be careful. And she didn't want Rachel exposed to more danger than she already faced. "Are you sure you weren't followed here?"

"Yes," Rachel said. "I was careful. No one even noticed me."

"You're probably right. There's no reason to, at least not yet. The police haven't determined why you weren't home, but they will. And when they do, they'll try to find you." She walked to the window and looked down the boulevard lined with cobblestone pavements and chestnut trees, flower pots splashing color across the urban landscape. Paris was just waking up. The wrought iron tables at the café across the street were filled with patrons, drinking coffee and reading newspapers. A man stood on the corner, his dog on a leash, and a small group of businessmen collected at the bus stop. Trucks rambled down the road; cars passed, the black sedans so common in the city, and she cringed when she saw some with small

Nazi flags on their bumpers. There were a few horse-drawn wagons, relics of yesterday, people riding bicycles, and an occasional taxi.

Claire noticed a woman standing across the street watching the building. She was about forty years old and wore her black hair tucked into a tight bun. She held a newspaper folded under the arm of her prim brown dress. She stood patiently, with no apparent destination. Maybe she was waiting for someone, a friend or lover. Or maybe she wasn't.

"You are sure no one saw you come?" Claire asked, closing the drapes.

"No, I don't think so."

Claire thought of her neighbors and the nearby shop owners. She wondered whom she could trust. She realized that Rachel couldn't stay in her apartment, but where could she go? Everyone else in Rachel's life was a Jew and couldn't help her – but Rachel knew that. That's why she had come to Claire.

She returned to the window and peered out. The woman still stood across the street, but the newspaper was no longer under her arm. Now a man stood beside her. He was older, glasses perched on his nose, a gray hat on his head. They were both facing the building. Claire couldn't tell if they were watching or not. But she couldn't take the chance.

She looked at the yellow star stitched on the left breast of Rachel's dress, the insignia that all Jews were required to wear. It would have to come off. "I have to find somewhere to hide you and your family," she told her. "How about the store basement?

"Will that be safe, with the bookstore just above?"

Claire looked at the young girl, afraid but strong. She was careful, and she could be trusted. Her life depended on it. But now, so did Claire's.

"Yes, I think so," Claire said. "You'll just have to be quiet during the day, while the store is open. Tonight we'll get your family, and then we'll find a way to get you out of Paris."

Claire looked out the window again. The woman and man were still there. A truck drove by, followed by another close behind it, the side panels painted with the name of a fish wholesaler. Once they passed, the woman and man were gone.

Chapter 4

There were four soldiers in the staff car. One stood in the passenger's seat, bracing his hand against the windshield. He had binoculars around his neck, an officer's cap and insignia. Two enlisted men rode in the back, machine guns straddling their laps. Paul looked towards the barn. Catherine and Sophie were inside, but so was the airman.

The Germans climbed from the vehicle and studied the trees that flanked the property. The officer, a slight man wearing round spectacles with black rims, nodded at Paul as he smoked a cigarette.

"Suche in den Wäldern," the officer commanded, his eyes still trained on Paul. "Search the woods."

The officer and driver moved in front of the barn, towards the river. The other two soldiers walked to the edge of the woods where the parachute had been. The officer waved to the fisherman standing in the boat, rod in hand, his eyes trained on the shore. He motioned to the officer, nodded his head, and pointed to the trees. The soldiers began searching the woods, poking their machine-gun barrels through the shrubs, kicking the soil. One soldier looked at the tree where the parachute had been, studying the damaged branches. The other examined the shrubs flattened by the airman's fall.

"Dieser Bereich ist gestört," the soldier called to the officer. "This area has been disturbed."

Paul's heart sank. He thought he had been so clever. But another Frenchman had betrayed him. The fisherman had seen the parachute and told the Germans.

Catherine and Sophie emerged from the barn. They walked quickly to the back of the yard, near the garden. The officer studied them for a moment. Then he looked at the barn.

"Sprechen Sie Deutsch?" the officer asked Paul. His eyes were dark, nearly black, and he had an eerie calmness that was frightening, almost evil. Although not intimidating physically, he still projected strength and power and a cold, callous cruelty.

Paul was terrified. He struggled to stay calm, but felt his entire body trembling. He spoke German fluently, as well as English, but he wasn't prepared to admit to either. He pretended ignorance and shook his head.

"What is your name?" the officer asked in accented French.

"Paul Moreau."

"Did we interrupt your lunch?"

"Pardon?" Paul asked, the plate rattling in his hands.

"You have food and wine. You must be hungry."

"Yes, I am."

The officer glanced at his watch. It was 10 a.m. Too late for breakfast, too early for lunch. He motioned for his men to come closer.

"We're looking for a British airman," he said. "Have you seen him?"

"No," Paul said. He feigned interest and concern, but wasn't too convincing. "Is my family in danger?"

"Perhaps," the officer said. He eyed Paul closely, taking a drag on his cigarette.

The soldiers by the tree were scraping away the dirt where the parachute was buried. A few more inches, and it would be exposed.

"It's very important that we find him," he said. "Do you understand?"

"Yes," Paul stammered. His eyes moved to the soldiers digging.

"Have you seen anything suspicious?"

"No," he said. He motioned to Catherine and Sophie. "We've been gardening all morning."

Catherine stared at the Germans, her arm wrapped around Sophie. She was afraid, although her lips were taut with defiance.

"Oberst, fand ich den Fallschirm!" one of the soldiers called. "Colonel, I found the parachute."

"Kommen," he called and motioned them forward. He waved to the fisherman, pointed to the woods, and then to the barn.

"We're going to look in the barn," he said to Paul. He watched him closely, studying his reaction.

Paul shrugged, trying to show no concern, but his stomach churned violently.

The officer walked to the door, whispering to the driver. He withdrew his pistol. The driver readied his rifle. Paul held his breath, fearing the worst. He turned towards his wife and daughter. "What are they doing, Papa?" Sophie called.

Paul showed an assurance he didn't feel. "It's all right, Sophie. They're looking for a missing man."

The officer entered the barn, weapon poised. The other two soldiers flanked the entrance. The Englishman couldn't escape.

Paul walked towards them, slowly and deliberately. He was three meters from the entrance when he heard the driver shout.

"Halt!"

He cringed, knowing his life was about to change forever.

Chapter 5

A narrow door in a corner of the bookstore led to a rarely-used basement. It contained a dozen bookshelves, partially filled with overflow from the store, while the rest of the room was crammed with stored items: shelves, baskets, containers, racks of old clothes, all of the things a family collects after occupying a building for over a hundred years. Claire hung a small bell on the door, which jingled when it was opened, to provide a warning to the Abzacs.

A small bathroom, just a sink and a toilet, abutted the rear wall. Claire placed a row of bookshelves in front of it, spanning the basement width and capturing the bathroom, creating a living space a few meters wide. She filled the shelves with books and baskets and clothes, making it seem as if they had always been there. An opening was cut at the bottom of one bookshelves, providing access to the hidden room. Behind the false wall of shelves, hidden among a few old chairs and cushions, was the Abzac family. Proud and independent, the family was gracious and thankful, knowing their lives depended on Claire.

She had smuggled them into the basement over the course of two days. The parents, Marta and Teofil, were resistant, unwilling to relinquish their independence. Teofil was the hardest, adamant that he should remain at his shoe repair shop, insisting he had done nothing wrong. Only

Rachel understood that they would be punished for what they were, not what they did.

The first day passed uneventfully, and then the second. Even though the family was uncomfortable, and obtaining the extra food a hardship for Claire, their anxiety began to ease. But the cautious, careful actions implemented to protect them did not. They adopted a routine, and Claire brought food to the family before the store opened, and then later at night after it closed. Sometimes, when her employees were distracted with customers, she took the family something during the day.

On Monday, Claire acted as surprised as the other employees when Rachel did not appear for work. She offered no explanation and merely shrugged, suggesting the young woman might have found a better opportunity. The others seemed to accept what she said, but all knew about the roundup of foreign Jews and suspected Rachel had been part of it.

That evening Claire walked to a café near the river and sat at an outdoor table. A few minutes later a man joined her, stocky and middle-aged, with green eyes and a shock of white hair. His hands were rough, he earned his living by using them, but his heart was tender.

"Henri, thank you so much for coming," Claire said in the hushed whispers a crowded café dictates.

"I've known you my entire life," he explained. "You said you were in trouble, so I came to help. Now tell me what happened."

Claire leaned forward, close to him, and told the story of the Abzac family. Henri listened intently, offered no judgment, and made no comment until she had finished.

"Why are you taking such a risk?" he asked.

"I know Rachel. It's the least I can do."

"It's dangerous."

"I know. But I feel like I can help them."

He was quiet for a moment, sipping chicory coffee. "And you couldn't help Jacques?" he asked, suspecting the real reason.

She felt like her heart had been tightly squeezed. "No," she said softly. "I couldn't help Jacques. And when Rachel appeared at my door, I wanted to help her. And now I want to help every Jew I can."

Henri Durant leaned forward, his hand on her arm. "Claire, many women lost their husbands. Just as you did. But they aren't fighting a war that has already been lost."

"I've made my decision."

He leaned back and looked at the determination on her face. It was a familiar expression. It was useless to try to change her mind.

"Don't underestimate the Germans," he advised her. "One mistake and they'll find you. And when they do, they will kill you."

"I know the Germans," she told him. "That's why I'm doing this."

Henri gazed at the river, the people walking along it, soldiers mixed with civilians. There was a building across the water with a large Nazi flag draped from a third-floor balcony. He studied it for a moment, its symbol so much more than a nation, so much more than a city's surrender, and considered her resolve. He felt what she was feeling, the pain of losing loved ones. The Nazis took whatever they wanted – lives, money, belongings – until you refused to let them take anymore.

"Who were the man and woman watching from across the street on the day Rachel arrived?"

"I don't know," she answered. "They may have been waiting for the bus. There's a stop on the corner."

"Or they could have followed Rachel."

She shrugged. "I'm not sure," she admitted.

"Have you seen them since?"

"No, I haven't. But I don't watch the street through the day."

"I think the Abzacs should leave now."

"Where can they go?" she asked.

He was quiet for a moment, pensive. "I will take them. My boat is docked a block away." He pointed to a fishing boat siting serenely, rocking gently in the current, looking like a postcard.

"Bring the parents and the boy first. Take them to the riverbank and let them approach the boat. I will talk to the boy, pretending to answer his fishing questions, and invite them onboard."

"Then get the girl, but restore the basement before you go. You will come also. Tell your staff you're going to your home in Giverny for a week or so. Do you understand?"

"Yes," Claire said. She was suddenly overwhelmed; she realized it wasn't a game she played – her life was at stake. "I'll go now."

"I'll wait until midnight," Henri said. "If you're not here, I'll return tomorrow evening. But you have to get them out of Paris."

She went back to the store, collected Stanislaw, Marta, and Teofil, and led them to the river bank. She guided them to a kiosk, where they waited while she purchased a newspaper. She discreetly pointed to Henri's boat and then scanned the front page as they walked past, no different from any other family strolling through the streets of Paris.

Henri was waiting on deck and, as they approached, he engaged them in conversation. He made a fuss over Stanislaw, and anyone watching would think the fisherman was satisfying the boy's curiosity. They chatted amiably, and Henri invited them to board.

Once satisfied they were safe, Claire made her way back to the store, merging with other pedestrians. She walked quickly, avoiding the soldiers who peered in the shop windows, ignoring the German staff cars that prowled the streets. Ten minutes later, she was hurrying down the basement steps.

"They made it," she said to Rachel.

"There were no problems?"

"No, but we must hurry."

She started removing books from the shelves. She cleared away the bottom shelf, exposed the opening, and Rachel climbed out to help. Once the first bookshelf was empty, they slid it against the adjoining wall where it had been originally. Then they started on the second one. It took them over an hour to rearrange the basement, making it look as it did only a few days before. Once finished, they made their way up the steps. The store was closed, the lights dimmed. Claire had already left a note for her employees, informing them she would be gone for a week. They went to the front entrance and Claire prepared to open the door, scanning the street for suspicious activity. She gasped and moved away quickly, guiding Rachel behind a shelf.

A woman, about forty, her black hair in a bun, and a male companion, older with glasses and a gray hat, stood at the bus stop. They had also been watching the book store when Rachel first arrived.

Chapter 6

"Bewegen sich nicht!" the soldier shouted. "Don't move!"

Paul heard sounds of a scuffle, men wrestling in the dirt, grunting, a cart falling over. Then he heard a gunshot, sharp and distinct. He peered into the barn. The officer was by the entrance. The soldier stood in the center of the floor in front of some hay bales. Tommy Dover lay motionless on the ground, a pistol in his right hand, his chest covered with blood. His eyes were open, blue and serene.

Paul turned away, sickened. He felt like he was going to vomit, but he knew he had to protect his family. He pretended to be shocked and screamed, covering his face with his hands, and slowly walked backwards, feigning horror. "Where did he come from?" he asked. "Thank you for saving my family. Who knows what he would have done to us."

The officer came towards Paul, his face showing no emotion. A soldier who had flanked the barn, closest to the road, came to his side. The soldier near the river walked to Catherine and Sophie. Both had the barrels of their machine guns raised. The officer looked towards the river, as if he sought direction. The fisherman waved, and then pointed to Catherine and Sophie. The officer turned to the soldier closest to him and nodded his head.

With no warning, the soldier swung his leather boot in an upward arc, his foot catching Paul in the groin. He cried out, pain spreading through every cell of his body, and fell to the ground, squirming into a fetal position and clutching his crotch.

"Stop!" Catherine screamed from the garden.

Her voice was faint, dulled by ringing in Paul's ears. The pain was the worst he had ever known. Any movement he made only amplified it.

"You helped the enemy," the soldier yelled in French.

"No," Paul gasped. "I didn't know he was there."

The soldier started kicking him savagely. His heavy boots flung into Paul's arms and legs and torso, pummeling organ and muscle and bone. Each blow sent shock waves through his body, each nerve screamed in pain.

"Please, stop!" Paul cried.

"Leave him alone!" Catherine yelled. She was coming closer.

Still the kicks came. The pain dulled, replaced by numbness. Just as he was about to faint, the attack stopped.

The soldier leaned over, screaming in Paul's face. "You hid the Englishman."

"No, I swear," Paul choked. "I didn't know he was there."

He started kicking again, but Paul no longer felt the pain. He was like a rag doll, tossed and turned, flailing and falling. Again, just as he was about to faint, the soldier stopped.

Catherine was screaming and crying, her voice vague and far away. Through glazed eyes Paul saw the officer look at him curiously, wondering if he was dying. Then he talked to his soldiers. Their voices sounded slurred.

"If you ever see the enemy again, you will report it," the officer ordered.

"Yes, I'll do whatever you say," Paul replied, fighting to stay conscious.

"Good," the officer said. "Tell everyone I spared your life. Do you understand?"

"Yes," Paul gasped, unable to believe they would let him live. "I understand." He was crying, tears streaming down his face, mixing with the blood that flowed from his mouth and nose. He was totally and completely humiliated, begging for his life.

"You must never forget," the officer advised. The monotone was frightening, sinister in its measured cadence.

"I won't forget. I promise."

The officer turned and looked at the fisherman, who again pointed to Catherine and Sophie. Then he motioned to the soldier who stood near them. Catherine was screaming and Sophie was crying. Both were pleading, begging the barbaric men to stop.

Paul closed his eyes tightly, hoping the horrible nightmare would end. Feeling helpless and defeated, he crawled like a coward at the enemy's feet.

Their boots crunched the grass, growing dimmer as they walked to the staff car. Then the motor started. A few seconds passed before the officer spoke again.

"You must never forget."

Two shots shattered the silence. Paul wept as blackness overcame him.

Chapter 7

"Move away from the door," Claire warned. "Quickly."

"What's wrong?"

"We're being watched by the man and woman that were here the day you arrived."

Claire glanced up and down the boulevard, searching for anything else suspicious. Pedestrians strolled along the street, looking in shop windows. Cars and trucks and taxis drove by. On the far corner, where a bar stood next to a clothing store, three men were outside, smoking cigarettes. Nothing seemed unusual; it was just another night in Paris.

"There's a bus stop on the corner," Rachel said. "Could they be waiting for the bus?"

"I doubt it," Claire replied, glancing at her watch. "We have two hours to get to the boat. We'll wait and see if they leave."

Rachel peeked from behind a bookshelf, peering out the door. "There's a black car parked across from the bakery," she said. "Behind the taxi. Two men are sitting in the front seat. What do you think they're doing?"

Claire looked at the vehicle. It was the type of sedan the Gestapo drove. The occupants could see both the building and the man and woman across the street. She looked at Rachel, quiet, ordinary, hardly noticeable – yet worldly and wise at sixteen. She watched and waited, listened and learned. It was easy to underestimate her.

"They look like Gestapo," Claire said. "But I can't be sure. We'll just have to wait. There's not much else we can do."

Ten minutes later, a second black sedan, the same make and model as the first, parked at the other end of the street, two imposing males in the front seat. Now each had a clear view of the bookstore and the apartments above it.

The man with the glasses and the woman with her hair in a bun were still across the street. Occasionally they spoke, making casual conversation as if they had never met before, but Clare suspected that wasn't the case. The man wore the same gray hat he had on when she first saw him. The woman had a black umbrella under her arm where the newspaper had been. Claire now had no doubt that the building was being watched; they were trapped.

She didn't want Rachel to know how serious the situation was. She was afraid, her body trembling, her mind searching for a solution that didn't exist. She wasn't prepared to confront the Gestapo. Not that anyone ever was. She tried to stay calm. She had to think. There had to be a way to escape and she needed to find it. There was a second store entrance in the vestibule, and the apartments had fire escapes leading to the alley behind the building. They could leave the store, go into the vestibule, up to her apartment, and out the fire escape.

"They're probably watching the back of the building, too," Rachel said quietly, as if she had read her mind.

Claire looked at her, surprised. "I didn't think of that," she admitted. "But you're right."

"What are we going to do?"

Claire didn't know what to tell her. There wasn't anything they could do. At least there was nothing she could think of. "I don't know," she said. "Maybe if we wait, they'll leave. They might think we're gone, or that we were never here to begin with"

Twenty minutes later, the man took off his hat and waved it back and forth, slowly and methodically. Then he placed it under his left arm. The passenger door to each car opened and a man got out and walked towards the store.

"Something is going on," Claire said, her heart beating faster. "I just don't know what it is."

"Should we try to use the fire escape?" Rachel asked, panic in her voice. "It could be our only chance."

"I think it's too late."

The men crossed the street, coming from different directions. They each surveyed the area, eyeing pedestrians and cars, trying not to appear suspicious as they converged on the store.

Claire and Rachel moved farther from the doorway, hiding behind some shelves. There was nowhere to go. Claire wished they had left the basement bookshelves in place. At least they could have hidden behind them. Or maybe they should have risked an escape through the alley. Claire grabbed Rachel's hand and held it tightly.

The men arrived at the same time. They walked into the recessed area that formed the front entrance, pretending to look at books on display in the window. After a moment had passed and none of the pedestrians seemed interested in them, they looked briefly in the store, but then turned to face the street. They never knocked, never tried the door to see if it might be open. They didn't seem interested.

Claire and Rachel watched anxiously from behind the bookshelves as the seconds ticked by. They waited for the men to act, expecting them to force their way through the door. But they didn't.

"What are they doing?" Rachel hissed. "Are they just going to stand there?"

"I think so," Claire said, confused by their behavior. "Maybe they're guarding the door, making sure we don't leave."

Just as she spoke, the woman removed the umbrella from under her arm, even though it was a pleasant evening, and opened it. She stood in the street, the umbrella over her head, looking a bit ridiculous.

"It's a signal," Claire said, watching closely.

The men in front of the store pressed against the display window, trying to hide in the shadows. Each removed a revolver from a shoulder holster.

The entrance door to the vestibule opened. A man exited and turned to walk down the street. The light from the street lamps lit his face. He was young, late thirties, tall and slender.

"It's Mr. Arcand," Claire said. "His apartment is next to mine."

Arcand paused just outside the doorway. He reached into his pocket, withdrew a pack of cigarettes, took one and lit it. He exhaled pensively, nodding to an attractive woman who happened to walk by.

The two men in the store entrance leaned back against the window. They watched Arcand closely, holding their pistols as if they were about to use them.

"Could they be here for him instead of us?" Claire asked, trying to make sense of what was happening.

Arcand stood there, studying the street. He looked at the man and woman, apparently dismissed them, and then turned to the car in front of the bakery. He seemed to study it intently, then glanced in the opposite direction, toward the second sedan, before his gaze returned to the man and woman. The men in the store front crept forward slowly, weapons poised. Arcand still hadn't noticed them; he was facing the street. The man and woman across the street turned, each facing a sedan. They waved their arms broadly, motioning the vehicles towards the store.

As if sensing danger, Arcand walked briskly down the street. Just as he passed the store entrance, the two men emerged from the shadows and grabbed him, pinning his arms and jamming their pistols against his back. The sedans left their parking spaces, eluding the vehicles traveling up and down the *Boulevard Saint-Germain*, and pulled forward, coming to a halt in front of the book store. Arcand struggled, pushing the men away and tried to run, but they easily overpowered him, forced his hands behind his back and handcuffed him. A car door opened and he was roughly shoved in; the men with the guns followed, flanking him in the rear seat. The man and women got into the second car, both in the back seat, and seconds later the vehicles pulled away, merging into oncoming traffic. The whole episode lasted less than three minutes.

Claire looked at Rachel, dumbfounded. "The Gestapo was watching the building," she said, still unable to believe their good fortune. "But they weren't looking for us."

Chapter 8

Paul Moreau lay in bed at his Giverny cottage, his head propped upon a pillow. He stared vacantly out the window, not seeing the grass that stretched to the Seine or the chestnut trees that bordered it, but he did notice the flowers that colored the landscape. Catherine loved flowers.

At the edge of the property sat a small knoll that climbed above the river, marred by two white crosses. Paul knew they bore the names of his wife and daughter. It was the most scenic place on the farm, rising from the riverbank to stand guard over the Seine as it rolled lazily past. Surrounded by trees on three sides, the branches painted the area in shade and hid the hill from the world, creating a sanctuary bathed in serenity.

Over a week had passed since the Germans came. And although he was starting to recover, the purple bruises beginning to fade, the mental anguish remained, ripping his heart from his body and dwarfing the physical pain that consumed him. It was a grief so overpowering, so debilitating, he knew he could never escape it.

His cousin Claire Daladier sat in a leather chair across from the bed. She had rescued the Abzacs and then remained in Giverny so she could care for him. Her efforts, when combined with their friend Dr. Durant's daily visits, ensured his condition was monitored and treated. She had just served him lunch, although he ate little. He kept gazing out the window, mesmerized by the beautiful flowers, tinted by nature in every color of the rainbow, blooming throughout the yard. Claire knew they were Catherine's passion. It was hard to look at them without thinking of her.

"I know it hurts," she said softly. She had lost a dear friend and a child she had treated as her own, two years after losing her husband Jacques. A likable man with a ready smile, he met a gruesome death at the end of a machine gun.

"And I know you feel the pain as badly as I do," Paul said softly, grateful for all she was doing.

He thought of her apartment above the family bookstore on the *Boulevard Saint-Germain*, close to his on *Rue de Poissy*, both Parisian streets on the Left Bank that were shaded by trees, blessed with buildings beautifully designed, surviving the centuries. But since the Germans came Claire spent more time at her home at Giverny, escaping the sights and sounds of a German occupation, leaving much of her bookstore's operation to her employees.

He didn't know how to grieve, or to overcome it – if that was even possible. He didn't know how to make the horrible nightmares go away. But he wanted to. "Do you think of Jacques often?" he asked quietly, hoping she could help him.

"It's a rare day when I don't," she said. "I try to justify it, but I never can. I always wonder why he had to die. It was so senseless."

He knew the feeling. It was overwhelming despair, complete and utter helplessness, an inability to comprehend the useless loss. It was drowning in a grief that choked the mind and heart and soul, consuming your entire being – thoughts, actions, beliefs. It was emptiness, a void that could never be filled, darkness so black that light didn't exist.

"But life is always worth living," she added with a shrug. "Isn't it?"

Paul managed a weak smile. In her case, life was worth living. She was young, barely thirty years of age. Men found her attractive; women found her congenial. She was intelligent, talented, and vivacious. She had much to live for.

"Why should I live when Catherine and Sophie didn't?" he asked. "Why should Jacques die in the prime of his life?"

A knock on the door interrupted their conversation. "How are we today?" Dr. Durant asked as he entered the bedroom. He was an older man, a bit overweight, with gray hair and round steel glasses, kind and compassionate.

Paul didn't reply. He again looked out the window, admiring the flowers. Would his death reunite them? Was Sophie with Catherine? He never had thoughts like these before.

Dr. Durant eyed him curiously and moved next to the bed. He started to examine him, poking and probing and checking. "Is there still blood in your urine?" he asked as he listened to his breathing with a stethoscope.

"A little," he said.

"Are you feeling stronger?"

"I'm better every day," he said. His eyes strayed to the flowers.

Dr. Durant watched his patient closely, his face showing concern. "Don't try to make sense of it," he said compassionately. "You won't be able to."

The doctor motioned Claire to the hallway. They whispered among themselves for a moment, and then left the house, walking out into the yard and down to the river.

Paul imagined Catherine and Sophie as he last saw them, standing in the garden. The ache was overwhelming. He thought of little Sophie, at the dawn of life, unable to realize the simplest of dreams. And Catherine, his friend and lover, so terribly missed.

He could hear their laughter, see their tears. He remembered even the most mundane moments, now so treasured, so sorely missed. A family dinner, with Sophie describing a day with her dolls in intricate detail as Catherine listened intently, hiding a smile. Or walking down the road, enjoying a summer stroll as Sophie skipped beside them. Sophie dancing across the yard, showing Catherine her latest creation, practiced to perfection. Catherine's penchant for hats, broad and floppy and hanging over her eyes. She wore them in the garden, hiding from the sun, while Sophie played beside her.

But now they were gone. And he was nothing without them.

Chapter 9

Claire and Dr. Durant walked passed the gardens, a mixture of flowers planted in a rainbow of colors, and paused to enjoy the view of the River Seine.

"The Abzacs are safe," Durant said. "They'll live with a farmer on the other side of the village, helping in the fields. You did the right thing bringing them to me."

"I didn't know who else to turn to. Or who else to trust. I could only think of you and your brother, Henri."

"I'm sorry you found Paul and his family," he said softly. "We had convinced ourselves that if we stayed in a small village and minded our own business, the war wouldn't impact us. How naïve and silly that seems now."

Claire's face was pale, her eyes glazed with sorrow, as she remembered the horrendous scene she confronted when she went to see her cousin, whose house was just down the road from hers. It was a surreal nightmare, ghastly and gruesome, horrific beyond belief. She had gone into shock after finding them, her mind unable to comprehend, and was wandering aimlessly down the rural road when Dr. Durant happened upon her. Knowing something was wrong, he stopped to help.

"It's something I wish I could forget," she said sadly. "But never will."

"I think it's time for us to take back France," Durant stated firmly. "We can't wait for the Germans to go away. Or for someone else to chase them away."

Claire thought of the satisfaction she felt in saving the Abzacs. Somehow she recovered a piece of what she had lost when Jacques died, or when she found Catherine and Sophie lying murdered in the grass. She also knew the risk, the overwhelming fear instilled by the Gestapo. But she still she wanted to help people, and now nothing would stop her.

"I'll do whatever you need me to," she offered, "but I want to help the Jews. They're suffering the most."

She knew he trusted her. He knew her as well as she knew herself. And he had known her mother and father just as well.

He picked up a twig and quickly drew a diagram in the dirt. It was a rough map of the Left Bank of Paris. "Let me show you something," he told her. "It's a secret I've kept for over twenty years."

* * *

Paul watched from the window as they lingered in the garden. Claire picked some flowers, roses of red and pink and yellow, and some lilies, and bunched them together. They strolled to the riverbank, watching the Seine as it meandered by.

A plate of ham and cheese and a tray of bread sat on the table beside the bed. The knife, long and slender, lay beside it. The blade glistened in the sunlight that filtered through the window. He stared at it, studying the curve of its handle and the chiseled sharpness of the blade.

He looked to the window. Claire held the flowers while Dr. Durant spoke. Their discussion seemed interesting; Claire listened intently as he spoke, his hands gesturing.

He knew it would be awhile before they returned. The walk back would take a few minutes, and their conversation seemed far from over. Paul looked at the table. The knife still lay there, innocent but deadly. He reached across the bed but it was just beyond his grasp, and he struggled to grab it, groaning, a sharp pain in his ribs. He couldn't do it. He returned his head to the pillow, gasping. Maybe if he shifted his torso and stretched as far as he could, he might be able to reach it, even though the pain would be intense – like he was attached to two horses running in different directions. He summoned his strength and tried again, stretching across the bed, barely touching the knife with the edge of his fingers. He put pressure on the handle, trying to roll it towards him. The blade came closer, and he was able to grasp the handle. He took the knife in his hand and collapsed against the pillows, moaning with pain, and waited for the throbbing to subside.

When he opened his eyes, Claire and Dr. Durant still stood on the riverbank. The doctor was drawing something on the ground with a twig.

Paul took the knife and placed it against his wrist, pushing the blade against his skin. He felt the sharpness and he closed his eyes, driven, convinced that no other path existed. He applied more pressure, feeling the blade prick the softness of his skin, the veins, blue and purple and vulnerable, crawling like a spider web up his arm. He pushed harder, feeling the pain, the knife about to break through. Then the back door creaked on its hinges, and he heard footsteps in the kitchen.

"Let me put these in a vase," he heard Claire say.

Paul sighed and surrendered. It took strength to take your life. And he was a coward. He had proven that when the Germans came. He heard the kitchen spigot. Claire was filling the vase. He tossed the knife back onto the tray. It landed near the bread, not quite where it had been, but he didn't think anyone would notice. He didn't want them to know.

"You haven't eaten," Claire said as she walked into the bedroom, followed by Dr. Durant.

"I did a little."

"You have to eat, Paul," Durant advised. "You'll lose your strength if you don't."

"I need to do more than lay in bed," Paul said with renewed resolve. He had chosen to live. Now he would make the most of it. "I need revenge."

Durant looked at Claire. "We were just discussing that in the garden.," he said. "We all want revenge. But revenge doesn't win wars. It gets people killed. Although that doesn't mean we can't fight back."

Paul was a bit confused. "Revenge is fighting back," he replied. "First, I want to kill the fisherman. And then the colonel."

"Emotion is dangerous," the doctor said. "But patience and cunning and intelligence are not." He pulled up a chair, his demeanor different, switching roles from doctor to mentor and confidant. "We have options. I've just discussed them with Claire. We can help people. And we can make a contribution."

"We have options?" Paul asked. "How can the three of us fight the Germans?"

"You don't have to be on the front lines to help win the war," Durant answered. "The Allies are starved for information. We can start there."

"How do we do that?" Paul asked. "I'm a banker and Claire owns a bookstore."

43

"You and Claire return to Paris," Durant said. "Attend German social functions and public gatherings. Blend in with the enemy. Obtain any information you can: eavesdrop in cabarets, get names of German officials, regiments stationed in Paris, planned troop movements, identify regiments on leave."

"Suppose we do learn something of value," Paul said. "Who do we tell?"

"Claire and I have enlisted my brother, Henri. And I will provide two more contacts for you in Paris."

Paul was surprised at both Durant's knowledge and Claire's involvement. "Dr. Durant, how long have you been involved in this?" he wondered aloud.

"A few months," he replied. "I called some old friends. They helped me get started."

"Old friends?" Paul asked. "From where?"

"From the Great War," he said. "I was more than a doctor then. Your father and I served together. We were engaged in espionage."

Paul was quiet for a moment. His father was killed in the war. The man he idolized, his hero, the man he wanted to be when he grew up, was stolen from him. The Germans had killed him. And they had murdered Catherine and Sophie. Now he wanted to kill every German he could.

"Are you all right, Paul?" Claire asked.

"Yes, I'm fine," he said. "How are you involved in this?"

Claire recounted the story of the Abzac family, and how Henri Durant had helped to save them. "The longer the Germans are here, the worse it will be for the Jews," she said. "That's what Dr. Durant and I were just discussing. I want to help more Jews escape."

Paul was shocked that his cousin, quiet and modest, mired in books her entire life, had the courage and ability to rescue a family. "Claire, I never thought you capable," he said.

"Which is why she's such a good candidate," Durant informed him. "She just saved four lives."

"I thought the Jews were deported to a colony in the east," Paul said. "Are they really in danger?"

Durant was quiet for a moment. He glanced at Claire, and then Paul. "Not many people know this," he explained. "The Jews are deported to the east, but to slave labor camps. Then they are worked to death. Others are murdered long before that."

Paul struggled to sit up in bed, sliding his sore body up against the pillows. "Then Claire and I should get back to Paris so we can get started," he suggested. "We'll get information, and we'll help Jews. But I also want to kill Germans. And the French who help them, starting with the fisherman. I want to kill him with my bare hands so I can look in his eyes while he dies."

"And how does a banker intend to kill Germans?" Durant asked quietly. "Are you a good shot?"

"No," Paul admitted. "I'm not much for guns."

"Knives?"

Paul shook his head.

"That's good," Durant said. "Because good shots and men with knives get themselves killed. Along with many innocent people. Especially around Nazis."

Paul was quiet, reflective. His eyes moved to Durant's. "It's something I have to do," he said softly.

"Bankers don't make good killers. For now, you'll obtain information. When you're able to control your temper, to quench your thirst for revenge, then you can move forward. Not before."

Paul looked away, sulking. He knew Durant was right, but he wasn't sure he could comply. He realized he didn't know how to kill Germans, but he wanted to learn. He couldn't help it.

There was an awkward pause before Durant spoke. "We have another issue to address."

"What is it?" Claire asked.

"Rachel Abzac insists on returning to Paris," he said. "She wants to fight the Germans, too."

Chapter 10

Eventually Paul healed completely, although he still needed some physical therapy under the guidance of Dr. Durant before his legs were fully functional. He regained complete use of his kidneys, which was the doctor's greatest concern, and the ugly purple bruises that covered his body gradually faded away. His mental anguish, and the guilt and sorrow that came with it, would last a lifetime.

It was early September when they returned to Paris, but little had changed while they were at Giverny. Flags with the swastika were evenly spaced down the *Champs-Élysées* and other major boulevards. The Hotel Meurice, across from Tuileries Garden, was still German headquarters. Other hotels housed German troops, as did private homes, where residents were expected to provide quarters for an officer or two. The headquarters of the Gestapo was still located on the posh Avenue Foch. And the English bookstore, W.H. Smith on the *Rue de Rivoli,* had a large swastika hanging above its entrance.

Paris had been peaceful the first two years the Germans were there. The enemy was fascinated by the fabled metropolis, unable to digest its splendor: the River Seine splitting the city in half, the graceful arches of the Pont Alexandre III Bridge, the flying buttresses of the Notre Dame Cathedral, or the lofty reach of the Eiffel Tower. At first they were more like tourists than conquerors, taking photographs and marveling at the beauty and culture. But their grip had gradually tightened, and they started to slowly strangle the city.

Food was rationed, with minimal amounts of milk and meat allocated to the people, turnips and potatoes still available in abundance. Most Parisians had small pots of vegetables growing on their terraces: tomatoes, radishes, onions, spinach or lettuce. Paul and Claire were more fortunate – they could obtain fruits and vegetables from their cottages in Giverny, and meat and cheese and milk from local farmers.

Claire went with Paul to his flat on the *Rue de Poissy,* on the Left Bank just across the Seine from Notre Dame. As Paul tentatively stepped across the threshold, he was flooded with memories. He could see Catherine cooking dinner, chatting idly over the counter as he sat in the parlor and read the newspaper. Or Sophie, sitting on the floor with her dolls, mimicking voices and holding conversations with imaginary playmates.

As he walked through the apartment, he was overwhelmed with emotion and started to cry. He held his hands to his eyes, trying to stop the tears as they rolled down his cheeks, but they only fell more forcefully, his body heaving and jerking. Claire hugged him tightly.

The parlor was Catherine. The Art-Deco furniture, so sleek and functional, had been her favorite design. It was tastefully mixed with Impressionist prints and amber Art Nouveau glass that dressed the end tables. For the first time, he realized how eclectic her tastes were, and even though he had disagreed when she purchased them, he realized how skillfully she blended them together. But now he would never be able to tell her. He could smell her perfume, see her books on the shelves, her robe draped carelessly over the chair beside the bed. Her clothes filled the closet; the bathroom cabinet was cluttered with her make-up. A high-heel shoe peeked shyly from under the bed, photographs of them together hung on the wall beside a charcoal sketch she had done of the Louvre.

They had met at the Sorbonne in 1925, both determined to change the world. Paul graduated with a degree in economics, earning much of his tuition employed as a bricklayer. Although he enjoyed the physical work, he was fascinated by finance, the intricate paths that money takes and the many uses it has. Catherine was an art major inclined towards the Impressionists; she painted or sketched every day, and the galleries that sprinkled the city sold most of her creations. She had just reached the point in her career where her name was easily recognized, and most saw a rewarding future for her. Now there was no future.

He passed Sophie's room, but didn't have the courage to enter. He looked from the doorway at the canopied bed, stuffed animals arranged around the pillows, meant to protect their owner. The toy chest with the clown's face, painted by Catherine, sat by the closet, where the open door showed tiny clothes draped from their hangers. A miniature unicorn of pink Murano glass sat on her dresser, beside the little make-up kit she used when playing mommy. But she would never be a mother. She would never be more than a five-year old child.

Claire led him back to the parlor, where he sat and stared. He clung desperately to the past, afraid to let them go, afraid to look and smell and feel what surrounded him, afraid to accept that they were gone.

Paul spent the next few weeks at Claire's flat. It was best that he avoided being alone. He didn't want his thoughts to wander in the wrong direction, the road he had almost taken at the cottage.

Claire helped him avoid painful memories, and one day while he was at the bank, she packed away the belongings of Catherine and Sophie and had everything moved and stored in Giverny. They could be saved for another day, when happy memories masked sad ones. He was upset when he returned to find the empty apartment, but he knew she was right; he needed as few reminders as possible, at least for a while.

Once the personal belongings were gone, Claire gradually replaced the photographs and glassware, and then the tables and chairs. She even had the walls painted. After three or four weeks, the apartment was far different from what it had been, and Paul started to look for tomorrow, with yesterday hidden in a special corner in his heart. Once his apartment had been redone, Paul and Claire decided to stay with each other, alternating between apartments, until he was comfortable being alone.

Paul received the invitation a few weeks after his return to Paris. It was to a social function that weekend, hosted by the Council for Economic Development, at the *Hotel de Crillon*. It heralded a new era of joint economic cooperation between German and Franco enterprises. As an officer of the *Banque de Paris,* he would be an honored guest. As Paul read the invitation, he saw that the event was sponsored by Julian Junot.

He was the most hated man in Paris.

Chapter 11

Dr. Durant reviewed the identity papers and rationing coupons one more time, and then handed them to the sixteen-year-old girl. "You are no longer Rachel Abzac," he said. "Your name is now Rochelle Allard."

She nodded, her face showing no emotion. Her brown hair was brushed straight back, exposing a face like any other teenage girl in France. She was plain, making no attempt to be beautiful, at least not through cosmetics or hair style, but it helped her blend in. And now, nothing was more important than blending in.

He looked at her gravely, trying to amplify the danger, opened the papers and pointed to the address. "Your flat is ten blocks from Claire's book store, just off *Rue Monge.* It's best that you avoid the employees there, since they know you are Jewish. You live on the sixth floor, in a tiny attic apartment."

"I know the area," she said, thinking. "And I know the street."

"The first three-months' rent has already been paid. Don't ask by whom. You will tell the landlord, a middle-aged woman named Margaret, that your Aunt Marie arranged for the apartment. That's all she needs to know, and in regard to the arrangements, that's all you need to know. The less you know, the better."

"I understand," she said.

Her face was passive but Durant guessed that her stomach must be churning, just as his had when he first started working for the Resistance. The detailed preparations only highlighted the risk. Life on a farm with her family was safe and secure, with little chance of discovery. They could be together, helping those who were kind enough to shelter them. And when the war ended, they could return to Paris.

Dr. Durant watched her closely. "It's a lot to ask of a teenage girl," he admitted. "Many adults who want to do it, can't. No one will find fault if you change your mind and stay in Giverny."

"Those that are missing are just like my family," she told him. "They came to Paris to better their lives, and the lives of their children. They struggled with a new language, lived in shabby flats with peeling wallpaper, fading paint, and dated colors. And they worked six or seven days a week for twelve hours a day in their own small shops or in restaurants or taverns or stores. And they did it gladly, because they chased a dream that promised a better existence."

"It's still dangerous, a risk you don't have to take, even if you do want to help them."

"I have to do it," she said. "Whole families are gone; their lives are nightmares. Someone has to fight back. If no one does, the Germans will take more and more, until there's nothing left to take."

"Stay here" Dr. Durant urged her. "Help your own family."

"No," she said, her resolve returning, her determination strong. "I'm going to Paris."

"You're certain?"

"Yes, I'm sure."

He studied her closely, admiring her courage, envying her strength. She could be trusted; he was sure of that. He knew he could give her ever-increasing responsibilities because she was capable and competent, brave and mature. She wouldn't fail him. "You'll work at the factory on the corner near your flat," he said, pointing to the map. "You start on Monday morning at six a.m. The factory makes boots for soldiers on the Russian front."

Rachel was listening intently, as if she knew her life depended on it. "I will do well. I know the work."

"Good," Durant said. "My brother Henri will take you into Paris at dawn."

"And how will I kill Germans?"

He marveled at her defiance, her courage, and her commitment. "You will obtain information about the factory," he informed her. "How many boots are made, where they are shipped, how they are shipped. What other products are made at the factory, and who tells them what to make."

"And how will I get that information back to you?"

"Every Sunday morning you'll go to the café adjacent to your apartment. Sit at a table outside, and a young man named Meurice will join you. If it's safe, he'll compliment you – your hair, or scarf, or blouse. If it isn't safe, he'll talk about the weather. Then you know you are in danger."

She nodded, then began memorizing the instructions. "What do I do it if isn't safe?" she asked. "How do I escape?"

"You will do what Meurice tells you to do," he said sternly. "That's how you stay alive."

She nodded, as if to accept his direction, but stared pensively.

"Are you all right?" Durant asked.

"I'll be entirely on my own," she said, sounding nervous and a bit overwhelmed, "for the first time in my life."

"You know where your family is," he said. "You can return at any time."

"I know," she said quietly. "But this is something I have to do. It isn't a choice, as it would seem to others, or a foolish obsession, as it seems to you. It's a part of me." She put her hand against her heart. "It's in here."

He studied the young woman, an adult in a child, and he understood. She was just like him.

Chapter 12

Julian Junot was a wealthy industrialist with business interests throughout Europe and Africa. His companies were wide-ranging: mineral excavation, food production, construction, locomotive and railcar design and manufacture, as well as an investment banking division in Geneva and a large commercial real estate portfolio. Started by his great-grandfather, the businesses had thrived and prospered, expanding under the leadership of successive generations. Junot had become chairman in his late twenties, when his father died in a plane crash. Some said his was the most effective in the entire lineage, even at such a tender age.

He was humble and modest; those who knew him claimed he was as comfortable with the poor as he was with the rich. He was known for his charity, providing funds for orphanages and helping the unemployed and those less fortunate. During the world economic collapse, many owed their lives to him, since his charities ensured that anyone without the means still had a hot meal every day. Then the Nazis came and no one remembered what a good man he was. They didn't want to.

He had little involvement in politics before the war, but when the Germans advanced on Paris and the government fled, he filled the void and brokered the city's surrender, giving the world's most beautiful city to the enemy without a shot being fired. The French army left one day; the Germans walked in the next. Junot's reward was oversight of the city, ensuring the needs of his German masters were always met. Parisians were horrified. In their eyes he had transformed from a benevolent industrialist to a hated traitor. He could never convince them otherwise and didn't bother to try.

The Germans, having subjugated the nation, were now integrating French culture and economic viability into that of the Greater Reich. The purpose of the banquet at the Hotel Crillon was to promote joint economic cooperation. It was there that Paul first met Junot, even though he already knew who he was. But then, all of Paris knew who he was.

He attended with Claire. They settled in among a hundred other guests, scattered two or four to a table. A large Nazi flag was draped from the ceiling of the far wall, the swastika consuming the room and choking those that shared the space. Paul recognized some Parisian businessmen, but was more surprised by those he didn't know. There were also German officers sprinkled among the crowd, some with French women. The enemy, it seemed, had taken everything Paris had to offer.

Paul and Claire scanned the room as they enjoyed their meal, salmon that was superbly cooked, so tender and perfectly poached that it flaked apart when prodded slightly with the fork. Apparently the Germans, and the French elite who joined them, weren't subject to rationing.

Paul glanced at his watch. It was 8 p.m.

"You're anxious, Paul. Why?" Claire asked. She had an amused look on her face, her brown eyes big and bright.

"I don't know what to expect," he said. "And I don't want to waste the evening."

A middle-aged woman at an adjacent table rolled her eyes. Paul couldn't tell if she was annoyed, apprehensive, or in agreement.

"Keep your voice down," Claire warned. "You may not be among friends." She studied him closely, as if wondering whether he should attend a public event with so many Germans. He was still too angry, the inner turmoil too volcanic.

Suddenly a tall, ramrod-straight German officer loomed over their table. He wore wire-rimmed spectacles, his gray hair cut close to the scalp. There was a red stripe down the leg of his uniform trousers, the mark of a general.

Paul's heart started to race. He hated all things German, especially those in uniform. He studied the man for a moment. He looked vaguely familiar, probably from the newspapers. Maybe he had even met him before. But it didn't matter. He hated him anyway. He realized how hard it would be to socialize with the Germans and the French who supported them. How could he pretend to be sympathetic to their cause? Especially when he wanted to kill every one he saw.

The general nodded a polite greeting, and then addressed Claire.

"How nice it is to see you," he said as he gently took her hand. "I'm so glad you're back in Paris."

She smiled, and offered brief introductions. She seemed to like him. "So how are you, General Berg?"

"I'm well," he said. "I trust you are, also?"

Paul was surprised. He didn't know she counted any Germans as friends, especially generals. Maybe that's where he had seen him before, in Claire's store.

"Yes, I am," she said. "I just needed some time in the country."

"Giverny?" he asked.

Paul watched warily. How did the general know so much about her? It seemed they were more than casual acquaintances. Maybe they were more than friends.

"Yes," she replied. "The family cottage. It's so peaceful there."

General Berg turned to Paul. "You have a remarkable cousin," he told him. "But I'm sure you're aware of that."

"Yes, I know," Paul said, still wondering what their connection was. Although Berg seemed too old to be a romantic interest, Paul suspected there was something between them. Berg did have a wedding ring on his finger. Not that it mattered in wartime Paris.

"I believe you promised me a rematch," the general reminded her.

"You're right, I did. And I'm available at your convenience."

It was then that Paul recalled another of Claire's talents. She was an amateur chess champion, quite renowned on the Left Bank of Paris. Her book store had several tables in and outside the store, used for chess, checkers, and cards. She was often in demand to participate.

"Excellent," he said eagerly, rubbing his hands together. "I'll look forward to it. I've been practicing with my aide, although he is definitely not as skilled as you."

He nodded to Paul and then returned to his seat a few tables away.

"I forgot about your talent for chess," Paul said, still wary of the warmth between the two. He didn't like Claire being so close to a German general.

"He's a customer at the store," she said. "When we play, he always talks about his granddaughters. He loves them dearly. I might have liked him very much, but..." She paused, searching for the right words. "He's a Nazi. And there are no nice Nazis."

Paul didn't reply, but considered her statement. He thought of the enemy as creatures, devoid of emotion or consideration for human life. He sometimes forgot they were people, just like him. And many of them were good people. The problem was, the majority were not.

A short, stout gentleman made his way to the podium. He tapped the microphone and, when satisfied that the sound system was adequate, he began to speak.

"Thank you for coming, ladies and gentlemen," he began. "I am Otto Ernst, from Berlin, Chairman of the Joint Economic Council."

He paused and took a sip of water. "The Economic Council is an organization formed to produce partnerships between French and German businesses. The primary purpose...."

"Is to steal French business," Paul whispered.

"Hush," Claire hissed. She glanced at those sitting nearby. "Paul, you had better be quiet. Don't drink any more wine!"

He was getting annoyed. The master plan was clear to him. "History will call the Economic Council grand larceny," he muttered.

"Bitte," the woman beside them said in German. "Excuse me."

Claire eyed him sternly. "Paul, pay attention," she told him. "No one is interested in your opinion." She nodded discreetly to a man in a Gestapo uniform who sat at the next table.

Otto Ernst was still speaking. "With our goal in mind, and knowing that more information will follow, I will now introduce you to our Paris sponsor, Mr. Julian Junot."

The attendees applauded politely. Paul studied their faces. He was curious to see who, after two years of German occupation, still remained French and who had climbed into bed with the enemy.

Junot stood up, walked to the podium, and shook Ernst's hand. Junot was a handsome man with finely formed features, slender and less than average height. His hair was black, tinged with gray at the temples. Dark eyes, bright and twinkling, gazed upon the audience. He appeared physically fit for a man of his age, which Paul judged to be early forties. He was meticulously dressed in a hand-tailored gray suit and blue silk shirt.

"Thank you, Otto," Junot said warmly. "And good evening ladies and gentlemen."

"I've known him for years," Claire whispered. "He's -"

"A traitor?" Paul asked innocently.

He felt someone tap his shoulder. He turned to find the man in the Gestapo uniform, leaning forward.

"Stille," he said sternly, pointing to the stage. "Hush."

Paul decided to be quiet. It suddenly seemed like a good idea.

Junot spoke for a few minutes, welcoming those in attendance, discussing Franco-German relations, but Paul wasn't really listening. He was fighting his temper, trying to control his rage. Just as Dr. Durant said he should.

"So in closing," Junot was saying, "I ask that you greet change with an open mind. Give the Joint Economic

Council a chance. And the greatest economic force in history will follow. So mingle, introduce yourselves to one another. We don't have lectures or presentations planned. Just a relaxing evening where you get to meet interesting and powerful people."

Otto Ernst scampered to the podium. "I'll be contacting you all over the next few days. Enjoy your meal and thank you, Mr. Junot." The German then led the audience in applause.

Paul shook his head. "Junot will hand everything in France over to the Germans," he whispered to Claire. Just like he gave them Paris."

"It's too soon to tell what will happen," Claire said.

"I know what will happen," Paul argued, "France will be a distant memory. It will be called Germany."

"Paul," Claire said, nodding her head toward the stage. "Junot is coming this way."

Junot was smiling, shaking hands as he walked through the crowd.

"Let's go," Paul said anxiously. "Before he gets here."

She looked at those nearby. They remained seated. "We can't leave now," she hissed. "It'll be too obvious."

He was two tables away.

"Who cares?" Paul asked. "I have no desire to meet him."

Claire gave him a nasty look. "Try to be polite," she advised.

"Claire, how are you?" an approaching man crooned. "I'm so glad you could come."

Junot took Claire's outstretched hand and kissed it lightly.

Claire blushed, and then made introductions. "This I my cousin Paul Moreau," she said, "and this is Julian Junot, one of my best customers."

Junot shook Paul's hand. "She's a fabulous saleswoman," he offered. "A look at my library will confirm that."

"I haven't seen you in a while," Claire said. "You're not buying books elsewhere, are you?" She wagged a finger at him, pretending to be angry.

He smiled, eyes twinkling. "No, of course not," he replied. "I wouldn't think of it. I've just been preoccupied."

"We all have," Claire said softly. Her eyes were trained on his, searching, and then she smiled again.

Junot turned to Paul. "Have we met before, Mr. Moreau?" he asked.

"No," Paul said, trying not to sound abrupt. Durant wanted them to mingle, but he was uncomfortable with Junot's cozy relationship with Claire. "I'm sure I would have remembered."

"Have you always lived in Paris?"

His question surprised Paul. He hadn't expected pleasantries. "Yes, we have," he responded.

"I have as well," Junot answered. "It's the most beautiful city in the world, with a culture surpassing any site or civilization. And its greatest day has yet to dawn."

"Really?" Paul asked. "That's hard to imagine. I think Paris's greatest day has passed, like a pleasant autumn. And a severe winter lies ahead."

Junot showed no offense. "And what do you think, Claire?" he asked.

Paul watched them closely. He couldn't help feeling like they were having some sort of private conversation, one that had nothing to do with Paris, but everything to do with the two of them.

"I think I agree with my cousin," she said softly, her eyes on his. "Paris had a fabulous past. But it's hard to envision a future."

"I disagree," Junot responded. "Paris has fabulous prospects. I think your time frame may be too short. Do you know the Chinese think in terms of generations? We in the West think in terms of weeks or months."

"Sometimes that's all life allows," Paul said, not interested in Junot's philosophy. Or his vision of Paris's future.

Junot looked thoughtful for a moment. "Claire, I wonder if you might be interested in joining a club I started," he suggested. "It's called the Bibliophile Society. We meet at my home a few times a month to discuss literature." Then he smiled. "And we drink a lot of wine. You're welcome, as well, Mr. Moreau."

"We would love to," Claire said.

"Good, I'll have an invitation sent to your store. My home is nearby. Right on the *Ile Saint-Louis*, on the *Quai d'Orleans.*"

"Yes, I know," she said. "It's just a few blocks away. Right across the river from Paul."

"Julian," someone called from across the room. "Mr. Deveraux is waiting to meet you."

It was Otto Ernst. He was talking to a white-haired man who looked slightly annoyed.

"I'm sorry," Junot said with a shrug. "I must go." He turned to Claire, his eyes still twinkling. "It was so nice to see you again. And a pleasure to meet you, Mr. Moreau."

Junot turned and moved across the room.

Paul looked at Claire, a bit angry. "Why were you being so friendly?" he asked.

"Because I have known him for many years and he is an interesting and charming man. He's one of my best customers."

"But you know what he is," Paul said. "And what he's done."

She rolled her eyes. "Paul, we were having a harmless conversation," she replied. "Nothing more. Besides, we need to mingle. Remember what Dr. Durant said."

Chapter 13

"Julian Junot, this is Andre Deveraux," Otto Ernst said. "Now, if you'll excuse me, I have other guests to attend to."

Deveraux was tall and stooped, with half-lens glasses perched on his nose. Slender, with white hair and a meticulously trimmed goatee, he gazed upon Junot curiously. "I've heard much about you, Mr. Junot," he informed him. "I was surprised when Otto said you wanted to meet me."

Junot nodded politely and said, "I've heard much about you, as well. I wanted to enlist your assistance."

Deveraux looked surprised. "I'm not sure what I can offer," he replied. "I'm a simple public servant, merely doing my duty."

"I realize that," Junot answered. "But you fill an important role. I understand you control the selection process for Jews collected in the round-ups, where they are sent, and when they are shipped east."

Deveraux stared at Junot, his pale blue eyes guarded and noncommittal. "I comply with the wishes of my German overseers," he offered, "much like you."

"Agreed," Junot said cautiously, tiring of the verbal jousting. "You have your duties and I have mine. Unfortunately, my primary occupation is that of a businessman. My service to the government of Paris is purely voluntary."

Deveraux smiled. "I know your family's history well, Mr. Junot," he told him. "Voluntary service is admirable. And if paid by the people of Paris, I'm sure you would decline, given your personal circumstances."

"I would," Junot replied. "But I speak to you, sir, as a businessman. Given my production requirements, I have factories to run. To do that, I need labor."

"I'm not sure I understand."

"During the last two round-ups, I was able to persuade the French police to divert some of the Jewish men to my employ. Personal favors that were greatly appreciated, and gladly returned, I might add. I give the Jews a room – they're slums really – and some slop to eat, and no pay whatsoever. They work in my factories, all day, every day."

"And how has that worked?" Deveraux asked, hiding his distaste.

Junot sighed. "Not as well as I had hoped," he admitted. "The men miss their families – not that I care – but one recently escaped. He's probably searching for his loved ones."

"I'm sorry to hear that, Mr. Junot. But I still don't see how I can help you."

"I have a better plan," Junot explained. "I'm looking for entire Jewish families. Then they can work side by side in the factory, even the children. There will be no complaints, no escapes."

Andre Deveraux cringed, his face pale. He didn't speak.

Junot watched his reaction. "Please, Mr. Deveraux, spare me your indignation," he advised. "What do you think happens to the Jews you send east? I've heard the rumors, just as you have."

"Mr. Junot, although I understand your problem, I'm not in a position to solve it."

Junot smiled faintly. "But I think you are, Mr. Deveraux," he insisted. "You underestimate your authority."

Deveraux's face tensed. "What are you trying to say, Mr. Junot?" he asked.

"I want some of the Jewish families released to me."

"I'm afraid that's impossible."

"I am willing to pay for them. Name the price."

"I'm not in the business of slave labor, Mr. Junot. The Jews are collected and sent east. That's all you need to concern yourself with."

Junot withdrew his wallet, removed a business card and handed it to Deveraux. "I still think we can help each other, Mr. Deveraux," he suggested. "I need cheap labor, desperately." He glanced around the room, ensuring no one was close enough to overhear. "And I'm willing to pay handsomely for it. But that should be a private agreement. Just between you and me."

Chapter 14

Claire Daladier left her bookshop at 12:45 p.m. and walked to *La Tour d'Argent,* an exclusive restaurant a few blocks away. She didn't tell her employees where she was going, which they found very curious, especially since she was nicely dressed in a violet skirt and lavender blouse, accented by a pearl necklace. They jokingly asked questions, offered conclusions, and suggested a plethora of alleged destinations, much to Claire's amusement. But she didn't reply, gave no reason why she was leaving, and didn't tell them how long she'd be gone, which only added to the mystery.

As she walked down the street she occasionally paused, pretending to gaze at a dress display in a shop window or to eye croissants in a bakery. She waited a few minutes, let all of those behind her pass and then examined who remained, searching for anyone suspicious. She knew she was being overly cautious, especially since she was only meeting someone for lunch. And even though it was a person she shouldn't be seeing, it was likely no one would notice, or even care if they did. But there was always the chance that someone might. And weeks or months later, they could connect the lunch meeting to another event and arrive at dangerous conclusions.

When she reached the restaurant it was crowded, as expected for that time of day. German officers dominated the patrons, their gray uniforms striking and intimidating. A general or two with crimson and gold collar patches adorning their uniforms were mixed with the others. Businessmen in tailored suits and starched shirts shared tables with nicely dressed women in blouses and skirts, expensive clothes common to those that frequented the establishment.

Claire nodded to the head waiter and then walked past him, her table reserved. She moved through the dining room, turned at the first aisle, and went to a booth shrouded with broad-leafed plants. The adjacent tables were occupied by Germans and she noticed no locals, not that she expected anyone she knew in such a posh restaurant. She sat in the booth, its high-backed green leather chairs offering more privacy to those that wanted to avoid prying eyes and ears.

She faced the window, which offered a generous view of Notre Dame. Claire studied it for a moment, the flying buttresses supporting it so slender, yet so strong. The structure seemed fragile, as if the spider-web of supports could fail at any time. Yet the building had stood for almost ten centuries. Strength, it seemed, was easily underestimated and could not always be determined. It made her think of Rachel Abzac.

A waiter arrived and offered a glass of Merlot which she accepted, and he left the bottle on the table. She was excited, her stomach queasy, almost like a little girl behaving badly. She reflected on what she was doing, which was months in the making, but daring and unconventional. She was conflicted – knowing the meeting was wrought with danger but wanting desperately to proceed, regardless of the risk. In a world teeming with death and disaster, any thread of happiness had to be clenched, coveted and protected, and she felt no guilt for what she was doing. She couldn't stop anyway – just like a train rumbling down the track. It would either discover new territories, exciting and unexplored, or crash, causing havoc and devastation.

Ten minutes later Julian Junot appeared and casually ducked into the booth, attracting little attention given the clientele. He was a regular customer; the patrons were accustomed to seeing him. The staff always gave him the utmost respect because he treated them well, chatting about their families and leaving generous tips.

As soon as he was seated, the waiter filled his glass, appearing to politely ignore the pair who wanted to be left alone, and then departed.

"Did anyone see you come?" Junot asked quietly.

"No," she replied. "I was careful."

"It's easy to explain should someone see us in a public place," he said. "But I don't want anyone to know how frequent our meetings will be."

"I understand," she responded. "It would only raise questions we don't need to answer. But they'll know soon enough."

Junot frowned, but didn't disagree. "Your cousin, Paul, definitely mustn't know," he insisted. "He's consumed with rage, which is understandable with what he's endured, but he's unpredictable – and that makes him dangerous."

"I realize he can't be trusted," Claire acknowledged, "and he would never understand."

"Is there anyone else we need to worry about?"

"My employees were very curious," Claire informed him, amused. "They asked a dozen questions, since I'm rarely dressed so well during the day. I finally told them I was meeting Voltaire – just to give them something to talk about."

He laughed and asked, "A French philosopher? Why not a German – Schiller or Schopenhauer?"

She rolled her eyes. "They were curious," she commented dryly, "but if I showed a sudden fondness for German philosophers, they would get extremely suspicious."

Junot smiled. "I suppose Voltaire is much better," he agreed.

"Surprisingly, they thought I was joking," she said, pretending shock. "And then I said I was going to play chess."

"Did they believe you?"

"Of course not," she said grinning.

"Playing chess is appropriate," he told her. "You can be the queen and I'll be the king."

"A king has such limited movement," she said coyly, "and always has to be guarded. I think you make a better knight – gallant and noble, able to leap over others to get what you want, often without them even suspecting."

The waiter interrupted them, arriving with the menu. Junot squinted in the dim lighting, scanning it casually, familiar with its contents, and then put it on the table. "The soup is always excellent," he informed her. "As is the beef bourguignon and calamari."

Claire rarely dined in such elite establishments; they were far too expensive. She was flattered and a bit intimidated, even though her mouth watered at the selections. The abundance of food made her feel guilty, knowing others barely had enough to survive. She realized how divided Paris really was. There were those who still had, and those who would never have.

"I'll defer to your judgment," she said, realizing that anything on the menu would be delicious.

"As you wish," he replied, and then selected beef bourguignon for both of them.

The waiter arrived, took their order, and left. They were alone again.

"How is business?" he asked.

"It's good," she answered. "The Germans are strong buyers. They've developed French tastes."

"I find that interesting," he mused aloud. "Germans develop French tastes, but few French acquire German tastes. I wonder why that is."

The pleasantries continued until the meal was served and then they ate, quiet and pensive, cautious and reflective. Both knew they stood on a dangerous precipice and any step had to be taken carefully.

It was only after their meal had been completed, and another glass of wine consumed, that the tone of the conversation became hushed, the wording cautious, the topic precarious. The discussion continued for almost thirty minutes, instruction and receipt, description and clarification.

Junot rose to leave. "You have many decisions to make," he said. "Once you take this step, it's difficult to go back, to return to what once was."

"I know the risks," she replied, not yet knowing if she wanted to continue. "And I know the rewards. I'll make my decision soon."

"I'll send you a message," he told her. "And then we'll continue our discussion."

Chapter 15

Shortly after 9 a.m. on Monday morning, Otto Ernst came to Paul Moreau's office at the *Banque de Paris*. He was short and heavy, almost as wide as he was tall, and he had a permanent smile etched on his cherubic face. It was hard to dislike him, even though Paul wanted to.

"I hope I haven't intruded," Ernst said. "But I'm charged with the integration of Jewish-owned businesses into the Greater Reich. I'm overseeing the merger between the Berlin Bank and the *Banque de Paris*."

"I wasn't aware the bank was being confiscated so soon," Paul said, feeling his face flush with anger.

"Merger is the preferred terminology," Ernst informed him. He seemed to expect resistance, as if it wasn't his first venture. "As you know, the Kohn family has owned the *Banque de Paris f*or over a century, and no one would ever dispute that."

"Agreed," Paul said tersely. "Every member of their family, past and present, has given their lives to the institution."

Ernst ignored his comment and replied, "I want to start with locations of all branch offices, liabilities and the loan portfolio, followed by a list of assets, investments, and deposits."

Paul couldn't believe how casually Ernst discussed stealing a family business that was a hundred years old. He had to do something to prevent it, but he didn't know what. He decided to stall for time.

"That may take a while for my staff to produce," he said, eyeing papers on his desk. "Maybe a few days. And then I'll have to review everything. As for the branch offices, if you give me just a minute I'll obtain their locations."

"Yes, of course," Ernst replied. "Please, take your time. Maybe today we'll examine the offices and tomorrow we can start with liabilities."

Paul walked across the hallway to his assistant's office. After a brief conversation to discuss what Ernst needed, he returned with the branch information.

"Is everything in order?" Ernst asked as Paul entered.

"Absolutely," Paul said as pleasantly as he could. "Here's the branch information. I can have a list of liabilities by tomorrow, assets later in the week. The loan portfolio won't be available until Wednesday, although I can assure you that our lending practices are sound."

"I realize that," Ernst assured him. "We've already done some preliminary checks. But the Berlin Bank is most interested in the loan portfolio."

"Why?" Paul asked. He thought assets would be their priority.

"Many of the loans will be called, particularly in the business arena," he explained, the smile now absent from his face. "Loan holders who can't repay their debt will be faced with foreclosure."

"You steal the business," Paul observed, "Jewish or not."

Ernst shrugged apologetically, as if the decision was not his. "Signs of a healthy economy, I'm told," he said. "Only the strong survive."

"Who benefits when the *Banque de Paris* becomes owner of these businesses?"

"The Berlin Bank will auction them," Ernst answered. "That will raise additional capital, improving the balance sheet of the bank."

"And of course, only German businesses will be permitted to bid."

"German law," he said tersely.

"The plan is to take many fine businesses, some of which have been family-owned for centuries, and give them to Germans," Paul summarized. "Is that correct?"

"Isn't that a bit harsh, Mr. Moreau?"

"Not really," Paul replied, trying to control his increasing anger. "What are your plans for assets?"

"Some tangible assets, like buildings, will be sold to raise capital," Ernst explained. "Securities will be reevaluated to determine if they're still suitable investments for a bank as large as our merged enterprise."

"What about liquid assets?" Paul asked.

"Liquid assets will be delivered to the main office of the Berlin Bank."

"So, in other words, liquid assets will be stolen?"

"A callous term," Ernst commented. "Let's say that they'll be used to their fullest potential."

Paul studied Ernst closely, digesting his statements. Some of the liquid assets might go to Germany, but not all of them. He would hide them so the *Banque de Paris* could claim them when the war was over.

Ernst seemed to observe Paul closely, his eyebrows arched. "Is there a problem?" he asked.

Paul managed a weak smile, masking his true feelings. "Of course not," he responded.

Ernst relaxed. "Excellent," he said, "I knew that we could work well together." He was quiet for a moment, studying the list of branch office, and then looked up. "The Joint Economic Council is having another dinner tomorrow at the *Hotel de Paris*, he said. "I'd be honored if you and your wife came as my guests."

Although Ernst's comment was innocent, Paul was consumed with grief, the pain sharp, as if his heart had been ripped from his body.

Ernst saw the agony on Paul's face. "Is something wrong?" he asked.

"No," Paul replied softly, his face pale. "My wife died a few months ago. It was my cousin who attended the last dinner with me."

Ernst reached across the desk and lightly touched Paul's arm. "I'm so sorry," he said sincerely. "I didn't know."

"Of course not. I wouldn't expect you to."

An awkward silence ensued. After a moment had passed, Ernst continued the conversation. "Can I expect you at dinner?" he asked.

Paul remembered his instructions from Dr. Durant: mingle with the enemy and obtain information. "I'd be honored," he replied.

Chapter 16

Paul had trouble sleeping and decided to take a stroll along the river. It was near curfew, so he didn't venture far from home and found both the streets and the riverbank almost deserted, other Parisians apparently fearing the curfew as he did. As he walked towards the water, admiring a clear sky, stars twinkling down on the city, a bus drove slowly past. Paul read the slogan on its side: *Junot Industries – Building a Better France,* over the image of a steel arch bridge, partially constructed. Paul was disgusted, knowing Junot would build all the bridges his Nazi masters needed, not that he deserved to build any bridges at all.

He was a few blocks from home, across from the *Île de la Cité,* when he heard distant cries. He walked faster, peering into the darkness, and saw a woman sitting on a bench, struggling, a German beside her. His arms were wrapped around her, pulling her towards him. Paul watched for a moment, not sure if he should intervene, when the situation worsened. She was shoved to the bench, with her legs thrashing, the German sprawled on top of her. His hand was over her mouth, muffling her cries. He wrestled with her dress, pushing it higher. His officer's cap lay where it had fallen on the cobblestone beside the bench.

Paul tiptoed towards them, ensuring no one was watching. He glanced at the buildings behind them, all were dark. No one was visible in the windows. He crept closer.

Both the German and the woman were too distracted to see him, the woman struggling, the German fighting her. Paul reached the bench without being seen and tugged at the collar of the German's coat.

"Get off her!" he said forcefully, his voice quivering.

The German turned, his face contorted in an angry snarl. He climbed off the woman, fumbling with his trousers, and moved towards Paul, who retreated slowly, holding his hands up in surrender.

"Leave her alone," Paul demanded while signaling he didn't want to fight.

The woman rose, straightening her dress, and watched, her hand covering her mouth.

The German swung his right fist at Paul and missed. He swung again, with his left, catching Paul's face with a quick jab, stinging his lip and drawing blood.

Paul raised his fists, swinging repeatedly and ineffectively. The German lowered his head and charged forward, shoving Paul to the ground, his head near the stone edge of the embankment, the river just below him. The soldier straddled Paul and started pummeling his face. Paul tried to block the blows with his hands and arms, or at least reduce their effectiveness, but some got through, hitting his eyes and nose and mouth. He could smell the alcohol on his assailant's breath, feel him panting, slowly tiring, as he wildly swung his fists.

Paul clung to his arms, trying to stop the assault, fighting to push the German off him. Then he saw the woman approach, tiptoeing forward, a large round stone in her hand. It was the size of a grapefruit, taken from the border of a nearby tree, smooth and polished. She cringed, finding the courage required, and slowly raised the rock above her head.

She brought it forcefully down on the German's head. He grunted, remained upright, looking shocked. Then she swung the rock again, sideways, hitting him on the temple. His body shifted and he tumbled off Paul, falling along the rock rim that bordered the Seine. Paul scrambled to his feet, blood dripping from his mouth and nose. The German rose to his knees, shaking his head slowly.

Paul rushed forward and pushed him, shoving as hard as he could. The soldier fell into the river and grasped at the rock retaining wall, his hands clinging to the stone. Paul stomped on the German's knuckles until he lost his grip and fell foundering into the water, waving his arms, his head bobbing above and below the surface.

"Hilfe! Ich kann nicht schwimmen," the soldier called desperately. "Help! I can't swim."

He drifted into the middle of the river, flailing, his head slipping below the water and then reappearing, choking and gasping. He tried to fight towards shore but couldn't, and again fell below the surface, several seconds passing before his face appeared, coughing and spitting out water, fighting to breathe. Finally, a few minutes later, he sank into the water and vanished.

Paul stood in shock, watching the man drown. When the head disappeared for the last time, he turned to face the stunned woman standing beside him. With a knowing glance their eyes met, a secret and silent pact was formed, and they each turned and briskly walked in opposite directions, leaving the corpse submerged in the Seine.

Paul returned home and looked in the mirror. His face was battered from the beating – his left eye swollen, his lips and nose bleeding. But he would be all right; it was nothing serious. And he could explain the injuries with some invented story: a fall down the stairs, a minor automobile accident, a mugging. He ached where the German's punches had landed and eased himself onto the sofa, sitting in a darkened living room. His thoughts were foggy, almost incoherent, as if the last hour had been a surreal dream. It had only taken a few minutes, but in that short span of time, a man's life had ended. Paul wrestled with his conscious, stabbed by pangs of guilt. Who was he to take another's life, even if it was the enemy in a world at war? He had no right to serve as judge or jury, even if death seemed a just punishment for a would-be rapist.

A small part of his torment slipped away. Maybe it was revenge, maybe it was the feeling that he had done something, taken action, ensured Catherine and Sophie hadn't died in vain. Someone had paid the price for their murder. It was still the enemy, even if it wasn't the one responsible. But most disturbing to him was that he had killed a man. And some part of him had liked it.

Chapter 17

Rachel Abzac quickly grew accustomed to the six flights of stairs that led to her attic flat; it wasn't much different from where she had lived with her parents. Her new building was ornate, if a bit dated, boasting an elegant spiral staircase with worn marble steps. The plaster cornices were cracked and crumbling, the paint and wallpaper faded, and the varnished hardwood floors were stained and dull. But Rachel could see that it had once been a beautiful building.

There were six apartments on each floor. Rachel's consisted of a single room with a bathroom attached and a kitchen: sink, stove and small refrigerator tucked under a cabinet. Since it was equipped with a bed, a bureau, a comfortable but worn chair, and two small tables, Rachel was delighted to have a home of her own. The flat had one window that cranked open, and she put three small pots on the ledge, planted with spinach, radish and onions. The rent had been paid three months in advance, she had no idea by whom, but it gave her the opportunity to pay her bills and build a small stash of cash.

She reported to work, as directed, and met the thirty people employed at the factory. They ranged in age from young, like her, to an elderly man. Their personalities were just as varied, from talkative to subdued, and happy to sad to miserable. Rachel was trained on a small machine that stitched the sole of the boot to the leather, although at times some sewing had to be done by hand. It was tedious work, repetitive, but she filled the hours watching the others in the factory, learning who might befriend her and who might not. She also studied the work others did so she could learn their tasks. In a matter of days, she excelled in several different positions, having leveraged her experience from her father's shoe shop.

By the end of her first week, she was an accomplished employee and had managed to ask a few innocent questions yielding valuable information. She needed to know everything about the factory, and she was confident she eventually would. All her coworkers seemed to like her, even if they weren't openly friendly, and it didn't seem as if any suspected she was a Jew.

On Sunday Rachel went to the café on *Rue Monge*, near both her apartment and the factory. She left her flat early and walked around the block where the café was located, both to see what clientele frequented the establishment and to try to calm her nerves. She dressed casually, but wore a red scarf supplied by Dr. Durant.

The outdoor section of the café was marked by wooden flower boxes, less than a meter high, defining an area for a dozen tables. The building had a large glass window, where those who chose to sit inside could still view the boulevard, flanked by green fluted pilasters, the paint starting to fade. Another dozen tables were scattered through the interior, along with a long counter displaying pastries, fruit, and baguettes.

All but one of the outdoor tables was occupied, most by German soldiers. Rachel sat on an empty chair, warily observing the enemy. It was on the edge of the café, near the sidewalk, and should have guaranteed privacy, but it was sandwiched between tables occupied by Germans. To her left sat four enlisted men in plain gray uniforms, a bit loud, laughing amongst themselves and not interested in what was going on around them. A single German officer sat at the table to her right, reading some papers as he sipped his coffee, a leather briefcase leaning against the table leg. Rachel wondered what secrets the satchel might contain.

She ordered a coffee, receiving the substitute most often used in Paris, toasted barley mixed with chicory. Her heart was pounding, her breathing labored. She pretended to be calm, casually watching the pedestrians pass, but she was actually so nervous she almost got up and left.

Ten minutes later, a man about twenty walked up to her table and sat beside her. He had piercing green eyes, sandy brown hair that hung over his forehead, and a chiseled face that was the most handsome Rachel could ever remember seeing. He sat down and smiled, his eyes sparkling, his teeth polished a bright white.

"I'm Meurice," he said. He grabbed her hand, as if to shake it, but held it. "I love your scarf."

Rachel was taken aback, not expecting to be romanced, but after a moment she relaxed and decided it was part of their cover. She left her hand in his, even though she was embarrassed and a bit uncomfortable, and smiled.

"Thank you," she replied. "I'm glad you like it. I'm Rachel."

He flashed the smile again and said, "Hello, Rachel. Are you enjoying your new job?"

"Yes, I am."

He slid his chair closer and, in hushed whispers, she proceeded to tell him all she knew about the small factory: where the leather came from, how many people worked there, where the orders originated, where the boots were shipped to, and how they were shipped.

Meurice listened intently, giving Rachel his complete attention, and didn't write anything down. But when two young women arrived and sat at a nearby table, his gaze left Rachel and shifted to them. At times he stared, punctuating his interest with a smile, but then, just when she thought he was not listening at all, he interrupted her.

"Who are the most dangerous people in the café?" he asked suddenly.

Rachel paused, confused by his question, and then furtively studied each of the tables. She ruled out the civilians and German enlisted men. She nodded at two German officers who shared a table closer to the café.

Meurice casually glanced at the customers, pausing to again smile at the two girls beside them. He then leaned closer to Rachel.

"No, not the officers. It's the two men against the café window. They are civilians, appear to be businessmen, but are probably much more. The leather gloves they laid on the table are similar to those issued by the German high command. They are either Gestapo, or high-ranking officials in civilian clothes. In addition, they whisper among themselves, much as we do, not wanting their conversation to be heard. We're posing us lovers, so such behavior is natural. For them, it is not."

Rachel was amazed. "I'm impressed with how perceptive you are," she told him.

"No need to be impressed," he answered. "But you must be just as observant. It could save your life. Do you understand?"

She studied his face, suddenly longing for her family at the farm in Normandy. "I understand," she said softly.

Their meeting took about thirty minutes. That was short enough to appear as friends to onlookers, long enough for them to get to know each other. When the discussion was over, Meurice issued instructions.

"There are three things you need to do. First try to learn who in the factory is friendly to the Germans. Second, try to think of ways to stop work, but not completely and not in an obvious way. Maybe a series of minor mishaps that force lower production rates. Once we have managed that, we'll see what the repercussions are. Do you understand?"

"Yes, I do," she said. "But what is the third thing?

He motioned to a movie theater across the street. "Next week we will meet in there," he instructed. "Sit towards the back."

Then he leaned over and kissed her, pressing his body against her before he stood abruptly and walked away.

Chapter 18

The *Hotel de Paris* was a century-old structure built of brownstone and accented with white stone moldings. Lavish in its design, with arched windows and decorative trim, it had an excellent reputation for both food and lodging. It sat on the right bank of the Seine, two blocks northeast of the Louvre, and was a favorite among Germany's military. The local elite, those whose lives were not dictated by ration cards, found its food irresistible and thought sharing the dining room with the enemy an acceptable trade for an entertaining evening.

"We must be pleasant and cooperative, regardless of who's here," Claire said to Paul.

"I'm trying," he replied with a shrug. "Just like Dr. Durant told me to."

"I know it's hard. But we have to become part of high society, at least the levels the enemy frequents. That's the best way to obtain information."

They entered the dining room, which was tastefully decorated with burgundy carpet and ivory walls, to find about two hundred people, many congregated around a bar at the end of the room. Fifty or so tables were scattered about, covered with gold tablecloths that matched the drapes. A dance floor dominated the remaining space.

There was the usual assortment of German generals, most with French women, immaculately dressed, pearl earrings and necklaces accenting their evening gowns. A sprinkling of Vichy officials, their faces familiar from the

Parisian newspapers, moved freely through the attendees but focused on their German masters, seeming to give them more attention. Free from elections with no constituency to satisfy, the people of Paris didn't seem as important as their German overseers. There were several actors and actresses – Madeleine Sologne, Danielle Darrieux, and Jean Marais among them – artists, writers, the German sculptor Arno Becker, and a sprinkling of businessmen, from those who ran restaurants to those who ran factories.

Otto Ernst stood at the edge of the dance floor and waved as they entered. Paul and Claire walked over to him, and Paul made introductions.

Ernst seemed impressed with Claire, his eyes not leaving hers. She did look stunning in her chic black evening gown, her hair framing her face with long, soft curls captured by barrettes. And she really seemed glad to meet him. She was much better at acting than Paul.

"Let's go to the bar and get some drinks," Ernst suggested cheerfully. "And then I will insist you have a good time."

As they approached the bar, Paul realized he knew, or at least recognized, about half those in the room. Some he despised; others he tolerated. None, at least after his initial glance, were ever counted as friends. Claire stopped to greet several customers from her store, briefly discussing recent purchases or new releases.

"There's Henri Bordeaux," she said as she pointed to a famous artist.

"Mr. Bordeaux is leading a cultural exchange between our two nations," Ernst said. "Artists, sculptors, actors and writers will all meet with counterparts from the other country."

"Maybe you can introduce me to some of the writers," Claire requested. "I can ask them to do readings at the store."

"I will right now," he offered. "There are a few by the dance floor, probably discussing their next novels."

They strolled across the floor, passing a steel magnate and a clothing manufacturer, both of whom were clients of the *Banque de Paris*. Then they met a German colonel who supervised rail transportation, and a man who processed the tons of fish that were sold in Paris each day. Ernst chatted with each for a moment before continuing.

"Claire and Paul, I want you to meet Alain Dominique, France's favorite journalist," Ernst said as he approached three men.

Alain Dominique was a handsome man with blue eyes and wavy blonde hair. A gifted writer whose articles were usually headlines, he was known for pre-war exposes critical of the French government. He had recently found a niche purporting the benefits of Franco-German relations.

"Claire, have we met before?" he asked, all but dismissing Paul.

"We may have. I own Daladier Rare Books on *Boulevard Saint-Germain*."

"Of course," he said. "That's where I've seen you. I've been there many times."

Ernst introduced them to two other writers conversing with Dominique: Louis-Ferdinand Céline, known for both his brilliance and his anti-Semitism, and playwright Jean Giraudoux, who was enjoying the success of his theatrical production, *The Apollo of Bellacc*. They discussed their works with Claire, the conversation dominated by technique and style, which excluded both Paul and Otto Ernst, who listened politely. Both writers were interested in showcasing their projects in Claire's store and, after they had made the arrangements, Ernst interrupted them.

"We had best be seated," he said. "They're preparing to serve."

Each table had room for six guests. Otto Ernst, Claire, and Paul sat together and, although there were place settings for three more, no one else sat at their table.

The first course consisted of *soupe à l'oignon au fromage*. They chatted amiably, sipping glasses of white Moulin-à-Vent wine, savoring the onion soup so superbly prepared. Other guests drifted in and eventually most of the tables filled. They had just finished their soup when a couple entered the dining room, pausing briefly in the entrance.

The woman was attractive, a stunning blue evening gown clinging tightly to her slender frame. Her blond hair was stylishly arranged, pinned high on her head to allow the light to reflect off her diamond earrings. Her eyes were a light blue, her lips outlined with faint red lipstick. Her companion was Julian Junot.

Otto Ernst waved them to their table.

"I'm sorry we're late, Otto," Junot said as they shook hands. "Claire and Paul, this is my wife Jacqueline."

She nodded and smiled politely, taking each of their hands in turn. Paul greeted her warmly; Claire seemed distant, almost intimidated.

"Claire is the owner of my favorite book store," Junot continued.

"Then you must know my husband well," she said. "He's probably your best customer."

"We have shared many pleasant moments," Junot said lightly, sparing Claire a reply. "And will continue to do so, I'm sure. Paul is with the *Banque de Paris.*"

"A man who works with money," she said. "You can't find a job more interesting than that."

They all laughed as the Junots were seated and the waiter served them.

"Otto, how are your business mergers coming?" Junot asked.

"They're progressing. Some more rapidly than others."

"I think it's marvelous," Junot said between mouthfuls of soup. "Combining two strong economies like Germany and France will benefit the consumer and the war effort. Just think of the efficiencies gained."

"What efficiencies are they?" Paul asked. Although he tried to sound polite and not icy, he wasn't entirely successful.

Expressing no offense or irritation, Junot explained, "Shared resources, consolidated billing operations, closure of non-profitable factories, a smaller, more centralized management team. The benefits are numerous."

"I've seen no benefits at the hairdresser," Jacqueline said. "I still can't get an appointment."

They all laughed. It was good that she lightened the conversation. Paul was feeling irritated, even though he hid it well.

Claire sensed his torment and managed to make eye contact. He smiled at her reassuringly. Sitting back in his chair, he sipped his wine, trying to relax.

The waiter returned with the next course. Claire, Junot, and Paul ordered steak, such a rarity in wartime Paris, so tender and delectably prepared it made the mouth water. Otto and Jacqueline selected chicken, expertly sautéed in garlic butter and served with a creamy mushroom sauce.

"Are there any solutions to the labor shortages?" Junot asked.

A slight frown marred Ernst's face. "Not really," he admitted.

"I have a marvelous idea," Junot said. "But no one seems interested. I would like to use as many Jews as I can get in my factories."

"I don't see the advantages," Paul said, trying not to sound shocked.

"First of all, we're no longer forced to feed them. They can make a contribution to the Reich, rather than being a drain on it, by supplying labor at a fraction of the normal cost."

"It's a sound concept," Otto Ernst said. "Of course, Berlin would have to approve any consignments of Jews. I suspect they're needed in the east."

Paul's knuckles turned white as he grasped the table. Junot should be dead. And he should be the one to kill him. But then he remembered Dr. Durant telling him he wasn't there for revenge, but to obtain information.

"Does anyone know where the Jews are sent?" Paul asked. "Or what happens to them when they get there?"

His question was met with apathetic stares and slight shrugs. Apparently no one knew, or they didn't care.

Junot suddenly reached into his pocket, as if he remembered something. He withdrew a business card and handed it to Paul. "I promised an invitation to the Bibliophile Society the last time we met," he reminded him. "I'd be honored if you and Claire came to our meeting this Friday."

"We'd love to," Claire said. "It sounds like fun."

"It is," he continued. "Otto, you're welcome, also."

"I'd like to, but I have to go to Berlin. I leave Thursday for a week or so."

Paul made note of his comment. If he could stall a few days, he could hide some of the bank's assets. All he needed was a plan. Ernst's innocent remark was the type of statement Durant had taught them to be attentive to.

"The Gestapo arrives," Ernst then said, interrupting their conversation.

Paul turned to the entrance. There, standing in the doorway and framed by the light of the chandelier, stood the man who had murdered Catherine and Sophie.

Chapter 19

"Col. Kruger," Ernst called out to him. "Come join us."

Paul grabbed a steak knife from the table and held it in his lap. He clenched it tightly.

Kruger walked towards them, but then stopped at a table where three German officers sat with mugs of beer. He chatted, nodded his head, his hands on the back of an empty chair.

"It's him!" Paul whispered.

Claire looked at him strangely, confused by his frantic expression.

Kruger pulled the chair from the table, as if he was about to sit down.

Ernst shrugged and said, "He must not have heard me."

"Paul, are you all right?" Jacqueline asked. "You look pale."

"I'm fine," he said as the others studied him curiously.

"Col. Kruger," Ernst called, much louder, waving his hand.

Kruger turned and saw him, and waved back. Ernst motioned him over. Kruger nodded to his companions and pushed the chair back toward the table.

"Paul, what's the matter?" Claire asked when the others were distracted.

Paul ignored her, watching Kruger as he walked towards them. He waited patiently, ready to plunge the knife in his heart, should the colonel recognize him.

Claire gave him a reassuring glance. "What is it?" she hissed in his ear.

"He killed Catherine and Sophie!"

She looked at Kruger, and then around the room. There were armed soldiers at the door and several officers among the guests.

"Paul, I know it's hard. But you have to stay calm. Pretend you don't know him."

Kruger stopped two tables away and started talking to a Vichy official who sat with two businessmen and their spouses. They chatted amiably, Kruger nodding, showing no expression.

"If he recognizes me, I'll kill him," Paul threatened.

Claire looked around at the people at their table. The Junots were talking quietly, enjoying their dinner. Ernst was watching Kruger.

"You will not kill anyone," she whispered. "Get control of yourself."

Paul was amazed at her strength, her control. "He'll know who I am," he insisted.

"Are you enjoying dinner, Paul?" Junot asked curiously.

Paul eyed Kruger frantically, and then turned to Junot. "Yes," he said. He tried to recover, making eye contact. "Very much so."

Junot nodded, smiled faintly, and leaned towards Jacqueline, talking softly.

Kruger laughed lightly, nodded politely, and left the adjacent table.

"You don't even know if he's the right man," Claire said.

Paul took a sip of water. His heart was racing, his palms sweaty. He held the knife tighter.

Kruger arrived at their table, his face passive, his owl-like eyes nestled behind black-rimmed glasses. He looked at Paul.

Paul was trembling. He met Kruger's gaze, certain recognition was a second away. He clenched the knife, poised to strike.

Kruger sat down while Ernst made introductions.

"This is Paul Moreau and his cousin Claire Daladier. May I present Col. Gerhard Kruger, of the Gestapo? He's an old friend, recently transferred from Normandy."

The colonel nodded at Paul, but didn't offer his hand. He studied him closely for a moment, his eyes narrowed. "Have we met, Mr. Moreau?" he asked.

"I don't believe so," Paul answered nervously.

He knew Kruger was the killer. Ernst said he just came from Normandy. All the pieces fit. Every muscle of Paul's body was coiled like a spring, ready to strike. His hand tensed, the knife ready.

"Mr. Moreau is an officer of the *Banque de Paris*," Ernst said. "Maybe you met there."

"I don't think so," Kruger said. He studied Paul a moment more and then shrugged.

He turned to Claire. "I know we haven't met," he said, nodding his head politely. "I surely would have remembered you."

"Claire owns a book store on the *Boulevard Saint-Germain*," Junot said.

"I've yet to go there. But I'd like to. I am an avid reader."

"Really?" Claire asked, intrigued. "What do you like?"

"German military history," Kruger replied. He smiled almost apologetically. "And I adore the English romantics. The poets, mostly, Byron, Shelley, Keats."

Junot showed surprise. "Not what I would have expected," he confessed. "Especially from the Gestapo."

"A passion I normally keep private," Kruger admitted sheepishly.

Paul wondered if he had the right man. The appearance matched. But would a lover of English literature order the murders of an innocent woman and child? Maybe he was mistaken? He relaxed his hand, holding the knife limply.

"Books are an escape," Jacqueline said. "Maybe you wished you lived in another time."

"Perhaps," Kruger responded. "I never thought about it."

"We have a club that meets on Fridays," Junot said, handing him a card. "It's devoted to literature. And fine wine, I suppose. Why don't you come? I've just enrolled Paul and Claire."

Kruger was thoughtful for a moment and then said, "It sounds interesting. I'll try to attend."

They were interrupted as the waiter brought salad and cheese, the third course.

As the dishes were set before them, Paul noticed Kruger staring at him for a moment and then turning away, looking puzzled.

Paul still held the knife, although he didn't know what to do with it. He nudged Claire. She touched his thigh, urging caution.

"What are you doing in Paris, Otto?" Kruger asked.

"Integrating Jewish businesses."

"And what becomes of the Jews?"

"We've just detained thirteen thousand," Junot said. "They're supposed to be deported to the east. I want to convince officials to let me use them in my factories."

Paul watched Kruger warily and then shifted his gaze to Junot. How could he treat humans like objects, things to own, slave labor? He would probably work them to death, and then simply replace them.

Kruger looked pensive. "It is an interesting solution," he mused aloud. "The Reich is rapidly building factories. We need labor to operate them."

A German soldier entered, paused near the entrance and searched the room. He looked at their table, squinted in the dim lighting, and then walked towards them.

"Colonel Kruger," he said, saluting smartly. "I'm sorry to disturb you, sir. But you're needed to address a delicate matter."

Kruger sighed and slowly stood. "Thank you all for a wonderful evening," he said, seeming reluctant to leave

After exchanging farewells with those at the table, he turned to Claire and Paul. "Claire, it was delightful to meet you," he offered. He bowed slightly, his face showing pleasure, almost expressing a smile – but not quite. He then turned to Paul. "It was good to see you again, Mr. Moreau."

Paul felt nauseous and faint, his entire body quivering while Kruger walked away. "He remembers me," he whispered to Claire.

"We don't know that for sure," she said. "It's an expression; he may have used it without thinking."

"I should have killed him."

Claire watched him warily. "No you shouldn't have. You would be dead if you had tried. You don't even know if he's the right man."

He knew that the odds of meeting the man who had killed his family in Normandy at a dinner party in Paris were remote. If it was true, he knew Claire wanted the man dead as much as he did. But they were significantly mismatched, a German colonel trained to kill versus a bank officer and a bookseller. It also wasn't the time or place, and any action had to be approved by Durant. And he was very specific. They were to collect information, not kill Germans.

"It was him, I'm sure of it," Paul insisted. "We are in danger."

"He didn't seem dangerous to me," Claire said. "He was soft-spoken and polite, mentioned English literature, and he's coming to Junot's book club. It didn't look like he had an uncontrollable urge to kill anyone. It's probably someone else."

She didn't sound fully convinced, but her explanation helped calm him. They had to keep looking forward, not backward.

"What are you two whispering about?" Jacqueline asked curiously. "Some dark family secret? Or the boring people at your dinner party?"

Claire laughed lightly. "Certainly not the dinner party," she informed them. "It's much more mundane. Whose turn is it to visit our grandmother? She can be exhausting." She rolled her eyes to accent her statement.

"Be kind," Ernst said, smiling. "We will all be old one day."

Paul surely hoped so.

Chapter 20

Rachel sat in her flat, the combined living room and kitchen barely four meters square, and thought about her meeting with Meurice. Something about it made her uncomfortable, but she wasn't sure what it was. He was careful, perceptive, knowledgeable, she certainly felt safe with him. He could identify danger, and he respected it. But did he know fear? Not like she did. But then, she had stood on a narrow ledge, six floors above an alley, while the French police knocked down the door to her apartment. Then she smiled faintly. Maybe it was because the two girls at the café got more attention than she did. Could she be jealous? She wasn't sure; it was a new emotion for her. But once identified, she dismissed it. She couldn't take risks or show weakness, and jealousy was a weakness.

She cooked some soup with the turnips, onions, and salt she was able to get with her ration cards. It was watery and tasteless, but had some nourishment. She knew that was most important; she had to maintain her strength. As she ate the soup, complimented by hard bread, she thought of her family safe on a Normandy farm. She knew Stanislaw loved it, tending the fields and feeding the animals. But she wasn't so sure about her parents. It would be most difficult for her father, a man who made and mended shoes his entire life, to plant wheat and milk cows. But she also knew it kept him alive. And hopefully he realized that, too.

She hoped they understood that she returned to Paris to help save the Jews and preserve their way of life. In her own way, she could contribute to Germany's defeat. She knew it would take time. But whether it took a week or a month or a year or a decade, some day they would be gone, and she wanted to be part of that.

* * *

Rachel found it was much easier to start the fire in the factory than she had expected. She noticed a metal waste drum against a wooden partition, adjacent to where leather was stored. The area was usually deserted in early afternoon. Workers got leather for production in early morning and just after lunch. Although some returned in late afternoon, if they needed more leather to finish their daily tasks, she wasn't concerned. She would have enough time to act.

She started by throwing paper in the bin each time she went to get leather. No one noticed that she was in the storage area more frequently than normal. Or no one cared. She was so quiet and hard working, that no one paid much attention to her. After she was satisfied that there was enough paper to sustain a fire, she put the small can of oil used to lubricate her machine into her dress pocket. Then she casually went to the storage area, carefully observing the other workers.

Just as she reached the trash bin, she saw Pierre, the shop foreman, walking towards the storage area. She froze, frantically looking for a place to hide. Although it was normal for her to be there, she knew workers would try to remember who was in the area just before the sabotage. She ducked behind the far side of the trash bin and pretended to buckle her shoe. There was a good chance he might not see her. And if he did, her behavior was easily explained. But a lingering doubt might exist after the fire was discovered.

She heard him rummaging through the leather, probably trying to find a piece that suited his needs. Just when the noise stopped, and she imagined he was about to leave, someone else approached.

"Pierre, may I leave fifteen minutes early today?"

Rachel recognized the voice of Minnie, a woman in her late thirties whose husband had been killed in the war, leaving her with three children. Most men felt sorry for her, Pierre among them. Others tried to date her, none with any success.

Rachel heard Pierre sigh, as if he were considering the matter. She imagined him scratching his graying beard, as if the decision was of such importance. He was a stocky man, late forties, liked by most of his employees. But he could be difficult at times.

"Yes," he replied, "I suppose so. But how will you make the time up?"

Rachel's heart was beating faster. She couldn't stay where she was if they continued to talk. How long did it take to buckle a shoe? If discovered, she would look like an eavesdropper; no one would believe her story. She held her breath, daring not to make a noise.

"I can make it up to you tonight," Minnie promised. "Right after dinner."

Rachel was shocked. She had no idea the pair were romantically involved. But at this point, she didn't care. She just wanted them to leave.

"That sounds fair," Pierre whispered. "I'm sure I can think of something to do with the time you owe."

Minnie laughed, and then it was silent. Rachel wasn't sure if they had walked away or not. She was just about to stand up when she heard movement, clothes rustling.

"Stop," Minnie said, giggling. "Someone will see. Control yourself and go back to work. Wait until tonight."

Rachel waited another minute and then tentatively stood, peeking over the trash bin. She looked carefully around the area, saw no one, and then poured the oil on the paper in the bin, soaking it. She hurried back to her work station but, as she rounded the corner, she bumped into Marc, a quiet man about forty, somewhat mysterious. No one really knew him. She was startled, her eyes wide, wondering if she had been caught. "Excuse me," she said, her voice quivering.

Marc merely nodded and moved on, not making eye contact. He didn't talk much.

Rachel returned to her machine and went back to work, keeping a wary eye on the storage area. Thirty minutes later, when she was sure it was deserted, she returned. It only took a few seconds to light the fire. Then she quickly returned to work.

Several minutes passed uneventfully, and then the commotion started.

"Fire!" someone yelled.

"Out! Hurry, everyone out!"

Smoke had begun to fill the building, traveling along the ceilings and then filling the space below. The fire had smoldered, finally caught and consumed the debris in the trash can. It had spread, the flames scorching the wall and threatening the ceiling. The workers evacuated, coughing and choking as they hurried down the steps. A handful remained to battle the small blaze, carrying buckets of water and stringing a hose across the floor from a spigot.

"Carelessness, I'm sure," said Minnie as they reached the street.

"Suspicious just the same," Pierre observed. As foreman for the shift, his pay was dependent on production. He looked at his watch, annoyed by the delay.

Rachel watched him closely, smiling that she knew his secret. She noticed Minnie move to the other side of the pavement. It seemed no one would suspect they were lovers. A French policeman arrived, and he and Pierre talked for several minutes. During the interim, workers finished extinguishing the fire and opened the windows to clear the smoke, and the remaining employees began to file back into the factory.

Rachel returned to her post. There was more damage from the water than fire. Unfortunately, some of the leather was soaked, and it would have to dry before it could be used again. With no leather for production, Pierre decided to release the workers for the day and, since it was Friday, the leather had the weekend to dry. Production would resume on Monday. Workers on the third floor had four hours of pay deducted from their wages.

As they filed out of the factory, Rachel was quite proud of herself. The fire had been easy to start. No one had seen her. And in their zeal to extinguish it, the workers had caused more damage than the fire had. She had stopped four hours of production. Maybe a handful of German soldiers on the Russian front would have cold feet.

The workers went down the stairway and out into the street, and there the line halted. Rachel waited patiently, wondering what the delay might be. The line moved slowly, if at all, and after fifteen minutes had passed, she reached the building's exit, twelve workers still in front of her. She looked to the front of the line and gasped.

The French policeman, aided by the factory owner and a German soldier, were questioning each worker.

Chapter 21

Dr. Durant organized the Resistance in Giverny, with its many links to members in Paris, with the aid of a mysterious British spy named Alexander. The Englishman came to France occasionally, but most of his communication with Durant was clandestine. As for Claire and Paul, they had met Durant once since their return from Giverny, on his brother's boat on the Seine.

The Resistance movement was designed so that few members knew the identity of more than a handful of other operatives. This prevented large numbers from being exposed if a single person, or an associated cell, was captured by the Germans. Still, the risk was significant.

Claire and Paul were assigned two contacts in Paris, both established by Alexander and Dr. Durant. The first was an antique bookseller, a tiny man named Louis who was never without his dog. He sold his wares from metal cabinets perched on the stone walls that rimmed the River Seine. This was common; dozens of booksellers lined the river banks. It was also convenient for Claire. As the owner of a rare bookstore, she often visited the sidewalk sellers, searching for volumes to stock her shelves. She was careful not to give Louis more attention than she gave others, and this communication method worked well.

The second approach, primarily for Paul, involved the night-shift janitor at the *Banque de Paris,* an older Spanish immigrant named Pablo. They exchanged critical information via a secret location, a picture in Paul's office with a false back. Since Paul arrived at work while Pablo was leaving, they also exchanged notes or had a brief conversation each morning.

Paul and Claire were amazed, after their first few months in Paris, at the information they were able to collect. Claire overheard discussions between German soldiers and officers in her bookstore, obtaining intelligence on troop movements and raw material shortages. Paul acquired financial data at the bank and via conversations with Otto Ernst. And finally, they learned further details at social events they attended. They were also cultivating their friendship with Julian Junot, regardless of how repulsive it was. If one of Vichy's leading officials trusted them, they could get valuable intelligence that assisted the war effort.

Otto Ernst arrived at the *Banque de Paris* shortly after 2 p.m. Paul had promised a copy of the loan portfolio, as well as a list of liquid assets, but he knew that if he stalled, he might be able to hide assets before Ernst returned from his planned trip to Berlin.

"Did you enjoy yourself at dinner?" Ernst asked as he entered Paul's office.

"Very much so," Paul replied.

"I'm glad you liked it. Julian Junot had many fine things to say about you when you left."

"Really?" Paul asked, surprised he had made an impression.

"Yes, he did. And Claire, too. He likes her very much. Always has, apparently. The book connection, I suppose. They both love books."

"That's true," Paul agreed. "They do have similar interests."

Ernst continued talking while Paul nodded politely. But he was distracted, his mind focused on delaying Ernst for a few more days.

"We're fortunate to have such wonderful jobs," Ernst said, again discussing business. "Now, if you'll get the loan portfolio and a list of assets, I'll have all the information I need."

"I have the loan portfolio here," Paul said, handing him the report.

"Excellent," Ernst muttered as he began to thumb through the many pages.

"Do you want to review it? I could explain the entries."

"No, I wouldn't know what I was looking at. The accountants at the Berlin Bank will do that." He leaned forward and whispered, "I really don't know anything about banks at all!"

"Sometimes I wonder if I do," Paul joked.

Ernst laughed. "You're a good man, Paul. We work well together." Then he sighed, adding, "I'm afraid I have to leave for Berlin today. It's quite unexpected."

"Is anything wrong?"

He shrugged. "No," he replied, "I don't think so. I just hope nothing impacts my ability to stay in Paris."

"What could jeopardize that?" Paul probed, seeking information.

"I'm afraid I'll be sent to the Ukraine," he whispered, glancing about nervously before leaning forward. "I really don't want to go. But I must do as ordered."

"I hope you stay," Paul said. "We're just getting started. You and I can do great things together."

"I know," Ernst agreed. "But if duty calls?" He glanced at his watch. "It's getting late, my friend. I need to go. Do you have the list of liquid assets?"

"Let me check. The last I looked my staff hadn't finished yet." Paul left the room and walked to an associate's office. He glanced down the corridor. Otto Ernst wasn't watching. Paul waited a few minutes, then returned.

A door opened and the bank president, Henri Kohn, walked in with Alain Dominique. Paul assumed the journalist was an important customer if Kohn was dealing with him directly, especially since he was about to have his bank taken over by the Germans. Paul thought it strange; he had never seen Kohn meet personally with any other customers.

"Everything all right, Paul?" he asked.

"Yes, of course. I'm in the middle of a meeting with Otto Ernst. How are you, Mr. Dominique?"

Dominique nodded as he and Kohn moved past. Paul shrugged, perplexed by their private meeting, but knew it was none of his business. He returned to his office.

"I'm sorry, Mr. Ernst," he said with feigned disgust. "They still haven't finished. A few more hours. I'm sure we'll have it by then,"

The smile left the face of Otto Ernst. He studied Paul suspiciously. "A few more hours?" he questioned.

Paul nodded. "I apologize," he said. "I didn't think it would take this long."

Suddenly Ernst stood, apparently convinced of his sincerity. "It doesn't matter," he responded. "I'll get it when I come back."

"Are you sure? They're almost done."

"No, it's all right," he said. "I'll be back Monday." He again glanced at his watch. "I'm sorry, I have a train to catch. Have fun at Julian's."

Paul nodded, smiling smugly. It would be an interesting party. It was his chance to avenge Catherine and Sophie. He was going to kill Col. Kruger, quietly and quickly.

Chapter 22

Claire studied the chessboard, her concentration intense. She reached forward with her right hand, paused and returned it to the table. She gave the matter more thought, and then moved the bishop to compliment her rook's position. "Checkmate," she said, sitting back in the chair.

Gen. Berg shook his head slowly, as if wondering how he had been so cleverly outmaneuvered. "Claire, you're amazing," he said finally. "I never saw it coming. But I should have."

She smiled. "Maybe your mind is on something else," she suggested.

"I don't think so," he said as he studied the board a moment more. "You used a classic military maneuver called the pincer movement. It's like ice tongs. When the enemy advances in the center, like I did with my pawns and knights, the two prongs wrap around him, like you did with bishops and rooks. Gen. Manstein is a master at it. In fact, he's just south of Stalingrad right now with something similar planned for the Russians. Let's hope that becomes a checkmate, also."

"I wouldn't know about Gen. Manstein's plans," she said, feigning a smile. "But maybe you can apply some of his techniques to your chess game?"

Berg laughed. He knew she was poking fun at him. "One more game," he requested, "and then I have to go. My aide and I are going fishing."

"All right," Claire agreed. "One more game. I have plans, also, some fresh inventory I have to price."

"Good," he said. "I think I can beat you this time. And maybe you can help me choose a gift for my granddaughter's birthday. Something French. She would like that."

"Is this for Gertrude or Astrid?"

"Gertrude," he replied. "She'll be eight this year. But you would think she's all grown up if you heard her talk to me. She's very protective. Sometimes I feel like I'm the child and she's the adult."

Claire laughed. "She sounds delightful," she commented.

"She is. So is Astrid, much more sensitive than her older sister. You would like them."

Claire enjoyed hearing about his grandchildren, certain they knew nothing of their grandfather's activities. "I'm sure I would," she replied. "Why don't you let them visit Paris sometime?"

"Perhaps I will," he said. "They would like it, I'm sure. Maybe in the spring."

* * *

Claire left the store after the chess match ended and visited the booksellers that lined the Seine. She purchased a book of eighteenth-century verse, a leather-bound volume on Italian history, and then stopped at the display owned by Louis, her Resistance contact. A small man with silver hair, his smile was warm and inviting, his friendship valued and long-lasting.

A floppy-eared beagle named Charles sat beside him. A constant companion, he was known for mismatched ears, one brown, the other black. He wagged his tail frantically as he looked up at Claire, eager and anxious.

"He wants a treat," Louis said, handing her a biscuit.

Claire kneeled and patted Charles gently, holding the treat and making him beg for it. When he successfully completed the trick, she gave him the biscuit and watched as he devoured it, licking his lips.

She stood abruptly, bumping into a German soldier who had walked up behind her.

"*Bitte,*" he said, nodding with a polite smile. "Sorry."

Claire nodded, surprised by his presence. The pavement was filled with pedestrians, Germans among them, but she hadn't noticed him so close to her. There were two other soldiers with him. One reached for a book and leafed through it, the other waited, watching the Seine.

Claire scanned the books casually, watching the soldiers warily. She found a nineteenth-century edition of Dante's *Inferno*, illustrated by the gifted artist Gustave Dore, and examined it closely. "Louis, how much is this?" she asked, holding it up.

He excused himself from another customer, an elderly man with a cane, stepped around the soldiers, and came to her side. He examined the binding, looked at the title page, and quoted a price. Then he whispered, "Wait until they leave."

Claire countered his price, the start of the negotiation, and pointed out a minor flaw. She was also stalling for time.

Louis considered her remark and examined the book once more. "Let me give it some thought," he said.

"I'll take care of this customer, and then we can discuss it further."

The German who had been watching the river left, followed by the second soldier. Only the man who had bumped into Claire remained. He was looking at a book, reading the first page.

Louis returned, took the book from Claire's hand, and surveyed the binding before leafing through the pages. He then offered another price. Claire pretended to consider his latest offer, watching the German closely. She selected another book, a modern version of children's nursery rhymes, and looked through it.

The German put the volume back into the cabinet, noticed that his companions were walking away and, with a last glance at the books, reluctantly pursued them.

Claire still held the two volumes. She pretended to examine them more closely until she was sure the soldiers were out of earshot. Then she offered a combined price for both of them.

"Do you have a message for me?" Louis asked softly.

Claire glanced around furtively and whispered, "Between the bills."

"That sounds like a fair price," he agreed. He wrapped the two books in paper.

Claire handed him some money. "Thank you, Louis," she said. "I'll see you soon."

She had slipped a note between the bills describing the military information she learned during her chess game with General Berg. It was only the beginning. She knew she could get much more information from him. And he wouldn't have the slightest hint she was doing it.

* * *

Later that evening Claire sat in a dark taproom at a secluded corner table, staring at the stage. Édith Piaf, a sultry singer and Paris icon, was singing *Le Vagabond*, the season's most popular song. An accordion player accompanied her, the rhythm moving and memorable. The room was lit dimly and filtered with cigarette smoke, but the mood was lively, the clientele upbeat. The majority of the men were German, primarily officers, generals and colonels. All had French woman at their sides, laughing and flirting. Music echoed, liquor flowed, laughter rung and, given the state of the audience, it was difficult to tell that a world war raged or that most Parisians struggled to feed their families.

Claire sat across from Julian Junot, sheltered from the patrons by a divider wall, drinking the finest Scotch that Paris had to offer. All in the nightclub knew him, women and men, French and German. Some feared him, a few admired him, but all respected him.

Claire sipped white wine from Bordeaux, feeling guilty for indulging in such a luxury. The wine was light, tickling the palate, and it probably cost more than she earned in a week. The entertainer, the food, the wine, the scotch, all amplified war-time Paris and the great divide between the elite and average citizen.

"I've given considerable thought to your suggestion," Junot said.

Claire sipped her wine. "It seemed the best way for me to contribute," she offered. "Do you think it will work?"

"Absolutely," he said. "Most would never understand why you do it, but I do."

Junot then stopped talking, nodded and smiled. A German general, tall and gaunt, his face scarred, the right ear missing and his right eye covered by a black patch, leaned in from the aisle to greet him.

"General Schneider, how are you?" Junot asked warmly. "May I present Claire Daladier?"

The general bowed slightly, polite and respectful. "I'm honored."

"It's nice to meet you," Claire greeted him warmly. She wondered where he had been wounded. Probably the Eastern Front, from where maimed soldiers returned daily, along with corpses. He stood crookedly, apparently plagued by additional wounds not visible.

"How is your son Rudolph?" Junot asked. "Is he still in Italy?"

"He is," the general replied. "And just promoted to captain."

"You must be proud of him."

"I am," General Schneider said, his face beaming. "He's a good man with a bright future." He nodded to Claire and stepped back in the aisle. "I didn't mean to interrupt. I just wanted to say hello. Enjoy your evening."

Claire waited a few moments, ensuring the general was gone, and then said, "He must have been horribly wounded."

"He was," Junot confirmed, "in Russia. He's in Paris on leave, soon to return to the Eastern Front. He's a fabulous military strategist."

"He must be very courageous to return to the battlefield."

"He is," Junot replied. "And there are many more like him."

"You seem to know most of the generals in Paris."

116

"I know them all," he said. "Those who rule France may someday rule the world. I can open doors for you that show a future you can't even imagine."

Claire studied him closely, wondering if she waded in water too deep. "I'm sure you can," she said softly.

"And that alone should show that you're making the right decision."

After they finished dinner, she asked Junot to drive his Mercedes to the Seine, and she got out of the car a short distance from where Henri Durant had his boat docked. She glanced at her watch, mindful of the curfew, and saw Durant sitting on a bench by the water, waiting for her. She watched Junot drive away, and when his car was no longer visible, she approached Durant.

"Hello, Henri," she said, greeting him. "Have we made progress?"

"Yes, we have," he replied. "It's a perfect plan."

"It still amazes me that your brother discovered it during the Great War," she said, visualizing the map Dr. Durant had drawn in the dirt while she was in Giverny.

"It was just as he remembered," he informed her. "We were able to access the location from three different points in the city. We're still working on the logistics, but we've already started to use it."

"I would like to see, especially if it's operational."

He was pensive for a moment. "Do you go to church?" he then asked.

She was confused by the question. "No, not normally," she told him. "At least…"

"At least what?"

She paused. "Not since Jacques died," she whispered. "There seemed to be no point. It's difficult to have faith when something like that happens."

He placed his hand on hers, to console her. "We've all lost loved ones," he offered. "It never gets easier."

"I know," she replied, "the pain is always there." She paused, reflective, and then inquired, "Why did you ask about church?"

"If you want to see the operation, go to *Saint-Étienne-du-Mont* on Thursday, at 7 a.m. Sit in the first pew. Hold rosary beads in your hands and wear a black hat with a veil, something appropriate for mass. Pray for ten minutes, and then light a candle to the right of the altar."

"And then what?"

"Then you'll see."

Chapter 23

Rachel's heart was pounding, her body trembling. They already seemed to know the fire wasn't an accident, but she didn't know how. Had someone seen her? The German and the policeman questioned the first worker in line, an elderly man who was very kind and liked by everyone. He smiled nervously, acting not as if he had something to hide, but afraid he would be accused of something he didn't do. She couldn't hear what they were saying. The German talked for a few moments and then pointed sternly to the front of the building. The worker went and stood against the stone wall, looking frail and frightened and very alone.

Pedestrians walked by nervously, knowing something was amiss but not wanting to be involved. Cars and taxis passed on the street, the passengers looking curiously out the windows. But for the most part, people tended to mind their own business. It was safer that way.

The next two workers, middle-aged women, were questioned briefly and permitted to pass. Then a young girl approached, but she was not even questioned. The German just waved her along. Rachel watched those in front of her being challenged and interrogated. Some were of no interest to the German and were allowed to leave. Others aroused suspicion and were ordered to stand against the wall. Maybe they had seen something; they could be potential witnesses. Maybe they had seen Rachel.

Ever so slowly the line moved forward. Rachel studied the process carefully, practicing the answers to the questions she expected to be asked. She needed an excuse, just in case someone had seen her. But it couldn't seem contrived. She studied those detained and tried to imagine what they might have seen her doing.

Most of the other workers were dismissed, with only a few detained, until only an elderly woman, a bit obese, stood between Rachel and the German. Six more workers were behind her. Three people now stood against the wall: the elderly man, a young girl who was known to have a child out of wedlock, and Marc, the man she had bumped into by the trash bin.

Rachel was afraid. She kept looking at Marc, trying to determine if he remembered their encounter. He didn't return her gaze, but merely stared vacantly ahead. His eyes were dull, a permanent pain etched on his face. Someone said he had lost two sons when the Germans invaded. But no one knew for sure. He barely spoke. He simply came to work each day and did what was asked.

She tried to appear calm. The German was imposing, a large man, intimidating. He towered over each employee, glaring at them as if they were guilty and had to prove their innocence, an arrogant smile pasted on his face. The French policeman stood beside him, deferring to the German, but talking to the factory manager and providing opinions on his employees and any involvement they may have had.

"Papers, please," the policeman said. He had a pair of half-glasses on the edge of his nose. He looked very official, administrative, not as if he captured many criminals or ever fought an enemy.

Rachel handed him her identity papers. As the policeman reviewed her documentation, the German studied her closely, searching her face, and gazing up and down her frame, looking for anything suspicious, almost as if she had something hidden.

"Rochelle came to work with us a few weeks ago," the manager said, using the alias on Rachel's documents. "She's one of our best employees."

"Where were you before that?" the German asked.

"In school."

He was looking at her shoes, but she didn't know why. She didn't think she had left any clues, no oil residue. She avoided looking down, suspecting a trap.

"Why are you working?"

"My mother died," Rachel answered. "She was very sick. Now I have to support myself."

"Where's your father?"

"He was killed in the war."

The French policeman finished studying her papers and handed them back to her. The German looked away, his attention diverted to the three workers leaning against the wall.

"You may go," the policeman said.

He gave her a faint smile, as if he was probably a nice man caught in a difficult situation. Maybe he had a daughter her age.

"Thank you, Rochelle," the manager said, offering a weak shrug. His eyes were apologetic. "I'm sorry for the inconvenience. I will see you Monday."

Rachel started to walk away but paused. She looked at those standing against the wall. She realized they were suspects, not witnesses. Or they would have detained her, also. No one had seen her.

"What happens to them?" she asked, looking directly at the German.

The German looked at her, surprised she had the nerve to speak. "We haven't determined that," he said in poor French.

She stood, unafraid, and faced the soldier. "They're all good people," she informed him. "And they're all good workers."

The manager looked timidly at the German. So did the policeman. Then, with a bit of admiration, all three watched the brave teenage girl walk away.

* * *

Rachel met Meurice in the movie theater. They sat in the third row from the back and watched the film, *Remorques,* starring Jean Gabin and Madeleine Renaud. The story was a good one, telling the tale of a tugboat captain who has an affair with a married woman, despite having a seriously ill wife. The theater offered Parisians an escape from the German occupation, and the movie houses were always full.

During the first fifteen minutes they observed those nearby as they watched the film. Meurice, with his keen perception, studied the patrons closely. Even though there were several German soldiers sprinkled in the audience, some of whom were only rows away, he finally leaned close to Rachel and provided the code.

He put his lips near her ear, almost touching her. "You look nice," he whispered.

She relaxed, and proceeded to tell him about the fire she had set at the boot factory. She gave a detailed description of how she had carefully planned and committed the act, how Marc had almost seen her, the extent of the damage, and the employees questioned afterwards. She described several other acts of sabotage planned.

"You need to space them far apart," he advised. "Don't do anything else for at least four weeks. Wait for the suspicion to wane. And next week, tell me the fate of the three workers detained. You are sure they weren't witnesses?"

"If anyone had seen me, the German soldier would have known. Nothing he did or said showed any suspicion."

He looked at those seated nearby; all were engrossed in the movie.

Rachel then provided information on the shipments received and sent that week, and where supplies came from and product was sent to. Almost all of the boots produced were sent to the Russian front, as they had been previously.

"The number of boots made and where they are sent equate to soldiers and their positions," Meurice explained. "It's valuable information and helpful to the war effort."

Rachel was proud of her contribution. "I can do more," she offered.

"We do have another role for you," he whispered.

"What is that?"

"We need a courier. You will pick up material, anything from printed leaflets to false identity papers. You will hold them until they need to be passed on, and then you will deliver them. It can be very dangerous. Are you willing to do that?"

"Absolutely," she said with no hesitation, knowing how great a risk she was taking.

Chapter 24

Paul left his house Friday evening with a small vial of cyanide in his pocket. He had convinced the local druggist that he needed it for rats in the alley behind his flat. He doubted the pharmacist believed him, but he sold it to him it anyway. Paul intended to mix it in Kruger's drink, hoping it caused a slow, agonizing death.

He planned to meet Claire by the *Pont de la Tournelle,* and from there they would walk to Junot's townhouse. He arrived early, as he always did, and while he waited he thought of the pain they endured, the lost loved ones, the overwhelming grief. Life used to be simple; now it was complex. Life used to be dreams; now it was nightmares. He remembered Giverny as a child. Claire lived just down the road, and a handful of cousins and friends, dead or dispersed throughout the world, had lived there, too. They romped through the fields, swam in a nearby pond, ran along the railroad tracks, played hide-and-seek. It was a time of innocence, absent of danger and fear. It was a time of discovery, learning life and love. It was a time mankind would welcome again, should it ever return.

He saw Claire in the distance and watched as she approached. There was a bounce in her walk, a smile on her face. She looked different. She seemed happy, carefree, but Paul didn't know why. There was a healthy glow to her cheeks, which had been absent for some time.

"You look excited," he said when she reached him.

"I am. Who wouldn't be?"

"It is hard to believe that we're going to a gathering hosted by a Vichy official, possibly the most powerful man in Paris. And that we're spending the evening at his luxurious townhouse, mingling with Parisian elite, all while spying for the Allies." He didn't mention the cyanide. He knew it was wrong. Dr. Durant had warned him. But it had to be done. He couldn't help himself. "And they have no idea that the information we collect could lead to their defeat. And when they fall, France will again be French."

* * *

The townhouse of Julian Junot was only seven or eight blocks from either of their flats, across the *Pont de la Tournelle* and onto the *Ile Saint-Louis,* one of two islands perched in the River Seine. *Ile Saint-Louis* was smaller than its sister, the *Ile de la Cité,* home to Notre Dame. The two islands were the city's birthplace and the focal point from which all other locations were measured.

The *Ile Saint-Louis* was the more romantic, frozen in the seventeenth century, somehow a village in the midst of a city. It contained boutiques, cafes, restaurants, markets and bakeries. Its inhabitants were an eclectic mix: shopkeepers, domestics, merchants, artists, with the quays that rimmed the river reserved for the well-to do.

They walked towards the isle, the pavements crowded with pedestrians, some stopping at kiosks scattered along the street that sold everything from fresh fruit to newspapers. The locals wandered the boulevard, sat in outdoor cafes and looked in shop windows. German soldiers mingled among them, usually in pairs or groups. They bought French goods, dated French women and ate

French food. The longer they were there, the more integrated into society they became, dictating and dominating, but still appreciating.

As Paul and Claire crossed the bridge, they saw two German motorcycles approach. Immediately behind them were two more, each equipped with sidecars, the soldiers armed with machine guns. They knew they usually served as escorts for important officials, and they watched curiously as a black sedan followed, Nazi flags sprouting from each corner of the bumper. The sedan was followed by two more motorcycles with identical sidecars, soldiers and machine guns.

"I wonder who that is," Claire said, eyeing the procession as it moved down the road.

"Who cares?" Paul shrugged. "Probably some general on his way to his mistress."

"It looked like someone more important than that."

They turned, walked two blocks down the *Quai d'Orleans,* the River Seine on their left. Just as they approached Junot's townhouse, Paul saw them.

They were across the street, along the river, walking briskly, perhaps hurrying home after a stop at the market. The woman was petite, with short strawberry-blond hair, two loaves of freshly baked bread under her arm. The child, a girl with curly blond hair, skipped beside her.

"Claire, look!" Paul's eyes were wide, his mouth open in surprise, his mind clouded.

She looked where he was pointing, but then turned to face him, looking bewildered. "Look at what?" she asked.

He started running across the cobblestone street. "Catherine! Sophie!" he exclaimed. He dodged a taxi, scampered around two bicyclists, and bumped into a pedestrian who stared at him angrily. Claire was right behind him.

"Paul, stop."

"Catherine! Sophie!"

The mother and child kept walking towards the bridge, as if they hadn't heard him. He went faster, running down the pavement.

"Paul! No!" Claire shouted.

"Catherine!" he said, grabbing the woman's blouse. "Catherine, it's me!"

The woman turned with alarm, fear flickering across her face. She was young, in her twenties. She pulled her daughter towards her.

"Excuse me, sir?" she asked, her voice trembling.

Paul stopped short, shocked and breathless. "I'm sorry," he stuttered as his eyes welled with tears. "Please, I'm so sorry. I thought you were someone else."

"Mama, who is that man?" the child asked.

"No one we know," the mother said. She nodded to Paul with a faint smile. "It was a mistake."

They turned and continued walking down the street. Paul was sobbing, tears dripping down his cheeks. It was a painful realization.

He felt an arm wrapping protectively around his shoulder. He cried a moment more, gradually got control and turned, expecting to find Claire consoling him.

"Are you all right, Mr. Moreau?" Col. Kruger asked.

Paul was startled and dazed. Fighting to regain his composure, he answered, "Yes, I'm fine. Thank you. I'm sorry I got so emotional. I thought they were someone else."

Claire stood just behind him, looking panicked.

Paul dabbed the tears from his eyes, fearing for his sanity, and looked at Claire helplessly. They both knew how dangerous Kruger was. And now he may have recognized Paul from Giverny, when Catherine and Sophie were killed.

Kruger gave Paul a sympathetic look and a last pat on the back. "It's all right," he said. "Rarely are people what they seem."

Chapter 25

Paul was still shaken as they walked back towards Junot's townhouse. He took a deep breath and tried to control himself – he knew his life depended on it. Claire was next to him, her arm wrapped in his, as they tried to pretend everything was normal. But they knew it wasn't. Kruger walked beside Claire, his face expressionless, as it always was. His tone, when he did speak, was calm and measured. If he was surprised by Paul's reaction, and there was no reason why he shouldn't be, he didn't show it.

When they reached Junot's home, Paul and Claire were overwhelmed by its beauty. Built of brownstone centuries before, with arched windows and white stone trim, it was the finest home on a street of fine homes. French doors opened to ornate balconies with white marble balusters that offered generous views of both the Seine and the Left Bank. It was a street for the rich, and his family had lived there for generations.

Paul grasped the brass knocker shaped like a lion's head and rapped on the door. It was opened a few seconds later by a smartly dressed man, balding, middle-aged but with perfect posture. His black eyes peered at them passively but politely.

"Hello," Claire said cheerfully. "I'm Claire Daladier and this is my cousin Paul Moreau. Mr. Junot invited us."

"And I'm Colonel Kruger, also a friend of Mr. Junot."

"I am Bernard, Mr. Junot's personal attendant. Please come in and make yourselves comfortable."

Bernard gave them a quick tour. He seemed proud of the residence, sounded a bit snobbish, but with every reason to be. The house was lavishly decorated with floors of Venetian tile and walls covered in Flemish wallpaper of varying shades of green, the design suggesting the fleur-de-lis. Plaster ceilings were coffered and sculpted into lavish floral patterns and the windows were accented by rosettes and fluted casings. Each room seemed more extravagant than the last, and there was hardly a lack of bookshelves for they covered at least one wall in each room and easily contained ten thousand volumes. Paul looked at the French influence in the design of the residence with disgust. It was too French for a man who had betrayed France.

Bernard escorted them to the second floor with a library, guest rooms and an office suite. He informed them that the whole house, including the kitchen and all the servants, were at the disposal of the guests. As Colonel Kruger left to discuss something with another German officer, Claire and Paul continued the tour.

They found Julian Junot on a second-floor balcony watching the Seine. He sat passively, as if immersed in thought. A wrought iron table stood beside him, a glass of wine and a worn copy of *Fathers and Sons* sat upon it. A moment passed before Junot realized they were standing there.

"Welcome, I'm glad you could come," he said warmly. "Bernard, can you get them a drink?"

Paul looked to Claire who nodded. "White wine will be fine," she said.

"Make it two," Paul requested.

Bernard nodded and disappeared.

"He's indispensable," Junot informed them. "The man keeps my entire life organized. I couldn't function without him. He's been with me over twenty years, and we still have no secrets. He's not only my attendant, he's my friend."

"You're fortunate to have such an able assistant," Paul said.

"I am," Junot replied. He took a sip of wine. "You just missed General von Stülpnagel. He always visits when he's in Paris."

Paul and Claire eyed each other uneasily. Von Stülpnagel was the German military governor for all of France. They were suddenly overwhelmed, feeling dwarfed by the magnitude of the circles they were infiltrating.

"We saw him on our way here," Claire said weakly. "Actually, we saw his sedan and escorts."

"He's an interesting man," Junot continued. "Absolutely brilliant. It only takes a minute to recognize that. It's obvious why our Führer trusted him to oversee France. I'll make sure to introduce you. You'll like him."

"He sounds fascinating," Claire said, aware of the information that could be gleaned from such an important man. "I would be very interested to meet him."

Bernard arrived with their wine, and they sipped pensively, studying the Seine.

Claire looked at the book on the table. "Turgenev?" she asked, referring to the author.

"Yes, I have a weakness for the Russians. Their writing is so passionate. How about you, Paul? What do you like to read?"

Paul thought for a moment. "Economics, I suppose," he replied, "because I'm a banker, and murder mysteries, because I like to think that I'm very clever and can predict who the killer is. But I never can."

Junot laughed. "Maybe if the murder occurs in a bank you'll be able to guess the ending," he joked.

"Perhaps," Paul said, forcing a smile. "What do you read? Other than Russian authors?"

"Everything. My mother was an avid reader and I inherited the trait. I like history, the classics, biographies. And I'm embarrassed to admit that I adore scandalous gossip. It doesn't matter if it's politicians, actors, musicians, friends or neighbors. Bernard gets me the tabloids the day they're published and I devour them."

Paul wondered if Junot ever considered the horrible things people said about him. If he was so interested in gossip, he must. He probably didn't like it.

They were interrupted when a German officer walked onto the balcony.

"General Berg, how are you?" Claire asked with surprise.

"Claire, how nice to see you. Are you here for the book club?"

"Yes, are you?"

"I am. But I actually live here. Julian has graciously opened his home to me."

"I'm sure you're enjoying it," she said. "It's fabulous."

"It is," he said and turned to Junot. "Julian, I'm afraid I broke one of your wine glasses, so I gave Bernard money to replace it. I told him to buy a whole set."

"Don't be silly," Junot replied. "It's only a glass."

"I insist. I'm your guest and you're a gracious host," Berg said firmly. He then turned to Claire. "Would you care for a game of chess?"

Even though it was the game that bonded them, they seemed to have an obvious affection for each other – or Claire was a fabulous actress. But she was much better at socializing than Paul, used to dealing with her customers, expressing interest in their lives. He was not, struggling both with casual conversation and the rage that consumed him, even though he did manage to control it.

Paul wondered if there was more to their relationship. Many Germans had French girlfriends, even those with wives at home. And Claire seemed to enjoy the attention he gave her. She was a young window in the prime of her life; her husband died over two years ago. Gen. Berg was a handsome man, tall, distinguished, respectful, even if twenty years her senior.

With everyone occupied or distracted, Paul saw the chance he had been waiting for. He put his hand in his pocket and rolled the glass vial of cyanide between his fingers. He strolled through the rooms of the second floor, finding guests scattered about, looking at books or engaged in conversation. He didn't see Kruger.

He walked down the steps to the first floor. Four men were playing poker at a table in the parlor. He paused to watch the game, joining other onlookers. There was a pile of francs on the table, much more than he could ever afford to risk on a game. The players studied both the cards in their hands and each other's expression. Their faces were solemn, and an air of tension dominated the room.

He moved past them, through the dining room wrapped in floral beige and red wallpaper, dominated by a long mahogany table with lions' paws feet, and went towards the kitchen, where he found the door closed. Without giving the matter any thought, especially given the party, he opened the door and walked in.

Junot's wife Jacqueline was locked in an embrace, the man's back to the entrance. They were kissing, sensually. As soon as they heard the door swing open, they jumped apart, startled and looking guilty.

The man was Alain Dominique.

Chapter 26

"Excuse me," Paul said, embarrassed. "I didn't mean to intrude."

"What are you talking about?" Alain Dominique asked sharply. He was glaring at Paul, challenging him.

"Nothing," Paul replied, "nothing at all. I should have knocked." He retreated toward the entrance, disengaging.

"Wait a minute," Dominique demanded.

Jacqueline blushed and grabbed his arm. "Alain, don't make it worse," she pleaded.

Paul held his hands up in a sign of surrender. "It's none of my business," he reassured them.

He turned and left, leaving Jacqueline nervous, Dominique angry. As he hurried through the dining room he thought of Junot's penchant for scandalous gossip. He didn't have to read the tabloids; he didn't have to wonder about friends and neighbors. He only had to look in his own house.

Paul wandered through the first floor again but couldn't find Kruger, so he returned to the library. General Berg stood in the corner of the room, talking to Bernard, Junot's personal assistant. At first he thought it a curious conversation, but he then remembered Berg lived at the residence. He probably knew Bernard well. Paul walked onto the balcony, hearing Claire's musical laugh echoing through the library. She and Junot were watching the sun set behind the Eiffel Tower. He couldn't hear what they were talking about, but he did notice they were sitting very close to each other, both smiling.

"The view is delightful," Junot said. "I love to watch sunsets, especially against the backdrop of Paris. It's so beautiful." He turned to Paul. "Are many guests here?"

"About twenty-five," Paul replied. "Some are in the library, talking or reading while a rather animated card game rages on the first floor."

"Jacques Chausse," Junot said. "He loves cards. Most of our gatherings have at least one game that lasts until dawn." He rose and sighed. "I had best socialize for a moment. I was expecting Colonel Kruger. Have you seen him?"

"He arrived with us," Paul informed him, "but I haven't seen him since."

As soon as Junot left, Paul turned to Claire and said, "I saw Jacqueline Junot in the kitchen with Alain Dominique. They were kissing."

"Are you sure it wasn't innocent?"

"Yes, I am," he said. "Not with a kiss like that. They must be having an affair."

"I wonder if Julian knows."

"How could he not? He's one of the most powerful men in Paris."

Claire thought about it for a moment. Then she looked at Paul and shrugged. "Maybe he doesn't care," she offered.

They returned to the library and mingled with the guests. When Claire was distracted, examining hand-painted water colors in a book about birds with an art professor from the Sorbonne, Paul again searched for Kruger. He wandered the house, fingering the glass vial in his pocket. As he moved from room to room, a picture of the home's owner began to emerge.

The wealth of Julian Junot was obvious, visible in the furnishings, the construction of the house, the ornaments that decorated the rooms, and the books that lined the shelves. But something else was evident, dominating his residence, his appearance, and his family's legacy.

It was a love of France. There were Parisian collectibles on tables and shelves, the paintings of Cezanne, Gauguin, and Renoir hung on the walls, pictures and maps of various stages in French history were displayed in cabinets and frames, weapons of French chivalry dominated one room, while the triumphs of Napoleon decorated another. The French Revolution and the excesses of the kings that preceded it were the theme of another room, while images of the Great War, the French defiantly refusing to allow Paris to fall, accented another. Almost every item in the house screamed of nationalistic pride. Why then, Paul wondered as he strolled through the house, would he suddenly become so devoted to such a horrid enemy?

Paul walked through every room except the bedrooms but couldn't find Kruger. He must have left shortly after arriving. Paul was disappointed, but he knew he would have other opportunities. He went to find Claire, who was now in the second-floor parlor with a handful of other guests.

"Are you having a good time?" he asked her.

She muttered a reply as Julian Junot entered the room. Kruger walked in behind him, expressionless.

Paul tensed, watching Kruger as he entered, holding a crystal goblet in his hand, half-filled with white wine.

Paul walked towards the colonel, trying to casually get near him, looking for a chance to sprinkle the poison in his drink. Kruger and Junot stood in a corner, talking quietly, and Paul watched as Kruger set his glass down on the table. He casually moved behind them, fingering the leather volumes on a book shelf.

Paul took the vial from his pocket. He used Kruger's body to shield his actions from those in the room. He removed the cap.

A woman across the room, one of Paris's renowned opera singers, laughed loudly. Both Kruger and Junot turned to face her, distracted by the noise.

Paul used the diversion to his advantage. He sprinkled the poison in Kruger's drink, returned the cap to the vial, and put it in his pocket. He discreetly shook the glass, stirring the poison with the contents.

Kruger turned back to Junot and continued talking. He picked his glass up, holding it by the stem.

Paul waited, his heart pounding.

Chapter 27

Kruger moved the glass to his lips.

Junot leaned towards him, whispering.

The glass stopped, the hand stationary. Kruger replied, without drinking.

Junot spoke, but then motioned to the study. Kruger nodded.

They talked for a moment more. The glass close to the lips, but not quite touching.

"Paul, we have to leave," Claire said. "It's close to curfew."

"In a minute," he replied, distracted.

Junot walked towards the study, motioning Kruger to follow, guiding him away from the guests. The discussion seemed serious, requiring privacy. Kruger put his glass down on a table next to the leather couch. A moment later, they were gone.

Paul stared at the wine glass, sitting unclaimed on the table. Bernard was already moving through the room with a tray, collecting glasses left behind. He picked up Kruger's. It blended with the others, some empty, some filled.

"Paul, come on," Claire urged.

With a last, lingering look at the glass, he turned and left. He had failed. But it was a good plan, one he could use again. He would never stop trying; he owed that to the memory of Catherine and Sophie.

The guests mumbled their thanks and farewells as they filtered quietly from the house. Jacqueline Junot stood in the first-floor parlor, smiling as each guest passed.

Paul watched her warily as she said goodbye to Claire. As he approached, Jacqueline's eyes pleaded for understanding. "Please," she leaned toward him and whispered, "don't tell anyone."

Paul squeezed her hand tightly. "I won't say a word," he promised. He didn't blame her, not with what she was married to.

Claire and Paul left together, hurrying through the streets of Paris, mindful of the curfew. They parted company at the bridge, traffic thinning as curfew approached, and she walked briskly to her flat. A German soldier rode by on his motorcycle, driving too fast, followed by a black sedan, probably the Gestapo. A taxi, equipped with a wood-burning engine, moved in the opposite direction, smoke trailing behind it. But for the most part, the streets were deserted.

As Claire reached the entrance to her apartment building, a vehicle turned onto the *Boulevard Saint-Germain*. The headlights shone briefly across the pavement, catching her in their glow. Just as she turned the doorknob, a German troop truck halted at the curb.

"What do you think you're doing?" a soldier called from the passenger's side window.

Claire glanced at her watch. "I'm just getting home," she replied. "There are still a few minutes left until curfew."

"No, there isn't," the soldier said. "You violated curfew."

He got out of the truck, a machine gun slung over his shoulder.

"No, I haven't," she said politely. She held her wrist up, and pointed at her watch.

Her reply, or the fact that she had the audacity to offer one, aggravated the soldier. He showed his displeasure by smacking her across the face. His hand bit sharply into her lip, causing a stinging pain and a trickle of blood.

"I said that you violated the curfew," the soldier repeated. "Don't argue with me. Get in the truck."

Two soldiers jumped from the rear of the vehicle and grabbed Claire roughly, shoving her into the back of the tuck. They ignored her protests, climbing into the vehicle behind her. Seconds later, the truck sped off, its destination unknown.

Other than the two soldiers, two men and a woman occupied the rear of the vehicle, three to each side, facing each other. The men, reeking of alcohol, and the woman, an apparent streetwalker, remained silent. Claire did also.

The vehicle traveled down the *Boulevard Saint-German* before crossing the Seine. The streets were empty, even as they moved down the *Champs-Élysées.* As the vehicle neared the *Arc de Triomphe* it slowed, allowing a German staff car to pass in front of it. A few moments later, the truck came to a halt at 84 Avenue Foch, the building that served as Gestapo headquarters. They were forced from the vehicle and into the building, one soldier prodding them with the barrel of his machine gun.

Claire was afraid. She didn't know what was happening, and the Germans weren't offering any information. Those with her didn't seem deserving of captivity either: two drunks and a prostitute. They had only violated the curfew. Why were they being delivered to the Gestapo?

"Do they intend to torture us?" Claire whispered to the other captives.

"They can do whatever they want to," one of the men hissed.

With fear on their faces, they were led into a large lobby that was brightly lit. Their captors placed them in the center of the spacious tiled floor and then walked in circles around them. The Germans examined them closely, placing their faces inches away and shoving them, just enough to make them lose their balance.

One of the soldiers poked Claire's crotch with the barrel of his machine gun, much to his companions' amusement.

"Stop it," she said firmly. "You can't treat me like this. I demand to see an officer."

The Germans laughed. Then they lifted the prostitute's dress, exposing black lingerie. She pulled her dress down, as flustered as Claire was.

They heard the sound of boots crossing the tiled floor, and an officer entered the foyer. The captives knew their fate rested with him, and a deafening silence filled the room.

He wore a captain's insignia, strutting about the room with an air of self-importance. He was short, with dull eyes, and he strolled pompously in a circle as he examined the captives. He studied the prostitute for a minute and then observed the two men who had been drinking. Finally, he turned to Claire.

"How did you come to violate the curfew?" he asked quietly.

"My watch must be slow. I thought I was home in time. These soldiers picked me up at the entrance to my apartment."

The captain smiled. "Do I look like an idiot?" he asked.

"No," she answered softly.

"Then why would you expect me to believe such a stupid story?"

"It's the truth."

"Where did you find her?" he asked the soldier.

"On the *Boulevard Saint-Germain*."

"Let me see your papers," the captain demanded.

Claire removed her credentials from her pocket and gave them to him. He looked through them casually.

"If I could telephone a friend, I'm sure he will explain everything."

The officer looked at her with disbelief. "And who, may I ask, is going to convince me to release you?" he questioned.

"General Berg."

"General Berg?" he asked. "You expect me to believe that you know General Berg?"

"A phone call will prove it. Better now than me calling him after I'm released."

The captain took a deep breath and turned to the soldiers. "Take the drunks to clean the toilets in the barracks," he commanded. "I want them spotless by morning."

"Yes, sir," a soldier said. He and a companion grabbed the two men and pushed them out of the room.

That left the prostitute and Claire.

"Take the whore to my office," he said.

He looked at Claire, studying her closely, before relenting. "Come on," he told her, "let's make that telephone call."

They walked toward a black telephone on a table by the entrance. The captain motioned to the phone. "Please," he said, handing her the mouthpiece. "And if you're lying, I will make it very unpleasant for you."

Claire dialed the phone, praying that someone answered. On the seventh ring, Bernard did.

She quickly explained her dilemma. A few minutes later, Berg was on the phone. Claire informed him of her plight and then handed the phone to the captain.

The captain listened, his expression changing from arrogance to disbelief. The conversation lasted only a minute. The captain didn't speak. His face paled, and then as the conversation continued, he turned crimson with anger and embarrassment.

"Yes, sir," he said into the phone. "I understand perfectly."

He placed the receiver back into the cradle and turned to Claire with a slight bow. "My apologies, Madame Daladier," he stated politely. "Come with me. I'll drive you home personally."

Chapter 28

When Rachel went to work that Monday, all three of Friday's suspects were present: the elderly man who always smiled, the young girl, and Marc, the sad man who had lost two sons when the Germans first attacked. None discussed what happened with the Germans, whether they were detained a minute, the entire weekend, or not at all, giving no indication what their punishment, if any, had been. All made it clear that they wanted to be left alone, and they focused on their assigned tasks.

Rachel watched the trio at their work stations, using the observation techniques Meurice had taught her. Her greatest fear was that any one of the three might have given information to the Germans. Or it could be worse. Maybe one of them already worked for the Germans. They could have been watching her, and were detained on Friday to report any suspicious activity. Meurice had been right to warn her not to sabotage the factory again – at least not for a while.

Marc spotted her studying him. Since he always kept to himself, and rarely spoke to anyone, it was unusual for him to acknowledge coworkers. His gaze met hers, cold and penetrating. Rachel shivered but refused to be intimidated. She did not turn away. Their eyes locked for several seconds.

Marc glanced away, briefly, and then nodded to the left.

Rachel turned to where he indicated and saw the foreman, Pierre, standing in the shadows by the stairwell. He was observing the production floor, ensuring each worker did what he expected, and didn't seem to notice Rachel watching. He studied those on the floor a moment more, and then opened the door and disappeared into the stairwell.

Rachel again looked at Marc. He motioned towards a sewing machine in the corner under the window. Minnie was operating the machine, running stitches along the soles of a pair of leather boots. As soon as she finished she stood, looked at everyone in the room, and then walked to the stairwell. After a last, furtive check, she opened the door and discreetly stepped through, rapidly closing it behind her.

Rachel looked at Marc. He winked at her and smiled.

* * *

Later that day Rachel had her first courier assignment. She went to a printing shop on the *Rue des Écoles,* next to the pastry store, wearing her red scarf. She was well suited for the role – an innocent teenager that seemed to mind her own business. Until you looked more closely.

The shop was small, not more than a counter and space for three or four customers to wait in line. The owner behind the counter was a stocky man, his hair starting to gray, his expression a bit surly. He smiled curtly and nodded as she came in. There was another customer in the shop, a businessman dressed in a gray suit. Rachel knew he could be friend or foe, indifferent or interested. She thought of what Meurice and Dr. Durant had taught her, to be perceptive and observant, to blend with the local populace. She looked at a display, a small table in the corner with four papers on it that represented different printing styles. She pretended to be interested, as if she were making a selection.

The customer soon left and Rachel nervously went to the counter. "I've come for Monsieur Bonnet's package," she said, using a prearranged greeting provided by Meurice.

The printer nodded, studied the red silk scarf for a second, and continued the conversation, verifying there was no danger. "How is Mr. Bonnet?" he asked. "Does he still care for his mother?"

"He is well. And his mother's health is improving."

"I'm glad to hear that," the printer said and, apparently satisfied Rachel was safe, he went to the back of the shop.

Rachel could hear noises, rummaging through shelves, doors opening and closing. She was nervous, wondering if she could trust him, even though she had no reason not to.

He returned a minute later with two packages, one a large bundle tied with string, the second a small box. "The bundle is for Monique," he continued. "She is small, like you, maybe twenty-five years old with short blond hair. Split it in half and give it to her in two meetings. Meet her in front of the camera store three blocks down on your right on Wednesday at 6 p.m. Wear a beige beret – that's how she'll identify you. She'll ask you for directions to the dress shop. If you're comfortable with her and those around you, and you think it's safe, tell her to go two more blocks and turn right. If you sense danger, simply say that you don't know where the dress shop is. Do you understand?"

Rachel nodded, absorbing the instructions.

"The box is important," the man said softly. "On Thursday at 5 p.m. you will sit on the bench by the Metro station entrance across the street from the theater. A woman will sit beside you and ask what time the train to Versailles arrives. You don't need to know her name. If it is safe, you will reply it has already left and give her the box. If it is not safe – if you're suspicious of anyone around you or think you may have been followed – say the train departs at 6 p.m. and leave with the box. Bring it back here. Do you understand?"

Rachel digested what she had been told, visualizing the clandestine meetings. "Yes," she said. "I understand."

The front door of the shop opened, ringing a little bell affixed at the top of the door frame. Rachel showed little interest, her business with the printer almost concluded, but she noticed the shop owner look to the entrance. His eyes grew wide, his face tensed.

Rachel turned and looked behind her. A German officer was walking into the shop. He was tall and straight, with an officer's cap and black leather gloves. He walked up to the counter, nodding to Rachel.

"Captain Donner," the printer said. "I have your order right here."

The captain smiled at Rachel. "There's no hurry," he assured him. "The young lady was first. Please, take care of her. I'll wait."

The captain turned to look out the window. Rachel and the printer made eye contact, sharing a frantic look.

"I think I have everything except the invitations," Rachel said, inventing a reason to remain. "But I can come back for them."

"No, I have them here," the printer said.

He turned to a rack behind him, stuffed with parchment and paper, orders filled with neat name tags attached, and a list of orders yet to be filled. He took a small stack of cards and wrapped them in brown paper, tying them in string.

"Here you go. That should be everything."

"Thank you," she said, nodding a discreet farewell.

Rachel grabbed the stack of papers, guarding the small box that she knew was most important. She held them in both hands and started for the door.

"Let me get that for you," Captain Donner offered.

"Thank you," Rachel replied, pulling the papers against her chest. She couldn't risk dropping anything.

As he opened the door he looked at her closely and said, "That's an armful for such a small lady. Are you sure you don't need help carrying it?"

"No, sir. I will manage."

"It's no bother. I can have a soldier accompany you."

"Thank you so much," Rachel responded with an innocent smile. "But I don't have far to go. That's very nice of you, though."

The captain clicked his heels together and nodded politely.

Rachel passed through the entrance and heard the door close behind her. She sighed with relief, her heart pounding. She realized the captain had not been suspicious, only kind. Perhaps he was the father of a teenage girl like Rachel, who now waited patiently for her father's return. He was probably a school teacher or a banker or a salesman when the world was not at war. But she also assumed, if the slightest suspicion had been aroused, he would react quickly and cruelly, just as he had been trained to do.

She hurried down the pavement towards her flat, nagged by an unanswered question. Who was Monique?

Chapter 29

Claire couldn't stop thinking about Gestapo headquarters. If their reaction to a mere curfew violation was that intimidating, what would they do if they suspected her of Resistance activities? Or worse yet, what if they actually caught her? She knew she had to be stronger, more cautious and conservative, avoiding risk and outthinking the enemy. She had to maintain the image of a demure bookstore owner, while planning and plotting the enemy's defeat.

She met Gen. Berg for coffee, alert for any information he might reveal, and thanked him profusely for intervening. He was annoyed at the Gestapo and apologetic to Claire.

"The curfew is designed to discourage subversive activity," he informed her, "not to harass law-abiding citizens. I'm sorry you were snared by such an overzealous soldier."

"It was frightening," she said, feigning fear and intimidation. "I had done nothing wrong. I'm sorry I had to bother you, but I didn't know what else to do. Now I don't know how to make it up to you."

He glanced around the café, and then placed his hand lightly over hers. "A quiet dinner might be nice," he suggested. "Just the two of us."

She smiled, offering encouragement, and moved closer. "I would like that."

* * *

Paul arrived at Claire's flat at 5 p.m. on Tuesday for dinner. The radio played softly in the background, a song called *J'Attendrai* by Rina Ketty.   The recording was several years old but had experienced a resurgence in popularity. The title, *I Will Wait For You*, had special meaning for many lonely people: Jew and Christian, women and men.

They had combined some of their meat rations and Claire made a thick stew, adding chunks of potato and carrots. Even though they had talked about the curfew violation at length, they discussed it further as she cooked.

"It was an unnecessary risk," Claire advised him. "We can't make mistakes like that. Why invite the Gestapo into our lives? We need to keep low profiles, creating no suspicion."

Paul studied his cousin, reflecting on her transformation. She was strong, cautious and cunning, and easy to underestimate. "You're right," he agreed. "Any interaction with the enemy that's not on our terms presents risk."

"I'm just grateful to General Berg. If it weren't for him, it could have been much worse."

Paul peered at her. "You seem to be very close," he said, sounding annoyed.

She looked at him with mild surprise. "Isn't that our objective," she asked, "to mingle with the enemy and obtain information? Berg and I share an interest in chess. So what? I know he's a Nazi general. I know he's one of the most dangerous men in Paris. But if I can use chess to get information, and can risk having a German general as a friend, then I will."

Paul dropped the issue. It was none of his business who her friends were, as long as it didn't jeopardize what they were trying to do. And he knew Claire was too smart to compromise their mission.

The news came on the radio while they were eating, providing glowing reports of German successes on the Eastern Front. A glorious victory was predicted at Stalingrad, but both Claire and Paul knew the battle was going badly for the Germans. They were surrounded, clinging to ever-dwindling territory. The newscaster then shifted to local news. They heard:

Today, in a real estate auction, Junot Properties offered the winning bid for the commercial real estate formerly owned by the Jew, Abraham Blum. Properties are scattered throughout the metropolis, and include an entire city block on the Rue di Rivoli, near the Louvre. Mr. Junot was quoted...

Paul turned off the radio. "I would rather not know," he said simply, returning to his meal. "Because I wouldn't be able to look at him if I did."

After dinner they sat in the parlor and enjoyed a glass of wine. Paul shared his next challenge with Claire.

"I have a balance sheet from the bank to show you. I have to alter it and then hide assets from the Germans. I'm hoping you can help me."

"What type of assets are we talking about? We can't do anything with stocks or bonds or real estate."

"No, you're right. But there are two assets stored in the basement vault. And that's what we will focus on."

"What are they?"

"Cash and gold," Paul said softly. "Tons of it."

He pulled the ledgers from his brief case. "Can you tell these have been modified?" he asked.

She looked through the balance sheets. The numbers were recorded clearly, legible and unblemished. She added up the columns of figures on a separate piece of paper and found the math correct. Then she held the ledger up to the light and looked for unusual markings.

"It seems legitimate," she said as she put it down on the coffee table. "And the numbers add up."

"Good," Paul said. "Then it worked. Because the balance sheet has been forged."

"How much are the numbers off by?"

"Ten million francs."

"That's a lot of money!"

"It's not that much, given the total assets of the bank. But I intend to hide it from the Germans."

"Paul, we need to be careful."

"Then I shouldn't hide the money?"

"Yes, of course you should. But we need a perfect plan, something foolproof."

"I realize that, but it's more difficult than it seems. And I still have to get the money out of the bank."

"What about the gold?"

"There are nine thousand two hundred and six gold bars, each weighing one kilogram. I changed the balance sheet to show four thousand two hundred and six bars."

She looked at him with amazement. The sheer wealth was overwhelming. "How much money is that?" she wondered aloud.

"About thirty million francs."

"And how are you going to steal five thousand bars of gold, each weighing a kilogram?"

"I'm not sure," he said. "But I don't have much time to do it."

Chapter 30

Claire went to the church, *Saint-Étienne-du-Mont,* on Thursday at 7 a.m. Located on the *Montagne Sainte-Geneviève*, it was built in 1535 and contained the shrine of St. Geneviève, the patron saint of Paris. Claire entered and, as she always had, marveled at the simple elegance of the structure, its polished stone, the spiral stairs that flanked the altar, the hand-carved walnut choir screen. It exuded beauty and grace, drawing the eyes ever upward, providing a glimpse of the glory of heaven.

She stared in awe, moving toward the altar, and sat in the first row, as she had been directed. She wore a black hat with a veil, and held rosary beads in her hands. She kneeled, praying for Paul and Catherine and Sophie and Jacques, and for Paris to again be free. When ten minutes had passed, she rose to light a candle at the altar.

She made the sign of the cross and kneeled, bowing her head and whispering a short prayer for the Resistance. She was barely there a minute when a priest appeared from the shadows, lightly touching her elbow. He wore a plain frock, was short and stocky, his face masked with kindness and compassion. About thirty years of age, his hair was black and short, his eyes brown, and the hint of a beard shadowed his face, as if a razor had been used with limited success.

Claire studied him curiously, her first impression one of implicit trust. His face, so gentle and serene, his eyes, so penetrating and sincere, portrayed a sensitive man who cared about the human race. She knew he was her contact, the man who would show her all she had been helping to build.

"I'm Father Nicolas," he said quietly. "I'll hear your confession now. Please follow me."

She rose from the bench and followed him into the dark recesses of the church. They left the altar, entering the corridor that flanked it, and continued to the rear of the church, down a narrow set of marble steps that led to a dimly lit basement. They passed many crypts: in the walls, free standing and imbedded in the floor. Finally, along the back wall, they came to a halt in front of a marble coffin. Beautiful in its simplicity, the lid was flat and polished, signs of a crack near the corner of the base.

"Here we are," the priest said softly, as if whispering out of respect for the dead. He reached forward and started to slide the top of the coffin off of its base, the smooth stone moving with little friction.

Claire tentatively peeked inside. She could see only an eerie blackness, but she felt an uplift of cool air.

Father Nicolas reached into the coffin, along the top wall, and the audible sound of a light switch toggling was heard. An instant later, the interior of the casket was lit with a pale glow. The coffin had no bottom, and Claire looked down a vertical steel ladder, attached to a wall of stone, descending down a seemingly endless shaft. She shivered as they moved closer.

"The ladder descends about fifteen feet," Father Nicolas said.

"Is that where we're hiding the Jews?"

"Yes," he said. "There are almost fifty now, the population growing rapidly. A few more arrived just before you."

"Is it safe?"

"Yes, as safe as it can be. This section of the catacombs is isolated from the others."

Father Nicolas explained that the Left Bank of Paris was home to underground caverns and catacombs, almost three hundred kilometers in total, up to one hundred meters below the surface. They were created centuries before, when the limestone was mined to build the monuments of Paris. This extensive network of underground caverns and canals, corridors and caves, were like arteries, winding and turning and climbing and falling throughout the subsurface of the Left Bank.

Claire listened politely, but Father Nicolas only confirmed what she already knew. He described what Dr. Durant had drawn in the dirt on the banks of the Seine while at the cottage in Giverny. As Paul rested in his bedroom, physically and mentally destroyed, Dr. Durant had explained an ambitious plan to use the catacombs as a defense network during the Great War. He and Claire resurrected the plan in part, altering its purpose to hide the Jews while safe transport for them was arranged.

The Resistance chose this section because it was isolated from the rest, and they could safely hide in just one segment, separated from the remainder. Right now, beneath the city's subways and sewers, the caverns contained a German bunker, bank vaults, and those closer to the surface, wine cellars and even a nightclub. In some areas, like this vein, the caverns were independent of the main excavations. And this segment had two other entrances, making it an ideal location for hiding the Jews.

Claire digested what he told her. "I have forged documents for the Rosenbergs," she informed him. "They'll be the first to depart."

"Their arrangements are still being finalized. When completed, they'll be escorted out of Paris, either to Switzerland or Spain. Come, let me show you," he said as they prepared to descend.

Chapter 31

Claire entered a cylindrical shaft made of cut limestone, a blend of beige with veins of vermillion and gray. The tunnel was man-made, the mortar strong and intact, hundreds of years old. She went down a vertical steel ladder anchored into the stone, firmly attached every meter or two. A string of electric lights, activated by the switch near the coffin lid, lit their path.

Father Nicolas came down behind her. "Don't worry," he assured her. "The ladder is safe and quite secure."

He stopped halfway down and pointed to a cache of stones, matching those in the cavern in size and composition, collected in a steel mesh net. He showed her a pocket cut into the rock, a handle inside the cavity, an attached steel wire running up the wall to the net. Activation of the lever allowed the rocks to fall to the ground, filling the exit and the first few meters of the cavity.

"The rocks can be released to conceal the entrance," he informed her.

The ladder descended five meters more before coming to rest on the rock floor. They stood in the bottom of the cylinder, its circumference narrow, with a low, slender exit leading to the catacombs beyond. The tunnels were originally excavated to access the limestone. The rock, so beautiful in texture and hue, and the mortar that held it together, were added for support after a series of cave-ins in the 1700's.

They left the cavity at the base of the ladder and walked into a slender tunnel, barely two meters square. The walls and ceiling were made like the cylinder, limestone cut and shaped, and mortared into place. Claire couldn't help but admire the beauty of the stone, even when used in such a rough state. The corridor angled downward in both directions, each path lit dimly by lights strung along the ceiling.

Father Nicolas pointed to the right. "This path leads to another entrance several blocks away," he said. "It's accessed just off the *Rue Monge,* by the *Rue des Écoles,* behind the flower store."

Claire was familiar with the location. "Right on the corner, next to the cafe?" she asked.

"Yes," he replied. "The stairwell is similar to this one, but located in a small tool shed in a secluded garden. It's been easy to smuggle Jews into the yard, down the stairs, and then to the cavern where they are currently housed."

Father Nicolas led her down the corridor to the left. They passed a graceful arch, somehow looking peculiar in a place where it was never seen, and a vertical support column constructed of random sized rocks, leaning precariously.

Claire paused to study the pillar. "That doesn't look structurally sound," she observed anxiously.

Father Nicolas shrugged. "It must be" he responded, "to have survived all these years. I always marvel at the skill of the master who built such a beautiful arch, while the pillar looks like it was made by a child."

The corridor continued for a hundred more meters before opening to a large empty space, low and wide. The open path curved sharply to the left and disappeared. It continued across the void, the path winding upward along the far wall forty meters across the darkness.

"Where are we geographically?" Claire asked. "The winding corridor is very confusing."

"We're below the fifth arrondissement, about halfway between the *Banque de Paris* and the *Sorbonne*," he explained. "There are tunnels leaving the cavern that contain reservoirs of fresh water, one used for drinking, the other for bathing, and a tunnel that leads to a deep vertical offshoot, an area used for trash and waste."

"Are the Jews in this cavern?"

"Yes, just past this bend," Father Nicolas said. "They have electricity, furniture, partitions for privacy, books and magazines, toys for the children. Most of the food is brought in through the church, a smaller amount via the access behind the flower store."

Claire considered safety, should one of the two entrances be discovered. She also wondered if other points could be used, so more Jews could be helped.

"Is this area completely isolated from the rest of the catacombs and caverns?" she asked.

"Yes, primarily through a cave-in that occurred a hundred and seventy years ago. But there is one more entrance. Exiting the cavern in the other direction, the corridor at the extreme end extends for a kilometer or more. It leads to a crypt in Montparnasse Cemetery, which is quite far from the *Saint-Étienne-du-Mont.* Due to distance, this entrance is not normally used to access the cavern. But it will make an excellent escape path."

Claire looked at the stone walls, graceful arches, and crooked pillars that supported the buildings above. She was amazed that the city hadn't completely collapsed, crumbling into the catacombs.

"Come," Father Nicolas said. "I'll introduce you to the families we're helping."

They continued down the winding corridor until they reached the cavern. The space was vast, but with low ceilings supported by pillars, with many smaller areas leading from the main.

As they approached, people stopped what they were doing, playing games, reading books, washing clothes, or tending children, and studied them closely. Based on their clothing, Claire could see that they were from all walks of life, young and old, peasant and professional. Small children peeked shyly from behind their parents, teenagers watched curiously acting brave and defiant, and the old merely observed, apparently wondering what was about to happen.

Claire smiled and greeted the odd assortment of people as they passed. Some merely nodded, others came closer, introducing themselves and welcoming her warmly.

"I'll get the Rosenbergs," Father Nicolas said while Claire mingled.

He walked behind some partitions perched against the edge of the wall and emerged a moment later with two adults, a young girl, and a small boy. They came towards Claire while Father Nicolas made introductions.

Jacob Rosenberg was a slender man with short black hair and full beard. He wore wire-rimmed spectacles, a yarmulke perched on his head. He explained to Claire that he was a rabbinic scholar, expert in the five books of the Bible and Hebrew history. His family wanted to go to

Portugal, via the escape route to Spain, where he could continue his teachings. He introduced his wife Rebekah, a petite woman with black hair and an olive complexion. She deferred to her husband as he spoke, smiled shyly, and minded her children. As she introduced them – little Anna was four, a child with dark eyes and an impish grin, and Josef was eight with spectacles similar to his father's – they stared at Claire in wide-eyed fascination.

Claire knelt down and spoke to the children. "How are you?" she asked, smiling. "Are you ready to take a trip?"

The girl grinned and shrugged, hiding behind her mother's skirt, but Josef took a step forward, and proudly spoke for the family.

"We're going to Portugal," he informed her. "My father says we'll make many new friends."

"Yes, I'm sure you will," Claire said. She stood and addressed the parents, handing them their documentation, forged by a local printer friendly to their cause.

Jacob Rosenberg studied the documents for a moment and then put them in his pocket. He took Claire's hand and held it in his. "Thank you so much for helping us," he said sincerely. "I know you risk your life by doing so."

Claire felt her heart swell and tears moisten her eyes. "I'm happy to do it," she assured him. "As you would do it for me."

Chapter 32

Beethoven's *Moonlight Sonata* echoed through the flat, calming the night with a melodic arpeggio. Paul Moreau sat in a pleated leather chair in the dimly lit parlor, a half glass of Scotch on the table beside him. On his lap lay a pad of paper, in his left hand a pen. In the center of the page he had drawn a circle. Within its boundaries he wrote the names Catherine and Sophie. From the circle, lines extended in three directions. On the first line, he wrote the word: fisherman. On the second he penned: Kruger. And on the third he wrote: Junot.

He studied the depiction pensively and took another sip of Scotch. After the word fisherman, he put three question marks, and then wrote: who. Next to Junot's name he wrote: deserves to die but serves a purpose. He then crossed out the line that connected it to the circle containing Catherine and Sophie's name. He stared at what was left, his hatred brewing. Next to Kruger's name he wrote boldly and in capital letters: KILL.

He raised the glass to his lips and drained the contents. He rose, went to the kitchen, grabbed the bottle of Scotch and refilled the glass. The sonata was just finishing, so he walked to the Victrola and picked up the needle, starting the piece at the beginning – for the fourth time. He returned to the chair and picked up the pad of paper, turning to the next page. In the center he drew a large circle, and in it he wrote: forty million francs. From the circle he drew a number of straight lines. On them he wrote: truck, coffin, German staff car, and then three lines with question marks. He was trying to identify any method imaginable for removing the cash and gold.

He took another sip of Scotch, flipping the pad of paper to the first page. He stared at the words Catherine and Sophie on the center of the page. With the tip of his finger, he rubbed the writing tenderly. Then he covered his face with his hands and cried.

* * *

Wednesday morning Otto Ernst sat in Paul's office, skimming through documents. "This is more than I imagined. Over a hundred million francs. And that's only the main office. There's more at the other locations?"

"Yes," Paul said, relieved his alterations had gone undetected. "But there's no gold in other locations. It's all stored here."

"I'd like to arrange transport to Berlin as soon as possible. May I use your phone?"

"Of course," Paul said, his heart sinking. "I'll give you some privacy."

He left the office and closed the door behind him. As he paced the corridor, his frustration mounted. How did he get into such a precarious situation? He should have hidden the gold first and then altered the balance sheets. This past weekend had been his chance, but he had wasted it. He waited a few minutes and walked back to his office. The door was open. Otto Ernst sat in the pleated leather chair in front of his desk, rustling through his briefcase.

"Bad news," Ernst announced, frowning. "The earliest Berlin Bank can arrange transport is Monday. We need a truck for the bullion, and armed escorts. I was optimistic to think we could move the gold so quickly."

Paul was relieved. "That should be fine," he responded. "It's been untouched for years. A few more days won't matter."

Ernst stood and shook his hand. "I suppose not," he agreed. "I think I have all I need. Unless you hear otherwise, I'll return on Monday, at 10 a.m."

After Otto Ernst left, Paul walked down the stairs to the basement. The vault, constructed of steel slabs imbedded in concrete walls, had been built in place as the building was completed around it. A tumbler lock allowed entry, its combination known only to a select few. Paul stood before the vault and sighed, considering the insurmountable task that lay ahead of him.

He looked around the rest of the basement. The walls were thick, made of brick faced with worn stucco. The room was empty except for the safe. At the other end, cleaning equipment and supplies were stacked against the wall: brooms and mops, buckets and bins, some wood and metal boxes, and rags. The basement vault was no longer used for daily bank business. It housed only the emergency reserves: funds that were rarely required. A smaller, more modern vault had been installed close to the offices.

Paul fingered the lock, slowly operating the tumblers. After inputting the combination, he felt it release, and he slowly swung the heavy door open. The vault was lined with shelves containing metal boxes, each housing five hundred thousand francs, and stacks of gold bars, each twelve centimeters long, one centimeter high, and six centimeters wide. Sitting on the shelves, were nine thousand two hundred and six gold bars.

Paul realized the cash would be easy to take. There was so much of it. He could remove ten million francs and rearrange the metal boxes. No one would notice. But the gold presented a different problem. He planned to take almost half of what was there. Anyone who had ever been in the vault would notice immediately.

He lifted one of the gold bars. It was dense. He wondered how to remove five thousand gold ingots, right under the nose of the German army. He glanced at the stairs. It was the only way out. He studied the gold bars again: all stacked neatly, ten high and five deep. Row after row after row.

He moved the first pile so there was room behind it. He stood the second stack on edge. The ingots consumed the same space. If each row was arranged this way, he could remove half the gold and create the illusion that it was undisturbed. But where would he put the ingots he removed? He stood in the center of the basement and stared at the vault, thoroughly demoralized, seeing no solution. He could never remove the gold in one weekend, not undiscovered. Dejected, he walked slowly up the stairs, went into his office, and closed the door. He sat behind his desk and put his head in his hands, closing his eyes tightly. Victory was elusive, but he refused to concede defeat.

Almost an hour passed before he realized he had made it much harder than it had to be. The solution, once he discovered it, was actually very simple. He removed a piece of paper from his desk and wrote a detailed letter to Pablo, the night janitor and his Resistance contact. Then he put the letter behind the picture on the wall, a method of communication they had previously arranged. His instructions were very important – a fortune in gold bullion and, possibly his own life, hung in the balance.

Chapter 33

Julian Junot drove his black Mercedes through the nineteenth arrondissement, along *Rue Manin* and then into *Parc des Buttes-Chaumont,* one of Paris's largest public parks. He entered a small parking area in the southwest corner surrounded by trees, turned off the ignition and waited.

It was 8 a.m. on a Tuesday morning, and there were no other cars in the lot. The day was crisp but clear and, as Junot rolled down the window, he could hear birds chirping, a woodpecker pounding on a nearby tree, and distant voices. He scanned the spaces between the trees and saw a young couple walking a dog, a man with a cane, and a woman sitting on a bench, scanning a newspaper.

It was ten minutes before the second car arrived. The driver entered the lot, parking several spaces away. He remained in the car, the engine off, until five minutes had passed. Then the door opened and a slender man with white hair emerged, half-glasses perched on the end of his nose. He walked furtively toward Junot's car, glancing in all directions, and then quickly opened the door and slid into the passenger's side.

"Good morning, Mr. Deveraux," Junot said as the man sat down.

"Junot," Deveraux nodded brusquely, staring straight ahead.

"What do you have for me?"

"Five families, twenty-eight people. Ten parents, six grandparents and twelve children."

"Where are they now?"

"In Drancy, the complex northeast of the city."

"And how will you get them to me without arousing suspicion?"

"They have been chosen for medical experiments," Deveraux explained. "They are at greatest risk."

Junot looked at him curiously and asked, "What do you mean?"

Deveraux studied Junot, searching for any signs of compassion. "Some of those at Drancy have been there over a year," he informed him. "Others, such as those I'm sending you, are dispatched quickly."

"I still don't understand."

Deveraux paused, thoughtful for a moment, and then replied, "Among those I am sending you are two sets of twins, two handicapped children and a veteran from the Great War who is one of the grandparents. He suffers from seizures and uncontrollable shaking from a mustard gas attack."

Sounding annoyed, Junot asked, "Why would I want these misfits? I do have businesses to run."

"Because the excuse I gave you is actually the truth. The Nazis are fascinated by twins, handicapped, and those afflicted. They are shipped as quickly as they arrive. The Nazis perform medical experiments on them, supposedly with horrific results."

"So why send them to me?"

Deveraux paused. "I suppose I'm trying to save them," he admitted. "Regardless of what people think, I do have a soul."

Junot sighed, digesting the latest revelation. "I suppose I can get some use of them," he said, disappointed. "But it's certainly not what I expected. When is delivery?"

"Thursday. They will arrive in the back of a closed panel truck, dark green, with *Jules Lafont, Grocer* in white lettering on the side."

Junot was quiet for a moment, and then directed, "You will arrange for the truck to be left in an alley at the Sorbonne, near the school of Philosophy. Leave the vehicle at 8 a.m., collect it at noon. Agreed?"

"Agreed," replied Andre Deveraux.

Junot withdrew a fistful of bills from his pocket and handed them to Deveraux. "It's all there," he said.

Deveraux quickly shoved the money into his pocket and then studied the landscape, ensuring no one watched. He reached for the door handle.

"Wait," Junot said, lightly touching his arm. "When can I have more?"

Deveraux sighed and sat back in the seat. "It depends on many things," he replied. "How successful we are tomorrow, who observes, who asks questions. If the Jews' exit goes unnoticed, then we can plan another delivery."

"I need all you can get me," Junot said. When Deveraux glanced at him suspiciously he added, "The old ones won't last very long."

Chapter 34

Rachel sat on the bed in her tiny flat, staring at the packages she had gotten from the printer. She was about to cross a delicate line, moving from a Jew impersonating a Christian, a teenage girl hiding from an enemy who wasn't really looking for her, to a combatant. It was a large step, and she wondered if it was worth taking. She could hide at the Normandy farm with her parents and brother, waiting for the war to end. But she realized the war might never end. Not unless she, and thousands like her, continued fighting for the cause. She knew it sounded naïve, as if she thought she was saving mankind, but the aggregate impact of so many, even when doing so little, would be significant. Ultimately, it was a battle of good versus evil; it was a fight worth winning. Maybe the enemy could be defeated by people like her, at least when their actions were summed. Tanks and ships and planes and guns might not be needed. At least that's what she hoped. Because then the killing could stop.

She ate some cheese and bread for dinner, leaving the crust, which was stiff and stale. She would add it to soup the next day. As she enjoyed her meal, drinking water to wash it down, she thought about how long she had stood in line to get it. She realized that, if the war lasted many more years, most of Paris would starve.

After dinner, she sat on her bed and removed the string from the package the printer had given her. The stack consisted of pamphlets, four pages long, that urged

Parisians to resist the Nazis, to demonstrate overtly and covertly, passively and aggressively. Using cartoons to illustrate points, the leaflets provided instructions on hampering the war effort.

Rachel realized that the innocent cartoons, which many would discard upon receipt, could lead to the death of anyone who possessed them. There was little risk to her, a courier. She was in danger only while they were in her possession, which was far different from the person who distributed them. She thought of Monique, the girl she must deliver them to, and she had a new respect for her, even though she had yet to meet her.

Rachel divided the stack in half, as instructed, and placed them under her cot against the back wall. In front of the pamphlets, she placed boxes that contained her clothes and were normally stored under the bed.

The smaller package was sealed, the brown paper wrapped tightly around the contents. This was the most dangerous item, the riskiest to deliver. She was curious, wondering what it was, but realized it was best not to know. She decided to hide the package in the oven, on a corner in the upper rack. It would be safe there until she delivered it on Thursday.

* * *

On Wednesday evening at 6 p.m., Rachel stood in front of the camera shop, wearing her beige beret and staring in the window at the displays. She had only been there a few minutes when a young woman approached. She had short blond hair, a broad smile, and seemed carefree and unconcerned as she strolled down the pavement. She stopped abruptly, standing beside Rachel.

"Can you tell me how to get to the dress shop?" the woman asked.

"Two blocks down and then turn right," Rachel replied.

"Good," the woman said. "I remember, although I'm not sure if that means we stop or continue."

Rachel was uncomfortable, a bit anxious. "We continue," she said softly.

The woman was not as careful as Meurice. She appeared to pay little attention to nearby pedestrians, didn't seem to notice people across the street or those riding by on bicycles or driving by in cars, even though they were mainly taxis. She did, however, warily watch three German soldiers, barely ten meters away, talking quietly and smoking cigarettes.

"I'm Monique," she said. "At least that's what everyone calls me. It's not my real name, though." She then glanced around and, apparently satisfied it was safe, leaned forward and whispered. "I can't tell you my real name."

"I understand," Rachel said. She didn't offer a name, real or imagined.

"Do you have something for me?"

Rachel ensured no one was watching and then handed her the pamphlets. The German soldiers seemed preoccupied, watching two French women cross the street.

Monique took the package and smiled. "Bring the rest on Friday," she requested. "Same place, same time. Use the same codes." Then she walked away.

Rachel shrugged off her doubts. The delivery had gone well; no one seemed to notice them. Even though Monique appeared unaware of her surroundings, she was probably more observant than it seemed. She was certainly watching the Germans, and she probably had surveyed the area before her approach and determined it was safe.

Rachel's next task was planned for the following evening. On Thursday at 5 p.m., she sat on the bench by the entrance to the Metro station, across the street from the theater. She studied cars, bicycles, buses, and taxis, ensuring none looked suspicious. She also observed the passing pedestrians, looked at those waiting to enter the theater, and scrutinized the German soldiers sprinkled among the people of Paris. Two were nearby, looking into a jewelry shop window. Rachel decided they were shopping for girlfriends back home, or for French girls they were trying to befriend.

She had been there a few minutes when a woman sat beside her on the corner of the bench, turned slightly, her back to Rachel. Was she waiting for a bus or a taxi, someone to exit the Metro station, or was she the new contact? Rachel couldn't be sure.

Several seconds ticked by silently. Rachel didn't speak, nor did she look at the woman. After a minute or two had passed, the woman turned slightly and asked, "Do you know when the train to Versailles arrives?"

The woman was very careful. She had taken several minutes to study the landscape after she sat down, and probably longer before she approached. She kept her face turned away, their bodies almost touching.

"It has already departed," Rachel said, carefully mouthing the code.

"You have a package for me?"

"Yes," Rachel replied.

She handed over the parcel, just as the woman turned to face her.

Each gasped, wide-eyed and open-mouthed at the sight of the other, but they recovered quickly. After a few seconds had passed, and each accepted the situation, the woman spoke.

"How are you Rachel?"

It was Claire Daladier.

Chapter 35

People hurried down the steps to the Metro to catch departing trains while others emerged, having just arrived. A crowd had gathered outside the theater, waiting for the current show to end and the next to begin. Rachel and Claire didn't want to attract attention by staying too long, so they left the *Rue Monge* and strolled down side streets, pausing to look into shop windows, always watching those they passed cautiously.

As they walked the streets of Paris, Rachel told Claire about the indoctrination Dr. Durant had provided: identity papers, an apartment with pre-paid rent, the job at the boot factory. She explained the information she gathered, the boots she made, and the fire she had set. She was proud of stopping production for a half day, telling Claire she knew exactly how many boots were not sent to the Russian front because of her. And then Rachel told her about the people she worked with, Marc, the man who had lost his sons, Pierre the foreman and Minnie his secret lover.

Claire listened intently, a slight smile on her face. Rachel talked continuously as they walked up one block and down the next. Claire hardly said a word, realizing how terribly lonely Rachel must be. With no friends or access to her family, she was completely alone. And now, at the sight of a friend, someone who cared about her, she rambled on, excited and happy.

When Rachel stopped talking, Claire tried to convince her that she should reconsider her Resistance activities. "Rachel, why are you doing this?" she asked.

"I have my reasons," Rachel replied. "Just as you do."

"But you're all alone. You've sacrificed everything."

"*Bitte,*" a passing German soldier said, stopping abruptly in front of them. Two other soldiers were with him.

Rachel hooked her hand in Claire's arm, pulling her closer. They both knew the parcel stuffed in Claire's pocket could cause their deaths if discovered.

Claire was startled but regained her composure. "Excuse me?" she asked.

The soldier looked at his companions, who shrugged and remained silent. The soldier then nodded slightly, and pointed to the street. "Theater?" he asked in stilted French.

Claire's body, so tense and taut, relaxed. "Directions to theater?" she questioned.

The Germans looked at each other, confused. "Theater," the first soldier repeated, slowly emphasizing each syllable.

Claire turned in the direction from which they came. "Straight down this street," she answered. She took her hand from her pocket to point the way, but the package accidentally fell out. It bounced on the pavement, landing at their feet.

Rachel bent over quickly, grabbing it, but so did one of the soldiers. For a moment they each tugged, the soldier looking at Rachel oddly. Then she let go.

Claire's eyes were wide with fright as the soldier stood up. He looked at the parcel curiously, turning it over in his hand, before giving it to Claire, nodding politely.

She smiled and casually put it in her pocket, but she could feel cold beads of sweat on the back of her neck. Once certain the package was secure, she continued giving directions. "Go to the end of the street and then turn right," she said, pointing. She held up two fingers. "Two blocks."

The soldiers looked at each other, shrugged and grinned, and then nodded politely. "*Danke,*" they each said in turn.

They continued on their way, moving down the pavement.

Claire sighed with relief. "I really didn't need that," she said as she turned to Rachel. "That could have turned out much differently. Did you learn anything?"

Rachel looked at Claire and smiled. "Yes, I did," she responded. "I learned that I'm not alone anymore. I have you as a friend."

Claire rolled her eyes and said, "Rachel, you don't understand how dangerous this is. It's not a game. Your life is at stake."

"I want to make a contribution, even in my own small way."

"But you could have stayed with your family, where it's safe. Why did you come back? The Germans will kill you, just for giving me a package like this. Is that worth losing your life for?"

"You're not telling me anything I don't already know."

"I'm worried about you," Claire said in a motherly tone. "And that's because I care about you. I don't want anything to happen to you."

Rachel was quiet, her fact taut, her arms crossed. It didn't seem her mind could be changed.

Claire watched her closely and sighed in surrender. "Your family is well," she said. "They seem happy, working the fields with the farmer, except they miss their daughter."

"I will be home when the time is right."

"And when will that be?"

"As soon as the Germans are gone."

They strolled a few minutes more, talking about the weather, which now offered the promise of spring. Rachel asked about the bookstore, concerned about her former coworkers, and they talked about the war and the German setbacks on the Russian front. But all too soon, each realized they must go.

"You will be bringing a similar package to me next Thursday," Claire said. "We'll meet on the same bench and use the same code."

"Is there anything else?" Rachel asked.

"Yes," Claire replied, making one more effort. "Go with your family. Before it's too late."

Chapter 36

Claire knew Rachel had motivated her to save Jews when the innocent teenager arrived at her door, frightened and confused, but she also owed it to Jacques and Catherine and Sophie. Savings Jews would be her cause, her contribution to mankind. And whether she saved one or a thousand, it was something she had to do. Much of what Rachel had said also applied to her.

Claire wanted to help her; she wanted to make sure she was safe. She couldn't convince Rachel to return to her family in Normandy and, after considering all the issues, Claire decided to integrate her into the network she was forming. She would have to find just the right assignment, something interesting but not too risky, intricate but not overwhelming.

She mulled over telling Paul just how much she had done to save the Jews. He knew she developed plans with Dr. Durant, but he didn't know any details. And he would never dream the operation she was now a part of actually existed. He seemed ready; he was behaving as Dr. Durant told him to. But she decided to wait a little bit longer. If he was able to hide the gold at the bank, without risk and without killing Germans, then she would tell him.

* * *

"I have great news," Paul said as he entered Claire's apartment.

She was sitting on the couch, the newspaper sprawled around her. "I can't wait to hear it," she replied.

He detailed his plan to hide assets removed from the bank's basement vault. She listened closely and, as shocked as she was by its boldness, she digested his comments and gave them her complete consideration. "Are you sure you can trust Pablo?" she asked.

"I'm certain."

"It's a tremendous amount of cash and gold."

Several moments passed and not a word was uttered.

"You're quiet," she said. "Have I discouraged you?"

"I trust Pablo, I really do. But the equivalent of fifty million francs in cash and gold would tempt anyone, even a saint."

"Have you told him about the money, or just that you need his help?"

"I asked him to get supplies and sneak them into the basement. He really has no idea what's going on. But I do need help. It's a very physical task."

"Then why tell him? You and I can do it."

"You're willing to help?"

"I am," she said, determined.

"It's a lot of work to steal that much cash and gold. Are you sure you're up to it?"

Claire smiled and replied, "I don't have anything else planned."

* * *

Paul arrived at the bank early on Tuesday morning. Henri Kohn, the elderly president, was already there.

"How are you?" Kohn asked.

"I'm good, Henry. And you?"

"My family is leaving Paris next week," he said softly, with just a hint of pain. "I don't think it's safe, at least not for us."

"I understand," Paul said with compassion. He realized it wasn't safe for any Jews, even the privileged. And it was getting worse every day.

"The Germans will be here Monday, won't they?" he asked.

Paul nodded. He could not look at Kohn and speak. The man had given his entire life to the bank, just as his father and grandfather had. Now it was about to be stolen.

"I wanted the right man to oversee the merger," Kohn said. "That's why you were chosen."

Paul wasn't sure if his statement had a hidden meaning. "Thank you," he replied. "I'm honored you trust me. It's a daunting task."

"It is," Kohn agreed. He glanced around the corridors and, when sure no one was nearby, he whispered, "It should be your crowning achievement."

Paul walked into his office and put his briefcase on the desk, wondering what Kohn's statement really meant. Although he wasn't sure, he knew he had to be careful. A panicked Kohn might think he could save his family by bargaining with the Nazis. Paul could be walking into a trap. Maybe everyone knew exactly how many gold bars and boxes of cash were in the vault.

Paul left his office and quietly made his way to the basement. As he entered, he saw that Pablo had not only understood his instructions completely, he had already started fulfilling Paul's request.

Toward the back wall, where the cleaning supplies were stored, was a small pile of dust and dirt, swept against the wall. Next to it were the supplies that Paul had asked for, stacked carefully on the floor.

Chapter 37

On Friday evening just after 5:30 p.m., Rachel walked to the camera shop, carrying the propaganda pamphlets under her arm protectively. She was still concerned about Monique, but she decided to proceed and observe more closely. She wished she had the benefit of Meurice's advice, but she had no way to contact him other than their meetings on Sunday mornings. And she couldn't avoid her new responsibilities for a suspicion that might be meaningless.

She arrived early and walked around the block, finding nothing unusual, only the steady stream of pedestrians who wandered the streets of Paris. She crossed the street and surveyed the camera store where they were supposed to meet, and the jewelry and pastry stores adjacent to it, but saw only shoppers who came and went and the people passing by. German soldiers and French policemen mingled with the crowds, but none seemed interested in anything except their own destinations. She walked to the jewelry store and studied the window display, marveling at the diamonds and rubies and emeralds, wondering who could afford them. She tried to decide what her choice would be, should she ever have the money, but each time she made a selection she found another even more beautiful than the last.

Promptly at six p.m. she moved in front of the camera shop. As she waited, she thought of how good it was to see Claire again. It had been months since they had last seen each other, from autumn to spring, but to Rachel, a whole lifetime had passed. She would never forget how Claire had saved her and her family, and she would be indebted to her for the rest of her life.

Monique arrived about ten minutes after six. "I'm sorry I'm late," she said. "Do you know where the dress shop is?"

Rachel looked around. Monique was a little too loud and, once again, she hadn't calculated the danger posed by those around them. Rachel had already done so, watching the traffic and passersby, but she surveyed the area again. There were four German soldiers across the street, near a café, but they were immersed in their own conversation. A French policeman walked a few meters away, crossing the street. A young couple with a baby in a stroller moved past them. Shoppers mingled near the adjacent pastry store. It seemed safe.

"Yes," Rachel replied, "two blocks down and turn right."

"Have you brought my package?"

"Yes, it's right here."

"Good, I'm in a hurry." She giggled, squeezed Rachel's arm, and said, "I have a date. I'm so excited."

Rachel smiled, but was still alarmed. "Good for you," she replied. "I won't keep you then."

"Next Wednesday," Monique reminded her. "Same time, same code."

Monique walked quickly down the *Rue Monge,* and then crossed the street, continuing down the other side. She held the package of pamphlets under her arm.

Rachel watched her uneasily. Although she had no reason to suspect her of anything but carelessness, she decided to follow her. She crossed the street and walked behind her, staying almost a block away, hidden among the other pedestrians.

Monique never looked back. Nor did she pay any attention to people on the pavement, young or old, man or woman, German or French. She seemed to have one intention, and that was to meet her boyfriend.

Rachel suspected she would deliver the pamphlets or take them home and then go for her date. She was surprised when Monique turned down a side street, walked up to a French policeman, and abruptly hugged him, package in hand.

* * *

"I've never met Monique," Meurice said that Sunday. "I think the printer knows her, but I'm not sure how."

"It's not just carelessness," Rachel informed him. "It's almost like she doesn't know what to do, or how to behave. She seems totally unaware of what goes on around her. I don't think anyone showed her, at least not like you showed me."

"Maybe you should teach her?"

Rachel was quiet, reflective. She had never considered herself an expert. But she could surely show Monique. "You're right," she replied. "I should teach her."

"That's a start," Meurice said. "But I still think the French policeman is a problem. Some can be trusted; most cannot. He might even be the one who distributes the pamphlets. He wouldn't be the first. But we have no way of knowing."

"What should I do?"

Meurice thought for a moment. "Tuesday night when you pick up the pamphlets, share your concerns with the printer," he advised. "He knows Monique. Your suspicions might be completely unfounded."

* * *

On the way home from work that Monday, Rachel felt like she was being followed. She stopped abruptly and looked back, but saw only the throngs of people so common to a large city. There was a French policeman talking to an elderly man with a cane, but he seemed to have no interest in her. Two German soldiers walked behind her, but when she paused and pretended to look in a shop window, they walked past chatting among themselves.

She ate sparingly when she got home and slept restlessly that evening. She woke earlier than normal, still worried about Monique. That morning on her way to work, she had the same eerie feeling about being followed. But even though she paused and peeked, walked slowly and then quickly, she saw no one. When she got to the factory, she began to plot her next act of sabotage. Fascinated by the electric panels, she began learning how to interrupt production by damaging fuses and wires. But it was too dangerous. If she tossed water or metal shavings into the panel, it would shut down the factory, but might kill her as well. She finally decided to obtain more information. Maybe she could ask Meurice.

She made her scheduled stop at the printer that evening. There were two other people in the shop, a middle-aged woman and a young girl. Rachel waited until they left, staring out the window at the street beyond. Once they were gone, and she was alone with the printer, she voiced her concerns about Monique.

"I've never met her," he admitted. "But she wouldn't have been chosen if she couldn't do it, just as someone selected you. I don't know who that was, nor do I want to know."

"She seems like a risk."

"Make this week's deliveries," he suggested. "If you're not satisfied, do not return next Tuesday. It's better to be safe and wrong, than right and at the mercy of the Germans." He gave her two packages, just as he had the week before.

"Is there another way out?" Rachel asked.

Yes," he replied. "Come, I'll show you." He led her to the back of the shop, into an alley, and onto a narrow side street. "Be careful," he hissed and turned to leave.

She walked to the corner and returned to the *Rue Monge,* a block from the printer's shop. She crossed the street and walked in the opposite direction, before retracing her steps and returning home. Again she saw nothing suspicious.

When she arrived home, she hid the large package under her bed, behind the cardboard boxes that contained her clothes, and the smaller parcel in the oven that she had never used. She considered a better hiding place, but a search of the tiny apartment offered no prospects. There wasn't enough room. She thought about trying to pry up a floorboard to stash the packages there, but the packets were too big.

It was just after midnight when someone knocked loudly on her door.

"*Öffnen Sie die Tür!*" a German called. "Open the door!"

Chapter 38

Paul strolled down the *Boulevard Saint-Germain* on Thursday afternoon. He loved to walk the streets of Paris, mingling with the people, studying the outstretched limbs of the chestnut trees, looking in shop windows or studying faces in outdoor cafes. He admired the architecture: quaint mansard roofs, wrought-iron balconies, and limestone buildings with ornate moldings. And in spring and summer, and well into autumn, beautiful flowers grew at the base of trees, in pots beside doorways, and in boxes under windows, splashing a kaleidoscope of colors on the urban landscape.

He was joining Claire for lunch, and he stopped in a corner café off the *Rue du Cardinal Lemoine* to buy tomato and cheese baguettes and two apples. While he regretted meat was so scarce, he thought Claire would appreciate the tomatoes, which were also rare. As he approached her flat he saw Alain Dominique exit the bookstore, a newspaper under his arm, and walk down the *Boulevard Saint-Germain* towards *Pont de Sully.* Paul wondered what he was doing there. Was he spying on Claire?

Dominique made him think about Jacqueline Junot. She was attractive, congenial, humorous, polite, truly a sweet person – except her husband had become a traitor. He didn't blame her for having an affair with Dominique, but he wondered what kept her with Junot. Was it money? Probably not, because he knew she came from a wealthy family. They had two small daughters; they must form the glue that kept the family intact.

"Claire," Paul called as he walked into her flat. "I just saw Alain Dominique leaving the store. Does he go there often?"

She came out of the kitchen and said, "He comes once a week or so."

"Is he one of your best customers?"

"No," she replied. "He rarely ever buys anything."

"Don't you think that's unusual?"

"No, I don't. It's a bookstore. People come in and browse all the time." After a moment's thought she added, "including you."

Claire sliced the baguette into four small sandwiches. As they sat at the table, eating and drinking glasses of red *Chateau Margaux,* she looked at Paul, proud of his progress. "I noticed you controlled your hatred for the Germans while planning the theft of assets from the bank," she said. "The mission, a form of revenge in itself, has given you a cause and an identity. You're excited about it, and I'm sure that after its success, you can safely assume more increased responsibilities. It's time; you're ready."

He listened intently as she told him about the caverns beneath the *Saint-Étienne-du-Mont,* the escape routes to the cemetery and the flower store, and the large cave that served as home to fifty Jews. She described the families, the escape routes, the logistics required to keep them alive, and the preparations needed to help them escape. And lastly, she told him about Rachel Abzac, acting as a courier for forged documents, determined to fight the Germans in whatever way she could. Paul was both amazed and impressed. He was shocked at the level of Claire's involvement. "I know I shouldn't ask, but who is helping you with all of this?" he wondered aloud.

"Dr. Durant made the initial arrangements," she said. "He knew about the cavern. He told me when we were in Giverny. But the plan only became reality in the last few months."

Paul realized she hadn't answered his question, but she would in time. "How many people do you think it can hold?" he asked. "It gets worse for the Jews every day. We have to save as many as we can."

"Your reaction was just what I'd hoped for," Claire responded. "It gives you a new battle to fight, a new cause to support. There are probably a few hundred people there now. Food is the biggest problem. We need to find a better way of delivering it."

"When can I see it?"

"Take care of the gold first," Claire told him. "And then I'll show you everything."

* * *

On Friday morning, Paul checked the basement to ensure his supplies were all there. When satisfied they were, he mentally rehearsed his plan. Claire would arrive just after closing, bringing dinner for her cousin. He had prepared his co-workers by saying he expected to work late Friday evening, and, perhaps a bit on Sunday afternoon, to ensure all was ready for the Berlin Bank. He had several offers for assistance, all of which he politely declined. By week's end, he had discussed his plans so often and with so many people, that none would think it unusual or suspicious if he remained after hours.

By late Friday afternoon, the bank had emptied except for Henri Kohn. Paul waited anxiously for him to leave, glancing at his watch. Claire was due shortly.

She arrived at five o'clock, playing her role perfectly. "Paul," she called called as she entered from an unlocked side entrance. "I brought you some dinner. Just because you're working late doesn't mean you can't eat."

Paul met her in the corridor, hoping his stern glance told her something was amiss. "Claire!" he said with pretended surprise. "That's so kind of you."

She entered his office and laid the food down. "The bread has just come from the oven," she said.

"It certainly smells good," Henri Kohn announced as he appeared in the doorway.

"Mr. Kohn," Claire said, startled. "I thought Paul was alone. I hope I didn't disturb you."

"No, not at all. I was just preparing to leave."

"Would you care to join us?" Paul asked innocently.

"No, thank you. My own dinner is waiting. Claire, it was nice to see you."

He turned and walked down the hallway. Suddenly the sound of footsteps stopped and then became louder. A second later his face re-appeared in the doorway.

"Paul," he said. "You're doing well."

And with this enigmatic statement, he turned and left.

Chapter 39

Claire and Paul ate bread and cheese and sipped red wine, consumed with nervous anticipation. Since Henri Kohn had just left, they decided to wait before starting. They couldn't risk having him return. Even though the Germans were stealing his family's bank, they couldn't be sure where his loyalties lay.

Fifteen minutes later, Paul walked to the side and front doors of the bank, studying the *Boulevard Saint-Germain* and the *Rue de Poissy.* When satisfied that Henri Kohn was gone, and no one else would be arriving, including Pablo who was off until Sunday night, he secured the side entrance. Then he energized the bank's alarm system, which had ably protected its assets for so many years.

When he got back to the office, Claire had neatly packed the remaining food, knowing they would be hungry later. Her expression was anxious, but eager.

They went down the steps to the basement and stood before the vault. They had spent several nights rehearsing their plan, discussing each minute detail. Now it was time to begin. Anxiously, Paul dialed in the combination, and the vault opened.

"It's five-thirty," Claire said, glancing at her watch.

"Let's get started. It's going to be a lot of work to steal forty million francs."

They entered the vault and removed ten steel boxes, ensuring each contained a million francs. Then they piled them outside the door. As Claire rearranged the remaining boxes, Paul turned his attention to the far wall. He moved all of the cleaning supplies, boxes and crates, storing them by the steps. Then he examined the materials that Pablo had left for him.

Lying haphazardly on the floor so as not to attract attention, and intermixed with the cleaning supplies, were several bags of mortar, sand, lime, and about thirty bricks. Two large buckets, one to fetch water, the other to mix the mortar, sat beside them. By the time Paul had cleared a working space, Claire had finished rearranging the metal strongboxes left in the vault.

"Do you think it'll work?" she asked.

"It has to. We can't steal all that gold bullion without being seen."

"So we'll hide it," she said.

"At least the German's won't get it. And when the war ends we'll return everything to the *Banque de Paris.*"

Returning to the vault, Claire picked up four bricks of gold and carried them across the basement to the far wall. She started stacking them in a row across the floor, with a slight gap between the bullion and the wall.

Paul carried a bucket upstairs and filled it with water. When he returned, Claire had made good progress. She had a row of gold bricks across the entire length of the floor.

"Are you maintaining a careful count?" he asked.

"Yes," she said, pointing to scraps of paper on the floor. "Don't go in the vault. You'll mess up my system."

"I won't. Besides, I have enough work here. We have a fake wall to build, remember?" Using the trowels and hand shovels he'd packed in his briefcase, Paul mixed the mortar in the other bucket. He stirred carefully to minimize the dust, mixing the first of many batches.

As Claire continued to stack the gold, Paul laid piles of mortar in the space next to the wall. He also broke up the existing stucco, inserting metal into the cracked mortar and laying it across the bullion, anchoring the new wall into the old. It was a tremendous amount of work, but they continued without complaining.

Paul soon established a rhythm, using the bricklaying expertise he had gained working his way through college. Eventually he passed Claire, and had to wait while she stacked the bullion. He watched her for a moment, her slender body slowing. He could see she was tiring.

"Just bring the gold to the edge of the vault," he told her. "I'll carry them to the wall and stack them."

"What about the strongboxes with the money?"

"We'll add those to the top. Then the weight of the gold won't crush them."

Studying the wall closely, Claire said, "I hope you calculated the right amount of gold and bricks."

"I did," he assured her. "I used to do this for a living, remember?"

They paused to rest after three hours. They had built a wall of gold bullion to a one-meter height, and Paul had put stucco over the first two-thirds. He tested the strength of the false wall. The density of the gold held it stable and the stucco tied it together. He knew it wouldn't last twenty years. But he was hoping it wouldn't have to.

Their pace slowed as the night wore on. The gold bricks, which were a kilogram each, seemed to weigh tenfold by midnight. But they continued to carry them from vault to wall, stacking and cementing them together before placing stucco across their faces. Paul used the thirty new bricks in five different locations, scattered across the wall. He would leave them exposed, creating the appearance that a real brick wall rested beneath the stucco.

By midnight they were two-thirds done. They paused, weary and sweaty, and ate the remainder of the bread, cheese, and wine that Claire had brought when she arrived. They sat in the basement and relaxed, enjoying their small feast and relishing the relaxation.

Claire wiped the sweat from her brow. "It looks like we'll finish by dawn," she observed. "I was beginning to wonder if we would."

"We have the whole weekend, but the mortar needs time to dry. Then I'll come back on Sunday and smudge some dirt on the wall. That'll make it look old."

"What about the boxes and cleaning supplies?"

"When we finish we'll put everything back."

"Why not wait until Sunday?"

"It wouldn't surprise me if Kohn came in over the weekend. Just to check."

With a sigh, Claire got to her feet and said, "Then I guess we should finish up."

"You're right," Paul said as he rose on tired legs. "It's back to work."

By 5 a.m. they had finished. Claire counted each brick that remained in the vault and then arranged the gold so it appeared undisturbed. As seldom as the vault was used, Paul was confident no one would notice. They closed the door of the safe and locked it securely.

The new wall housed all the gold bullion, as well as the metal strongboxes along the top. Even the bags that the cement came in were hidden, tucked in the narrow space between the bullion and the existing wall. The stucco covered everything, tying it together. They had cleaned up, washing both buckets thoroughly, and storing them against the new wall, just as they had sat beside the old. Then they put the cleaning supplies beside them.

When they had finished, they stood at the vault and surveyed the basement. It was hard to notice much of a difference, especially with the dim lighting. Pleased with the results, they thought it unlikely anyone would know the wall was worth forty million francs. They waited for daylight and then quietly left, walking quickly back to Claire's house, tired but successful.

They wrote a detailed report, using the latest codes provided by Dr. Durant. They described the number of gold bars and metal strongboxes, the construction of the wall, and their efforts to ensure it appeared original. Knowing how devastating discovery of the document would be, they brought the letter down to the Seine and gave it to Henri Durant. They knew his brother would have it within hours. Now, if anything ever happened to them, the hidden assets of the *Banque de Paris* could be found.

Chapter 40

Rachel bolted from bed, her heart pounding. She looked frantically around the room, searching for a way to escape, but found none. Her flat had only one small window, operated by a hand crank. It didn't open fully and she could never fit through it. And even if she could, it led to a slate roof with a steep pitch.

She couldn't hide. The flat was too small, barely the size of a large room. Even the ceiling was low and angled. She looked under the bed. They would find the pamphlets; they may not see the documents hidden in the stove.

She heard the rifle smash against the door and saw the jamb splinter as the door burst open.

"*Bewegen Sie sich nicht!*" a soldier ordered, his rifle drawn. "Don't move!" He strode into the apartment, followed by an officer and another soldier.

Rachel froze, her eyes wide with fright. She started trembling, her body shaking, her heart racing. She wrapped her arms around her torso, covering her flimsy nightgown.

"*Suchen,*" the officer commanded. "Search."

The officer pointed a pistol in Rachel's face. The soldiers tore the apartment apart, ripping cabinet doors off their hinges. They yanked the cardboard boxes from under the bed, dumped the clothes on the floor, and rummaged through them. Then they found the packet of pamphlets.

The soldier gave one of the leaflets to the officer. He paged through it and then handed it back.

"*Sie sind verhaftet,*" the officer said. "You are under arrest."

Rachel started crying, fighting to hold the tears but failing. She was terrified, completely alone, painfully aware of what a dangerous game she had played. Now it could cost her life.

The soldiers continued to search. They overturned the mattress, slicing it with bayonets. Then they opened the tiny refrigerator, spilling the contents onto the floor.

Rachel eyed the stove nervously. They opened the oven and peered inside. They didn't see the documents hidden in the corner of the upper rack.

"*Zieh dich an!*" the officer ordered. "Get dressed!"

She shivered as the Germans' prying eyes watched her lewdly. She removed her nightgown, quickly replaced it with a functional red frock, and sat on the cot, putting on her shoes. She tried to buckle them but couldn't, her hands were shaking so badly.

The officer tired of waiting. "*Nehman Sie weg,*" he directed. "Take her away."

They grabbed her roughly and shoved her towards the door.

"*Warten Sie!*" the officer called. "Wait!"

The soldiers paused, holding her between them, each squeezing an arm.

The officer walked to the bed, something attracting his attention. He kneeled, reaching behind the bedpost, and retrieved a necklace. He took it in his hand, fingering the pendent. It was the Star of David.

He turned and looked at Rachel slyly. "*Du bist ein Jüdin,*" he said.

Chapter 41

A human chain of German soldiers entered the vault, continued up the basement steps, traveled through the corridor to the side exit, stretched out onto the pavement, and ended in the street beyond, passing gold bars from one set of hands to the other. An armored truck with *Berliner Bank* painted on its side was parked by the street entrance, a German troop truck assigned as escort.

Paul watched the vault being emptied, Henri Kohn and Otto Ernst standing beside him. He marveled at the wealth the Germans were stealing, but gloated over the riches hidden in the fake wall a few feet away, as secure as when the gold lay buried in earth. He looked at Henri Kohn, seeing his face etched with sadness. Paul could imagine how Kohn felt, losing a bank that had been in his family for generations.

As the soldiers emptied the vault, they joked that they would someday tell their grandchildren about all the gold ingots that had passed through their hands. They worked quickly, emptying shelf after shelf, the ingots disappearing and leaving behind a trail of dust.

"This is a great day for the *Banque de Paris,*" Otto Ernst said.

Paul hid his disgust. The bank existed in name only. Its assets were being stolen.

Henri Kohn turned to Otto Ernst. "I have done everything you asked," he said quietly. "Will you keep your word?"

Paul was surprised by his tone and demeanor. The authoritative bank president had vanished, replaced by a pleading puppet.

Ernst did not reply, but instead looked at Paul. "Last week I asked Henri to review the ledger you provided," he informed him, "just to validate the figures. And he's been watching you closely ever since. In return, he'll be rewarded."

"I even came down to the vault and counted each gold bar," Kohn said.

Ernst eyed Paul sternly. "Is there anything you would like to tell me?" he asked.

Paul could feel beads of sweat on his forehead. How much did Ernst know? And why had Henri Kohn betrayed him?

"No, I don't think so," he said, shrugging. He searched Kohn's face, looking for a clue.

"You're positive?" Ernst asked. "Because if there was, now would be the time to do it."

Paul's heart began to race, his breathing rapid and shallow. "Yes," he stuttered. "I'm sure."

One of the German soldiers turned, his machine gun slung over his soldier. He watched Paul, and then averted his gaze to Ernst, as if waiting for direction. Ernst touched him lightly on the arm and nodded for him to return to his duties.

"I'm afraid I don't understand," Paul continued.

"There were thousands of gold bars in the vault. Agreed?"

"Yes," Paul said slowly.

"And it's all there?"

"Of course," Paul said, feigning indignation. "Where else would it be?"

Ernst looked at Kohn. "What did you determine, Henri?" he asked.

"When I counted the gold ingots, I found that . . . one was missing."

Paul sighed with relief. Kohn must have counted the gold on Saturday, after he had finished hiding it. And he must have reviewed the ledger after it had been altered. Maybe he and Claire had miscounted; maybe an employee had stolen an ingot at some point in the bank's history. Or Kohn could have erred. But one missing ingot was certainly not that important.

"I don't know how to explain that," Paul admitted. "I never thought to actually count the gold bars."

Ernst watched him closely and then started to laugh. "Paul, you're too easy," he joked. "If you had decided to steal the gold, you would have taken a lot more than one ingot. So, our count was off. It's close enough. Maybe Henri miscounted. Who knows? We're tallying what gets loaded on the truck. That will be the final determination."

"I assume our business is finished?" Henri Kohn asked.

"Yes, Henri, of course it is," Ernst said. "You did well." He handed him a packet of documents. "As you requested, safe passage for your family. I have papers for thirty-seven people."

Kohn leafed through the documents, ensuring everything was there. He saw Paul watching. He shrugged, almost apologetically, and said, "Next weekend I'm taking my family and friends, cousins and grandchildren, to a vacation home we own in *Rosas,* just over the border in northern Spain."

Paul looked into Kohn's eyes and saw that he was pleading for understanding.

"You've earned a rest," Paul said, knowing Kohn was saving the lives of those he took with him. "You've given your life to the bank. You must be exhausted."

Kohn smiled weakly, seeming pleased he had Paul's acceptance. "Thank you," he said softly, lightly touching his arm. Then Kohn's expression changed to one of satisfaction. "Paul," he said, "there's a reason why I chose you to work with Mr. Ernst. I knew you would execute the transfer flawlessly."

It was then that Paul realized Kohn knew exactly how many gold bars were in the vault − before and after he hid them. He was honored Kohn had chosen him to do what could be done to save the bank. "Everything is waiting for you," Paul said. "Should you ever choose to return."

"That's much appreciated," Kohn said, understanding the cryptic message.

"Paul, Berlin Bank is pleased with your cooperation," Ernst said. He rested his hands on his big belly. "Few Frenchman can visualize the benefits of combining our nations' assets."

"We can only hope that all joint ventures have a similar outcome," Paul said humbly. When satisfied that Ernst was not looking, he winked at Henri Kohn.

* * *

Pablo was leaving Tuesday morning just as Paul arrived. He stopped and nodded and then bumped into him lightly. When Paul got to his office, he found a note in his jacket pocket. He closed his office door and looked at it. Scratched on the paper was a cryptic message:

BOOKSELLER 4 p.m.

Chapter 42

Claire arrived twenty minutes early for her meeting with Rachel at the bench across from the theater. She walked around the block, ensuring it was safe. Pedestrians filled the streets, some waiting in line at the theater, others shopping in stores or sitting in outdoor cafes, watching those who were watching them. German soldiers strolled by, a few with French women on their arms, but none seemed to notice her. Sedans and taxis and buses and bicycles all passed uneventfully, hurrying to their specified destinations. After scrutinizing the area, she determined that it was just another evening in occupied Paris.

A man passed, walking quickly, making eye contact furtively. Claire avoided him and turned away, stopping to look in a shop window. She watched his reflection in the glass, waiting while he passed. She decided he was harmless, only admiring her, and not interested in what she was doing. A few seconds later he disappeared, turning at the next corner. Once he was gone, she studied her own image and was surprised by what she saw. She looked drawn and tired, much older than she really was. Stress, danger, and grief had etched lines in her face and created black circles under her eyes.

She thought of Jacques, whose loss was still so difficult to cope with. They were happy, enjoying life, until the Germans killed him. She smiled, remembering the day he proposed. They were drifting on the Seine, sharing a weathered rowboat that had only one oar. They enjoyed the afternoon, kissed and caressed and then he clumsily withdrew the ring from his pocket. He was so sincere, so in love, as he asked her to share his life. She accepted with no hesitation.

He was born and raised in Giverny, and they had known each other since they took their first steps. And from the time she realized that boys were different from girls, she noticed that Jacques Daladier was a shade handsomer, a bit smarter, and a lot more interesting than any of the rest. Casual acquaintances, given Claire's summer residency, their friendship deepened with the years, blossomed to love, and led to marriage. Sadly, they had no children.

Losing Catherine and Sophie was even harder. Their deaths were senseless – they fought no war, stole no secrets, and threatened no one. But she mourned privately, unlike Paul, who wanted to kill every German he saw. When they died so brutally, and so close to her losing Jacques, a piece of her died with them.

Claire turned the corner and saw the bench was empty, which meant Rachel was late. She walked across the street and stood on the corner, pretending to wait for a bus. From there she could watch the bench without arousing suspicion. Five more minutes passed and Rachel still had not arrived. Claire walked to the end of the block, crossed the street, and approached the theater. Ten minutes later, there was still no Rachel.

She continued walking the neighborhood, glancing at her watch, studying the people, a horrible sense of dread grasping the pit of her stomach. She wondered if Rachel had been betrayed.

Forty minutes later she knew something was drastically wrong and there was no point in waiting. She went to a phone booth, put a coin in the slot and dialed the number. A man answered the phone.

"The package didn't arrive," she said softly.

* * *

An hour later she was sitting next to him, his hat pulled low over his forehead, hiding the upper part of his face. In the darkness, no one could tell his identity. They sat on the bank of the Seine, staring at the water. Two lovers were nearby, laughing and flirting, and the man studied them for a moment before he spoke.

"I'll find out if the Gestapo has her," he said guardedly. "It may take a few days."

"We don't have a few days," Claire said desperately. "She knows me, she knows Durant. She could expose everything."

The man sighed, annoyed at the complication. He was always careful. "If she is with the Gestapo, I'll get her out," he said firmly.

"How"

"We'll invent some sort of medical emergency and then claim she has to be moved to a hospital."

"But how can she fake an illness if she doesn't know to do so? We have no way of getting a message to her."

"She doesn't have to fake an illness," the man said.

"Then how will it work?"

"I'll supply the doctor."

Chapter 43

The cell was dark and cold, clammy and smelling of earth. Rachel lay on a bare cot, shivering, with no blanket and no light. Her body ached, pummeled and punched, battered and bruised. The attacks started when they left her apartment, the guards pushing her down flights of stairs, kicking her forward, making her crawl from the lobby to the black sedan that took her to Gestapo headquarters.

She tried not to cry, but couldn't help it. The pain in her stomach and back, her bruised legs and arms, her heart racing with fear, were all more than a sixteen-year-old girl could bear.

They took her to Gestapo headquarters on the *Avenue Foch*, pushing her into the building with the barrel of a machine gun. They kept her in the lobby, tears rolling down her cheeks, her body quivering, every muscle aching, her lips and nose bleeding, while they assembled all the soldiers in the building. They gathered around her in a circle, and lined the walls from the lobby to the cellblocks. They made her take off her clothes, shivering under the stare of a hundred Germans. She tried to cover herself with her hands, shrinking with embarrassment and humiliation as she was displayed before them. The shame hurt more than the beatings, more than the kicks and punches or the tumble down the apartment stairs.

As the soldiers leered at her naked body, she was led down the hallway, devastated by the hoots and hollers and whistles. She was taken to the basement, past a row of cells to the end of the corridor, handed a thin smock, and shoved into the cell, surrounded by darkness.

She sat on the floor crying, aching and bleeding, humbled and humiliated. Several minutes passed before she summoned the strength to dress, found a bare cot in the darkness, and sat on it. Barely an hour elapsed before they came to get her. A German officer led her down the corridor to a room with a single light dangling from the ceiling, a sparse chair beneath it. Two Germans waited, an officer who studied her curiously, and a burly man with a shaved head, heavily muscled arms, and a lewd grin, wearing tight leather gloves. The muscled man tied her to the straight-backed chair and stepped back, standing near the officer. They stood there, whispering, watching her.

She started crying, knowing she had walked into a world far more dangerous than she ever could have imagined. She was terrified of what was to come, hoping she could withstand the beatings and praying she wouldn't weaken and betray her friends.

The stocky man walked up to her slowly, his heels pounding the concrete floors. He stood beside her, quietly and waited for the officer's signal. When it came, a discreet nod of the head, he smacked her across the face with the palm of his leather-gloved hand.

The slap drew blood, dripping from her lip, which was already cracked and bruised. She cried out, tried to control herself, but the tears fell faster and the stinging pain lingered.

He took a thin black cloth from his back pocket and wrapped it around her head, blindfolding her. The room grew silent, an eerie tension growing with each passing second. Rachel could hear her heart beating wildly inside her chest, air escaping her lungs. She sat quietly, crying softly, waiting for the next blow.

Almost a minute passed. Then he hit her again, higher on the face, stinging her cheek and eye. He punched her in the stomach, forcefully, and the air was rapidly expelled from her lungs. She gasped, choking, struggling to breathe, feeling her life slipping away.

The officer started asking questions, but she could barely hear him. She agreed to whatever he said, not knowing what answer he expected or even what question he asked. It seemed like a horrific dream, the German's voice vague and faraway, distant and dwarfed. She wondered if he already knew, as he asked questions in a measured, methodical cadence, that she would say or do whatever he wanted to avoid being hit.

It didn't work. A few minutes passed and then the fists came again, the punches combined with slaps on the back of her knees, the top of her foot, her elbow, her ears, her kidney, all areas that when battered cause excruciating pain. In a matter of minutes, every muscle in her body was bruised, twisted and torn. She had given them no actual information, but only because they hadn't asked. And she had confessed to every crime they accused her of, including the worst. She admitted to being a Jew.

She awoke on the cot in the cell, surrounded by darkness and overwhelmed with pain. Her mouth was swollen and filled with blood, which leaked out around her lips, dripping onto the cot and the simple frock she wore. She couldn't move. It hurt too much.

There was no way to estimate time. She didn't know if she had been there hours or days. She only knew there was a gnawing ache in her stomach and parched dryness in her throat. She knew that she had been stupid to trust Monique. Her intuition had told her not to, every warning imaginable repeated several times. But she hadn't listened, and now she paid the price. As she lay there consumed with pain, she thought of her family, her parents and little Stanislaw. She missed them so badly. Now she might never see them again, might never hug them or tell them she loved them. Her parents would never know how much she appreciated all they had done for her. They would never know her gratitude, because she had never described it, had always taken them for granted.

Why did she ever think she could wage a one-woman war against the Germans? What did she think she could accomplish? She had done nothing but interrupt the production of boots for a few hours and transfer pamphlets and documents from one person to another. But she was a Jew. And that combination would mean her death. She wondered if they would torture her again, and how much more she could take. How quickly would she talk if they asked for names? She had to protect Claire at all costs. That much she decided. Claire had saved her family. If it meant her death, Rachel would not betray her.

She wasn't sure how long she had been in the cell when a steel plate beside the door opened suddenly, a sliver of light filtering in. A tin plate was pushed though the opening, resting on a shelf attached to the wall. Then the little door was closed.

"Fish," said a voice from the hallway.

Rachel was famished. She reached for the plate, grabbed morsels of fish with her hand and shoved it into her mouth. The fish was salted, probably herring. It was too salty, but she ate it anyway.

An hour later her tongue began to swell against her bloated, bloody lips. It was slight at first, but after another hour passed it become painful, the thirst overpowering, consuming all of her thoughts. She would do anything for the slightest moisture, if only a single drop of water, to wet her parched throat and mouth. She ran her tongue along the dirty stone walls, seeking dampness, competing with insects to find it, searching for anything to alleviate the thirst.

Several hours passed. She lay in agony, her throat dry and swollen. Only a drop or two of condensation found on the wall alleviated her thirst. And it wasn't enough. It only teased her, making the pain worse.

Suddenly the door opened and the light inside the cell was turned on. It was blinding, even though the source was a single bulb that hung from the center of the ceiling. Rachel shielded her eyes.

Two soldiers walked in, carrying a wooden box between them. They sat it against the wall and left. The light remained on.

Rachel slowly rose from the cot, every muscle of her body aching, looking curiously at the long, narrow wooden box. She approached it tentatively, fearing a trap. She took a step forward, peering across the tiny cell, and then took another step. Finally, she reached it, looking closely.

It was a coffin.

Chapter 44

Paul strolled along the *Quai de la Tournelle,* waiting for four o'clock. The booksellers lined the wall that edged the street above the river, practicing their trade as they had for over a hundred years. The pleasant afternoon had brought the people of Paris from their parlors to the streets, enjoying the shops and outdoor cafes now that winter became spring. Paul walked to the third booth from the corner, to the bookseller that he and Claire used as a contact.

"Mr. Moreau," Louis said with a nod. He bent over to pat the head of the beagle that never left his side, his eyes furtively surveying the landscape. "You have a meeting," he whispered.

Paul picked up a book, pretending to examine it, and asked, "When?"

"You'll enjoy that," Louis said loudly for any who might be watching. "It's a biography of Napoleon." He lowered his voice. "Five o'clock."

"It looks interesting," Paul said as leafed through the volume. Then he whispered, "Where?"

Louis motioned down the steps that led to the river's edge. "It was written in 1822, just after Napoleon's death," he informed him.

"Who am I meeting?"

"An old man. Or at least someone disguised as one."

"His name?" Paul asked quietly, putting down the book.

"Alexander."

Paul knew it was common for the Resistance to arrange meetings with only an hour's notice. The Gestapo had less time to react, should any member already be compromised.

At five o'clock Paul went down the stone steps that led to the cobblestoned banks of the Seine. He didn't see anyone that seemed a likely contact. A pair of lovers sat some distance away, watching the river wander by, and a tramp, dressed in ragged clothes rummaged through a trashcan.

Paul sat on a nearby bench and waited as ten minutes quietly passed. The couple walked away, arm in arm, and he watched a few boats meander down the river. A mother pushing a stroller paused to wrap the blanket tighter around her baby and then moved on. The tramp still picked through the trash.

He waited five minutes more. The tramp left his trash can and came closer. Paul looked away, certain he wanted a handout. He hoped the man would leave if not encouraged.

The tramp sat on the bench beside him. "I'm Alexander," he whispered.

Paul was startled, surprised a bum was his contact. Alexander was Durant's superior, the leader of the Resistance for all of northern France. He had expected something more, someone elegant and refined, polished and pretentious. "I'm Paul Moreau," he answered.

"Don't look at me," Alexander instructed. "Watch the boats as I speak."

Paul nervously obeyed. Their behavior seemed risky, meeting where the prying eyes of Paris could see them so easily. He wondered if that somehow made it safer, less suspicious.

"There is a man here in Paris who is doing great things," Alexander said. "He is known as the Fox. Few people know his true identity." He turned to look at the street behind them and studied the landscape for a moment, saw no threat or danger, and then glanced at the riverbank. When satisfied no one was watching, he continued.

"The Fox needs assistance," he informed him, "but there are few people he trusts. He knows what you did at the *Banque de Paris*, and he thinks you are capable."

Paul was flattered but alarmed. "How does he know about the bank?" he asked.

"It doesn't matter. But he does."

They were quiet a moment as Paul digested the information. "What does he need my help with?" he asked quietly.

"He has a hundred Jews hidden somewhere in Paris. And more come every day."

Paul thought of Claire and Dr. Durant using the catacombs to hide the Jews. Maybe he could combine their operations.

"How will we get the Jews out of the country?" Paul asked, knowing Claire faced the same problem.

Alexander studied the river a moment before replying. "Two printers, one on the *Rue de Toulene* next to the theater and the other on *Boulevard de Hausmann* by the butcher, will forge their papers. You must approach the elderly gentleman in each establishment. Be sure that no one can hear you. You will then say that the winter was warm this year. That is the code for your initial contact. Do you understand?"

"Yes," Paul replied. "The winter was warm this year."

"They will help you. But you still need to find a way for the Jews to escape, routes to neutral nations."

"Where will I meet the Fox?"

"In a public place like this, when darkness comes. Your code name is Sparrow."

"I'll have little notice?"

"Yes," he said. "And under no circumstances, even if it means your death, will you ever reveal his identity. Are you prepared to make that commitment?"

Paul thought of Sophie and Catherine. The pain had not diminished. "Yes," he said solemnly, "I am. But I have two requests."

"What are they?"

"First, I want to kill Colonel Kruger," he said. Even though he tried to hide it, the hatred was obvious in his voice.

Alexander gently patted his knee, apparently familiar with Paul's past, and said, "You may not kill Kruger, or any other German – at least not now. You must do nothing that attracts attention. You'll risk the entire operation if you do. What's your second request?"

"I want to kill Julian Junot."

Alexander studied his face, wrought with desire for revenge, and said, "That will be up to the Fox."

Chapter 45

Paul remained on the bench after Alexander left, quietly reflecting. He wondered where the Fox had hidden the Jews. How close was his operation, both in concept and location, to Claire's and Dr. Durant's? How many others were helping? He knew that when the Germans first conquered Paris, over one hundred and fifty thousand Jews were required to register with authorities. Now, three years later, he doubted half were left. Some had fled, or used fake identities to blend with society. And many others had been taken by the Germans or French police.

He knew that helping the Fox would be risky. He would have to control his thirst for revenge and do as he was told. There could be no mistakes. But danger didn't bother him. He didn't value his life as he had before Catherine and Sophie were killed. He thought of them often, denied life when it was only beginning, and he missed them so badly; he felt a void that he could never fill. He thought about Claire, saving the Jews, in part because she couldn't save Jacques. He understood why it was so important to her. It made her feel like she had some control when, in reality, she had none at all. Paul felt the same way.

Paul realized that revenge was a selfish component, but he was also striving to better the human race, just as Claire was. They could save people; children would grow to adults; parents would become grandparents. They could enable people to live their lives, not fear for their lives. And even though he couldn't bring Catherine and Sophie back, he could help others. And that's what he would do.

Two teenage girls walked by, chatting and giggling, their discussion a mystery. Maybe it was a boy, or a friend who had done something foolish, or their schoolwork or strict parents. They were learning about life and love, just as girls of their age should, regardless of the German occupation, and this reminded him of Rachel Abzac, a teenager imitating an adult. A girl who was allowed to choose freedom or the hell she had just left. She chose hell, fighting an enemy she could never defeat. But he supposed she got simple satisfaction in the fight, not the result. To Paul, she symbolized the very meaning of courage. And he was surprised by how much he had learned from one so young.

* * *

As Paul walked home from the bank the following day, he paused to look at a horse-drawn carriage, a Victorian relic misplaced in the twentieth century. They had grown more common as petrol became scarcer. Paris was going backwards, not forward. When he turned to continue walking, a man bumped into him.

"Excuse me," Paul said.

The man nodded, a hat pulled low over his forehead. "In your pocket," he hissed.

Paul reached into his shirt and felt a folded piece of paper, a message from the Resistance. He studied the street, making sure they hadn't been seen. The *Boulevard Saint-Germain* was a busy avenue, bustling with pedestrians. The people passing, whether German or French, were involved in their own lives. They didn't care about his.

He hurried home, occasionally looking over his shoulder to ensure he wasn't followed. Once he entered the sanctity of his apartment, he unfolded the note.

SIT AT THE THIRD TABLE NEAREST THE STREET AT THE CAFÉ DU PARIS AT 8 P.M. ORDER A GLASS OF MERLOT. I'LL ARRIVE AT 8:10.

Paul arrived at the *Café du Paris* a few minutes early, and ordered a glass of merlot. Music played in the background, an accordion accompanied by a guitar, with a woman singing a sad song of lost love. It was a moving melody, and for a moment he was mesmerized by the music. He eyed the customers curiously, wondering if the Fox was among them.

Precisely at 8:10, a slender man sat beside him, unshaven and a bit disheveled. "It's a pleasant evening," he said softly.

Paul studied his face, which wasn't familiar. The man's hands were rough, calloused – he earned his living outdoors, not from the comfort of an office. He wasn't what Paul expected. He envisioned the Fox as a man who led people, inspiring them, convincing them to risk their lives for the glory of France. The man didn't fit that mold.

They sat quietly. Paul was nervous. He didn't know what to expect. Or whether he was supposed to speak or just listen.

Finally, after a glance at his watch and a final look about the boulevard, the man said, "So you met Alexander yesterday."

"Yes, he wants me to help you. And I will. Regardless of what you need."

"Are you aware of the danger?"

"Yes."

"Have you seen what the Gestapo does to those who oppose them?"

Paul thought of Catherine and Sophie. The anguish returned, and, for a moment, his eyes misted. "Yes," he replied, "I know what the Gestapo does. More than most."

"And you'll take that risk?"

"Yes, I have to. I owe it to loved ones I lost."

The man looked at Paul with a flicker of compassion. He understood the pain. Maybe he felt it, too. "The sacrifice has just begun," he whispered.

Paul rubbed tears away. "Let me help," he urged. "I won't disappoint you."

The man glanced around the café. He watched a waiter pouring coffee for two German officers. They chatted for a moment, but posed no threat.

"Do you remember where you met Alexander?" the man asked. "On the bench by the Seine?"

"Yes, of course."

The man glanced at his watch. He seemed satisfied with the time. "That is where you will go now," he directed.

Paul looked at him, confused. "Why?" he asked.

"Go," the man said as he rose from the table. "The Fox will meet you there."

He vanished, merging with passing pedestrians. Paul rose from the table, baffled by the man's role. What was the purpose of their meeting?

The Seine was three blocks away. The steps to the riverbank were dark, as were the cobblestone sidewalks beside the murky water. He made his way to the bench, finding the area deserted. He watched a cat explore the trashcan that Alexander had probed the day before. He waited ten minutes, but neither saw nor heard anyone. Maybe the Fox had been unable to come.

Wondering how long he should wait, he looked at his watch. It was 8:50. Should he wait an hour more? Or should he stay until curfew?

Ten minutes later he heard footsteps. He dared not look; he didn't want to appear anxious or suspicious. He sat still, pretending to enjoy the evening. When the footsteps grew louder, he turned and looked briefly. It was a German soldier. He could see a machine gun slung over his shoulder. Paul felt his pockets, ensuring he had his documents.

The soldier paused, fumbling with a cigarette.

Paul ignored him, but the soldier still walked up to him. He held out his cigarette, asking for a light.

"I don't smoke," Paul said.

The soldier shrugged and put the cigarettes back in his pocket. Paul turned and studied the river, showing he didn't want to be bothered. But it didn't work.

The German sat on the bench beside him. He sighed and crossed his legs.

"I'm waiting for someone," Paul said, hoping he would leave.

The soldier said nothing. He watched the river.

"I'm waiting for a friend," Paul repeated more forcefully.

The soldier leaned closer. "I know," he said. "You're the Sparrow."

Paul was startled, his heart thumping against his chest. Was this a trap? How did the German know? It didn't seem possible. There had been too many precautions.

Paul thought of the intermediary. Could he have been followed? The silence was awkward and deafening.

He had only seconds to make a decision. Should he trust this man? Was it the Fox in disguise? It could be. No one would suspect a German soldier of being a Resistance leader. "Yes," Paul said softly, taking the most dangerous gamble of his life. "I am the Sparrow."

"And I am the Fox," the soldier said as he turned to face Paul.

It was Julian Junot.

Chapter 46

Rachel stared at the casket, her eyes wide and disbelieving. She looked away, the coffin too overwhelming to confront, and sat on the cot, defeated, praying for death. Emotionally drained, psychically beaten, the salt from the tears stung her bruised and battered lips. She wanted her father. Stern and stoic, Teofil Abzac was also kind and compassionate. He had solved all of her problems, and she had assumed he always would. Now, when she needed him most, he wasn't there.

She was learning she wasn't as brave as she had thought. Unlike Joan of Arc, a teenager like her who was destined to defeat a hated enemy, Rachel didn't have the courage and faith to succeed. She was just a girl gone from her parents' protective shadow and painfully alone.

The coffin sat by the wall, speaking louder than any voice ever could. She knew it was probably there for psychological impact, but would eventually be used. If the beatings continued, she couldn't survive more than a few days. She lay on the cot, struggling to swallow, aching from bruises, and prepared to die. An eerie acceptance crept over her, and calmness replaced the anxiety.

She remembered as a child she had been at her grandmother's death bed, watching her waste away, the life draining from her body. Now she wondered if their minds shared the same images – heaven or perhaps the fires of hell. She thought of family: mother, father, brother Stanislaw, and aunts and uncles and cousins still in Poland.

And she thought of her classmates and friends in Paris. Had the French police come for them, also?

She glanced around the dank cell, dimly lit, and she suddenly missed the blue sky, the cottony clouds that traveled through it, rain that fell from it, cleansing the ground and merging with earth. She pinched her nostrils closed with her fingers, trying to avoid the cell's odors, longing for the scent of a rose or her mother's perfume. She heard only silence, but missed the graceful melody of a beautiful song, or the pleasant chatter of those she loved. She longed to caress the faces of those she missed, but her knuckles were swollen from repeated blows, denying her hands the slightest movement. She so desperately wished for a simple glass of water, the most heavenly gift a gracious God could give, to ease the dryness in her throat and moisten her swollen tongue.

She wasn't sure if she had slept or fainted, but she awoke when the door to the cell opened, creaking on rusty hinges. A German soldier walked in, followed by a man in civilian clothes carrying a black bag.

She blinked in the harsh light, wondering what fate awaited her, a different pain or another torture.

"Is this the girl with stomach pains?" the doctor asked, moving toward her.

"I suppose," the soldier said. "It's the only Rachel here. Do you know who summoned you?"

"I don't remember," the man replied. "One of your officers called me, afraid she would die before he got the information he wanted. You should know his name. Why would you expect me to?"

The soldier shrugged. "She is registered as Rachel," he said. "That's all I can tell you. I don't know who called you."

Rachel studied the scene unfolding, bewildered. She was not sick; she was dying, but not from disease. They were killing her. Could this man really be there to help? Or was it the next step in their plan to destroy her?

The man sat on the edge of the cot. He opened his bag and removed a stethoscope, listening for several seconds in different locations. Placing his hand on Rachel's abdomen, the palm flat against her frock, he applied varying degrees of pressure, his eyes pleading, as if directing her to respond.

"Is this where it hurts?" he asked.

He was there to help, somehow she knew that. She followed his direction, cringing, not faking the agony since her body was wracked with pain. She only had to move to feel it.

"Yes," she gasped. "The pain is unbearable."

The doctor poked and prodded, searching for the pain's source. He examined her for several moments, his look concerned. He sighed, shook his head slowly, and turned to the guard.

"It's appendicitis. I have to get her to a hospital."

"But she can't leave. The captain isn't done questioning her."

"If I don't operate, she'll be dead by nightfall."

"Wait," the soldier said. He disappeared into the hallway, closing the door.

The doctor leaned forward and whispered in Rachel's ear. "Do as I say," he directed.

She nodded meekly. He moved away as the door swung open.

The soldier came back in. "We'll take her to the Jewish hospital," he said, "but she'll be placed under guard."

"That's fine," the doctor replied. "Now I just have to save her life."

Chapter 47

Paul stared at Junot, his eyes wide and disbelieving. He had been betrayed. And now he wondered if Junot would kill him.

"I'm surprised," Junot said softly, poking the machine-gun in Paul's side. "I thought you were a good Frenchman, loyal to the Third Reich."

Paul felt the cold sharpness of the barrel, the consequence of carelessness. How did Junot find out? Where had he made his mistake? He had no answers. But he knew he had to remain calm to find them, even though his heart pounded against his chest and his breath came in short, rapid bursts.

"You're quiet," Junot continued. "Do you think I will shoot you?"

"I'm not sure."

"Care to explain?"

"I have nothing to say." Paul decided to gamble, to grasp the unimaginable and hope it was real. "Are you the Fox?" he asked.

"I claimed to be, didn't I? You're wondering if you've been betrayed, aren't you?"

"Yes," Paul whispered.

"Do you think I'll have you arrested?" he asked as he again poked Paul's ribs with the machine-gun. "Or should I kill you?"

"I don't know," Paul said meekly. A sickening feeling washed over him. He had failed. Now he could never avenge Catherine and Sophie.

"Who is the Fox?" Junot asked.

"I'm not sure," Paul replied. He wondered how Junot found out about the meeting. Where was the real Fox? Was he dead?

"Why are you so certain I'm not the Fox?"

"Because I know you."

"Maybe you only think you know me."

There was an awkward silence. Paul didn't know what to believe. Julian Junot had to be the enemy. How could he not be?

"You want to kill me, don't you?" Junot asked.

Paul turned to face him. He couldn't hide the hatred in his eyes. "Yes," he stated, "I do."

Junot studied him for a moment, his eyes searching intently. "That's good," he responded. He removed the gun from Paul's ribs and put the weapon down. "Then you're the right man to help me. All of France should want me dead."

"And they do. How can you betray your country?"

"I don't. I only appear to. There's a massive difference."

"You're lying. I've heard you."

Junot smiled. "You heard me?" he asked. "What did I do, talk like a traitor? What act did you witness? Name a single thing I did, not said, that betrayed my country. You won't be able to."

Paul was tiring of the word games. "That's not true," he said. "No one has done more harm to France than you."

"Really? And how is that?"

Paul thought for a moment, and then said, "You convinced the French army to evacuate Paris. The city surrendered without a fight and you gave it to the Germans."

"That's true. I did give Paris to the Germans, but only temporarily. Would you rather have it destroyed? It was the only way to save it. It'll be French again. And it will be as beautiful as it ever was."

Paul remembered when the Germans came, demanding the city's surrender or they would bomb it into oblivion. Junot had intervened. The French army, already in disarray, retreated. The Germans arrived the next day. But the city was intact and undamaged.

"But still, you gave it to the Germans," Paul insisted.

"I did. But I also saved it. Would you rather have the Notre Dame Cathedral destroyed? Or the Alexander the Third Bridge lying in the Seine – even when the city would have fallen anyway? Or was it better to let the Germans borrow it?"

Paul digested his logic. Paris was the most fabulous place on earth. Even when marred by swastikas. And that was because of Julian Junot. It was just very difficult to see.

"Do you understand?" he asked.

"Yes, I think so. It's hard to make sense of it all."

"You need to think in longer terms. Don't you remember me telling you that on the night we met, at the dinner party? We suffer and sacrifice now so our children can lead a better life. And so it has been throughout the ages."

Paul felt a stab of agony. He thought of Sophie, trying to envision her as an adult with children of her own, in a Paris that was French, with no swastikas. But he let the image vanish, it was too painful. Sophie would never be anything more than an innocent child. He was starting to understand Junot. But he still wasn't sure he should. There were too many unanswered questions, too many inexcusable behaviors. "What about Jewish businesses stolen by the Germans?" he asked. "What did you pay for the properties of Abraham Blum? I'm sure it was a small percentage of their worth."

Junot glanced around, ensuring no one was nearby. He looked up the steps to the street beyond and along the walls that bordered the pavement. He then turned to Paul and said, "The businesses will be returned to their rightful owners. It will just take time. Abraham Blum is a friend of mine. I did all I could to prevent the Nazis from taking him away. And I would have paid any price to save his properties. When the war is over and he returns, he can have it all back."

"I doubt if businesses will ever be returned," Paul said, tiring of the verbal jousting.

"Paul, the Germans have defeated us. They can steal any business they choose. It could be much worse."

"Why help them?"

"Because we have no choice; it's the best way to save lives. And when the Germans are defeated? What will happen then?"

Paul was quiet. He was no longer interested in what was being said.

Junot watched his reaction. He changed tactics. "Do you think I don't know about the false wall in the bank basement?" he asked.

Paul tensed. "I don't know what you mean," he replied.

"I realize no one is supposed to know. But some do."

Paul turned and studied his face. The grim expression was gone, replaced by a plea for understanding.

Paul wavered, but still suspected a trap. "What about the Jews you take, like slave labor, so they aren't deported?" he asked.

"They stay alive, don't they? I suspect there are much worse places for them. Do you really think the Germans have Jewish colonies in the east? I don't. I think they have slave labor camps. And I think much worse than that goes on there."

Paul was convinced. Alexander said the Fox was the most valuable agent the Allies had. Junot had skillfully countered every point argued. His tone implied a desire to be understood, as if he needed a friend or someone to confide in, if nothing else. While the free world depicted him as the monster of mankind, he was quietly trying to save it. And no one knew the truth. Not London, or Washington, or Paris. Not even Jacqueline Junot.

"I am at your service," Paul said quietly.

He grasped Paul's hand and shook it firmly. "Thank you, my friend," he replied. "It's difficult. I need the help."

Paul marveled at the sacrifices Junot had made to the war effort, risking riches and reputation. And he was just getting started, acting alone.

"We have to be careful of the time," Junot said as he glanced at his watch.

"Do you have anyone else that helps you?"

"Yes," Junot answered. "A woman, very gifted. You'll meet her next. But it will only be the two of you."

"Tell me about the Jews."

"There are three hundred hidden in different locations, but we recently created a staging area. A hundred are there now. We'll give them new identities, help them out of the country, or hide them in rural areas. It depends on their preference. But we need to get started as soon as possible. There are many more coming."

Chapter 48

Paul sat in Junot's library drinking coffee. It was genuine, not the chicory that he had endured for the last two years. He savored the aroma, held the liquid in his mouth so it bathed his tongue, and let it slowly trickle down his throat.

"You're enjoying that, aren't you?" Junot asked, smiling.

"Yes, it's delicious. I didn't realize how much I missed it."

"Bernard will serve breakfast in a moment. First I want you to meet my other assistant. I don't think I could function without her."

The door to the library opened, swinging slowly on its hinges, obstructing Paul's view. He pictured the faces of the women he had seen at Junot's parties, assuming he must have met her before, but couldn't imagine who it might be.

She wore a beige blouse with a brown skirt; she was curvy but not voluptuous. She was petite, easy to underestimate, quietly attractive with a faint, fish-hook scar on her left cheek. Her eyes were big and brown and bright, marred with a hint of pain, although a smile came easily to her face. She could be any one of a million other women in France, simple, ordinary, but somehow the aggregate of her characteristics made her complex, interesting, extraordinary.

Paul rose, wide-eyed and confused. Something wasn't right. "Claire, what are you doing here?" he asked.

"I was invited," she said softly. "I work with Julian."

Paul sat down, surprised, a bit ashen, struggling to understand. He ran the events of the last year through his mind. He knew Claire was involved in hiding Jews; she had told him about the catacombs. But she despised Junot. Or at least she had appeared to.

"Why wasn't I told?" he asked quietly, hurt and a bit embarrassed.

"Because you weren't ready," Junot answered. "And you didn't need to know. But that's all changed."

They sat in the library, sheltered and secluded, sharing secrets, easing burdens, and at times shedding tears. Junot offered a thorough explanation of the operation, its founding and purpose, as well as its challenges. He didn't explain how Claire came to work with him; Paul wondered if the omission was intentional.

After breakfast they toured the catacombs. They entered through the church with the help of Father Nicolas. Paul was most interested in meeting the refugees, learning their names and talking to the families. He wanted to hear their dreams and nightmares, absorb their histories, and discuss their futures. After hearing their stories, heart-wrenching tales of separated families, lost businesses, and stolen ambitions, Paul, Claire and Junot walked the entire length of the corridors, envisioning the plan going forward.

Afterwards they ate lunch in an outdoor café, feeling uncomfortable in public, but knowing they would now be seen together often. Then they visited other locations where Jews were hidden, like the *Sacré-Cœur Basilica* in Montmartre and two other smaller churches. Paul and Claire learned, as they traveled the city, that the entire operation that hid and fed and clothed those in need of rescue was funded by Julian Junot.

They returned to the townhouse and shared a quiet dinner. The team had been formed; Junot assisted by Paul and Claire. Once the initial shock dissipated, and they began to address the intricate logistics needed to hide, support, and then disperse hundreds of Jews in a city occupied by the Nazis, they realized what a difficult task lay ahead.

Paul watched Claire while she summarized their activities. He was surprised by both her ability and devotion to the cause. It didn't fit her image, but he tended to think of her as his younger cousin, skipping though the fields of Giverny. He had been speechless when told she was Junot's assistant. Although they didn't discuss how it happened, and he realized the less he knew the better, he couldn't help wondering. He finally assumed it was arranged by Dr. Durant, and left it at that.

"Let's go through our plans for tomorrow," Junot said.

"At dawn the Rosenbergs depart through the church after morning mass," Claire said. "Mother and father and two children. They take the train to Bordeaux and will then be guided across the border into Spain. From there they will go to Portugal."

"At 10 a.m., the brothers Dior leave through the flower shop," Paul said. "They will take the train to Dijon and then cross into Switzerland."

"And at 7 p.m. Mademoiselle Dupree and her two daughters will be taken to the banks of the Seine, where they will sneak aboard the boat of Henri Durant. They will go to a small village in Brittany with new identities."

"Good," Junot commented, sounding pleased. "I think we're ready."

"If we move ten people a day it will take a month to rescue those we have now," Claire said. "But even at that rate, we can only save 3,600 people a year."

"A single round-up of Jews netted 13,000," Paul said.

"And we can't always send ten people a day," Claire added. "It depends on the trains and chosen destinations and the availability of Henri Durant and —"

"Claire," Junot interrupted softly. "We'll do the best we can. No one can ask for more. I continually request more resources for my factories. So far, the Germans haven't cooperated. But if they do, there's that many more Jews we can save."

He moved his hand to cover hers, briefly caressing it. Claire looked at him and smiled, contentment crossing her face. Junot moved his hand away.

Paul was startled by their intimacy. Or had he imagined it? "How did you discover the catacombs?" he asked, still watching them closely.

"Dr. Durant," Claire explained. "He had explored them as a student at the Sorbonne, but during the Great War his intelligence unit planned to use the vein that started at the flower shop on the *Rue Monge*. They had traced it to one other entrance located in the tomb of a family whose names have been erased by time."

"The good doctor had stumbled onto a unique section of the catacombs," Junot said. "It's isolated from the rest."

"Although his plan was never implemented, he explained it to me in Giverny," Claire continued. "He thought Jews could be hidden there if the proper infrastructure was constructed. He drew me a map in the dirt while we were on the river bank and you rested in your bedroom."

"Then Claire, with the help of trustworthy Resistance leaders, proved the plan feasible," Junot said. "The access in the *Saint-Étienne-du-Mont,* and the priests' participation, was added later, when a central repository was established. From there the Jews can be safely evacuated or given new homes and identities."

Claire went on to explain that, with contacts provided by Durant, she had enlisted people faithful to the priests at the *Saint-Étienne-du-Mont.* With their help, almost twenty in number, methods of filtering food through the church was created. The deliveries became commonplace, disguised by a charity organization started by Father Nicolas to provide food for the poor. No one would guess that only a small percentage of the food collected was given to the less fortunate, the majority was used to feed their charges. Some goods were also delivered via the flower store entrance, but not as effectively.

Once a pipeline for necessities had been established, the tedious planning to support the escapes was addressed. Claire and Junot had spent countless hours arranging a series of safe routes, advised by Alexander and Dr. Durant. Since the supply of human refugees would be replenished rapidly, it had to be quick and efficient.

They prepared three escape routes. With the aid of Durant, assisted by Pablo the bank's janitor, they developed a path to Spain; the Rosenbergs would be the first to use it, taking trains into southern France where members of the Resistance would help the refugees cross the Spanish border. Pablo's contacts would then assist them.

The second path, developed with Louis, the bookseller, and tested first by the brothers Dior, used the train to the town of Dijon. There, Resistance members would move the refugees into Switzerland. Alexander arranged a support group to help them once they arrived.

The third method, already proven by the Abzacs, used Henri Durant, who arrived daily to sell fish, normally leaving near dusk. Used sparingly due to the risk to Henri Durant, this path would move the Jews to Normandy and distribute them into rural areas of northern France with the help of Dr. Durant. His method, designed for families, posed the most risk since they remained in the country. But it was favored by Junot, who felt the Germans would never suspect such a daring plan existed.

Some Jews were simply given new identities and then returned to the city. Hidden among the masses, they lived Aryan lives with Christian exteriors, their Jewish interior preserved and protected.

At dawn the following morning, Claire went to *Saint-Étienne-du-Mont*. She wanted to be with the Rosenbergs as their journey began. Although her participation was symbolic, it was important to her. It was their first rescue attempt; she wanted to ensure it went perfectly. She entered the church, meeting Father Nicolas near the entrance. He stood waiting, his eyes wide, his face flushed.

Claire looked around, ensuring they were alone. "Is everything all right?" she asked.

"No," he hissed. "The Germans are here."

Chapter 49

Rachel's eyes fluttered open. The lights were bright and hazy, and she squinted at them for a few minutes, trying to focus. The room smelled of alcohol, and she tried to remember where she was, but couldn't. Her mouth was dry, her body aching, and she was weak and tired, fighting to keep her eyes open.

"You're awake," a voice said. "How are you feeling?"

She recognized the doctor, the man who saved her from the Gestapo, standing by her bed.

"Tired," she said hoarsely.

"I'm afraid I had to remove your appendix," he whispered. "I didn't want to. But the Gestapo sent a soldier to observe. Don't worry, though. You'll be all right."

She didn't understand. But it didn't matter. She only knew he had saved her.

"You need to rest," he advised her. "You were close to death."

She nodded weakly and grabbed his hand. "I don't know how to thank you," she murmured.

He squeezed gently. "Don't bother," he told her. "Help someone else like I helped you."

It was two more days before her strength began to return, helped by liquids given intravenously. Her body was still bruised, the purple blotches starting to fade, grim reminders of the Gestapo, and her abdomen was tender from the surgery. She remained in bed, immobile, but for the first time in many days she felt like she would survive; she felt new strength coursing through her veins.

She knew she was in the Jewish hospital, even though nothing identifying her faith was displayed. German guards patrolled the hallways, machine guns slung over their shoulders, as if they expected to attack the sick only because they were Jews. They watched all the patients, whose futures they had already determined, never letting them far from sight. But at least she wasn't being tortured. An operation was a small price to pay to prevent that.

She had gotten her life back; she had been blessed with a second chance. Now she had to make the best of it. She thought about what the doctor said: help someone like he had helped her. That's what she would do, help other people, and she would never stop – not for as long as she lived. She filled the idle time by planning her escape, even though she knew how difficult it would be with soldiers patrolling the hallways. Her room was on the third floor; she couldn't leave by the window. But as she watched hospital personnel come in and out and walk up and down the corridors, she found the solution.

The doctor visited daily, measuring her progress. She never learned his name, but she knew, for whatever reason, he had decided to save her life. She thanked him every time she saw him and he seemed genuinely touched. But after she had been in the hospital for three days, he took her chart and sat on the edge of the bed. "We have to get you out of here," he said softly. "The Germans know you're improving and they want to question you. They'll take you back to Gestapo headquarters or they might send you to Drancy."

"I have a way to escape," Rachel said simply, determined to control her own destiny.

He looked surprised, perhaps underestimating her, just as others had done. He looked at the door. No one approached; no one seemed near. "How?" he asked. "Soldiers are everywhere."

"I need a nurse's uniform. And then I'll walk out of the hospital."

"I'll get you the uniform," he said. "Do you think you can walk on your own?"

She nodded and told him, "I already have. I've been able to walk up and down the corridor three or four times without tiring."

"Strolling through the hallway is much easier than walking past a dozen Germans, out of the hospital, and onto the streets."

"I'll be able to do it."

"Do you have somewhere to go?"

"There's a fisherman who will help me. I only need to get to the river."

The doctor reached into his pocket and withdrew some money. "Take this," he said. "I'll return with a uniform."

* * *

An hour later, Rachel heard a loud noise at the end of the corridor. Taking advantage of the disturbance, she walked out of her room, limping slightly, dressed in a nurse's uniform. She looked down the hallway where a gurney had crashed into the wall, an intravenous device falling to the floor and spilling. She saw two German soldiers halfway down the corridor, watching the commotion.

She moved across the hallway, into the stairwell, and started down the steps. When she reached the second floor, she heard footsteps. Someone was coming up the stairs. It was risky; she couldn't tell who it was. She opened the door and walked onto the second floor, eluding them. She found it very much like the third floor, a long corridor with patient's rooms on either side, and a nursing station in the center. At the far end she saw an exit sign, another stairway. She stood straight, ignored the gnawing grip from the stitches in her abdomen, and started walking. It was deserted, except for an elderly man in a wheelchair outside his room.

She was fifteen feet from the stairwell door when she heard a noise behind her. Looking back, she saw a German soldier exit a patient's room, an anxious look on his face.

"*Krankenschwester, hierher zu kommen. Beeilen! Dieser Patient braucht Hilfe,*" he said. "Nurse, come here. Hurry! This patient needs help."

Chapter 50

Just before lunchtime, Paul sat in his office looking through loan applications. Henri Kohn was gone, no longer running the bank his ancestors had built. Paul assumed he was in Spain, waiting until the Nazis were defeated and his family could return to Paris to reclaim what was rightfully theirs. In the meantime, the bank's daily activities continued unaffected: loans were granted, investments made, savings accepted, and property foreclosed upon. Only the vacant office where Henri Kohn had spent the majority of his life reminded employees of his absence, and how coldly the German's had erased one hundred years of family history.

There was a light tap on the door and Paul looked up to see the portly frame of Otto Ernst standing in the entrance.

"Paul, how are you?" he asked, a smile adorning his face.

Paul rose to greet him. "Otto," he said, "it's nice to see you."

A tall man with thinning gray hair entered the office behind him. He wore a black suit that hung loosely on his slender frame. His face was defined by a hawkish nose and dark eyes, almost black, that studied Paul curiously.

"Paul Moreau, this is Oskar Bouchard, from Freiburg," Ernst said. "He is the new bank president."

Paul nodded respectfully, finding Bouchard's handshake limp and clammy. A German with a French last name. That was interesting. "It's nice to meet you," he offered.

"I expect to rely on you heavily," he told Paul, skipping the pleasantries. "To begin with, I would like to be briefed on your daily routine, your level of oversight, investment portfolio, and projected profits for the next quarter. I expect that information today."

"Of course," Paul said. "Whenever it's convenient for you."

"And have someone move my things into my office," he continued. "The boxes are in the Mercedes outside."

Paul felt his face turn crimson. He wasn't accustomed to being dictated to. "I'll have one of the tellers take care of that right away," he responded.

"Good," Bouchard said crisply. "I appreciate it."

Paul left the room and summoned a teller. When he returned, Ernst and Bouchard were in the vacated office of Henri Kohn. He poked his head in. "Your belongings will be brought in momentarily," he informed him.

Bouchard ignored him; Ernst shrugged.

Paul turned to leave, closing the door behind him. A second later, it opened.

"Do you have a moment?" Otto Ernst asked.

"Yes, of course," Paul replied, hiding his anger.

Ernst moved closer and quietly said, "I just wanted to tell you that I've been summoned back to Berlin."

Seeing the worry on his face, Paul said, "Otto, you always go to Berlin. Why are you concerned?"

"This is different. I don't think I'll be returning."

Paul turned to face him. He had learned to like the man, even if he was the enemy. "If that's the case, then good luck to you," he said, shaking his hand firmly. "Please keep in touch."

Ernst smiled and nodded. He seemed touched by Paul's warm wishes and sincerity. "I will," he said. "I promise."

Paul left his office for lunch, ducking into a café around the corner and sitting at an outdoor table. He ordered a sandwich and opened a newspaper, reading distorted descriptions of the battles on the Russian Front. The headlines screamed of Nazi victories, but all knew they were retreating under Russian advances. With a new Allied front in Sicily, the Germans were on the defensive

When his lunch arrived. he noticed his sandwich had layers of cheese but no meat, and a single leaf of lettuce. If he could find the time, he would spend a weekend in Giverny so he could stock up on food that was scarce in the city – fruit, vegetables and meat. Still scanning the headlines, he sipped ersatz coffee while he ate his sandwich, but was interrupted by a man who pulled the chair away from the table beside him and abruptly sat down.

"May I join you, Mr. Moreau?" he asked, even though he already had.

"Mr. Dominique, what a pleasant surprise," Paul said, finding the visit strange since the man rarely acknowledged him. He wondered why he would join him for lunch.

Dominique had a cup of coffee in one hand, a buttered croissant in the other. "It's a beautiful day, isn't it?" he asked "I just love the warm weather."

"I think we all do," Paul replied politely, but warily. "Winter is too depressing: cold and dreary, damp and gray."

He wondered why Dominique would seek him out, and then exchange pleasantries.

Dominique coughed lightly and seemed to study his croissant before watching a pretty girl pass, slender and sleek. She turned, caught his gaze and smiled. He brushed the wavy blonde hair from his forehead, seemed to study her a moment more, and then focused his blue eyes on Paul. "An image is rarely what it seems," he said mysteriously.

Paul had no idea what he was talking about. He glanced at the girl, assuming the comment referred to her, but couldn't make the connection. Instead he pictured Dominique's hands caressing Jacqueline Junot's back.

"That's so true," Paul said cautiously. "The eyes often mislead us."

"Then we agree; anything can be misinterpreted. Or even imagined."

Smiling faintly, Paul addressed the issue delicately. "I'm not sure I understand," he said. "But let's assume that I did see something. I suppose it might be different than it seemed."

Dominique smiled, but in a superior way, almost arrogantly. "I was referring to the bank," he said.

Paul felt his heart leap in his throat. He tried to remain calm, to appear uninterested, but he suddenly felt claustrophobic, fighting for air, caught in a cage. He shifted in his chair and said, "I'm sorry. Really, I am. But I don't know what you're talking about."

Dominique sipped his coffee. He seemed to enjoy an awkward silence, taking another bite of his croissant. He chewed thoughtfully, took another sip of coffee, and then lit a cigarette. "But we do agree things are not always as they appear," he insisted.

"Yes, I suppose."

Dominique leaned closer, the smile leaving his face. His eyes grew cold, his demeanor stern. He exhaled smoke, which the slight breeze blew into Paul's face. "I have noticed that something is not right at the bank," he said. "I don't know what it is, but I think you do. And you will tell me. Even if I have to force you."

Chapter 51

Julian Junot was parked on the *Rue de Rivoli*, just past 4 p.m., when the passenger's side door to his sedan opened. Andre Deveraux ducked inside and sat down.

"I've been concerned, Mr. Deveraux," Junot said sternly. "It's been a long time since our last business. We had been doing well, especially with the weekly deliveries."

"It gets harder every day," Deveraux informed him. "I don't think you realize."

"Or I don't care," Junot said apathetically. "What do you have for me?"

Deveraux shook his head slightly, disturbed by Junot's tone. "I have two pregnant women, near term," he said, "and their husbands, two small children, under the age of five, and a great-grandmother, probably in her eighties."

Junot turned to look at him. "You must be joking," he said. "You expect to be paid for that?"

"It's the best I can do."

"I'll take them," Junot said, "but I do have factories to run. I can't wait this long between shipments and then have five of the seven delivered unable to help. You have to do better."

"I can't."

"You will," Junot directed. "I need more with each delivery, and I need them weekly."

"The delivery will be made tomorrow morning at 6 a.m. at Paris Hospital, near the maternity ward. The cargo will be in an ambulance. It will be parked for two hours."

Junot pulled some francs from his pocket. "They'll be picked up, as agreed," he said. "Here's your fee."

Deveraux counted the money and then put it in his pocket.

"What about next week?" Junot asked.

"I can't," Deveraux replied. He turned to face Junot, his face flushed. "Don't you know what is happening?"

Junot looked at him innocently. "No, I don't," he admitted. "Tell me."

"I thought you ran the Paris Vichy?"

Sounding annoyed, Junot answered, "I'm involved in the Paris Vichy. I don't necessarily run it. Enlighten me; what is going on?"

"The Nazis took over Drancy two weeks ago," Deveraux said, his hands trembling. "The French police will no longer apprehend, or oversee, the Jews. The Germans will round them up, or collect them randomly in the streets, and take them to Drancy. From there they will be shipped east, quickly, probably within days of arrival."

Although Junot was very much aware of the situation, he pretended ignorance. "Will that change our arrangement?' he asked.

"Mr. Junot, you more than anyone should understand the Nazis. Not only can I no longer help you, but the Nazis have threatened to ship me out of Paris. On the same train with the Jews."

Junot looked at him, feigning surprise. "What a tremendous injustice that would be," he said, meaning not a word of it.

Chapter 52

Claire stood in the church vestibule, just inside the entrance, and looked at Father Nicolas with wide-eyed surprise, her heart racing. She never dreamed the Germans would find them. She ran the events of the last few days through her mind, wondering where they had been betrayed.

"Two guard the door," Father Nicolas whispered," just inside the sanctuary. A third is near the altar."

"Where are the Rosenbergs?"

"Still in the cavern."

Claire was relieved. It wasn't as bad as she had thought. "Are they searching the church?" she asked.

"No," he answered. "Come, I will show you." He motioned her to proceed, as if she were attending Mass. He walked to the side and stood in the shadows, hidden from parishioners.

She pulled the veil over her head, dipped her hand in the holy water and, facing the altar, made the sign of the cross. She proceeded into the church, respectful as always, awed by the majestic beauty that was so overwhelming, only to find two Germans flanking the sanctuary entrance. Their weapons were at their sides, ready if needed.

Claire moved past them, disgusted that armed soldiers stood in a place of worship. As she made her way up the center aisle, she noted there were two or three dozen people in the church, scattered throughout, offering a sampling of the city's residents. Dominated by elderly pensioners and retirees who started their day with the Lord, there was also a sprinkling of businessmen, wives, and more than a few college students. When she reached the third row from the altar, she genuflected and made the sign of the cross, and sat by the aisle. A German officer sat in the first row, ramrod straight, his head bare. It was General Berg.

She wondered if he was there to attend the service, or if he merely observed, prompted by information obtained. Did he know he sat twenty meters above a cavern hiding over a hundred Jews, four of whom were supposed to escape at any moment?

Father Nicolas emerged from a door near the altar and moved to the pulpit. He opened the Bible, cleared his throat, and began the service. He acted as if nothing was unusual, his words soothing the congregation, as if German generals always sat among them.

Claire watched Berg closely as the Mass proceeded. He had yet to see her. But he rose when prompted, kneeled when required, and made the sign of the cross in unison with the others. He gave every indication that he was a loyal Catholic, that he knew the prayers and hymns common to the church. Claire studied the red and gold epaulet on his uniform – the mark of a general. With the world waging a war the Germans had started, it seemed almost obscene to find one of their leaders worshipping the same God as those he conquered.

When communion was served, Berg stood in line with the rest, separated from Claire by a half dozen parishioners. As Father Nicolas placed the thin wafer in his mouth, the General's eyes were closed, his hands joined in prayer. He returned to his seat, head bowed, and continued to pray, his eyes closed. Claire took communion and returned to her seat unnoticed.

The Mass took fifty minutes. When it ended, Berg rose and walked towards the entrance. Claire stood at the end of the row. It was only then that he saw her. He smiled warmly and nodded, and motioned for her to go before him.

She could feel his presence behind her, looming like a shadow. But as the congregation filed from the church, he acted no different than the others. When they reached the entrance, the two German soldiers filed out, waiting on the church steps. First Claire, and then Berg, dipped their hands in the holy water and made the sign of the cross.

Father Nicolas stood by the door, greeting each worshipper as they left. As Claire approached, he eyed her sternly and nodded slightly. She understood; she should not linger. She could not lead the Rosenbergs to freedom. Someone else would have to.

Berg paused when he reached the priest. "I enjoyed your sermon, Father," he said. "It was so relevant to a world in turmoil."

"Thank you," Father Nicolas replied, gracious and accommodating. "You are always welcome. Please, come again."

"I intend to. It's such a beautiful church, an architectural masterpiece that offers spiritual solace. What a brilliant combination."

Claire stood to the side, listening, judging Berg's sincerity. It seemed that church offered him an escape from the war, just as it did the others. All sought compassion from a benevolent God, it seemed, even Nazis.

"Claire, it's so delightful to see you," Berg said as they left the church.

"I was surprised to find you here," she replied, and then realized it may have sounded offensive. "Although I'm not sure why."

He shrugged. "I'm not your typical German general," he informed her, "but I think you know that. And it seems we have more in common than chess."

She smiled, finding it hard to believe he was the enemy, but not for long. The sudden image of Catherine's and Sophie's brutal murders served as a quick reminder. Or Jacques falling to the ground, riddled with German bullets. "You're right," she said after a brief pause. "I'm sure there are many interests we share."

"I wanted to thank you for helping me choose books for my granddaughters," he continued. "They loved them."

"I'm glad," she said. "I thought they might. I enjoyed helping you."

Motioning to his car, Berg asked, "May I offer you a ride? We can stop and have breakfast."

Claire knew if she refused it would arouse suspicion. She would go with him. Maybe she would learn something. "Thank you," she said, smiling sweetly, her hand on his arm. "That would be nice."

Chapter 53

Rachel stopped abruptly, her heart pounding.

"*Kommen!*" the German said. "Come!"

She entered the patient's room, her stomach churning, her body trembling. An elderly man lay in bed, coughing and wheezing and struggling to breathe. A glass bag hung from a metal rack, a tube inserted into his left arm. As she came closer she saw his eyes bulging, his hands on his chest. She stood there, not knowing what to do, but trying desperately to appear as if she did.

The German eyed her strangely. He moved beside her, looked closely at the patient, and nudged her forward.

She put her hand on the patient's wrist, pretending to take his pulse. His expression didn't change; his face was pale, his eyes vacant. Saliva dripped from his mouth.

"I'll get help," she said. She couldn't treat him, but she had to do something. He might die if she didn't. She walked briskly into the hallway, glancing back to see if the soldier followed. There were no nurses, no doctors, no one she could summon. She saw only a woman pushing a cart filled with trays of food down the hallway.

"Get a doctor, quickly," she told her, pointing to the room. "That man is having a heart attack."

The woman looked at her strangely, but complied, scampering down the hallway.

The German was confused. "*Was falsh ist?*" he asked. "What is wrong?"

Rachel offered no reply, hiding her panic and trying to stay calm. She looked toward the stairwell door, and then back to the German. "I'll be right back," she said. She walked across the hall, pushed open the door, and started running down the stairs.

"Halt!" the German called.

She scrambled down the steps, the soldier right behind her. When she reached the first floor she bolted out the door and down the corridor, ignoring the wrenching pain in her abdomen. She searched frantically for an exit and found one at the end of the hallway. As she ran towards it, she saw a soldier sitting on a chair by the doorway. He gazed down the corridor curiously, watching the nurse run towards him, the German soldier chasing her. He stood, picking up his rifle.

Rachel turned into another hallway, scrambling past a reception desk as two startled women watched her. Running down the corridor, she swerved around an orderly mopping the floor and kicked his bucket over, its contents spilling on the floor. The German slowed, slipping on the sudsy water, struggling to maintain his balance.

"*Kommen!*" he shouted, his anger growing.

Rachel kept running, gaining distance. The soldier gingerly crossed the wet floor and continued after her. She approached an exit that led to a side street, but turned a corner instead and ducked through a doorway, finding herself in a linen closet. She saw walls lined with shelves, towels and sheets and washcloths piled on them – and no place to hide.

She stood beside the door, her heart pounding, gasping for air and holding her abdomen, the stitches pulling, the wound seeping. She placed her ear against the door, listening. It was quiet. She waited a few minutes and slowly opened the door, peeking into the hallway. The exit was at the far end, ten meters away. She only had to make it that far. Then she could leave the hospital and make her escape to the street beyond. She opened the door farther, finding no one in the corridor. She waited a minute more, still heard nothing and flung open the door.

The German was standing there, his rifle pointed at her chest.

Chapter 54

Paul always arrived first at the bank each morning, well before the branch opened or any others came in. He felt more productive at the beginning of the day, and it gave him the opportunity to see Pablo. When he entered the bank that morning, Pablo was dusting a bust of Marcel Kohn, the bank's original founder.

"Good morning, Pablo, how are you?"

Pablo's eyes grew wide and he held a finger to his lips, signaling caution. "I'm well," he replied.

Paul looked at him strangely. "Is everything all right?" he asked.

"Yes, how are you?" he asked. He then pointed to one of the offices.

Oskar Bouchard poked his head out of his office doorway. "What are you two talking about?" he queried.

Paul was startled. Glancing at his watch, he asked, "You're in early, aren't you, Mr. Bouchard?"

"Yes, I suppose. Pablo, I want the bookshelf in my office cleaned before you go. When the light shines through the window I can see dust on the top shelf. It's very annoying."

"Yes, of course," Pablo replied. "I'll do it now."

Paul stood in the hallway, shaken. He had to be more careful. He had been within seconds of saying something he might have regretted.

He went to his office and looked through some papers. He was distracted, trying to hear the discussion in

Bouchard's office. A few minutes later Pablo came out, walked down the hallway, and stopped at Paul's door.

"I should dust your bookshelf, also," he said. He glanced back in the corridor to ensure he wasn't followed. He moved behind the desk, dusted the bookshelves, and warily watched the door. When Bouchard didn't appear in Paul's doorway, Pablo leaned forward and handed Paul a slip of paper.

"A meeting with Alexander," he whispered.

Paul buried the paper in his pocket, beneath his keys. "Thank you, Pablo," he said loudly enough for Bouchard to hear. "Have a nice day."

Paul waited over an hour before he removed the note. It provided detailed instructions on where to meet Alexander on the Metro, the subway that ran beneath the streets.

* * *

Just before 7 p.m., Paul caught the train for Montmartre. He sat in the last car, the third seat from the back – as the note directed. There were several other passengers: traveling businessmen, students, German soldiers, housewives. He scanned a newspaper, waiting for his contact.

The train was just past *Rue Saint-Vincent* when a well-dressed man, complete with hat and cane, sat in the empty seat beside him. It was Alexander.

"You're doing well with transports, my friend," he whispered. "Especially the trains."

Paul was surprised by his clothing, since he was dressed as a tramp when they had first met. For a moment he wondered if it was the same man.

"I need a favor," Alexander continued. "It's extremely important and very dangerous. I would not normally ask you to do something like this, but I have no other choice." He turned suddenly and looked out the window at the passing darkness. A German major walked towards them, an armed soldier beside him. They paused, studying Alexander curiously.

"Papers, please," the officer said in French, holding out his hand.

They withdrew their papers and handed them to the officer, who glanced at Paul's and then briefly scanned his face. He took much greater interest in Alexander.

The seconds ticked by slowly. The major examined the documents closely, fingering the paper, checking the authenticity. He put them to his nose, inhaling, smelling the ink.

"Is something wrong?" Alexander asked.

"Perhaps," the major said tersely.

"You're not going to chew on them, are you?" Alexander asked with mock seriousness.

The major eyed him coldly. "You're very funny," he said, showing no amusement.

The major paused, his eyes trained on Alexander's. Neither blinked, neither spoke, neither changed their expression. The soldier fingered his rifle.

"Where are you going?" the major asked.

"To Claude's," Alexander replied. "It's a restaurant. Have you ever eaten there?"

"You are friends?" he asked, turning to Paul.

"Yes," Paul said nervously. "We've known each other for years."

"Really?" the major asked. "Why do I find that hard to believe? Tell me how you met?"

"At the Sorbonne," Paul answered, his stomach churning. "While attending the university."

The officer looked at Alexander and said, "I'm going to separate you. Then we will see if you have the same answers."

The officer whispered to the soldier, who led Paul toward the car's entrance. Once they were five meters away, standing by an elderly man and woman seated by the door, the major continued questioning Alexander.

"Tell me what your friend studied."

"*Er studierte Finanz. Ich studierte deutschen Philosophen,*" Alexander said in perfect German. "He studied finance. I studied German philosophers."

"You speak German?" the major asked, sounding surprised.

"*Natürlich spreche ich Deutsch du dummer Esel!*" Alexander said sharply. "Of course I speak German, you stupid jackass!"

"I beg your pardon," the major declared indignantly. "I could have you shot for talking to me that way!"

"I doubt it," Alexander said harshly, "because you're making a grave mistake, Major."

Sounding flustered, the German replied, "I don't understand."

"I know you don't. But you're harassing a Gestapo agent infiltrating a Resistance group. If it's ruined due to your incompetence, I will have you sent to the Russian front."

The major turned ashen. "My apologies," he stuttered. "I didn't realize." He motioned for the other soldier to return, and he and Paul came back down the corridor.

"Here are your papers," the major said to Paul. "Everything is in order."

Paul returned to his seat and he and Alexander watched the Germans walk away.

"What did you tell him?" Alexander asked.

"That I majored in finance and you were an art student. I couldn't think of anything else," he answered sadly. "Catherine was an artist."

"It's all right," Alexander said. "They're gone now."

Paul breathed a sigh of relief. Alexander was clever. He would have known what to say. He returned the papers to his pocket, his hands trembling.

By contrast, Alexander was calm and cool. Paul realized it wasn't the first time he had been confronted by the Germans, nor would it be the last. He lived dangerously, an Englishman planted in France, his accent not quite right, the risks not worth taking. But he took them anyway.

Alexander studied those still in the car. A German soldier napped a few seats away. A housewife sat across from them, her arms laden with packages. More people were near the front, a group of students clustered together, the rest scattered throughout the car. He seemed content. He placed a piece of paper in Paul's pocket.

"Get off at the next stop," he said. "We can't risk the Germans coming back. I'll be in touch."

"Wait a minute," Paul said.

Alexander's brow knitted. "What is it?" he asked.

"Can I kill Kruger?"

"No, absolutely not," he replied, irritated. "I told you that before. You can not do anything that jeopardizes the operation or endangers the Fox. I thought I made that clear."

Paul rose from the seat with no goodbye and stood near the exit. When the train halted and the doors opened, he left and didn't look back. A few minutes later, he caught the train returning to the Left Bank. It was only when he sat down and surveyed the people around him, ensuring it was safe, that he withdrew the paper from his pocket. The scribbled message was cryptic. It listed a series of numbers: 4:19:2120:172.

Chapter 55

"In the Name of the Father and of the Son and of the Holy Spirit," said the man in the confessional.

Father Nicolas urged him to continue. "May the Lord be in your heart and help you to confess your sins with true sorrow," he said solemnly. He then muttered from the scriptures, speaking softly in Latin. He was perplexed, the voice across the partition familiar. He finished, and then listened intently.

"Forgive me, Father, for I have sinned. It has been six weeks since my last confession." The man behind the partition paused, cleared his throat, and then continued. "I have lied to my daughters," he admitted. "I pretend to be what I'm not, and they suffer from my masquerade."

Father Nicolas noticed that his wife wasn't mentioned. "Why would you lie, or pretend to be what you're not?" he asked.

"I want to help others. But I need to protect my daughters from what I really am, because I love them so much."

Father Nicolas considered the sin the man confessed. Were his actions wrong in the eyes of the Lord? He felt more like a confidant than a theologian. "Isn't the pain your daughters feel only temporary?" he asked. "Won't the day arrive when your secret is revealed, and they will know their father made great sacrifices for the good of others, those far less fortunate and in far greater danger."

"The secret can never be revealed."

"Why?" Father Nicolas asked.

"Because those that are saved will always be in danger, as will I, for saving them. The fanatics who commit such horrific crimes will endure, their numbers too many to be brought to justice. And someday, they will seek revenge."

"So by keeping your secret for all eternity, you believe that you are protecting your children from those that commit these unspeakable crimes."

"Yes, I gladly sacrifice everything, including my life, to save those I can. In turn, to protect my children, no one must ever know what I've done."

"But in the eyes of God, you commit no sin by sparing your loved ones the truth. You have no sin to confess."

The man sighed deeply and said, "Maybe I just need to hear someone say that I'm doing the right thing, that I'm a good man."

Father Nicolas was silent for a moment, his heart heavy. "In God's eyes you are, Mr. Junot," he assured him. "And that's all that matters."

Chapter 56

"My world revolves around my family and my Faith," Gen. Berg said. He and Claire sat in a café, his two bodyguards at the next table. "It seems the war has taken everything else. But I'm fortunate to have my wife, Elsie. She is strong where I am weak."

Claire sipped her coffee, nibbled on a croissant, and said little. Berg was sharing his thoughts: his hopes for the future, his regrets from the past. She didn't know why, but she encouraged him to continue. She might learn something interesting.

"How did you and your wife meet?"

He smiled, reminiscing, and said, "She was visiting a cousin who lived near me. I was twenty, she was eighteen."

"You started dating?"

"Yes, I thought she was the most beautiful woman in the world. And I still do."

"How about your children?"

"I was blessed with three: Gertrude, mother to my granddaughters, Heinrich, a soldier in Italy, and Wilhelm. Gertrude is like me, tall and slender and talkative. So is Heinrich. He does well in the military and is already a captain. Wilhelm favored his mother, slight, pensive, an intellectual. He was killed in Poland at the beginning of the war. He never should have been a soldier." He took a sip of coffee and looked out the window, studying a light rain that washed away the sins of the evening before. "But I insisted," he continued. "I thought a few years in the military would teach him discipline, make him less of a dreamer. It was only when I lost him that I realized the ability to dream is rare; it was his gift. God was good to him. But I was not." He again looked out the window, wiping away a tear. He cleared his throat and then sighed. When a moment had passed, he continued. "And you?" he asked, his eyebrows arched. "No husband or children?"

"I was married but had no children. Jacques was a good husband." She paused, not knowing whether to continue, not knowing if she should share. "He died, during the first attacks," she told him. "Although now it seems so long ago."

"Then we share more than church and chess," Berg said softly. "We share pain."

They were quiet for a moment, watching the rain fall from dark clouds crossing the horizon. Claire looked at Berg's bodyguards at the next table, never far from their leader. He was an important man; his life was always in danger.

Berg sat up straight and turned away from the window. "Enough sadness," he said. "Let's discuss something fun. When is our next chess game?"

"Whenever you want," Claire replied. "I look forward to your company."

"Then I must find time to visit the book store."

They chatted ten minutes more and then Berg looked at his watch. "I'm afraid we must go," he said reluctantly.

They got into the back seat of the sedan, the bodyguards up front, and drove through the streets of Paris. The rain stopped, clouds passed, and a weak sun appeared, rays reflecting off puddles in the cobblestone street to form tiny rainbows.

"Thank you for breakfast," Claire said as they approached the bookstore.

"You're welcome. If I don't get to the store, I'll see you at Mass or the Junots'. Or another dinner date, perhaps?"

"I would like that," Claire said, smiling warmly. "Whenever it's convenient for you." She stepped from the car and thanked the driver. Then she looked at her watch. The Rosenbergs had left Paris, destined for Portugal. She entered her building's vestibule, closed the door behind her, and leaned against the wall, emitting a sigh of relief. Her first family had escaped.

* * *

Claire entered the *Restaurant Polidor* to meet Julian Junot at a table they frequented often. It was tucked away in the rear of the room, sheltered by shadows, and hidden from other patrons. The food was superb, a luxury in a city that had lost opulence, forgotten extravagance, except for those who could afford it. The restaurant, like many others sprinkled throughout the city, still offered whatever was wanted as long as money was no object. Junot, who insisted she always have the best, was waiting for her when she reached the table. He rose, helped to seat her, and kissed her on the cheek.

"You look radiant, as always," he said.

The waiter appeared with a bottle of Merlot and they moved away from each other, although he still held her hand. He was beyond caring who noticed. When the waiter left, he lifted his glass.

"To us," he said.

They clinked glasses and sipped their wine. Then he leaned forward and kissed her.

Chapter 57

Rachel was handcuffed and shoved down the hallway and out the exit. She was led around the corner to a black Peugeot where another German sat in the driver's seat; the engine was running. The rear door was opened and she was forced inside. The soldier scrambled in beside her, leaning his rifle against the door and withdrawing his Luger from its holster.

She shifted in the seat, trembling, and moved as far away from him as she could. Leaning against the far door, she peered at him from the corner of her eye. His pistol loomed large, although not pointed directly at her. Feeling a bit braver, she turned and studied him more closely. He was looking straight ahead, his jaw firm, his face tense.

They drove to the end of the street, to a checkpoint. The gate was lowered, and a German soldier sat in a chair beside it, reading a newspaper. He wore a pistol in a holster attached to his belt. He walked up to the driver's window as they approached and looked inside.

The German in the rear seat pointed the Luger at Rachel's face. Her heart was beating wildly; her hands in her lap, shaking. Her eyes focused on the gun.

"*Wo nehmen Sie?*" the sentry asked as he leaned in the driver's window. "Where are you taking her?"

"*Gestapo-Hauptquartier, dann Drancy,*" the driver replied.

The sentry looked in the back seat, saw the pistol in Rachel's face, and then slowly scanned the interior of the sedan. He nodded to the driver, returned to the checkpoint, and raised the gate.

Rachel felt her heart sink. All effort had been for naught: almost tortured to death, enduring an unneeded operation, the risks the doctor had taken to save her. She would die anyway.

The sedan advanced slowly, moving under the raised gate and then continued down the street. The German in the back seat lowered the pistol. She turned to face him, shaken and afraid.

His eyes were wide, his breathing erratic. He seemed as afraid as she was. His uniform fit poorly, and he now held the pistol carelessly, as if he didn't intend to use it. Something wasn't right.

"*Gehen!*" he said to the driver. "Go!"

The driver did not turn, he merely lifted his right hand in acknowledgement, and pressed the accelerator down, driving faster than permitted on the streets of Paris. Rachel struggled to see his face but couldn't. He sat low in the seat, and only his helmet was visible from the rear of the vehicle.

The car sped down *Rue Santerre*, away from Rothschild Hospital. There was little traffic and the sedan went faster, weaving in and out of the cars on the road. A few minutes later they crossed the Seine.

Rachel was confused. She spun around, watching the river. The hospital was in Paris's twelfth arrondissement, on the right bank of the Seine. Gestapo headquarters was also on the right bank, but some distance away. They were going the wrong way. They continued on, the river vanishing behind them as they moved deeper into the Left Bank. Rachel wondered if there was another Gestapo headquarters. Or were they taking her out of Paris to an internment camp? But it couldn't be Drancy; that was in the opposite direction. Now she was afraid of the unknown.

They drove ten minutes more and the sedan came to a halt in front of a church, the *Saint-Étienne-du-Mont*. Several pedestrians were near the car: a young woman leading a child by the hand, an old man, and three German soldiers walking down the pavement, still thirty meters away. The soldier in the back seat looked around nervously.

"Give me your hand," he said in flawless French.

Rachel looked at him in disbelief. Her hands remained in her lap.

He looked frantically down the street at the approaching Germans. There were beads of sweat on his forehead. "Quickly!"

She lifted her hands. He grabbed the handcuffs, inserted the key, and unlocked them.

"Go in the church," he directed her.

Rachel was dumbfounded. Were they really French, or pretending to be French? She glanced at the driver. He stared straight ahead, as if he didn't want his face seen. And three Germans were just ahead. It seemed like a trap. Maybe they would shoot her and claim she tried to escape.

"Ask for Father Nicolas," he told her.

She realized he meant it. She left the sedan and started up the church steps. When she turned to look, she saw the sedan slowly moving away from the curb, turning left at the next intersection, avoiding the approaching Germans. Rachel walked up the steps, looking nervously in all directions, still suspicious. The soldiers had almost reached the church, but they were talking among themselves, laughing and joking. They were close enough to see their faces. They were young. They weren't watching her.

She pushed against the carved wooden door of the church. It opened silently, as it should for a house of worship, perfectly balanced on large brass strap hinges. She entered, awed by the interior: stained glass windows, hand-painted murals, sculptures, carved pews, an altar flanked by decorative columns, and spiral staircases glittering with gold trim. She paused and stared, overwhelmed by the beauty, and for an instant all thoughts of Germans were gone.

As she admired the church, a man stepped from the shadows, dressed simply in a brown frock. His face was soft, sincere and honest, and he touched her lightly on the arm. "Rachel?" he asked.

She nodded, afraid to speak.

"You're safe now," he assured her. "I'm Father Nicolas. Come, we must hurry."

He led her through the corridor, down the steps into the church basement. It was dimly lit, slightly dank, littered with crypts and coffins of marble and granite. He took her to the back, through a series of rooms defined by stone walls and arched entrances, and led her to a crypt that stood against the wall, slightly elevated. He then slowly slid the marble lid aside. "Quickly," he said. "Don't ask questions."

As he moved the top aside, uncovering the coffin, he flicked on a light switch, exposing a vertical metal ladder. He motioned for her to descend.

She knew this was the path to safety, and that many people had risked their lives to get her there. She was overwhelmed with gratitude for her unknown saviors: the doctor who got her out of Gestapo headquarters and into the hospital, the soldiers in the staff car who were obviously not Germans, and now this good priest. And there would be more. She knew that.

"Thank you so much," she said softly.

She climbed into the coffin and started down the vertical steps, descending underground about five meters. She could see a rock corridor at the bottom, a cylindrical hallway that traveled in two directions. Just as her foot stepped off the last ladder rung and touched the cavern floor, she saw a man waiting for her.

He was of medium height, about thirty-five years old, well dressed in a dark business suit with a blue tie. He had black hair and dark eyes, and a deep sadness etched on his face that was so overpowering it left an everlasting impression, read instantly by all who met him.

"Hello, Rachel," he said. "I'm Paul Moreau."

Chapter 58

The next meeting of the Bibliophile Society was Friday evening at Junot's home. Alain Dominique, General Berg, and Colonel Kruger were in a parlor off the library, its entrance marked by a broad sweeping arch with a carved keystone. They huddled closely, immersed in a private discussion, their voices low.

Claire, Paul, and Junot sat in the study, within view of their conversation. Bernard entered occasionally, providing drinks or hors d'oeuvres as did Jacqueline Junot, chatting with the Germans, flirting with Dominique, and ignoring her husband. He pretended not to notice.

Paul eyed Kruger, hiding his hatred, incensed that he had failed to kill him. He wrestled with Alexander's order not to try again. It was hard to accept, but he had no other choice. He couldn't risk lives for his personal vendetta. He told Claire and Junot about both Alexander's urgent request on the train, including their encounter with the Germans, and his impromptu meeting with Alain Dominique. Although he had spoken to Dominique when he arrived, there was no mention of their lunch at the café. He acted like he barely knew who Paul was.

"He's a journalist," Claire reminded him. "He's probably looking for a story."

Paul shook his head. "I don't think so," he cautioned. "He's been at the bank several times. And I've seen him snooping around the book store."

Claire rolled her eyes. "Or he could have been buying books," she pointed out.

Junot watched the wine swirling in his glass. "Don't underestimate him," he advised. "Or his friends. They're dangerous. Dominique suspects something and he's trying to prove it. Don't let him outsmart you."

They were all quiet for a moment, sipping their wine, reflecting, perhaps, on their own encounters and interfaces with Dominique.

"What do you think Alexander meant?" Claire asked. "He sounded so desperate."

Paul looked at the paper, passed it to Claire and then Junot. "I have no idea," he admitted.

"It must be a code," Claire suggested. "Maybe the numbers stand for letters."

"But why twenty-one twenty together," Paul wondered aloud. "It doesn't make sense."

"It could be an address," Junot offered.

"And the other numbers might be a street," Paul said.

Bernard entered the study, filling their wine glasses.

"Bernard, take a look at this," Junot requested. "We think it's some sort of code."

The personal assistant, trusted by all, studied the paper and then handed it back. "Twenty-one twenty could be a time."

"Or it might refer to the scriptures," Claire said as she walked to the nearest bookshelf.

Bernard finished filling their glasses and then took the bottle to the adjoining room, where Kruger, Berg and Dominique continued their discussion.

"Here's a Bible," she said, leafing through the pages. "Verse 4:19 is 'We love because he first loved us.'

Nothing for 2120, and Psalm 172 is 'My tongue will sing of thy word, for all thy commandments are righteous.' They might have hidden meanings."

"What did Alexander say on the train?" Junot asked.

Paul thought for a moment. "He spoke about transports and trains," he answered. "And he mentioned needing a favor. I thought he was referring to moving the Jews out of Paris."

"Perhaps," Junot said, biting a fingernail.

"He may want us to sabotage trains," Paul proposed.

Junot stood, paced the floor, and said quietly, "That would kill people. And I have no interest in taking lives. Only saving them. Alexander knows that."

Paul watched Junot for a moment, considering his statement. "I suppose everyone has boundaries," he said, "limits they can live with, justified in their own minds."

Junot shrugged. "If we don't," he advised, "we should."

"If Alexander's message refers to a train, it must be an important one," Claire said, still trying to decipher the message. "Or why use a code?"

"Maybe it's a train schedule," Junot said.

"Today is the sixteenth of April," Paul offered. "So the first two digits, 4 and 19, could be a date."

"Three days from today," Claire said. "Assuming you're correct, that leaves two numbers: twenty-one twenty and one hundred and seventy-two."

"Bernard may be right," Junot said. "Twenty-one twenty is military time for 9:20 p.m. I'll check the train schedules."

He stepped into an office that adjoined the study and made a telephone call. A few minutes later, he returned.

"What did you find out?" Paul asked.

"A train leaves Paris for Berlin on April 19th   at 9:20 p.m. And guess what number it is."

"One seventy-two," Claire guessed.

Junot nodded and said, "We've solved Alexander's code."

"What's so significant about this train?" she asked.

"From what I've just learned, someone very important is aboard."

"And we must remove them?" Paul asked.

"Yes," he replied. "His name is Hans Brinkman, known as Johnny Helman for the last five years. He lived in London, near Trafalgar Square. But he spent most of his time traveling the countryside."

"A German spy," Claire said.

"He just escaped from England, minutes before his arrest."

"And we're going to return him?" Paul asked.

"If we can find a way to do it."

Chapter 59

After dinner the next day Paul and Claire sat in the parlor, relaxing with a cup of coffee. He studied his cousin's face, innocent and inquisitive, and wondered if anyone would ever suspect she was in the Resistance. He had known her his entire life, and he still found it hard to believe.

"Otto Ernst was called back to Berlin," he informed her. "He doesn't think he'll be back."

"That's a shame," she said. "I'm sorry to see him go. He's one of the good Germans." She thought about it for a moment, adding, "Maybe he was the only good German."

"He brought the new president to the bank before he left. His name is Oskar Bouchard. I guess the French name makes him legitimate." Paul shook his head with disgust and said, "He probably betrayed someone to the Gestapo. That's why they gave him the bank."

"Think about what Julian said," Claire advised. "It's temporary. Don't try to make sense of it."

"But it's still wrong. They stole the bank from a good family."

"I know," she agreed, "but we're trying to change it. We just can't fix it overnight."

He looked at her, studying the dark eyes, so bright and sincere. "You're right," he admitted. "I just wish we could do more. I wish I could kill Kruger."

"Maybe you should focus on all the good we're doing with the Jews. Look at the lives we've saved. And there are many more to come."

"You're right. I realize that. But I miss Catherine and Sophie. I think of them constantly, no matter what I'm doing. And I always will."

"So do I," she said. "But Alexander doesn't want us to kill any Germans, and for good reason. He doesn't want our operation compromised."

Paul was silent, studying her closely. "Let me tell you a secret," he said. "I don't care what Alexander says. If I have the opportunity, I'll kill Kruger."

"I get revenge by saving people," she replied sharply, "and you should, too. If you kill Kruger, you will risk everything, including many more lives than your own."

He sighed and put his head in his hands. Sometimes he felt like he was losing his mind. He then looked at her apologetically. "You're right, of course," he admitted. "I'm being selfish, but the urge is irresistible. I know at some point I won't be able to control it. Just don't tell anyone. It's my secret."

"I won't," she said, her eyes trained on his, "because we all have secrets."

* * *

Paul met Julian Junot the following morning and described his conversation with Claire. "She made a very cryptic comment about having a secret," Paul informed him.

Junot frowned and said, "I hope nothing is wrong."

"I just can't imagine what she could be hiding."

Junot was pensive for a moment. "I'm sure it's nothing," he said. "I know we have to be careful, but she can be trusted implicitly. We both know that."

"What do you think it is?"

"I think she is an exceptional woman," he said. "Brilliant, compassionate, attractive. She has a heart as big as Paris. Her laugh is infectious. But she is very lonely. Maybe it's a man. It would be good for her."

Paul was irritated. "I don't think you know her as well as I do," he reminded him. "Claire lost her husband during the German invasion. I doubt she's thought of a man since."

Junot was quiet, waiting a moment before replying. "Wasn't that more than two years ago?" he asked.

"It doesn't matter. She would tell me if there was a man in her life."

"She may want privacy until she's sure about the relationship, convinced her feelings are real."

Paul considered his comment. "We're very close," he said, "and have been all our lives. I can only think of one reason why she wouldn't tell me."

"What is that?"

He looked at Junot, the corners of his lips turned into a frown. "If the man is German," he offered, "that would explain her secret."

"Is there anyone she's been spending time with," he asked, "at social events or chess matches? Are there any Germans she may have mentioned?"

Paul thought for a moment before replying. "Yes, there is," he said tersely. "It's Gen. Berg."

Chapter 60

It took a few days for Rachel to stop thanking Claire Daladier for saving her life. And when Claire introduced her to Julian Junot, who came to the catacombs one morning, she could not stop staring at his shoes. She knew what true craftsmanship was from working in her father's shop and the boot factory, and his shoes defined it. The leather was soft, probably Italian, the workmanship exceptional, with not a stitch visible, and the polish so deep that the shoes reflected even the dim light of the cavern. She guessed they cost more than all the money her father made in his shop in an entire month.

"Rachel, are you all right?" Claire asked, interrupting her admiration of Junot's shoes.

She smiled shyly. "Yes, I'm sorry," she said. "I've worked in my father's shoe shop my entire life and I have never seen shoes as beautiful as yours, Mr. Junot."

Junot laughed, a bit embarrassed. He studied the teenager, her hair pulled back exposing a simple beauty that was strong and elegant. "Thank you, you're very perceptive," he observed. "I suppose they are inappropriate for the catacombs."

Rachel looked at his suit, hand-tailored, his silk shirt and tie, his hair, so immaculately barbered that it lay on his head perfectly, more like a work of art than a haircut. Everything about him reeked of power, sophistication, and money. She knew she could have gone her entire lifetime without meeting anyone like him, and he was certainly not the man she would expect to find in a cavern underneath the city of Paris.

"Rachel, I've been struggling with your future," Claire informed her. "After your narrow escape, I can't let you return to Resistance activities."

Rachel was both relieved and disappointed. Her hatred for the Germans ran even deeper, given the humiliation and torture she had endured, but she also feared them, more than she ever thought possible.

"I don't think I can do it anyway," she replied softly. "Even as badly as I want to."

"We thought of a better assignment," Junot said. He waved his hand to the small colony of Jews spread out before them. "You now know what we do here," he continued. "You know how the Jews arrive, receive new identities, and are then given their freedom."

"Yes, I see," Rachel acknowledged. "It's a good thing you are doing." She turned to Claire. "Just as you did for my family."

"What if we taught you how to run the operation?" Claire asked. "You would be fighting the war, but not be exposed to the enemy."

Rachel looked at the tiny village of partitioned walls with bags and suitcases and boxes and crates stacked against them, storing people's lives. She knew what an effort it took to feed and clothe so many people. And she knew she couldn't do it.

"I would love to. But I don't know how. I wouldn't even know where to begin."

"I will help you," Junot offered. "It's no different than operating a business. It just takes some organizational skills, which I can teach you."

Rachel was astonished that this man, whom she had never even met and had already helped save her life, was willing to share so much of his knowledge and unique abilities. It was an opportunity she knew came rarely, if at all, and when it did, it had to be taken advantage of.

"If you're willing, I promise to be the best pupil you ever had," she vowed.

* * *

Rachel was a quick learner, participating in Junot's daily lessons that ranged from developing and maintaining a budget to the logistics required to feed, clothe, and create new identities for three hundred people. At first she oversaw the operation under Claire's tutelage and, when that proved successful, she began to manage it alone. She excelled, and she loved it. Although she recognized the danger if ever exposed, she found it rewarding and less risky than confronting the Nazis on the streets of Paris. She could help many different people and she wasn't exposed to the Gestapo.

With a new-found appreciation for life after almost losing her own, she dove into making the operation as efficient as possible. First she established different zones in the cavern. She assigned one area to clothing: storage, manufacturing, altering, and fitting, all to ensure those about to leave were well-equipped. She arranged a small barber's area where hair could be cut or colored, mustaches and beards groomed, if needed. And she established a document center, well-lit with a table and drawers, cameras, proper paper and ink, so identification papers could be stored, created, or altered, eliminating the need for the public printers that Rachel never forgot led to her capture by the Gestapo. Two former printers took over the production of documents, choosing to remain and practice their craft, helping others and foregoing their place in line to start a new life. And lastly, she developed storage areas for food and beverages. She even managed to house chickens in a distant cave, providing fresh eggs for the inhabitants, and to harvest mushrooms that grew in the caverns.

The quickly maturing teenager assigned tasks to those waiting, utilizing the skills they possessed to earn their livelihoods. She recruited bakers and barbers and cooks and tailors and seamstresses, all working for the greater good, all contributing to the secret community. Others collected and disposed of trash, received and stored supplies, and cleaned the area. Teachers taught children, carpenters made benches and tables and toys, bankers showed those willing to learn the intricacies of finance, and former policemen kept order and stood guard over the two escape routes: the rear of the flower store and the tomb in Montparnasse. Shippers and logistics experts made the arrangements and organized the escape routes which would enable hundreds of refugees to start new lives. An intricate and interdependent community was established, governed by the people, with the objective of saving as many lives as possible.

They formed an operation that was much more efficient, able to process ten Jews per day, which was their original goal, and often the number increased to fifteen or sometimes twenty per day. They developed multiple escape routes, enlisting farmers and rural villagers, and recruiting Resistance personnel.

The overall population changed constantly; those escaping were replaced almost immediately by those arriving. Rachel provided a brief indoctrination to each group that came, explaining the rules and determining their strengths, skills and any special talents they might possess. Among one group of new arrivals, she noticed a tall, slender young man with sandy brown hair and piercing green eyes. He seemed startled to see her, staring at her intensely, as if wondering if he had the right person.

Rachel smiled when she saw him. "Hello, Meurice," she said simply. "How are you?"

Chapter 61

Claire sat in the parlor, a glass of wine in her hand, reflecting on how different her life had become since meeting Rachel Abzac. She had arrived clutching a centuries-old Talmud, a bit intimidated, but awed by the shelves of old books. Her family had hoped to earn extra money by selling the heirloom, if it had any value. Rachel had been stunned when Claire named a price. The ensuing discussion, with Rachel's eyes straying to the shelves beyond, had led to an offer of employment. It was one of those chance meetings that had changed both their lives forever.

Rachel had come close to losing her life. If she hadn't escaped, she would have betrayed Claire, and the Gestapo would have tortured her to death. The Gestapo always got what they wanted.

Her new role now was far less dangerous, far more appropriate, and Julian and Claire were pleased with her ability to grasp the intricacies demanded by the colony. It was an important position, almost equal to theirs. And she was doing well, responsible and accountable, and deftly managing the inflow of Jewish refugees and the new lives that were created for them.

A picture of Jacques, his face lit with a broad smile, sat on the table beside her. She looked at it, reminisced, and took a sip of wine. They had lived a good life, from the fields near Giverny, where they had romped as children, to the streets of Paris, where they had walked as adults. But

Jacques was gone. And she had come to accept that, the ache a little duller, the tears less frequent.

Catherine and Sophie were different; their deaths hurt more than Jacque's. Especially Sophie, her life gone before it started. Their loss was senseless, only demonstrating the cruelty of a country that conquers another. Claire wondered what twisted justification they invented for their heinous crimes. She understood Paul's obsession with killing Kruger; she often thought of doing it herself. And maybe someday she would. But she wrestled with how a man who discussed great English poets at a dinner party could brutally murder a defenseless mother and child. It didn't fit. But maybe that's how maniacs behaved.

She set the wine on the table and went into the bathroom, filling the tub. Then she soaked, the warm water washing memories away. As she continued to reminisce, she realized no matter how wonderful, the past was gone. And it was never coming back. Only the dawn lay before her and whatever adventures it delivered. She washed, changed her clothes to a casual dress that accented her figure, and then fussed in front of the bathroom mirror, putting on make-up. She used little, a bit of rouge and some eye shadow. Just as she was finishing, someone knocked on the door. She looked at her watch, marveling at his punctuality, and opened the door. "Come in," she said, glancing down the hall to ensure no one saw him.

Julian Junot entered and handed her a bouquet of flowers, lilies, the symbol of royalty.

She was flattered. He always spoiled her. "They're beautiful," she said.

"I know it's risky for me to come. But I thought it would be nice for us to be alone."

"No, it's fine," she replied. "The neighbors may talk, but I don't care anymore. I'm tired of hiding." She led him into the parlor and poured him a glass of wine. Then she put the flowers in a glossy Roseville vase, so beautiful it rivaled the lilies.

They chatted for a while, about the weather, business at the book store, the different battles and fronts that dominated the war. But both knew he hadn't come for conversation. As their discussion continued he moved closer, holding her hand, and then putting his arm around her. Then he kissed her, softly and sensually, gently exploring her mouth, his hand stroking her hair. He lightly nibbled on her neck and ears as his hands moved to her back, caressing the curves.

She moaned softly, pulled him closer, her arms wrapped around him. She drank in his scent, felt the muscles in his back, her hand traveling across his body, moving through his hair. When they separated, she felt her heart racing, every cell in her body responding to his touch. He kissed her again, harder, more insistently, his touch more demanding. She pulled away, breathless, and stood up. Then she reached for his hand and led him into the bedroom.

Chapter 62

"We know from Alexander's code that the German spy Brinkman is returning from England," Paul said when he and Junot met for coffee. "The question now, is how do we get him off the train?"

"We pose as Gestapo officers and board the train while it's stopped in Paris. Then we get Brinkman off."

"There's just one problem. I speak German fluently. You don't."

"I can manage a few phrases," Junot said.

Paul frowned. "Which only increases the risk," he commented.

"It's a risk we'll have to take."

"What if we're recognized?"

"We'll use disguises: moustaches, glasses, just enough to alter our appearance. I'll book a hotel room near the train station. We'll meet there a few hours before. Claire can help us."

"Won't that look suspicious?" Paul asked. "The three of us go into a room and emerge as different people. How will you get the room? You can't register as Julian Junot."

"Bernard will get the room. He can say it's for a high-ranking German officer and his mistress, a married socialite. It's safe. No one keeps track of who comes and goes in large hotels, especially when they're Germans."

"Then the last detail is getting Brinkman off the train and out of France," Paul said.

"He's in cabin 6A and there's one man with him," Junot informed him. "Most likely an escort, someone assigned to get him to Berlin."

"How do we kidnap him? Are you sure it's easiest to go on the train and remove him?"

"I think so," Junot answered. "We pose as Gestapo and present papers requiring transfer of custody."

"We should have a lookout, someone who has the car ready."

"Claire can do that."

Paul sipped his coffee. He was pensive, digesting the plan, evaluating options. "Where do we take him once we get him off the train?" he asked.

"We can have some of the Jews going to England take him with them."

"There is a route that might work," Paul suggested. "We use a network of farmers through northern France and into Calais."

"Are there three or four men available to send with Brinkman?"

Paul thought of those hidden in the catacombs. "Yes, I think so," he replied. "I'll have them staged at the first farmhouse. We just have to get Brinkman there."

"I can take him," Junot said. "Unlike most of Paris, I still have an automobile. Claire can come with me. It'll be a good cover. You return home on the Metro."

"Too much risk for you," Paul said.

"It's worth it. Brinkman is too valuable to the Germans, too devastating to the Allies."

"Where do we park your car?"

"On the alley beside the train station," Junot said. "We'll give Brinkman some sedatives, tie him up and lock him in the trunk. I'll drive him to the farmhouse with Claire and the refugees can take him to England."

"That leaves Brinkman's guard as the last detail."

"Make the forged order from some fictitious general in Paris. The guard's name is Captain Josef Hoffman."

"What if Hoffman doesn't believe it?'

Junot's face grew taut. "Then we take him, too," he said tersely.

Chapter 63

"Rachel, I'm so relieved you're alive," Meurice said as he stood with new arrivals deep within the catacombs. "I was certain Monique had betrayed you."

"She did," Rachel replied simply. She stared at him defiantly, her arms folded across her chest. Memories of torture and humiliation flashed through her mind, phantom pain stabbing her body. How could he expose her to Monique? He had seemed so careful. She wanted to punch him, swinging her fists wildly, pummeling his face. But she couldn't, and merely stood there, her lip quivering, fighting not to cry.

His face was anxious, cringing, as he watched her reaction. "At least nothing happened," he sighed. "And you're safe here."

"Something did happen," she answered angrily. "I was captured by the Gestapo, tortured for three days, humiliated in front of a hundred soldiers, and forced to lie beside my own casket. I was rescued by a doctor who convinced the Germans I would die unless he removed my perfectly good appendix. They couldn't let that happen, not before getting the information they wanted, so they sent me to the hospital, where I escaped after my operation. Other than that, it had no impact at all."

His face turned gray; his eyes mirrored compassion. "I am so sorry," he said. "If I could have taken your place, I would have – and you know that. Please forgive me."

"If it weren't for Claire, the Gestapo would have killed me. I couldn't even..." She started crying, even though she tried desperately not to. Her body jerked, the tears flowed, and she covered her face with her hands. She hated to show weakness.

Meurice took her in his arms, pulling her close and whispering, "I would never do anything to hurt you. Surely you know that."

"No, I don't," she sobbed, gaining control of herself and wiping away the tears. "You could care less. You were always more interested in other women."

"That's not true," he said softly, releasing her. "I only pretended to flirt, so you would think I was worldly and mature."

She studied his face, finding sincerity, although at first she didn't believe it. "Why would you do that?" she asked.

"Because I wanted you to find me attractive," he admitted sheepishly.

"I do, but not because you flirt with other women. Because you're handsome and intelligent and interesting."

He smiled. "Thank you," he said. "You're very special, too."

She grinned, blushing.

"I take full responsibility for what happened. If you forgive me, I promise I'll make it up to you. Even if it takes my entire life."

She paused, painful memories lingering. "I'll try to forgive you," she said softly, "but it won't be easy."

"I should have been smarter," he confessed. "I know better. Monique should have been checked more closely, by me and others. She made me uncomfortable, she was too carefree, and wasn't properly trained. But I assumed, due to those who referred her, that she knew what to do and how to be cautious. Now we know she didn't, and her carelessness almost cost you your life. I would have never done anything that exposed you to danger."

Believing him at last, Rachel hugged him again, pulling him close, holding him tightly and feeling his strength. "I know you wouldn't. But you were so careful when we met. How could you be fooled so easily?" she asked.

"I was very stupid," he admitted. "There's no other explanation."

"Were you caught, too?"

"Almost," he said. "I came home from work and saw the Gestapo surrounding the building I lived in. I watched from across the street, sitting in a café, drinking a cup of coffee, never dreaming they were there for me. It was only after an hour had passed, and other residents had come and gone, that I realized the truth. I left, spent the night hidden among trashcans in a nearby alley, and told my Resistance contact the next day. He knew I was Jewish, and took me to an elderly man's house on *Rue Jussieu*. I was there for over a month. Then I was taken here. Are you waiting to escape, also?"

Rachel smiled. "Not really," she said. "At first I was taken here because it was safe. I was supposed to join my family in Normandy. But I still wanted to fight."

Confused, he asked, "Then what are you doing here?"

"I'm in charge of the operation."

"What do you mean?"

"I run everything," she said. "That's why I gave your group the indoctrination."

His eyes widened and he saw her in a new light. "You do?" he asked. "I'm sorry, but I'm very surprised. Not because I have any doubt that you are capable, but because it is a tremendous responsibility for one so young."

"Young?" she asked. "I just turned seventeen. I'm a woman – and maturity is measured by experience, not age. How old are you?"

"Twenty. But I'll be twenty-one in six months."

"Twenty? So you're a wise old man?"

He laughed. "No," he admitted, "I suppose not."

She took him by the hand. She was proud of her accomplishments and wanted to show him. "Come," she urged, "I'll give you a tour of the facility."

"Maybe you can teach me?" Meurice asked, as Rachel led him forward. "Then I can help you."

"I can," she said coyly. "But you'll be leaving soon. We'll arrange a new identity for you, teach you skills if you need them, and let you return to the outside world."

"I know that, but I still want to help – even if it's only for a short while."

Meurice seemed amazed by the complexity of the operation. Rachel explained how she had been tutored, but didn't mention Julian Junot or Claire, explaining in detail how much she had learned about the business world, from finances to logistics. He listened intently and told her, "You can take what you learned here and start a business after the war. Or more than one business if you want."

"I have much to be thankful for," she said softly, truly feeling fortunate. "I will never forget all that people have done for me."

Rachel had everything running smoothly, and Meurice grew more impressed as each minute passed, taking an intense interest. She explained how food and consumables were obtained, waste was removed, the self-sufficiency provided by a printer, barber, tailor, and baker. She told him about the escape routes and those who supported them, and how to select which refugees would remain in Paris with new identities, which were earmarked for farms and rural villages, which would go to Switzerland, Spain, or England. As the days passed, he came to assist Rachel, working at her side, helping, doing whatever he could, and he came to see her as a much stronger person than he had ever imagined, like a diamond, with many different facets.

Their first challenge was to increase the number of Jews who could be rescued or assimilated into French society. It was Meurice who thought of the simplest solution, especially for those chosen to remain in Paris. Rather than relying only on the escape routes to the cemetery or the outbuilding behind the flower store, he offered a plain alternative.

"The priests here at the church have mass daily and three masses on Sunday," he said. "Why don't we use the church more aggressively? Instead of letting a few people per week filter from the church, after dark or when no one is near, we can let two or three people walk out with each mass. They can sneak upstairs and sit in the rear pews, as if they're attending the service. Then when mass is over, they can walk into the streets of Paris, blending with the city's residents."

"Claire told me they tried that once," Rachel informed him. "And a German general came to the service."

"It shouldn't matter, as long as we're prepared," Meurice said. "He would think they were parishioners, attending the service just as he was. We will all have to learn the mass, but that shouldn't be too difficult."

Rachel was pensive for a moment. She didn't like to take risks. But she realized the German general wouldn't be at every service. "They won't be able to carry their belongings," she said. "And most will never part with their remaining prized possessions – which is whatever they have in their suitcases."

Meurice thought for a moment. "Clothing is easy to solve. We can provide them with money. If it's only trinkets or personal effects, maybe we can deliver them to their new apartments, or even meet them on the street after mass. And some people, like me, came here with nothing. They can leave with nothing."

Rachel considered his idea but was still cautious. When you are tortured by the Gestapo and survive, it changes everything about you. It had certainly changed her. "We'll try it," she told him, still sounding skeptical. "But only with those who can leave with nothing but their identity papers."

Chapter 64

Paul stood in front of the mirror fussing with his collar. He was dressed as a German captain, complete with sidearm. A false moustache was glued to his upper lip, and powder lightened his hair, giving it a grayish color and making him appear ten years older. Junot wore a colonel's uniform. His appearance was altered by black horn-rimmed glasses that provided a look of authority. A false scar on his cheek, which Claire had applied with makeup, gave him battlefield authenticity. "How do we look?" Junot asked.

Claire studied them closely, knowing their lives depended on deception. "You're sure about the insignias, the division you belong to, things like that? Missing minor details can cost you your lives."

"I was told everything is accurate," Junot confirmed. "And I trust the contact completely. The uniforms are authentic German Wehrmacht with officer caps. A captain's yellow shoulder insignia contains two golden clusters; a colonel's meadow green shoulder insignia contains two golden clusters."

"It's important that everything is correct," she said as she combed Paul's hair, feathering the gray and then adjusted Junot's glasses, bending the frame so they sat squarely on his nose. She stepped back, eyed each closely and then announced, "I think we're ready." She could tell they were nervous. Neither had ever faced the enemy, not as combatants, not posing as Germans. If caught, they would be shot as traitors. She realized they knew this, and suspected their pulses raced a little faster, each breath a little more labored.

Junot glanced at his watch. "We had best be going," he informed them.

They left the hotel by a rear entrance and strolled to the train station. Junot's car was parked behind some trash cans in a nearby alley, the license plate altered.

"I'll be waiting at the car," Claire said. "Be careful. And if you sense anything wrong, abort the mission."

* * *

Paul and Junot left the hotel, walked into the night and then entered the brightly lit train station, a cavernous area servicing multiple tracks, the roof supported by ornate Art Noveua columns. The station was not only functional but, as with all things in Paris, it was architecturally beautiful, simple but elegant, functional but striking. The station was crowded with German soldiers and citizens in equal numbers and, given the bored look of those in the lobby, none seemed suspicious. As they walked to the gate where train #172 was waiting, no one seemed to notice them.

"Wait!" Paul hissed suddenly. He led Junot behind a group of people waiting to board, suitcases in hand.

"What is it?"

Paul pointed across the platform. Alain Dominique was walking from Brinkman's train. He moved briskly across the station, but not towards the exit. They watched as he disappeared into the crowd.

"Do we continue?" Paul asked, fearing a trap.

Junot was silent for a moment, staring at the path Dominique had taken. He nodded his head. They boarded the train, walking slowly through the cars until they stood at compartment 6A.

Paul opened the door and saw a man sitting to one side. He motioned to Junot. Then he entered.

"Heil Hitler!" Paul announced as he and Junot entered and saluted.

The two men rose and returned their salute, studying them curiously.

"Ich bin Kaptain Schrotter," Paul stated "I am Captain Schrotter."

"Ich bin Colonel Heinz," Junot said.

Since Paul was far more proficient in German, he dominated the conversation. He withdrew the forged papers from his pocket and handed them to the captain. "We have orders to take Brinkman to Gestapo headquarters," Paul explained in German.

"My orders are to take him directly to Berlin," the confused sentry said as he scanned the papers.

Junot and Paul tensed, their hands close to their side arms.

"What's this all about?" Brinkman asked. He was a small, wiry man about forty years of age. A swarthy complexion and tiny black eyes made him look more like a street hood than a German spy.

"Colonel Kruger of the Paris Gestapo has been asked to obtain some information from you," Paul said. "You will only be delayed a day or two. Then you'll return to Berlin."

"I just got done talking to the Gestapo," Brinkman griped.

"I know that," Paul said, feigning exasperation. He wondered if it was Dominique. Although surprised, he pretended not to be. "There are still some items that need clarification."

Brinkman's eyes narrowed. "But I'm looking forward to going to Berlin," he told them.

"Two days enjoying the French women won't hurt you," Paul joked. He looked at Junot and winked. "I don't think I would complain."

Junot smiled and added, "Nor would I."

Looking more relaxed, Brinkman answered, "I suppose you're right. A few days in Paris won't hurt."

"What am I to do?" his escort asked.

"Continue to Berlin," Paul said.

"I can't. My orders are to stay with Brinkman. I must go with you."

Paul could feel beads of perspiration form on his forehead. He was beginning to panic, his heart thumping like a drum.

"Take these papers with you to Berlin," Junot directed. He played the role of colonel perfectly, but with strained pronunciations.

The sentry stared at him curiously, as if alerted by the accent. He started to speak but stopped, and instead scanned the papers.

"Come, Mister Brinkman," Paul said, as if the issue were final. "Colonel Kruger is waiting. I think he has some entertainment scheduled for this evening."

"Just a minute," the sentry said, standing, as Paul opened the compartment door.

Paul froze and turned to look at Junot. There wasn't the slightest hint of fear on his face. He was completely composed, calm and serene.

"Yes, Captain?" Junot asked with raised eyebrows.

The soldier studied him for a moment and asked, "I just give these papers to my contact in Berlin?"

"Yes," Paul said for Junot, afraid to let him speak. "And if your commander has any questions, he can contact Colonel Kruger. He is responsible for the alteration in your orders."

"Yes, sir," the sentry said, apparently resigned to the change in plans. He sat back in the seat.

"*Auf Wiedersehen,*" Paul concluded curtly, tossing him a half-hearted salute.

They guided Brinkman from the train and into the station. He followed eagerly, seeming excited about a stay in Paris.

"A little vacation will be nice," he said as they crossed the lobby and exited into the darkness of the street beyond. "I've never been to Paris."

They started walking down the street, Brinkman between them. Just as they reached the alley, a man approached. He was stocky, dressed in civilian clothes, hunched over with his head down, the brim of his hat low over his eyes. When he reached them, he withdrew a pearl-handled knife from his pocket, the blade glistening in the moonlight. Without warning he plunged it viciously into the stomach of Julian Junot.

He grabbed Brinkman. "*Laufen!*" he said. "Run."

Chapter 65

Junot gasped, doubled over, and then slumped to the ground. His hands covered his abdomen, blood seeping through his fingers, staining his German uniform and dripping onto the gray cobblestone.

Paul was stunned, not knowing what to do. He started to chase the fleeing Brinkman who ran towards the station. The man who had stabbed Junot was across the street, watching. Suddenly he started shouting and waving his arms. *"Polizei! Jemand stach ein deutscher Offizier!"* he yelled. "Police! Someone stabbed a German officer!"

Paul stopped abruptly. He had to help Junot and they had to get away. He quickly retreated and bent over the prostrate body. Claire ran from the car, reaching Junot just as Paul did.

"What happened?" she asked.

"I don't know," Paul said, his heart racing. He checked Junot for vital signs. "A stranger walked up and stabbed him. Brinkman escaped. Dominique was in the station. Maybe he's behind it."

"Polizei!" the attacker yelled again, pointing at them.

Pedestrians paused on the pavement, wondering whether to intervene. One man shouted for a doctor. Others started to tentatively walk towards them.

"Is he hurt badly?" Claire asked.

Paul couldn't tell if he was breathing or not. "Julian!"

Junot's eyes opened, vacant and dazed. They focused on Claire. "I'm all right," he mumbled.

Paul knew he wasn't. "Come on," he urged. "We have to go."

Claire ran to the car. She got in the vehicle and drove it down the alley, screeching to a halt beside them. Paul opened the back door, lifted Junot in and then climbed in beside him.

Police sirens wailed, the sounds coming from different directions, the noise rapidly growing closer. Claire drove the car out of the alley, the tires spinning wildly. Junot's assailant stood on the corner, ready to guide the police vehicles, still yelling to attract attention. As the car sped away, he moved into the street, pointing at them. Claire made a quick left and then another. She passed the first police car as it sped to the scene, its lights and sirens blazing, and then turned right.

A second police car approached, its flashing lights visible, and she turned into an alley, extinguishing the head lamps. The vehicle passed and she pulled out. She sped down the street, made two more rights, and headed towards the Seine, slowing the vehicle.

"Take him to my townhouse," Paul told her. "I'll park the car in the alley after we get him into the house."

"We have to get a doctor," Claire said.

"We'll use the man that helped Rachel."

Paul removed his uniform jacket and bunched it against the wound, hoping to absorb the blood.

"Julian," he said softly.

Junot's eyelids fluttered, his face contorted with pain.

"We're taking you to my house. Then we'll get you a doctor."

Fifteen minutes later the car came to a halt in front of Paul's townhouse. The street was almost deserted, but not quite. A few couples walked arm in arm, enjoying the moonlight, watching the Seine drift by.

Paul opened the car door and clumsily pulled Junot from the vehicle, struggling with the weight. Sweat soaked his forehead and he gasped from the exertion, but he managed to get Junot to stand. He looked up and down the street. A few taxis and automobiles drove past, but no Germans. If he could manage to keep Junot upright and get him up the steps and into the flat, they stood a chance.

"Claire, get the door."

She scampered up the steps and opened the door, holding it as Paul approached.

A few blocks away, a black sedan moved slowly down the street.

"Gestapo!" Claire hissed.

Chapter 66

The car crept forward, inching towards the townhouse. It veered closer to the curb, as if pulling up to a residence, but abruptly turned down a side street, moving away from the river.

Paul sighed with relief and leaned against Junot. "Julian, you're going to have to help me," he told him. "We're almost there." He held his arm around him, struggling to hold him upright. They staggered up the first three steps, one by one, wrestling to reach the next. Claire met them halfway, propping him up from the other side.

They reached the fourth step, with three more to go, when Junot started to slump. His face was pale, noticeable even in the dim moonlight. Blood was seeping through his clothing, soaking Paul's jacket pressed against his stomach. They let him rest briefly to regain his strength. His breathing was labored, his pulse weak. They had to get him inside.

Paul eyed the boulevard in both directions. A man walked his dog towards the river, pausing to let the animal sniff the base of a tree. He stared at them for a moment then looked away, either not noticing anything amiss or not caring. Sometimes it was better to mind your own business.

"Is that man watching us?" Claire asked.

"He probably thinks we're all drunk," Paul answered.

They pulled Junot up another step. He weakened with each moment, and the load became heavier, but they pushed forward. They made it up the second of three remaining steps and struggled to reach the next, pausing at the entrance.

Junot's head slumped against his chest. He was gasping, conscious, but barely. He was dying.

"We have to keep moving," Paul said. "The sooner he's resting, the better he'll be."

Claire took a deep breath and braced herself. "All right," she said, "I'm ready."

"Julian, we're moving again."

Junot clutched his stomach, gritted his teeth, and nodded.

The black sedan returned, slowly rolling around the corner.

"It's the Gestapo again!" Claire hissed.

They led him through the opened door. Blood dripped on the cobblestone. The car came closer.

Claire crossed the threshold, leading Junot forward. Paul held him upright, guiding him from behind.

The car crept even with them and stopped. Paul could feel them watching.

"Just walk through the door," Paul whispered.

With a groan they made it across the threshold.

Claire turned to close the door behind them. "They're rolling down the window," she warned.

"Captain, can you come here?" the soldier asked gruffly.

Chapter 67

Paul turned and smiled nervously, conscious of his German uniform, now conspicuously missing the jacket. "Let me get the colonel in first," he told them. "He's had too much to drink."

The German eyed him suspiciously and an awkward moment passed. Finally, he waved his hand and said, "Yes, Captain, but please hurry."

Claire and Paul led Junot into the parlor. They stumbled forward, guiding him to the couch.

"Cover him up," Paul directed. "Just in case they come in."

He turned and started for the door.

"Be careful," Claire said. "And try to keep them out of the house."

He scampered down the steps and walked to the curb. He put his hands in his pocket, wiping off the blood, and leaned into the open car window.

"Yes?" he asked, noting the soldier's rank was lieutenant.

"Do you need any help, Captain?"

"No, we're fine. We just left a party. The colonel had a little too much fun, if you know what I mean."

"Who is the woman?"

Paul hesitated, searching for a response, and then said, "She's a friend of the colonel's."

The soldier smiled knowingly. "I understand," he responded. "Maybe the colonel shouldn't drink so much."

The soldier motioned the driver forward and the car slowly pulled away. Paul was so relieved he almost fell to the pavement. He ran up the steps and into the house and saw Junot lying on the couch, his eyes closed, his face a ghostly gray. He moved the jacket and saw that it was soaked with blood. "He's going to need a doctor," he announced anxiously.

"Give me the jacket," Claire directed. "Go change your clothes while I remove his. We have to get rid of the uniforms."

Paul returned a few minutes later dressed in his own clothes. Claire sat by Junot, who was covered with a blanket, holding a towel against the wound. She picked up his uniform, collected Paul's and rolled them into a ball. Then she tied them tightly with string and wrapped them with black cloth, tying them again.

"I'll throw these in the building's furnace," she said.

When she left, Paul moved the blanket, and then the towel. Blood oozed from the wound, which was on the left side, just below the ribcage. It was jagged, the surrounding skin discolored.

"How are you feeling, my friend?" he asked softly.

"My strength is slipping away."

A few moments later he heard the door close. Claire had returned.

"Did you burn them?" he asked.

"Yes," she replied. "No one saw me."

"Can you bring more towels?"

She returned with two towels and some tape. Paul took the largest and placed it against the wound, applying pressure, stemming the flow of blood, and secured it with tape. Claire took the smaller towel, which was damp, and wiped Junot's face.

She bit her lip, her face ashen. "I'll get the doctor," she offered.

"Is it safe?"

She motioned to the telephone. "We'll call," she said. "He can tell us what to do."

He wavered, but stood firm. "No," he warned her, "the telephone isn't safe."

"What about Father Nicolas? Can he help us?"

"Yes, he can, but not until tomorrow."

"We have to do something," she cried. "We can't wait until morning. He'll die."

"I'll be all right," Junot whispered. He grasped Claire's hand, holding it tightly. "Just stay with me."

"Paul, we have to do something. What about Alexander?"

"We can't reach him," he said with dismay.

"I can call the doctor from a public phone."

Junot still clung to her hand, but his grasp was weakening.

"It's past curfew. Too risky."

Before he could stop her she ran out the door and onto the deserted street beyond.

Chapter 68

Paul watched from the door as Claire disappeared around the corner. There was nothing he could do. He couldn't leave Junot or chase after her, putting everyone at risk. He paced the floor, looking at his watch, and waited. After thirty minutes passed, he sat beside Junot and removed the towel, checking his wound. The applied pressure was working; the bleeding had slowed. Junot's eyes were closed, his breathing irregular and labored.

Two hours later Claire returned with an elderly gentleman carrying a black leather bag. He seemed shaken, probably from being awakened so late at night and then eluding the German patrols.

"Claire! Thank God you're safe."

She kissed Paul lightly on the cheek. "I couldn't find the man who helped Rachel," she told him. "This is Doctor -"

"No names, please," the doctor whispered.

He went to the couch and knelt beside Junot. If he recognized the famous face he didn't show it. But then no one would expect the Resistance to help a Nazi collaborator. He probably assumed it was someone else.

"Will he be all right?" Claire asked.

"It's hard to say," the doctor replied, probing the wound. "How long was the knife?"

"I'm not sure," Paul said.

The doctor examined his patient for a minute before standing abruptly. "I'm going to have to operate," he informed them.

Thirty minutes later, he was ready. Junot lay sprawled on the dining room table, old bed linens beneath him. A small serving tray stood beside the table, containing the sterilized tools of his trade. The chandelier was positioned directly above his abdomen. The doctor gave Junot a needle, a sedative that rendered him unconscious. Then he studied the wound, the scalpel in his right hand. He looked up and, after realizing they were standing there watching him, he smiled politely. "It would be best if you waited in the other room," he said softly.

"Of course," Paul replied. "You're right. We shouldn't be here for this."

"I'll call you if I need you," he told them. "It will take hours rather than minutes. First I have to cleanse the wound to remove bacteria and debris, and then I'll have to enlarge it with a scalpel to assess interior damage. If repair to organs or damaged tissues is required, it'll be morning before I can assess his condition."

Paul led Claire into the parlor and sat beside her on the couch. Tears had streaked her makeup, her face was pale, her breathing shallow.

"He'll be all right," Paul said, although he had no confidence that what he said was true.

Claire sighed and looked away, but didn't reply. She closed her eyes, as if trying to will away the night and believe it was nothing more than a nightmare.

Paul watched her closely, surprised she was so upset. "The waiting is the hardest," he said, referring to the operation.

"It always is," she replied, her face etched with lines of worry.

Paul paced the floor and then stood at the window, watching the Seine in the moonlight. Paris was quiet at night during the occupation. The city was dying, little by little, just like Junot.

Claire sat on the couch, her legs tucked under her, and sipped a cup of coffee. Paul knew that she had seen enough death: Jacques, Sophie, Catherine, her parents, friends and cousins. Death was part of life; sorrow made happiness that much sweeter, pain balanced pleasure. But it never seemed that way when death and pain and sorrow dominated and overwhelmed, dictating every thought and deed.

"Do you remember when we were children?" Paul asked, turning away from the window. "We used to have so much fun. When did life get so hard? It was so simple."

"It got hard when the Germans came," she said softly. "And it gets harder every day."

"Our yesterdays offered so much more promise, dreams of the future, thoughts of perpetual happiness. And then before we even realized what was happening, it was all stolen."

"When I reflect on what was, I realize how innocent we all were," she commented. "We never understood the brutality mankind is capable of."

Paul was quiet for a moment, considering her statement. He then asked, "Are you ever going to tell me your secret?"

She looked at him, her eyes searching, but didn't reply.

"I promise not to reveal it."

Still she didn't speak.

"I think I know what it is," he said.

She looked annoyed, but replied, "All right, if you think you know, tell me."

He summoned the courage to speak, knowing she might be offended. "I think you have a lover," he said, trying not to sound accusing. "And I think that man is General Berg."

She started laughing, shaking her head. "General Berg?" she asked incredulously. "Paul, are you insane? He's a Nazi. How could you ever think that? You would make a horrible detective." She chuckled a moment more, watching him in disbelief.

Paul felt confused and hurt, wondering how two cousins who had shared their lives couldn't be honest with each other. He watched her reaction, waiting for a reply, wondering how he could have been so wrong.

"I do have a lover," she said finally. "And it's Julian Junot."

Paul stared at her, his mouth open but unable to speak. "Julian Junot?" he asked finally. "How is that possible?"

"Apparently, it's quite simple," she replied, "because you were obviously fooled."

***

It was almost 4 a.m. when the doctor joined them in the parlor. His face was drawn; he was tired. He slumped into a chair and sighed.

"Will he be all right?" Claire asked.

The doctor shrugged. "It's hard to say," he replied. "I'll know more in a day or so. For now, he needs to rest."

"Should we move him into a bedroom?" Paul asked.

"Yes, we should," the doctor replied. "He'll be much more comfortable. He should sleep another five or six hours."

"Would you like to use a guest room?" Claire asked.

"Please do," Paul added. "You can't leave now anyway. Why not sleep a few hours?"

The doctor shrugged and said, "That may be a good idea. Then I can check on the patient before I leave. Assuming he's still alive."

Chapter 69

"You look like good Catholics to me," Rachel said.

Aaron and Freyde Roth stood before her, a married couple in their fifties. He wore a brown suit, white shirt and dark brown tie, his gray hair combed back from the forehead. Her black dress and pearl earrings were simple, yet stylish, her black hair long and straight, resting on her shoulders. Nothing about their appearance would lead anyone to suspect their heritage.

"Don't be nervous," Rachel continued. "This will be easy. Sit near the back of the church, and do what everyone else does, just as you practiced. Kneel when they kneel, stand when they stand. Mumble softly to yourself, as if you're praying, and no one will suspect anything. If Germans come in, they're only attending the service, just as you are. Don't be afraid."

Meurice watched Rachel with admiration as she supervised the Roth's escape, her demeanor calming both him and them. "And when the Mass ends, exit the church and walk onto the street, merging with the people of Paris," he added.

"This is important," Rachel said. She made the sign of the cross. "Remember, Catholics do that often."

Meurice mentioned the holy water at the church entrance, and Rachel described its use. "Just dab your fingers into the water, don't splash. Then make the sign of the cross."

The Roths were shaken; their faces showed their nervousness. They looked at each other, as if wondering if they could proceed, but knowing they had to. "Is there anything else?" Aaron Roth asked.

"Communion is just like I told you," Rachel said. "The priest will place a slender wafer in your mouth. Again, just do as the others."

They were obviously uncomfortable. But before they could voice their concerns, Meurice looked at his watch and nudged Mr. Roth's elbow.

"Come," he said. "It's time."

Rachel led them up the vertical ladder from the cavern, Meurice just behind them. They climbed through the crypt, smoothing their clothes as they stood in the church basement. Rachel brought them to the back of the church, Aaron Roth holding his wife's hand tightly.

Meurice waited near the stairs that led to the crypts. Rachel hid in the aisle beside the nave, invisible to those in attendance. During the weekdays only a few parishioners appeared, rarely more than twenty, but she didn't know who, if any, attended Mass daily. If there were any that devout, they would know that the Roths had never been there before, and that might arouse suspicion. She was nervous, knowing this was new, and that she would have to identify the risks and adjust her plan accordingly.

The Roths moved to the back of the church, stood in the entrance a moment as Rachel had directed, and then dipped their hands in the holy water and made the sign of the cross. They proceeded to a row of seats near the back, genuflected and again made the sign of the cross, and sat down by the aisle. Given the many rows of seats, it was not likely anyone would be near them.

There were about twenty-five people attending mass, scattered throughout the church, but most sat close to the alter. Promptly at 6 a.m., Father Nicolas emerged from a side door and walked to the pulpit. He eyed those attending, knowing that today would be different from all others. He was just about to commence the service when the carved wooden doors creaked on their brass strap hinges. He paused, waiting for the late arrival, and then looked on, a bit shaken.

Three Germans entered the church. Two flanked the entrance, standing respectfully at the rear of the church. The third walked towards the pews, the sound of his leather boots echoing on the floor. He was no stranger to the priest, or to the parishioners. It was General Berg. He nodded to Father Nicolas, looking embarrassed that he was late, and walked down the center aisle. He stopped just in front of the Roths, genuflected and made the sign of the cross. He turned and nodded to them, smiled politely, and sat in the seat in front of them.

Rachel watched from the darkened aisle, her heart thumping wildly. She knew Berg didn't know them, and that they weren't in danger, but she was still afraid. It wasn't worth the risk. Why had she let Meurice convince her? The lives of two people were in danger.

The priest nodded to the General and then to those at the door. He fingered the Bible on the lectern, and opened it to the first of several pages he had marked. He looked up, about to start his sermon, when again the doors creaked on their hinges.

With the second interruption in as many minutes, those attending the Mass turned to see the distraction. An elderly woman in the first row looked at the Roths curiously, studying them more closely than the German general, whom she had seen at Mass before. A middle-aged man two rows away looked also. Two other attendees – one who clutched his own Bible and looked like a young theology student and another who appeared to be a frumpy middle-aged housewife – also turned to observe the disturbance. Since all in the church had seen each other at daily mass before, they each glanced at the Roths before looking to the door.

As if his suspicions were also aroused, General Berg turned, looking at the couple curiously, his face displaying a sudden wariness. But then he shifted his gaze from the Roths' nervous faces to the church entrance.

Chapter 70

Col. Kruger entered the church, his gaze scanning those in attendance. He saw the Roths, uncomfortable and shifting nervously, and Berg sitting in front of them. Those who had been focused on the Roths shifted their attention to the newcomer. General Berg might be an occasional guest at morning Mass, but no one knew this intruder.

Kruger nodded, looking embarrassed, and proceeded to the pews. When he reached General Berg, he whispered a greeting and sat in front of him. He did not genuflect, nor did he make the sign of the cross.

General Berg seemed to forgot the Roths, even if the others did not. He shrugged, apparently questioning Kruger's message, eyed Father Nicolas apologetically, and then leaned forward for clarification.

Father Nicolas wisely began the service, taking advantage of the distraction, and the congregation turned to face him. He pretended not to notice the two German officers trying to communicate, talking loudly to discourage them.

The worshippers frowned at the colonel's mysterious and inappropriate behavior, and an aura of tensions gripped the congregation. Rachel watched from the shadows, wondering why the colonel was there. Did he come to get Berg? Did a military matter demand his attention? Or was he there for the Roths?

Father Nicolas continued the sermon. The churchgoers pretended to listen, stealing furtive glances towards the rear of the church, their gaze alternating between the Germans and the Roths. The Jewish couple sat erect, confused and afraid, daring not to move. Two German soldiers stood behind them, a general and colonel sat in front of them. They were trapped. Father Nicolas continued the service, emphasizing a specific word, or using dramatic gestures. The parishioners kneeled, the Germans and the Roths mimicked them, and the Mass continued.

Col Kruger turn and whispered to Berg again, waiting for a lull in the service when Father Nicolas paused to turn the pages in his Bible. An elderly gentleman with wire-rimmed spectacles cast him an angry stare, and Kruger nodded, aware he was being disrespectful. His inappropriate behavior was confirmed by General Berg's glare.

Ten minutes into the service, Kruger again turned and spoke to General Berg. He motioned towards the entrance, indicating that they should leave. His solemn expression implied it was important. Berg sighed and shook his head, appearing angry. He left his seat, genuflected and made the sign of the cross, and exited the church, following Kruger. The two soldiers left immediately behind them.

Rachel moved stealthily from the side corridor, staying in the shadows of the far wall, avoiding the peripheral view of the congregation. She tip-toed to the entrance, entered the vestibule, and peeked through the outer door.

She saw a German staff car, two small Nazi flags mounted at each end of the front bumper, sat by the curb. The two German soldiers stood beside it, while Kruger and Berg stood on the front steps, engaged in an animated discussion. As Rachel watched anxiously, they retreated to the sedan. Berg seemed annoyed, his face showing disgust. They climbed into the rear of the vehicle and then the car moved slowly down the street towards the Seine, leaving the church behind.

She sighed with relief and went back inside. She returned to the shadows, but managed to attract the Roths' attention. Using hand motions, she assured them the Germans had gone, and that they should follow the original plan and quietly exit when the Mass was completed. From there, they must go to their prepared destination.

The good priest continued his sermon, moving a bit faster than he normally would. He knew it was critical to get the Roths on their way. He had no way of knowing what the colonel had whispered to the general, or if it involved his church. They might be back. Twenty minutes later he gave communion and proceeded to the concluding prayers, seven or eight minutes shorter than normal. When the Mass ended, the congregation departed and, as the Roths walked to the exit, Mr. Roth felt someone tap him on the shoulder. He turned to find the elderly gentleman with the wire-rimmed spectacles who had given Col. Kruger the icy stare. Father Nicolas stood behind him, an anxious look on his face.

The Roths exchanged nervous glances.

"Welcome to our church," the man said softly. "If there is anything you need, anything at all, we will help you. And if your friends need help, we're glad to assist."

The middle-aged housewife standing behind him said, "I'm pleased that you joined us for worship. During the week, the same people normally attend this service. We'll make sure that you, or anyone else who might attend, are welcomed."

"Thank you," said Mr. Roth. "Thank you all." His wife nodded and smiled weakly.

"We're honored to have you with us," said the theology student. "And any of your friends."

The congregation guided them to the door, where Father Nicolas quietly wished them well. They left the church, nodded discreetly to the parishioners who had welcomed them, and made their way down the street, descending down the steps at the closest Metro station.

When all the parishioners had gone, Father Nicolas moved to the back of the church, down the darkened side corridor. He found Rachel waiting for him, hiding by the steps that led to the crypts.

"This will work," he said proudly. "There are good people in this congregation."

Chapter 71

The doctor emerged from the guest room just after 9 a.m., finding Paul and Claire in the kitchen making coffee. They went into Claire's bedroom where Junot lay peacefully, his eyes closed, his breathing regular. His abdomen was wrapped in gauze, a trail of blood on the cloth forming a vertical line just beneath his ribs.

"How is he, Doctor?" Claire asked anxiously.

"He's doing well," the physician said, checking Junot's vital signs. "Better than I expected."

"Is he hurt badly?" she asked.

"It could have been worse. He could have bled to death. I was able to repair the internal damage. I just want to have a look at the incision." He peeled back the gauze to inspect the four-inch sutured line. The skin around it was discolored and bruised, and the wound still seeped a bit of blood. "There's no sign of infection," he said, replacing the bandage and taping it to Junot's side.

He reached into his black bag and withdrew two vials of pills. "Give him a pill from each bottle every four hours," he directed. "One is for infection; the other is for pain. Let him rest another six hours or so before he tries to get out of bed."

"How can we ever thank you, Doctor?" Claire asked as she withdrew some bills from her handbag.

He held up his hand, shaking his head, and said, "No thanks are needed." He pointed to a pile of bloody towels in the corner of the room. "You had best get rid of those. I'll be back at eight tomorrow morning."

Once the doctor left, Claire broke down weeping. "I can't let anything happen to him," she sobbed.

Paul held her tenderly, surprised by her reaction. She was normally so strong, with walls around her emotions, rarely letting anyone in. "Don't worry," he promised. "Nothing will."

At noon Paul called Jacqueline Junot. Bernard, Junot's butler and personal assistant, answered the telephone.

"Mrs. Junot is away for a few days," he said.

"Do you know when she'll be back?"

"Probably not until the end of the week," he answered. "Why? Is something wrong?"

"No," Paul said, trying to be casual. "I just wanted her to know that Julian is at my house. He's rather ill. The flu, I believe. Anyway, the doctor was just here. He left a bottle of pills and told him to get some rest."

"Should I come pick him up?"

"No, he's sleeping now," Paul said. "Suppose I have him call you in a few hours?"

"That would be fine," Bernard answered. "Good-bye."

Junot awoke at 2 p.m. Claire was sitting beside him when his eyelids fluttered open. He gazed at the ceiling, unfamiliar with his surroundings and then gazed around the room.

"You're at Paul's house," she said as she gently touched his arm. "Everything is all right. Do you remember what happened?"

"Yes," he said faintly, as if rolling the events through his mind like a motion picture. "It wasn't good."

Then he paused, grimacing and looked at her. "But I'm glad I'm with you."

She smiled. "I'll get you some water," she told him.

"You'll have to call Bernard and explain your absence," Paul said. "I told him you had the flu and were staying here. He said Jacqueline was away until the end of the week."

"I'll call him later," he replied. "The medicine has me groggy."

Claire returned with a glass of water, propped him up and gave him a drink. He took several sips and then lay back down.

"How are you feeling?" Paul asked.

"Actually, I'm in quite a bit of pain."

"The doctor left some pills," Claire said. "Let me give them to you. One is for pain and one is for infection. He'll be back tomorrow morning to examine you."

Junot swallowed the pills, his face pale, his lips dry and swollen.

"What will you tell Bernard?" Claire asked.

"I'll say I'm going to Calais for a week to arrange the merger of a shipping firm. I'll also have to call my secretary. She'll wonder where I am."

"The doctor said the next few days are crucial," Paul told him. "You need to rest as much as possible."

Claire put a damp cloth on his head. "Don't worry," she whispered. "I'll take care of you."

Chapter 72

The doctor arrived the following morning, quickly crossing the threshold when Claire opened the door. "How is our patient?" he asked. He walked towards the bedroom, giving no indication he knew the identity of the man he had operated on. But everyone in Paris knew Julian Junot.

"He's been resting quietly," Claire replied.

"Good," the physician said. He moved to the bed. "He's awake."

"Yes," Junot said softly, his face pale and drawn. "I want to thank you for saving my life."

"No need," the doctor said. He pulled away the sheet and began to remove the gauze, exposing the wound. "I am a doctor. I repair broken bodies." He looked at Junot directly. "And I ask no questions."

"I'm very grateful," Junot told him. "If there is anything I can do for you, anything at all, please ask."

"I'll keep that in mind," he said, looking at the wound. "The incision looks good. Are you taking the medicine?"

"Yes, I've been giving it to him every four hours," Claire responded.

"Who will monitor him?" the doctor asked. "It's Monday morning. I assume you both work. He can't be left alone."

"I'll watch him," Claire said.

"See that he takes the medicine. It's important, especially to fight infection." The doctor glanced at his watch, as if arranging his day. "Also, you should change the bandage this evening. I'll leave some gauze and solution to clean the wound."

"Is there anything else?" Claire asked.

"No," he said. "Just make sure he rests. He can start to eat today – soup, juice, and some bread. I'll return Wednesday morning at eight. If all is well, we'll no longer have to see each other."

"Do you expect a full recovery?" Paul asked.

"I think so," the doctor said as he started for the door. "But it will be several weeks before he feels normal again." He nodded his goodbyes and exited to the *Rue de Poissy*.

"I have to get to the bank," Paul said after the doctor had left. "Are you sure you'll be all right?"

"Yes," she said. "I already phoned the store and told them I wouldn't be in. I'll attend to Julian."

"Call me if there are any problems."

* * *

Paul avoided calling Claire or coming home for lunch. He didn't want to deviate from his normal routine or make Claire think he was uncomfortable leaving her alone with Junot. But he couldn't help worrying. As the day wore on, he got more anxious, and, by 2 p.m., he decided to leave the bank. There was nothing pressing, no transactions that needed his attention, and since he occasionally left early to compensate for the nights he worked late, he thought it would be all right. He rose from his desk, yawned and stretched, and started down the corridor to Oskar Bouchard's office. As he walked toward the exit, he overheard people talking. He paused and listened.

"We'll wait one more week," Bouchard was saying. "Then we'll contact the Gestapo. They will be very interested in the information we have to offer."

"How reliable is the source?" a second man asked. It was a voice Paul didn't recognize.

"The most powerful man in Paris told me," Bouchard answered.

Paul hid in the shadows, anxious for information, but afraid to be caught eavesdropping. He barely breathed, he was so afraid of making noise. He listened intently.

"The most powerful man in Paris?" the unknown voice asked. "Julian Junot told you?"

Oskar Bouchard laughed. "No, you idiot," he said. "Julian Junot is a puppet. He has no power at all."

"Then who is the most powerful man in Paris?"

"Alain Dominique."

Chapter 73

Paul entered the townhouse just before 3 p.m. and found Claire waiting in the parlor, reading the newspaper.

"Quiet," she whispered. "Julian is sleeping."

"How is he?"

She shrugged. "I'm not sure," she said warily. "The pills make him very tired."

"That's probably good. He needs rest. It'll help him regain his strength."

"How was your day at the bank?" she asked, watching him closely.

"Unusual, to say the least."

"What happened?"

He quickly recounted the conversation between Oskar Bouchard and the unknown visitor. She listened attentively, letting him finish before she asked any questions.

"Could they be turning someone in to the Gestapo?" she wondered. "Or do they have information to offer?"

"I suspect someone is not cooperating with them," Paul said. "But I'm not sure with what."

"What about Dominique?"

"I don't know why anyone thinks he's the most powerful man in Paris, especially given his occupation. He's a journalist."

"But he has a way of appearing wherever there's trouble," she observed. "Could that be what they were talking about?"

"Maybe," he said. "He was at the train station when Julian was stabbed. And I've seen him at the bank several times." He paused, thinking of other times their paths had crossed. "Or maybe it's something else, something we don't know or understand."

"Like what?"

"Maybe his cover is that of a journalist, but his real role is much different."

Junot awoke an hour later. His face was drawn and his eyes glassy, signs of both weakness and the narcotics he was taking. But color had returned to his face and a slight smile showed his condition was improving.

"How are you today?" Paul asked.

"Much better," he replied. "I'm growing stronger by the minute. But I do apologize for being such a burden to you."

Paul smiled. "You're no burden," he said. "I only wished I could have stopped the stabbing."

"I don't think anyone could have. I suppose Brinkman got away."

"Yes, he did. I'm not sure what tipped someone off. But I'll find out."

Junot turned away, glancing out the bedroom window. There was a small courtyard behind the building, but only the trees were visible from the bed. He studied the twisted branch of a chestnut tree.

"What can I get you?" Claire asked, seeing him so moody and pensive. "Some soup, perhaps?"

"Thank you, soup would be nice," he said softly.

When Claire went to the kitchen, Junot turned to Paul and asked, "Is everything else going smoothly?"

"Yes," Paul replied. "The operation at the church is going well. Rachel sees to that, although she did have a scare recently. Gen. Berg appeared at the church service as she was evacuating a Jewish couple. But it worked to our advantage. We learned that the daily parishioners will support us."

"Are there any problems?"

Paul paused, hesitant to raise the issue, but said, "Funding, as always."

Junot frowned. "As soon as I'm able," he promised, "I'll get more money."

"We can last another week or so," Paul said. "But we're starting to run out of food."

"Is there anything else?"

"Yes, there is. Oskar Bouchard," Paul said. "What do you know about him?"

"The new bank president?"

"Yes."

Junot considered the name for a moment. "Not too much," he replied. "Someone owed him something. That's how he ended up at the bank."

"Could he be involved with the Gestapo?"

"Sure, anyone could."

Paul hesitated. He couldn't bring himself to ask about Alain Dominique. It would pry into his personal life. But then, he probably didn't know his wife was having an affair with Dominique.

* * *

Later that evening, Paul described his conversation with Junot to Claire. "But I couldn't ask him about Dominique," he said. "Not with what is going on between him and Jacqueline."

Claire was quiet. She was in no position to comment. She was sleeping with Jacqueline's husband.

"Bouchard said Dominique was the most powerful man in Paris?" she asked.

"Yes, but how will we ever find out what he meant?"

"There is one man who will know."

"Who?"

"Alexander."

Chapter 74

Paul left a message with Pablo requesting a meeting with Alexander, but didn't provide a reason. A day passed with no reply, and then two days later he was instructed to meet with Louis, the bookseller.

Paul and Claire walked to the Seine, finding Louis on the *Quai de la Turnelle*. The bookseller's cabinets were open, displaying his wares, and his floppy-eared beagle lay on the pavement at his feet. As Louis and Claire chatted amicably, discussing the purchase of some books for her shop, Paul paged through a volume about East African birds, beautifully illustrated with watercolors.

"You might enjoy this one," Louis said casually as he handed Paul a book from under the table. "Take a minute to browse through it."

It was about the early exploration of Africa and, as Paul opened it and studied the title page, he saw a handwritten note tucked between the pages. He furtively removed it and slipped it into his pocket. "Are you ready, Claire?" he asked.

She stopped in mid-sentence and eyed him strangely. "No, I'm not," she said, and returned to her discussion with Louis.

Knowing the Resistance provided little notice in regard to meetings, and not wanting to chance reading the note with so many people nearby, Paul anxiously tugged at her arm. "Come on, Claire," he said impatiently. "We can return tomorrow."

"Paul, will you relax," she scolded. "I'm talking to Louis."

The bookseller winked at Paul and grinned, well aware of his dilemma. "Suppose I hold these books for you," he said to Claire. He moved six leather volumes from his display and put them under the table. "You can think about it and return tomorrow."

"All right," she replied, rolling her eyes. She looked at Paul sternly and said, "I guess we have to go."

"I'll see you tomorrow," Louis assured her with a smile. "The books will be waiting."

Paul nodded and led Claire away.

"What is wrong with you?" she asked. "Couldn't you see I was negotiating with Louis?"

"I was given a message," he explained. "It was in the book he handed me."

She stopped and looked at him. "Then why didn't you say something?" she wondered aloud.

"I couldn't. There were too many people around."

"Read it," she urged.

Paul glanced around and, when satisfied he wasn't being observed, he removed the note from his pocket. It read, "Be at the emergency room of the Paris General Hospital at 4:15."

Paul handed the note to Claire and glanced at his watch which read 3:45. The hospital was ten blocks away.

"You had better hurry," she said as she returned the message. "I'll go to your house and wait for you there."

They parted, and he turned toward the hospital.

"Paul," she called when he was a few feet away.

"Yes?"

"Be careful.

* * *

A man met Paul at the door to the Paris General Hospital emergency room. Although he was dressed like a doctor, wearing a long white lab coat, a stethoscope dangling from his neck and a pair of black horn-rimmed glasses, Paul recognized him as Alexander. "Come this way, please," Alexander requested as he led him away from the waiting room.

They walked down an empty corridor and turned into a room on the left. It was an unoccupied patient's room.

"Take your shirt off and lie on the bed," Alexander said softly.

Paul did as directed.

Alexander sat on a stool beside the bed, his back to the door. He held the stethoscope to Paul's chest, acting as if an examination was in progress.

"What is it that you need?" he asked softly.

"Information," Paul replied.

"Go on."

"Alain Dominique," Paul said.

"*Abwehr*," Alexander said with no hesitation.

"What?"

"*Abwehr*," he repeated. "It's the Nazi intelligence agency. His cover is a journalist. He's extremely dangerous. Be very, very careful."

"I will," Paul said, surprised by the revelation. "How about Oskar Bouchard?"

"I can't place him."

"The new president of the *Banque de Paris*."

"Oh, yes. He's a Gestapo informant. No one of any importance; he doesn't have any power. Any more questions?"

"No," Paul said. "That's it."

"Be wary of Dominique," he clarified. "He's caused more than one man's death."

"I will," Paul promised. He thought of different places where he had seen Dominique, some accidental while others seemed planned, as if he knew Paul would be there. "He seems to be everywhere I am."

"Then you need to determine why," Alexander advised. "He either suspects something, or you share the same objective. Either explanation is dangerous. Think about it. We almost lost the Fox. That should be warning enough."

Paul was quiet for a moment, reflecting. It was more than a coincidence that Dominique was at the train station. But how did he know they would be there? Alexander was right. It had almost cost Junot his life.

Alexander looked behind him, listening intently to ensure no one approached. "Anything else?" he asked.

"I want to kill Kruger."

"I told you many times that you may kill no one. It would risk the operation and expose the Fox. And it just isn't worth it." He saw the disappointment cross Paul's face and he looked at him with compassion. "I shouldn't do this," he added, "but I will."

Paul leaned forward, listening closely.

"It's not what you think," Alexander said softly. "Kruger only obeys orders, which is still no excuse, but that's what happened."

Paul looked at him strangely. "No, it is what I think," he said curtly. "I saw it. So I don't understand what you're saying."

Alexander glanced at the door, ensuring it was closed. He then looked around the room and, when satisfied it was safe, he continued.

"Sometimes a fisherman is really a general."

Chapter 75

Whenever Rachel had a few stolen moments to herself, she usually thought of her family, wondering how they were, and what their life was like on the farm near Giverny. She missed them terribly, and realized that little Stanislaw was growing up, enjoying his childhood without her. But she risked her life to protect and preserve what they once had, hoping to have it again. And she knew that someday her family would understand, appreciating all she did for them. But for now, the cavern had become her life; the refugees were her family. She started each day by ensuring breakfast was prepared for the three hundred inhabitants. Then she supervised food deliveries, document creation, clothing manufacturing and modifications, barbers, waste removal, and the many chores assigned to members of their colony.

A major part of Rachel's day involved the selection process: this meant which Jews remained in Paris with new identities, who went to rural areas, and who were escorted out of France, seeking refuge in Switzerland or Spain, with a select few destined for England. Some were given the option of joining the Resistance movement, and a surprising number did. Most of those stayed in Paris, while the remainder worked the rural routes that others took to safety and freedom.

Meurice had become her loyal lieutenant, their original roles reversed. The pupil had learned from the teacher and then had become the master. She taught him how to run the colony, the logistics involved in sustaining it, risks involved in maintaining it, and the rewards reaped by ensuring hundreds of Jews avoided captivity. He waived his turn to escape, allowing a middle-aged tailor go in his place. When his turn came up again, he declined and an elderly scholar of the Torah went instead. It was soon obvious to all who knew him that he wouldn't be leaving the catacombs – not as long as Rachel was there.

Just after he declined his second planned departure, he and Rachel were sitting on a bench in a secluded area of the cavern. They often met there at night, away from the prying eyes of the colony, and discussed their day, their yesterdays, and their tomorrows.

"That's the second time you missed your opportunity," Rachel said coyly. "Why are you staying?"

He was quiet for a moment, then replied, "I like helping others."

She smiled. "You can help others in many different ways," she told him. "Even from Switzerland, where you would be safe."

"Perhaps," he said evasively. "But I like it here."

"This dark, dingy cave is hard to call home," she said. "Sunlight is precious; we risk our lives to enjoy it, and it's hard to get fresh air. Why do you like it here so much?"

"This is my home."

She reached over and grasped his hand.

He was surprised, not expecting her to be so bold, but he held her hand in his.

"What happened to the flirt I first met?" she asked.

He paused nervously. "You are different," he replied.

"How?"

"I can't explain it."

She turned and kissed him. He was startled at first but then responded, pulling her closer, caressing her back and shoulders. He planted tiny, tender kisses on her face and neck and ears before returning to her mouth.

It was Rachel's first kiss. And it couldn't have been better.

She awoke the next morning and smiled. Meurice lay beside her, partially clothed, sleeping soundly. She covered her nakedness with the sheet, wrapping it around her and pulling it up to her neck. Then she drifted off to sleep again.

Meurice woke her an hour later. He had brought breakfast, two pastries and some juice. "How did you sleep?" he asked.

She shyly dressed, self-conscious of his gaze. "Quiet!" she hissed. "I don't want the others to hear."

He smiled. Although walls defined the tiny space that Rachel had as her own, it was difficult to keep secrets in a close-knit community where all services were shared.

She could imagine the woman in the neighboring space listening to the sounds of their lovemaking and then telling her neighbor who told her neighbor. She suspected that by the time she and Meurice had fallen asleep, all three hundred citizens of the cavern knew they were lovers.

After a hasty breakfast, Meurice and Rachel escorted two young brothers, Raymond and Henri, destined to become Resistance members, up the ascending corridor to the flower shop on *Rue Monge*. They paused just before climbing the ladder up to the outbuilding that led to their escape. Rachel and Meurice shook their hands and wished them luck.

"We can't thank you enough," Raymond said to Rachel. "You're the little general of the catacombs".

She smiled, pleased with the compliment. "Are you sure you understand everything and have memorized your route?" she asked, always cautious.

When they nodded, she climbed the ladder and peeked from the outbuilding to ensure they could leave without attracting attention. They then departed, walking the streets of Paris, merging with passing pedestrians, taking a taxi or riding the Metro, vanishing into the metropolis. The brothers were destined for Cessy, close to the Swiss border, where they would help Jews, Allied airmen, and hunted Resistance members escape.

Rachel and Meurice made that journey several times during the day, usually escorting families at dusk, when they were less likely to be seen. They also used the church, having Jews attend mass and then filter out with the congregation, while a few others left the church at various times during the day. Even when General Berg attended, it was clear he was there to worship, and never seemed to suspect that some in the congregation were escaping from Nazis. Rachel and Meurice cautiously shuffled days and times of departures so no one became suspicious. As they knew only too well, not all Frenchman were trustworthy.

They used the escape route via the cemetery in Montparnasse sparingly, usually only once or twice each day. Although it effectively camouflaged the escape, the tunnel exit, hidden in a crypt, was some distance from the cavern where the refugees were housed. It was effective, few would doubt visitors emerging from a cemetery and fewer would note when they had entered or how long they had been there. It was the distance that minimized its use.

Meurice eventually found a more efficient way to use the cemetery route, often selecting large groups of eight to ten people but then releasing them in sets of two or three spread over several hours. Although this procedure meant he was often gone for much of the day, it allowed the operation to move refugees almost as quickly as they could issue them new identities and plan their escape routes. And the exit in the *Montparnasse* tomb was safe, hidden by a false wall. If someone entered from outside the crypt it appeared as if the corridor had been blocked with stone. But a small hole was made at the base, and effectively camouflaged, so the exit could not be viewed by intruders. Then they slid a boulder aside to access the exit.

And so the Resistance workers adopted these practices as their daily routines. Meurice routed escapees to Montparnasse; Rachel took them through the flower store. Others left via the church. Although someone left the compound every day, there were few days when large numbers escaped. Still, they were capable of safely evacuating up to one hundred Jews per week.

At night, those in the colony managed to entertain themselves. They told stories, held religious services, celebrated birthdays and anniversaries, read books and played music. While waiting for their escapes, they formed friendships, forged business relationships and enhanced their lives The entire operation was running so smoothly that no one thought anything could go wrong.

Chapter 76

The elderly man walked his dog through the cemetery almost every day. He liked to look at the names engraved on the tombstones and imagine what the people had been like when they were alive. It was his normal routine, for he was a pensioner with little else to do and his basset hound was his favorite companion.

He was far off the road, deep into the cemetery, studying the names on a mausoleum that contained many generations of an entire family. As he peered through his thick glasses, reading the family tree, he saw two men appear to walk directly out of an adjacent tomb. The stone wall of the crypt, which was always sealed, seemed to float open on hinges. Facing away from the street, the tomb was nondescript, and rarely attracted his attention since it was in a state of disrepair and seemed abandoned. Even the names chiseled in the marble could barely be read, and no one had been added in almost a hundred years.

He wondered if he was imagining things. Could the two men be caretakers? They might have been cleaning the crypt, taking care of the grounds. Maybe he had just never noticed them before. The men were about forty, their hair black, one slender and one stocky, and he noticed that they glanced furtively in all directions before walking to the end of the cemetery and standing by a marble marker, perhaps only pretending to honor the dead.

The basset hound tugged on the leash, eager to explore new territory, trying to lead his master forward. The man walked a few steps farther, now hidden from the two men. He peeked around the corner of the mausoleum, ensured they didn't see him, and watched the old tomb.

The men continued to stand there, hands folded and heads bowed, appearing to reminisce or utter short prayers, but stealing glances at both the street ahead of them and the cemetery behind them. When ten minutes had passed and they still remained, the old man assumed that nothing was amiss and his failing eyesight had gotten the best of him, or that his mind was playing tricks as it so often seemed to do.

It was then that he saw the front of the tomb swung open again, as if on hinges, and two women emerged. They were dressed in simple green and blue frocks, one with brown hair in a bun, the other with black hair that hung to her shoulder. They waited at the tomb, and a minute later three children appeared, two boys and a girl ranging in age from five or six to fifteen. They moved quickly to where the men stood, and the entire group walked out of the cemetery and onto the street beyond. They walked a half block down the street to the Metro, then descended the steps to the train below.

The man led his dog to the tomb where the people appeared to have exited, and he pushed on the stone door. It did not move. He pushed again, more forcefully, but nothing happened. He examined the door and the rest of the crypt, studying the weathered marble, but noticed nothing amiss. But then he saw scrapes on the floor, as if the stone had swung in a small arc, marking the base as it travelled. He examined the area closely, but could find no more clues.

Intrigued by the mystery he had discovered, he led his dog out of the cemetery, letting him stop to sniff the corner of a tombstone near the street. When he reached the entrance, he paused, not sure if anything should be done about the people that seemed to walk out of the crypt. He didn't want anyone to think he was crazy. But then he noticed a French policeman standing by the corner. After considering the matter for a moment, he walked over to him.

"*Monsieur*," he said, tapping him on the shoulder. "Can I show you something?"

Chapter 77

Paul's mind was flooded with memories: the fisherman standing in his boat near Giverny, nodding to Kruger, issuing orders, Kruger doing exactly as he was told. Now he clearly understood. According to Alexander, the fisherman was a general. His mind wandered through conversations and meetings, to the dinner when he first arrived in Paris. Gen. Berg, who was Kruger's superior, had said that chess, his granddaughters, and fishing were his greatest passions. Paul remembered the boat near Giverny, the sunlight reflecting off the spectacles, the broad hat that covered most of the face, the frame, tall and slender and erect, the motions to Kruger, the authoritative direction. And then he knew. Berg had ordered the deaths of Catherine and Sophie.

He had to kill him, but he didn't know how. It had to look like an accident or a natural death, like what he had planned for Kruger, or the entire operation built by Claire and Junot would be at risk. Even though blinded by rage, he forced himself to think logically and to consider the Jews. He couldn't tell Junot or Claire, or Alexander or Durant, because they would try to stop him. They wouldn't let him do it. They would reason with him; tell him it wasn't worth it. But he knew what he had to do, and, for him, there was no alternative.

"It's for the rats," Paul said to the druggist, after he had asked for a vial of cyanide. It was the same story he told a different druggist when he got the poison for Kruger.

An elderly man with a small shop on the *Rue Saint-Victor*, Paul suspected the druggist knew exactly what he wanted cyanide for. But the man seemed to decide it was not his business and did not press the issue.

"You have to be very careful with it," the druggist said. "As I'm sure you're aware. One vial could kill a human within ten minutes, after an agony of contortions and death throes. So you'll only need a few drops for rats."

"Of course," Paul said. "I'll scatter it on some food in the alley."

"It's also effective when mixed in wine or whiskey," the druggist said softly. "Should the rat be inclined to drink it."

Chapter 78

Paul Moreau sat in his Parisian apartment, listening to Chopin's *Prelude in E-minor*. He was writing in a notebook, focused on the architectural floor plan sketched on the page, making notes in the margin. The drawing depicted the third floor of Junot's townhouse – the study, an adjoining parlor, a bath and Junot's private office on one side, and two spare bedrooms and another bath on the opposite side. General Berg occupied the corner bedroom, the larger of the two.

Getting into the townhouse would be easy. He could wait until Junot was gone and tell Bernard he wanted to borrow a book from the library, leaving a note to explain its absence. Junot lent books all the time and Paul was trusted by all in the household. Entering Berg's bedroom and getting him to ingest the poison would be far more difficult. There had to be an easier way.

Eventually the solution came to him, and it was much simpler than he thought. He didn't need to force entry or take unnecessary risks. He walked to a small wine rack beside the kitchen cabinets. It housed fifteen or twenty bottles, some common, others not. He located a rare bottle of Sauternes, selected both for its exclusivity and the bulbous cork that sealed it. He examined it closely, ensuring it met his needs, before using a single-edged razor to carefully slice the foil wrapping the cork, and then delicately removed it, ensuring it didn't tear. He laid the foil on the table and grasped the cork, rotating it slowly, and eased it from the bottle. Delicately fingering the vial of cyanide, he sprinkled the poison into the wine. After re-inserting the cork, he wrapped the foil around the neck and glued it into place. He examined the bottle closely and was satisfied no one could tell it had been tampered with. Then he got a small piece of paper and wrote the following note: "Enjoy. Junot."

He taped the note to the bottle and put it in his briefcase. Then he walked out.

Chapter 79

Julian Junot healed quickly, the knife wound and subsequent operation leaving a scar but no permanent damage. He remained at Paul's for over a week, as did Claire, and they reveled in the domestic bliss that they rarely had the opportunity to enjoy. When Junot returned home, he spent another week minimizing his movements, and then resumed a full work schedule, running his businesses, appearing to comply with the wishes of his Nazi masters, and funding and overseeing the rescue operation for the Jews.

His relationship with Claire was far less clandestine than it had been. After almost losing his life, it no longer seemed so important to be secretive. He knew his marriage with Jacqueline was over; he knew about her affair with Alain Dominique. And now he often thought about how fruitless and senseless the whole charade was.

He met Claire at *Le Stella*, a restaurant in the 16th arrondissement. It was one of his favorite eateries, although not as private as others. It was frequented by the Parisian elite, all of whom knew who he was, but he didn't care. He wanted to be with Claire. And if the whole world knew that, it didn't matter to him.

They ordered wine from Bordeaux, onion soup, and steak tartar, a veritable feast in a city where most treasured their ration cards, even though they offered only enough food to survive. Just the aroma from the steak made the mouth water, as did the trays of food carried by the waiters, filled with chicken and fish and meat and vegetables.

"You're quiet this evening," Junot observed.

She was subdued, pensive; the glow that normally lit her face was dimmed.

"Julian, I need more," she said softly.

He knew what she meant, but he was surprised that she said it. He was quiet, watching her, letting her talk, his eyes trained on hers.

"I can't keep doing this," she continued. "I love you. You know that. But I can't be your mistress. It's not fair to me or you. And it's not fair to Jacqueline."

"Jacqueline is no angel."

"That's not the point. It's about me. I can't deal with the guilt. And I can't continue hiding, keeping everything about us a secret."

It was nothing he hadn't already considered. So why was he so surprised to hear her say it? Hadn't he thought himself that they were ready for more, that they deserved the happiness they found in each other's arms? "Can you wait until after the war?" he asked.

"Wait for what?"

"I'll divorce Jacqueline, and we can be together."

"I don't want to wreck your family."

"Then what is it that you want? Do you think the family will remain intact if you leave me?"

She was silent, brooding.

"I haven't seen Jacqueline for three days," he said. "Sometimes I go weeks without seeing her at all. She lives her life; I live mine."

She sighed, tired and confused. "I don't know what I want," she admitted.

"But I know what I want," he said, taking her hand in his. "I want to be with you. So if that can't wait until the end of the war, and our life together must start now, then I am prepared to do that."

She searched his face for a sign of sincerity, and found it. She leaned across the table and kissed him lightly, pulled away, and then kissed him again. When they broke apart, he looked at the nearby patrons and saw that they were watching them. "Let's go," he whispered.

He motioned for the check and paid the waiter. He helped Claire rise from her chair and they walked to the exit.

As they stood briefly in the doorway, a gun shot rang through the night. A piece of concrete chipped off the wall.

The bullet missed Junot's head by inches.

Chapter 80

Paul was surprised at how easy it was to gain access to Junot's townhouse. When Bernard answered the door, he merely pointed to his briefcase, said he had two borrowed books to return, and that he wished to borrow two more. Bernard showed no hesitation.

"You know the way," he said as he opened the door. "Please make yourself comfortable."

"Thank you," Paul replied. "I'll let myself out when I'm finished." He made his way up the stairs to the library. It was quiet. No one seemed to be home. He opened his brief case. The two books he placed inside to show Bernard, if challenged, would serve just as well as the two he supposedly borrowed. There was no need to disturb them. He moved through the library and into the parlor, walking softly, listening intently. Then he stepped into the corridor that led to the guest bedrooms. His heart was racing; he could hear each nervous breath he took. He saw no one and heard no one.

A small eighteenth century table sat just outside General Berg's room. Paul walked towards it, after ensuring no one was in the corridor. He again opened his briefcase and removed the wine bottle, gently placing it on the table. The note attached to it was plainly visible. He turned and left, quickly and quietly, walking down the stairs and out the front door. No one had seen him.

* * *

The following afternoon Paul stopped at a newsstand on his way home from the bank and purchased a newspaper. The headline announced progress on the Russian front, predicting the defeat of all Russian forces, even though they now threatened to enter Poland, the German army retreating in front of them. Paul sat on a bench and opened the paper, scanning the front page. On the lower left he found a smaller article, apparently added just before printing. He read the headline: *"GENERAL BERG FOUND DEAD."* He looked at the newspaper with smug satisfaction. The article showed Berg's picture. He was smiling. But he would never smile again, just as Catherine or Sophie would never smile again. Paul started reading the article, which detailed Berg's military career. A hero in the Great War, he had risen rapidly through the German high command. It mentioned his faith, and his devotion to his family, especially his two granddaughters, and his hobby, which was chess. The article claimed he was revered by his troops and would be sorely missed.

Paul kept reading, wondering if a cause of death had been identified. The article continued on page five, and Paul thumbed through the pages and continued reading. The story mentioned Berg's replacement, a General Helmut Schmidt, currently stationed in Normandy. There was a photograph of General Schmidt. He was tall and slender, stood ramrod-straight. His gray hair was close-cropped, but balding on top, and he wore wire-rimmed spectacles.

Paul stared at the photograph. He then turned back to page one, to Berg's picture. He was tall and slender, ramrod-straight with wire-rimmed spectacles. His gray hair was close-cropped, but not balding. He returned to page five, where the article described General Schmidt's military

354

career, his family, and his favorite hobby, which was fishing. Paul remembered something Otto Ernst had said, when Kruger first appeared. He had said Kruger had just been transferred from Normandy. Berg had always been stationed in Paris. Kruger's commander, when Catherine and Sophie were killed, would have been Schmidt, not Berg.

Paul flipped the page back to Schmidt. He covered the top part of his head, as if he had a fishing hat on. Schmidt could easily be mistaken for Berg.

He had killed the wrong man.

Chapter 81

The Lerners were a large family: mother, father, two daughters, two sons, and the grandmother. They were carefree and happy, the children skipping through the cavern, the adults chatting among themselves. They were accompanied by the Berkovich family, who were quite the opposite. Stern and taciturn, mother and father and two teenage boys, they rarely smiled or seemed to enjoy themselves, always appearing to have serious issues to address.

Meurice was leading both families to the cemetery exit. As they approached, he laughed with the Lerner children, mingled with the adults, and spoke quietly with the Berkovich family. He stopped them all near the exit, and again repeated their instructions. They must exit the crypt in three groups, the children scattered among them. The Lerners would leave the cemetery, walking three blocks north where a black truck waited for them, *Pierre DuPont, Antiques and Collectibles* painted on its side, the rear door open. They must climb in, and the driver would take them to the outskirts of Paris where Resistance members were waiting to guide them to Switzerland.

The Berkovich family were to use the Metro, travelling to the last station south where an old man with a black Labrador retriever waited to guide them three more blocks. They would then climb on a horse-drawn wagon and be taken into the country, destined for a dairy farm.

After Meurice had finished the explanation, and was certain both families fully understood, he peered through the peephole to ensure it was safe, as he had done dozens of times before.

He stopped short, shocked by what he saw. Standing before him, just on the other side of the rock in the cave below the crypt, was a French policeman. He was talking to three German soldiers, and Meurice could hear other, more distant voices, also speaking German. .

He stepped back, closing the access port quickly and silently. He turned to the families, putting a finger to his lips. He pointed down the long corridor from which they had come.

They stared at him wide-eyed, fear on their faces. The children looked to their parents; the adults had no answer. They could only do as Meurice instructed.

He moved rapidly, urging them onward, helping the grandmother, hushing the children.

"We must hurry," he said.

"Is everything all right?" Mrs. Lerner asked, worried and afraid.

Meurice didn't want to alarm them. "Just a change of plans," he said. "We'll be using an alternative route." Throughout the journey, as he guided them quickly and silently back to the base, he wondered how he had been discovered. Where had he been careless? When had he made the mistake that could now cost all the Jews in the compound their lives?

When they reached the main cavern, he warned Rachel and a handful of others who helped administer the colony. They frantically discussed a course of action, knowing how critical time was, and how important it was to protect the access into the church.

"We don't have much time," Rachel said. "And we can't take any risks."

"Even if they do get through the crypt, they may not even find us," said one of the helpers, a man named Peter. "Many of the corridors lead to dead ends."

"Or they may not even find the entrance," said Simon, another helper.

"Yes, they will," Meurice informed them. "It's only a matter of time."

"But we don't know that for sure," Peter disagreed.

"We can't take that chance," Rachel said. "Better to get everyone out and hide the entrances. Too many lives are at stake."

"But that will shut down the entire operation," Simon said, his eyes wide.

"We'll start over," she said grimly. "It's our only option."

A dozen young men, slated for posts in the Resistance, volunteered to move halfway down the corridor, delaying an enemy intrusion into the compound. In the meantime, Rachel decided to release as many Jews as possible through the flower store and the church. Both exits were readied for closure; a pile of rocks was staged above the entrance, ready to fill the area with stone.

The assistants organized the refugees into two different lines. The first, the smaller of the two and led by Rachel, would exit through the church. The second, led by Meurice, would leave through the flower store. They assembled quickly, taking only the most prized possessions they could carry, and moved towards their destination, quietly and orderly. Families remained intact, friends joined friends, as they stood single file, advancing as quickly as they could safely move through the exits.

Then, from a distant location down the corridor, they heard the first gunshot.

Chapter 82

The refugees moved frantically through the cavern, the sound of gunshots causing panic and pandemonium. Rachel managed those ascending the ladder the best she could, urging caution and patience and trying to appear calm, which was difficult when all knew their lives were in jeopardy. Meurice did the same, systematically guiding groups of two or three down the corridor and out the exit, filtering onto the *Rue Monge* beyond. A lookout stationed at the flower store ensured it was safe, and he helped to regulate the flow of Jews out of the catacombs. He then guided them onto the street, directing them to take different avenues and alleys, merging with the pedestrians that wandered the city streets.

Again they heard shots fired, two and then three. They heard shouts, frantic voices in both in French and German, issuing orders, screaming warnings. The noises came closer; the men guarding the corridor were retreating, buying time for the Jews in the colony to escape.

At the top of the ladder, Father Nicolas helped people out of the crypt: grandmothers, toddlers, mothers and fathers, scholars and laborers. He tried to calm them, telling them it would be all right, that they were safe. But he knew in his heart, as they did, that they had nowhere to go. They would elude the Germans and the French police, at least for now, but they were destined to wander the streets aimlessly and would have nowhere else to go but the apartments they had abandoned, waiting anxiously for the knock on the door that signaled their demise.

The battle in the corridor continued, the Jewish fighters shouting to each other, gradually retreating, stalling, planning their own escape through the flower store exit, delaying the enemy as long as possible.

Rachel urged people onward, limiting the possessions they took, ensuring families were together, keeping them moving as safely and quickly as possible. She had to protect the church; she needed time to sabotage the entrance. She looked at the line. There were twenty people left. "Please, hurry," she hissed.

She guided them up the ladder to where Father Nicolas was waiting. The other priests directed each where to go, most out the side door, a few out the front. They hid some in chambers, allowing the others to disperse before they were released, the old and feeble, the young and naïve.

Only five or six Jews remained in the cavern when Rachel saw the shadows of the Jewish fighters looming on the corridor wall. Time had run out. She got in line behind the last Jew, hoping the rest could hold, keeping the enemy at bay for a few more minutes – at least long enough to protect the church. If they came any closer, the remaining Jews would have to flee to the flower store. The refugees moved quickly, one after the other climbing the ladder until only Rachel was left at the bottom rung. Just as she was about to depart, warily watching the approaching enemy over her shoulder, she felt someone grab her, pulling her close. It was Meurice.

"Good bye, my love," he said. He hugged her, kissing her frantically.

"Hurry!" Rachel cried.

"Meet me in Tuileries Gardens," he called as he ran down the corridor towards the flower store exit.

Rachel scrambled up the ladder and released the rocks that buried the exit into the church, hiding it forever. She would meet him in Tuileries Gardens. If they survived.

Chapter 83

Paul Moreau sat in the Paris Café on *Rue des Ecoles*, enjoying a croissant for lunch. It was made with cheese, no meat, lettuce, or tomato, but Paul didn't complain. He watched people pass on the street as he ate, wondering how much of the war news was fact, and how much was fiction. He was surprised when an elderly man joined him, carrying a cup of ersatz coffee and shuffling on a cane. His hair and moustache were white, his glasses thick. It was when he sat down and issued a greeting that Paul realized it was Alexander.

"You're in extreme danger," Alexander informed him. "You never should have killed Berg."

"How did you know it was me?"

"Everyone knows. You must leave Paris immediately or Dominique will kill you."

Paul was startled, but defensive. "They have no proof," he argued. "The papers said nothing about how Berg died. And no one is watching me, including Dominique."

"Everyone is watching you. If you don't leave, you'll die. Don't you see what's going on?"

Paul was hesitant. He felt stupid, like a schoolboy who failed his lesson. "No, I don't," he admitted. "I killed Berg by mistake." He looked at Alexander, pleading. "You should be pleased. A Nazi general is dead. If I was in the military, you would be giving me a medal."

"It doesn't matter. You implicated the Fox. Why did you kill Berg in Junot's house? Dominique has tried to kill the Fox twice. Once with Brinkman, and then again last night. Now you have a target on your back, too."

Paul was afraid. He thought he could kill Berg without anyone knowing, even if he did kill the wrong person. He thought he could hide in the city's shadows, helping the Jews and minding money at the bank. Now everything was very real, very dangerous.

"There's more," Alexander continued. "The Germans and French police have found the cemetery entrance into the cavern. They're fighting their way in now. The Jews are escaping through the church and the flower store."

Paul was shocked. He thought of Rachel and Meurice battling for their lives. And Claire, just as exposed. "What should I do?" he asked hoarsely, his throat suddenly parched and dry.

"Tonight, after the sun sets, Henri Durant will be docked under the *Pont de Sully*, hidden by the bridge. You, the Fox, and Claire must get on his boat. He'll take you to a safe house near Giverny. You can hide there until the danger passes." He stood and vanished, still hobbling on the cane but moving much more quickly than when he arrived.

Paul went home and filled a small bag with personal effects, money and important papers. He made his way to the bookstore, alerted Claire, and they went up to her flat. He told her about Alexander's warning, the attack on the Jews in the cavern, and the need for their immediate departure. Then he told her about killing Berg. "We have to get ready go," he said, eyeing the clock.

"I can't, I have to help Rachel," she replied with no hesitation. She started for the door, leaving Paul in the parlor.

"Claire, stop," he said, racing after her. "It's too late to do anything. Just pray that they escape. And that's what we have to do."

She paused, her hand on the doorknob, feeling helpless.

"I told you what Alexander said. Dominique is trying to kill Julian. And now he's trying to kill us, too."

"He's right," she said, sighing in surrender. "Someone took a shot at Julian while we were leaving the restaurant last night. They barely missed him."

"You have to contact him right away. Tell him to come here."

Claire went to the telephone. She called his office, but he wasn't in. She tried his house. He wasn't home. She left a message with Bernard to have him call her.

They waited two hours, pacing the floor, watching the street from the windows, not knowing if they were already being hunted. They grew more anxious by the minute, their chance to escape waning.

"Are you upset about Berg?" he asked while they waited.

She frowned. "No, not really" she replied. "Berg would have killed me if he had to. But you didn't have to kill him. You only made things worse."

"I thought he was responsible," he said meekly.

"But he wasn't," she countered, glancing at her watch. "It's almost seven o'clock."

"Do you have any other way to contact him?" he asked.

"I'll try his office again."

There was no answer. The office was closed.

Paul looked at his watch. "We have to leave without him," he urged.

"No, I won't," Claire insisted. "I'll wait for him."

Just after 8 p.m., there was a melodic rap upon the door, like a signal, and it opened quickly. Julian Junot burst through the entrance, rushing into Claire's outstretched arms.

"Julian, I've been worried sick! Do you know what's going on?"

"Yes, I just left the church," he informed them. "I've been helping Rachel."

"Is she safe?" Claire asked anxiously.

"I don't know," he replied, "but I sure hope so."

Chapter 84

"At least Rachel got out of the catacombs," Junot continued, "but I don't know about the others."

"We have to get out of Paris right away," Paul said, citing information Alexander had provided.

"How were we betrayed?" Claire asked. "And how could Dominique know so much?"

"I don't know," Paul mused aloud. "But we don't have time to figure it out. Come on, Henri Durant is waiting for us."

There was an insistent knock on the door, loud and demanding. They exchanged anxious glances, knowing there was no way out, only the fire escape. And if the Germans were at the front of the building, they were at the back, too.

"I'll get it," Claire said, her heart sinking.

She walked to the door, Paul close behind her. Tentatively, she peeked through the peephole.

"It's Kruger!" she hissed.

They froze, fear etched on their faces.

"Julian!" Kruger called. "I know you're in there. Let me in. It's important."

Junot nodded to Claire. Reluctantly, she opened the door.

"Hello, Claire," he said as he entered. "I'm sorry to intrude."

"What's wrong?" Junot asked.

Kruger sighed, and motioned to the parlor. "Maybe we better sit down," he suggested.

He sat on a chair, his back to the kitchen, while Paul and Junot sat on the sofa across from him. Claire stood near Kruger.

"I'm afraid you're in danger" Kruger informed them. "I think the Resistance is trying to kill you."

Junot looked at Paul with amazement and then addressed Kruger. "But that's preposterous," he muttered.

"No, I'm afraid it's true," Kruger replied. "I came to escort you to Gestapo headquarters for your own protection – before anything happens to you."

"But we were just about to have dinner," Paul said, feigning an innocent astonishment.

They all knew Kruger was lying. But they didn't know why. He could easily take them into custody. Why was he being so cagey? Was he stalling for time?

"I'm sorry," Kruger offered, "but we have to leave. We can all go in my car."

"Let me turn off the oven," Claire said, walking into the kitchen.

As Paul and Junot tried to change Kruger's mind, Claire looked out the kitchen window leading to the fire escape. There were no Germans in the courtyard, so the rear of the building wasn't guarded. That meant Kruger was alone. That's why he was stalling; the Gestapo were on their way.

She eased open the kitchen drawer, slowly and silently. Then she withdrew a butcher knife, holding it behind her. "I hope dinner isn't ruined," she called from the kitchen, her voice drowning their murmured conversation. She walked back into the parlor, saying, "I can try to heat it up when we get back. Paul, it's that stew that you like so much." She walked behind Kruger, withdrew the knife from behind her back, and slid the blade across his throat, pulling it forcefully towards her, severing his carotid artery.

He gasped as blood squirted from the wound, soaking the front of his tunic. His eyes bulged as his hands moved to his throat, trying to stem the flow, blood seeping through his fingers.

Paul and Junot watched with astonishment, mouths open, eyes wide. Kruger slumped over in the chair, the blood still spilling from his body

"Claire! Are you all right?" a shocked Junot asked as he moved to her side.

She was pale and trembling, her face contorted with hatred. "Yes, I'm fine," she answered, even though they could tell she wasn't.

Paul scrambled to Kruger's body, taking a morbid satisfaction in watching him die, the life slowly draining from his body.

"You're not the only one that grieved," she said to Paul. "And you're not the only one that wanted to kill Kruger."

Junot held Claire protectively. "We have to get out of here," he warned.

"I checked the fire escape," she told them. "There's no one in the back of the building."

"Then we have to hurry," Junot advised. "Before there is."

Claire stared ahead, not moving, still in shock. "Wait."

"What is it?" Junot asked.

She pointed to Kruger and said, "Get him out of my house."

Junot and Paul looked at each other.

"How?" Paul asked.

"Down the fire escape," she suggested.

Paul and Junot removed the sheet from the bed and wrapped Kruger's body in it. They didn't know if he was dead or dying, but they managed to get him out of the kitchen window and onto the fire escape landing. It was raining, the steel landing and steps glistening and wet.

"How do we get him down three flights of stairs?" Junot asked.

"Gravity," Paul said sarcastically.

He kicked Kruger's body off the platform, and it bounced and rolled off the steel ladder, tumbling downward and landing with a loud thud in a puddle in the courtyard below, sounding like a melon when it hits a stone wall.

The shade to a nearby window opened and a man looked out. They could see him, his face pressed against the pane, peering into the darkness.

"Hurry," Claire urged. "Someone is watching us."

Scrambling down the ladder, Claire glanced over her shoulder to see the man slowly replace his shade, covering the pane and disappearing behind it.

It was raining harder as they hurried down the fire escape, anxiously looking for Germans. They paused at the base of the ladder, ensuring no one else was watching them. As they exited the courtyard, they peeked around the corner of the building, looking for the black sedans so common to the Gestapo, but saw nothing. Then they separated, Paul walking a few meters ahead, a broad-brimmed hat hiding his face, while Claire clung to Junot.

Just as they reached the street corner, they saw a German troop truck screech to a halt in front of the courtyard entrance. They continued walking, hurrying from the scene, as a half dozen soldiers got out, weapons ready.

All three knew they had escaped by minutes. They moved through the streets of Paris, suspicious of every pedestrian they passed, wary of every vehicle. Their hearts raced; their foreheads were dotted with sweat. They measured each step they took and the remaining distance to Henri Durant's boat, counting the meters to freedom, summing the seconds they had to live should they fail to escape.

The rain subsided as they walked towards the river, leaving the cobblestones slippery. A drizzle replaced the downpour, dripping down the streetlights. A man passed, walking his dog, both wet, unprepared for the rain.

Paul hurried forward, his heart racing, cringing with each sedan that passed. Alexander's warning had been urgent, demanding, so unlike a man known for calmness and the ability to think clearly. He wasn't sure where the breach had occurred, but the Fox had been exposed, and Paul was the known killer of Berg. Somehow, it didn't make sense. No one knew he killed Berg. How could they? And no one knew who the Fox was, except Claire and him and Alexander.

Then in a tumbling rush of tangled thoughts, he remembered the first meeting of the Bibliophile Society, his tour of the Junot residence, and his introduction to Bernard. Junot had described him as more than a servant. He was a friend, the only man who knew all his secrets.

It had to be Bernard. Only he could expose Junot. Only he knew that Paul had been in the Junot residence, supposedly in the library, the day that Berg was killed. Bernard knew of the many meetings Paul, Claire and Junot conducted in the sanctity of the library, and he knew about Junot's affair with Claire. And only Bernard, through

Jacqueline Junot, was exposed on a daily basis to Alain Dominique. Suddenly, the jigsaw puzzle was complete.

He looked back. Claire and Junot walked arm in arm, escaping the old and confronting the new. They whispered as they walked, smiled and cuddled, the danger growing more distant the closer they got to the river bank. They seemed relieved and excited, anxious for tomorrow, yesterday forgotten.

When they reached the wall overlooking the river, Paul looked down to see the boat docked on the edge of the water. Durant was watching from the bow, nets and fishing gear dangling over the edge, stored for later use. He saw Paul coming and made preparations to depart, not waiting a minute longer than needed. He knew the danger; he knew how important it was to whisk them away to the safety of Giverny, where the Resistance would hide them and protect them.

Paul walked past the stone wall and down the fifteen steps that led to the cobblestoned patio bordering the Seine. He looked around anxiously. There were few pedestrians; the rain kept people inside. The riverbank was safer; he couldn't be seen from the street. Even though no Germans were visible, he was sure they sat in nearby cafes, watching the rain, sipping coffee.

As he approached the boat, Henri Durant came to the edge. He leaned forward and offered an arm to help Paul aboard. "Hurry," he hissed. "We have to get underway."

Paul scrambled in. Claire and Junot were coming down the steps. Ten more meters and they would reach the boat. Durant started the engine and prepared to cast off.

When Claire and Junot were five meters away, a black sedan screeched to a halt by the steps. They all turned in alarm, staring at the vehicle.

It was the Gestapo.

Chapter 85

"Hurry!" Paul shouted, his eyes fixed on the sedan.

The front doors opened and two German soldiers scrambled from the vehicle. Alain Dominique exited the rear, a rifle in his hand.

"Cast off!" Paul called to Henri Durant.

Junot and Claire reached the boat, fear etched on their faces. Junot moved Claire forward, shielding her body with his own. Paul extended a hand, helping her on board. Claire took his arm, and Junot steadied her from behind, both hands on her waist. She stepped on to the boat as it bobbed in the water, struggling not to fall. Paul looked back at the Gestapo. The soldiers were scrambling down the steps, racing towards the boat. Dominique stayed on the street and raised his rifle. He crouched behind the wall, his elbow on the capstone, and took aim.

"Julian, take my hand," Paul urged. "Hurry!"

As Junot stepped on the boat he slipped, falling to the cobblestone. The rifle shot sounded simultaneously, echoing through the night. The bullet missed him, the fall saving his life. He crawled to the boat on his knees, diving onto the vessel as Paul pulled him on board. There was a cry behind him, followed by a gurgling sound. He turned, alarmed and confused.

Claire fell heavily to the deck, the bullet intended for Junot finding her instead. A red dot the size of a coin appeared on her chest, near the breastbone, and then gradually expanded. Blood oozed from the wound, spilling from her coat, running down her side, and dripping onto the deck.

Junot moved to her side, holding her, pleading, praying, begging a merciful God to help her. Tears streamed down his face, his chest heaving, as her blood dripped onto the deck, the puddle growing larger.

Durant eased the boat away from the dock just as the German soldiers rushed towards it. He opened the throttle, speeding down the Seine. The soldiers stood at the edge of the bank; one pulled his pistol from the holster, the other removed a rifle from his shoulder.

Dominique fired again, the bullet imbedding in the hull, above the water line, inches from where Junot was lying on the deck. Other shots were fired, but as the boat moved away they flew harmlessly overhead or disappeared into the wood of the cabin.

Life drained slowly from Claire's face, her color turning white and then gray. She gasped and coughed, struggling to breath, clenching Junot's arm, her knuckles white.

"Claire, no!" Junot shouted, tears running down his cheeks.

She raised her arm, clutching him tightly. Then her grip eased, slowly relaxing, until her hands fell to the deck. Her eyes stared vacantly ahead, lifeless and cold.

Junot wept, his tears dripping on her lifeless body. "Why couldn't it be me instead?" he sobbed. "Why couldn't it be me."

Chapter 86

The Allies came that June, landing on the Normandy beaches and then liberating Paris. But they were too late to save Claire. Paul and Junot buried her next to Catherine and Sophie, on the knoll that overlooked the Seine. Junot remained in Giverny, grieving, until the Allies came, but he then returned to Paris. Given the Allied advance and the chaos it created, the Gestapo were no longer interested in him. He was able to broker the city's surrender without a shot being fired, twice saving Paris from destruction. But even after the war ended, he would never let his true role be known. He would always be identified as the man who betrayed Paris.

Jacqueline Junot remained in Paris, still married to Julian, still leading a separate life. Tragically, she died in an automobile accident a few years later. For Paul, she symbolized the calamity of war, caught in the conflict's crosshairs. The man she loved, who she thought was a traitor, couldn't give her the attention she needed, so she thought she had found it in the arms of Alain Dominique, France's true enemy.

The Abzac family survived, sheltered on the Normandy farm. After the Allies liberated Paris, they returned to their shoe repair shop in the eleventh arrondissement. The shop still exists today.

Rachel and Meurice escaped the Germans, as did all of the Jews in the cavern except the brave few who lost their lives fighting the enemy. They remained in Paris, hiding, until the city was liberated, and then married after the war, eventually having three children. Rachel now owns a global shipping empire; Meurice oversees a world-wide operation that brings those who persecuted the Jews to justice.

Alexander remained in Paris until the war ended. He supposedly lives in Cornwall, writing mystery novels under an assumed name.

Alain Dominique disappeared soon after the Allied invasion. He reportedly went to Africa, then Syria, before vanishing completely. Bernard, his accomplice, was never seen again. His whereabouts remain unknown.

Shortly after the war ended, and life had become as normal as it could be, a young woman named Geneviève Mandel came to work at the bank. Attractive, with long black hair and an olive complexion, she was also intelligent, and witty. But even her extroverted personality couldn't hide the sadness in her eyes. When Paul saw the number tattooed on her wrist, he knew she had lived a hell he could only imagine.

She was a survivor of Ravensbrück, a concentration camp in northern Germany. Her husband had been killed trying to escape shortly after their apprehension, and her twin sons, three years old, were taken from her upon her arrival. One evening, she and Paul shared their pasts with a bottle of wine, weeping for hours, clinging to each other for strength and hope. He promised to help her, and they started searching for her sons, enlisting the aid of anyone they knew who could help, but they found no promising leads. The search continues, and will likely never end.

As is so common with those whose hearts have been broken in a way that can't be mended, Paul and Geneviève soon became inseparable, finding strength in each other, and slowly learned to live and laugh and love. There was much they shared; she was fleeing her own demons, just as Paul was.

They were married in late 1946 and had two children. Their youngest daughter, Deidre, eventually became the manager of the Daladier Rare Book Store, while their son Marcel went on to become an officer of the *Banque de Paris*, employed by the descendants of Henri Kohn.

Paul often thinks of the past, usually when he visits the graves of Catherine and Sophie and Claire. He misses them terribly, Catherine his best friend and lover, Claire his constant companion. He remembers Sophie as he last saw her, dancing around the yard with imaginary playmates, frozen in time. But he takes solace in knowing that all of heaven now loves her as much as he does.

EPILOGUE
Paris, France
July 1, 1976, thirty years later

The casket was perched in the front of the room, surrounded by roses, carnations, and lilies. The coffin was ornate, as it should be for a man of his wealth, trimmed with bronze vines of ivy that traveled its length. Paul realized as he gazed upon it, that he witnessed not only the passing of a man but the end of an era that should not be forgotten.

Tears welled in his eyes. He looked away from the casket, the image too overpowering, the realization too heart-wrenching.

As he studied the room, he saw that about twenty people had come to pay their respects. Most sat in chairs arranged in rows, while others whispered in small groups. Two women, with families at their sides, sat in front of the coffin. He realized they were Junot's daughters. A half dozen men stood by the entrance, two smoking cigars. Seeing one glance at his watch, Paul suspected they would remain only a respectable amount of time before departing.

The rest wandered the room. Some admired the flowers. Others consoled the daughters. He didn't recognize anyone. He would have thought, of those who knew him, that some would have come to say goodbye. But none did.

A small bench sat before the coffin, topped with a red velvet cushion and flanked by white lilies. Paul made the sign of the cross and kneeled, despite pain from his arthritis. It was only then that he looked at the face. Years had chiseled lines into it and his hair was white. But for the

379

most part, he looked the same as he did all those years ago. Only now he was at peace – the stress and tension were gone from his face. Paul could feel tears dripping down his cheeks, and he reached into the casket and touched his hand. It felt like stone but he held it anyway. He regretted they had drifted apart. And so much had been left unsaid. But it had been difficult. They shared memories they each wanted to forget, visions that haunted them, nightmares that woke them.

Paul knew he mourned one of France's greatest heroes, and a man who would never let it be known. It just wasn't like him. Only a few knew his secret. Years before he had made them swear they would never tell, and they never did. Paul wiped the tears from his face, ignoring the stares of those who didn't know who he was, and wondered if anyone else really grieved. Junot's daughters did. But they didn't know him as Paul did; they didn't know what a great man their father had been.

Paul walked to the rear of the room and found Father Nicolas standing quietly. His hair was white, and his frame a bit larger, but he still looked the same. He greeted Paul warmly, sharing his grief, helping to shoulder his pain.

The door to the church opened and a man and women entered. They were about fifty, the woman in a plain black dress, the man in a black suit, a yarmulke covering his head. It was Rachel and Meurice. Those in the room turned to the entrance, shocked. Why would two Jews attend the funeral of the man who had done so much to confine and condemn them?

Paul greeted them, and saw that the door of the church remained open. Behind them stood a line of people dressed in similar fashion, black dresses and suits, the men wearing yarmulkes.

"Some of those he saved wanted to come," Rachel said simply, but elegantly, as she was always able to do. She then led the line to the casket.

Paul stared in awe at the show of appreciation. He exited the church and saw that the line stretched down the street, for blocks on end, thousands of people, quietly waiting to show their respect.

A television news crew stood on the street, its cameras rolling, an anchorwoman reporting. She was saying, "… and so the mystery remains. Why would thousands of Jews attend the funeral of a man who did them more harm than anyone in Parisian history?"

Paul realized then that his story must be told. The world should know what he had done, the sacrifices he had made, and the risks he had taken. It was the right thing to do. It's what he would have done had their roles been reversed.

He considered the secret he had kept for so many years and his promise to never reveal it. It would be all right to break it now.

Julian Junot was dead.

The End

CPSIA information can be obtained
at www.ICGtesting.com
Printed in the USA
BVOW03s2152150917
494860BV00001B/3/P